SAN DIEGO DEAD

MARK NOLAN

To my loyal readers.

CHAPTER 1

Pacific Ocean, off the coast of San Diego, California

Jake Wolfe and his dog, Cody, sat in a small Zodiac-style inflatable boat, drifting on the ocean in the dark of night. The electric outboard motor was dead, with a bullet hole in the tiller's onboard computer.

Sharks circled, bumping the boat and waiting impatiently to rip both man and dog limb from limb. Sleek and dangerous apex predators with multiple rows of sharp teeth, most of the animals were approximately six feet long. The largest one circling the boat now, however, looked to be ten feet or more.

Jake knew he and Cody were up the proverbial creek without a paddle, and he cursed whoever had taken the oars out of this dinghy. He cursed himself too, for not double-checking to make sure the boat was fully equipped.

Beside him, Cody panted, tongue hanging out while gazing at the salty sea all around them, obviously thirsty for a drink of fresh water. The dog was a yellow Labrador and Golden Retriever mix with wavy hair, and intelligent brown eyes that seemed to look into your heart and sense what you were feeling.

Jake scratched his dog on the nape of the neck. "I'm sorry I got us into this, buddy."

The former war dog, trained again as a service dog, was one of the most intelligent and highly skilled animals on the planet. Staring at Jake with wise eyes, he lifted one paw and put it down.

Jake nodded at him. "Do something?"

Cody barked once.

Without warning, the largest, most aggressive shark bumped the boat harder, jostling the occupants.

Cody snarled and Jake studied the big shark. He felt a chill as he wondered how much it weighed. Enough to flip the dinghy over if it leapt onto the gunwale.

"Sorry Sharkzilla," he said, "but you have to go."

Drawing his stolen pistol, he took aim at the predator and fired a round at the base of the dorsal fin, into its trunk. The wounded shark dove below the surface, trailing a plume of blood. Other sharks attacked the dying one in a feeding frenzy, abandoning the drifting boat for a moment.

"That'll get rid of the big guy and keep the rest of them away from us for a little while," Jake said.

He ejected the pistol's mag to count how many rounds were left. He was running low—not good. Sunrise was a long way off, and he didn't have his phone or his handheld VHF marine radio with him.

Hopefully, none of the sharks would bite the inflatable dinghy and sink it. One of the individual airtight chambers had been shot and was deflated, but the rest were holding up, so far.

If he and Cody could survive until sunrise, they might live through this. But it was a big, endless ocean with millions of square miles of empty water covering one third of the planet. They could vanish into the Pacific without a trace and die of thirst or end up as shark food, their bodies never found.

CHAPTER 2

Earlier that night...

At one of San Diego's most luxurious beachside hotels, Jake Wolfe walked down a hallway, wearing a black tuxedo. Impersonating a room service waiter, he felt naked without his pistol, phone or ID as he moved toward the door of an expensive suite, pushing a cart that held a chrome dinner tray topped with a dome.

According to intel from the President's Operational Emergency Team (POETs), an Above Top Secret clandestine black ops group Jake worked for on occasion—a high-value target was staying in the suite. Jake had orders to kill him.

The target, Zef Krasniq, was a member of New York's Albanian mafia, now involved in piracy off the west coast of the United States. He and his gang forcibly boarded sailboats and motor yachts on the Pacific Ocean, attacked the crews, and sold the stolen watercraft to a Mexico-based drug cartel for smuggling purposes. He didn't care if families with children were on board. He'd sell the prisoners into forced labor, or worse—much worse.

The man had been designated a terrorist threat, but while the Coast Guard was actively searching for him, he constantly changed boats and phones and managed to elude the authorities.

Jake had unique skills, learned in his service as an infantry Marine deployed to combat, and later on black ops missions for the CIA's paramilitary branch. Once he'd been briefed about the piracy, kidnapping, and potential harm to children, he'd volunteered to help protect America from the threat.

Yesterday, in a rare stroke of luck, the target had shown up in San Diego on a camera with facial recognition software. Jake and Cody had immediately flown down from San Francisco on the luxurious private jet of a patriotic multimillionaire named Bart Bartholomew.

As Jake walked up to the suite door, a tall, broad-shouldered bodyguard in a well-tailored suit blocked his path. "Put your hands against the wall and spread your feet so I can search you."

Jake smiled and obeyed like an intimidated, submissive sheep. "Sure, no problem. I heard your paranoid boss was a big tipper. Hope it's true." He placed his white-gloved hands on the wall and spread his feet.

The bodyguard patted him down, then lifted the dome off the dinner tray to check inside. He replaced the dome, checked inside the cart's closed doors, and held a mirror on a stick underneath. Satisfied, he spoke into a tiny radio on his wrist. "Clear."

Another tall, muscular, and dangerous-looking man opened the door from inside and beckoned Jake to enter. He held a pistol with a silencer attached. "Leave the cart and bring the tray in here."

Jake picked up the tray and carried it into the suite. The door closed behind him on automatic hinges.

The bodyguard pointed with his free hand. "Set it on the dining table."

Jake did as he was told and replied cheerfully, "Okay, there you go. Enjoy your meal, sir." He held out the room service bill expectantly.

The man stood between Jake and the door, blocking his exit. "Wait a minute."

"Are you wondering if I accept tips? The answer is yes," Jake said, smiling to mask the tension he felt.

A bald, bullnecked man with a pockmarked face and a cruel smile walked into the suite's dining room and sat at the table. His cold blue-gray eyes glinted with a threat of violence. "Have a seat," he said to Jake, gesturing at the chair across from him. He spoke with an accent.

Jake gave him an innocent look. "Pardon me?"

"Sit down!" The man Jake recognized from a photo of Zef Krasniq, cursed and drew a pistol identical to the one held by the guard. Both men aimed their weapons at Jake.

Jake acted surprised, raising his eyebrows and opening his mouth. He obediently sat at the table across from the man. "What's this about, sir?"

"Taste the food, so I know it isn't poisoned."

"The hotel doesn't let us—"

"Taste it!" He raised the pistol and aimed it between Jake's eyes.

"Well, if you put it that way." Jake calmly picked up silverware from his table setting and tasted the Caesar salad, loaded baked potato and medium-rare filet mignon. "Delicious."

Krasniq watched him closely. "Now taste the wine."

"I thought you'd never ask," Jake said with a bold wink. He expertly popped the cork and poured himself a glass of the absurdly expensive French Bordeaux. He swirled and sniffed and took a drink. "Magnificent. You are a man of good taste who knows his rare wines. Hopefully, someday, I'll have enough money to buy a bottle of this. Maybe I'll sell a kidney."

Krasniq nodded at the flattery, as if Jake was only stating the obvious. "Pour me a glass."

Jake poured and then held the bottle poised near his own glass. "I could taste it again if you want to be doubly sure it's safe to drink."

The target finally smiled, apparently amused by this ballsy waiter. "Sure, go ahead. We'll drink a toast. These men don't appreciate excellent fine wine." He turned to the guard. "Cover him."

The guard sat on Jake's left and rested his elbow on the tabletop, aiming his pistol at Jake's chest. Jake blinked twice, poured himself another splash of wine and set the bottle on the table, off to his right.

Krasniq held his glass up in a toast. "To wine, women and song."

Jake raised his glass in reply. "I'll gladly second that."

They drank, and afterward the pirate studied Jake for a moment. "You're cool under pressure. Fearless, even."

Jake shrugged a shoulder and said nothing.

"Are you a war veteran?" the man asked.

"Yes, I served in the Marine infantry as a MOS 0311 with multiple deployments overseas."

"What does MOS 0311 stand for?"

Jake recited from memory. "MOS 0311 is the military occupational specialty code for a Marine Corps rifleman. The mission of my rifle platoon was to locate, close with and destroy the enemy by fire and maneuver, or to repel the enemy's assault by fire and close combat."

Krasniq nodded. "And did you? Fight and kill the enemy?"

Jake stared at him for a moment. "Yes. Many times, many enemies."

"Good." The man smiled in satisfaction. "I can always use someone like you in my business. Why don't you come and work for me on my security team?"

Adjusting his tie, Jake took another sip of wine, then gestured to the guard aiming a pistol at him. "What, and leave all this?" he joked.

The bald man chuckled and began eating his meal, taking a bite of medium-rare steak and savoring it. "In my experience, every man has his price. Your starting pay would be a thousand dollars a day, and you'd enjoy all the fine wine and liquor you care to drink. The only downside is you could get shot if you're weak, but I doubt you are; otherwise I wouldn't be making this offer. How does that sound to you?" He took a sip of Bordeaux and gazed at Jake from behind half-closed snake-like eyes as he awaited a reply.

Jake acted as if he was pleasantly surprised, putting a big smile on his face. "It sounds like I'm damned glad we met. After my deployments, every job back home seems dull, and I could definitely use that kind of paycheck. You're very generous, sir."

"As a civilian, have you continued practicing at a firing range to keep your shooting skills up to par?"

"Yes, of course," Jake said, and he moved so fast he caught both men by surprise. He grabbed the wine bottle in both hands and slammed the thick bottom straight down on the guard's gun hand, crushing the carpal bones of his wrist against the hardwood tabletop.

The guard screamed in pain, then fired a round at the wall in reflex and let go of the pistol for a second as he yanked his hand backward in agony.

Jake picked up the silenced weapon and shot the guard in the forehead before turning the weapon on Krasniq, who was reaching for his own pistol. Jake shot him in the chest, knocking him and his chair backwards onto the floor.

The target was down, but there was no time to breathe. Behind Jake, the suite door burst open.

CHAPTER 3

The hotel suite door swung closed automatically behind the guard as he aimed his weapon.

Jake took cover, ducking and using the other guard's dead body in the chair as a shield. He expertly shot his attacker several times, dropping him to the carpet.

The guard fell, firing one final round, intent on taking Jake with him as he died. The bullet went through the dead body, shattering a tall vase of flowers on a side table behind Jake.

Jake went around the table and found the high-value target still alive, lying on the floor and moaning as his bleeding wound slowly drained his life away.

The pirate spoke to Jake in a hoarse voice. "Get me to a doctor, and whatever they're paying you, I'll pay you *millions* more!"

Jake stood over him, glaring down with no mercy and threatening him with the pistol. "What happened to the people you kidnapped from boats? Where are the children? Talk to me!"

The man sneered. "I sold them to a trafficker."

Jake cursed and kicked him hard in the side, making him cry out in pain.

"Who's your boat buyer? Give me a name."

"I'll never tell you," the man said with a wet cough.

"Where can I find him?" Jake pressed his shoe down on the man's chest wound.

The man bellowed in agony and glared at Jake with hatred as he choked out his dying words. "He'll find *you*. You're a dead man!"

"Speak for yourself," Jake said, and he shot the HVT twice in the head. *Mission accomplished.*

Moving quickly, he dropped the pistol he'd been firing, grabbed the target's weapon off the table, checked that it had a full magazine and hid it in the back waistband of his pants under his tux jacket.

He picked up the empty wineglass with his DNA on the rim and put it in his jacket pocket, wrapped the filet mignon in a large white linen napkin and went out the door, placing the Do Not Disturb door hanger on the knob.

He had a feeling he might be forgetting an important detail, but he followed orders and focused on immediate mission exfiltration. Hurrying out of the building, he ran down some wide wooden steps to the beach and jogged across the sand in the moonless dark night, stopping at a gray inflatable dinghy near the water.

Jake's adopted war dog, Cody, stood there faithfully obeying orders to guard the boat and wait for his handler to return.

"Cody, pee now. Pee there." Jake pointed at a spot next to the boat.

While serving in the Marines, Sergeant Cody had been trained to empty his bladder on command before going on a ride in a boat, Humvee or helicopter. He obediently peed on the sand.

Jake pointed. "Get in the boat."

Cody jumped in, and Jake pushed the dinghy into the surf. He waded into the water, climbed aboard, started the electric motor and zoomed away into the darkness of the ocean.

The ten-foot-long boat with its quiet motor was similar to those he'd used on a few night missions in the Persian Gulf, and he deftly controlled it like an old hand.

As he looked back at the shore, he noted there were only a few people out on the beach, due to the dark sky, waning crescent moon and sporadic rain. They weren't paying any attention to the man who appeared to be a hotel employee.

Cody sniffed at the linen napkin and salivated, his tongue hanging out.

"Your nose doesn't miss a thing." Jake unwrapped the steak and set the napkin on the wooden bench seat. "Go ahead, that's for you, Cody."

Cody devoured the medium-rare beef as if he'd never had a steak before and another dog might try to take it away from him.

"Remember to breathe between bites," Jake said with a smile.

As they sped away from shore, Jake thought he'd made a clean getaway, until he heard a two-stroke outboard motor starting up. A skiff gave chase in the dark, its motor being pushed hard.

His pulse quickened and he cursed his luck. The race was on and the killing would continue, but who would die next?

A man in the pursuing boat fired a suppressed pistol. Jake saw the flash in the dark and heard the "snap" sound a bullet makes as it flies past in close proximity.

"Cody, lie down and stay low."

Cody obeyed instantly and kept his eyes on Jake, awaiting further orders.

Jake reached for his phone, patting his empty pocket and then cursing as he remembered he was required to do this mission "dark." He'd be disavowed if he was caught or shot.

Cody pawed at Jake's pocket, as if asking him to make a call.

Jake shook his head. "Sorry, no phone or radio allowed this time. It's just you and me, buddy."

Cody watched him with trusting eyes.

Jake felt a weight on his heart. He'd protect his dog at all costs. This mission had better not go all the way sideways.

He aimed his pistol at the boat gaining on them. Now he knew what he'd been forgetting when leaving the hotel suite. He should've grabbed the partially full mags of ammo from the other pistols.

The pursuing boat had a more powerful engine and it continued moving closer.

From time to time the person on board fired a suppressed round at Jake. One lucky shot hit the electric outboard motor's tiller and killed the small onboard computer. The display screen went dark, the motor died and the propeller spun to a halt.

Jake lay down next to Cody as their dinghy lost power and the skiff quickly gained on them. He held his pistol in both hands and aimed over the stern as the pursuing boat came closer.

He waited until he could see the outline of the man chasing him. When the man fired his pistol and the gun flash lit his face, Jake fired several carefully aimed rounds in return.

One bullet found its target, and the man fell into the water with a cry of pain as his skiff roared off in another direction, out of control.

Dark shapes appeared in the water as sharks flocked to the fresh blood, their dorsal fins cutting the surface.

The sharks began feasting while the bleeding man was still alive. He desperately splashed around and screamed as they bit off body parts and ripped him to pieces.

Jake cursed at him. "That's what you get for shooting at my dog!"

Cody snarled, exposing his teeth.

Once the sharks had devoured their prey, they began prowling and circling the powerless dinghy, bumping against it and trying to knock Jake and Cody into the water.

"How do I get us into these crazy situations?" Jake asked out loud.

Cody woofed at him as if he was wondering the same thing.

In San Francisco, Sarah Chance paced the floor of her studio apartment. She stared at her phone, worried that Jake wasn't answering her texts.

She tried calling him, but her call went to voicemail again. This was unusual. Jake was a total bad boy in many ways, but he never ghosted on her, or gave her the cold shoulder like some of the indifferent guys she'd known.

He and Cody were on a trip to San Diego, and she was planning on joining them to go whale watching. Why had Jake suddenly gone silent?

She feared they might be in danger. Recently, she'd learned a little about Jake's secret life after accidentally witnessing him terminate three terrorists who had been planning to explode a bomb under the Golden Gate Bridge and kill innocent people.

Jake had saved lives, but why did he have to be the one to do it? There were plenty of special forces veterans who could perform that dangerous work instead of him.

She placed one hand on her stomach. Her period was late, but she hadn't told him yet; hadn't told anyone except her doctor. She'd never been pregnant before and was wrestling with the heartbreaking choice of whether or not to go through with it. Everyone she knew had strong opinions, and she was afraid to talk about it. She'd never felt so scared and alone.

Could Jake step up and be a good father to their child? Or would he always be risking his life defending America against enemies? She admired him for his service, but it wasn't the life for her. Sorry, but she was a veterinarian and her job was to heal the sick, treat the wounded and put smiles on the faces of her cute four-footed patients.

She prayed that Cody was okay. The dog had stolen her heart. She loved him, and okay, she was falling in love with Jake too, but she had her doubts about the possibility of any long-term relationship together.

She hadn't planned on becoming a single parent in her mid-twenties. It took a heroic effort and great amounts of love, time and money. She had plenty of love to spare but was short on time, and money was tight in this city. San Francisco was becoming impossible to afford unless you held a high position in one of the wealthy tech firms or internet startups. The middle-class people, like teachers, nurses and firefighters were being squeezed out of town by the new ultra-rich.

A few months of dating Jake and getting to know him was not enough time for her to make a commitment like having a child together. In fact, she'd never really imagined herself marrying, having two kids and a house with a white picket fence. Right now she was totally focused on building her business, and barely had time for a boyfriend, let alone a baby.

Sarah stopped pacing and stood in front of the window to gaze out at the city lights and the Pacific Ocean. How would Jake react to the pregnancy news? He was a man, raised Catholic. She had no idea what he might say.

If she was going to end the pregnancy without including Jake in the decision, it made sense to visit the women's clinic right away while he was out of town. She had barely enough time to do it tomorrow morning before she flew down to meet him for a few days of vacation. She couldn't make an appointment, but a doctor friend would help her in an emergency.

What should I do?

She was a strong woman, but the early-pregnancy hormones made her feel more emotional than usual, and she began to cry. She looked out at the water with tears on her face. "Why aren't you here when I need you, Jake?"

CHAPTER 4

In Washington, D.C., Secret Service Agent Shannon McKay worked late as she often did. It was past midnight, yet she remained at her desk in an office located in the secret tunnels below the White House, known as the Catacombs.

One of her assets in California had conducted a dark mission tonight, but he hadn't arrived at the rendezvous afterward. *Had he been captured, wounded or killed?*

She thought about Jake Wolfe for a moment. The man was a loose cannon, but he got results. Jake and Cody helped protect America from deadly threats, and they did it their way or not at all.

She'd learned to compromise with the two Marine veterans who'd come home from battles overseas but never fully adjusted to peacetime. They were civilians now, but once a Marine—always a Marine. That was the key to understanding them. Sergeant Cody was worth his weight in gold, but Jake often went rogue. He had a temper and a protective streak in him that overruled his orders. The dog wouldn't listen to anybody else, though, so you had to take them both together or not at all.

She raised a hand and rubbed the back of her neck as she looked at a computer screen displaying a map of Southern California's coastline. "Where did you disappear to? Don't die on me now, when your country needs you the most."

Cody meant more to her than just a chess piece on the game board. He and another highly intelligent service dog named Skye had mated. The breeder said they'd been carefully selected and matched as the two smartest dogs in America, maybe in the world. When their exceptional puppies were born, Jake planned to have the best and brightest one trained as a guide dog for McKay's blind daughter.

She grabbed her desk phone and made a call to San Diego. "Send Easton and Greene on a search and rescue mission. Don't give me any excuses! Do it right now and report back in five minutes, or I'll find someone else who can."

Slamming the phone down, she cursed a blue streak, then took a deep breath and drank a gulp of cold, stale coffee.

"Dammit, Jake!"

～

Secret Service Agent Greene nodded at her partner, Easton, and they ran across the deck of a Coast Guard cutter toward a waiting H-65 Dolphin. They both ducked under the spinning blades and climbed inside. The helo lifted off immediately.

As they flew over the coastline, Greene sent a text to McKay while the pilot conducted a search pattern, looking for the inflatable boat, or bodies in the water. A lit dashboard display showed two photos: one of a young man in his mid-to late twenties with dark wavy hair and devil-may-care eyes, the other of a golden dog who stared at the camera with intelligent brown eyes, one brow quirked up as if questioning why his picture was being taken.

Easton, a broad-shouldered man who rarely smiled or engaged in small talk, sat in the copilot's seat and studied a screen featuring the feed from night vision cameras aimed below.

Greene sat behind Easton and next to the Coast Guard rescue swimmer. She ran a hand through her auburn hair and gazed out the window at the endless ocean. She'd protected Jake's life once before and would do it again, but mostly she was concerned for Cody. She felt a strong affection for the dog. They shared some kind of bond she didn't understand but loved and appreciated. Maybe Jake wasn't so bad either.

"Circle around again," she said.

The pilot nodded and banked the copter as he turned.

Jake sat with Cody in the powerless dinghy, his stomach in a knot as he experienced his worst fear; that his dog might be harmed.

The sharks returned, their taste for blood not yet satisfied, and resumed bumping into the sides of the boat.

Suddenly a shark leapt out of the water, bellying onto the dinghy gunwale and lunging at Jake with its mouth wide open.

Jake quickly leaned back in an attempt to keep the boat from flipping over and used both feet to kick the shark as hard as he could in its throat under the gaping mouth, deflecting the beast to the side. The animal slid off the boat and disappeared under the water's surface.

Moments later, another shark copied the move and launched itself partway onto the boat with its jaws gaping. Jake pulled his feet away just in time to avoid the bone-crushing bite.

The dinghy bobbed and rocked and almost flipped over, but Jake shifted more of his weight backward and kicked the shark in the eye with the heel of his shoe.

The animal thrashed and fell back into the water with a splash, circling around for another try.

Cody barked frantically and pawed at Jake.

"Cody, lie down!" Jake drew his pistol with his right hand and held Cody down with his left.

When the next shark tried bellying onto the gunwale, Jake shot it through the eye, killing it instantly. The shark sank back into the water and the other sharks feasted on it right next to the boat, causing the dinghy to bounce and sway as the water churned all around as if it was boiling.

Jake stretched out flat in an effort to distribute his six-foot length and weight to prevent the boat from capsizing. Cody lay right by Jake's side, partners through thick and thin. Jake kept one hand on his dog and made sure he didn't get bounced into the water. He held the pistol in his other hand, ready to shoot the next shark that showed its face over the gunwale.

He saw Cody suddenly raise his nose, look up at the sky and tilt his head as if listening. A moment later, Jake heard a helicopter approaching. The whump-whump-whump of rotor blades was a familiar sound to the war veterans.

He sat up and fired his pistol again, this time wounding one of the sharks furthest from him, making it bleed and temporarily drawing the rest away from the boat.

The copter hovered overhead, and its lights revealed it was painted dark orange with a white stripe. Jake had never been so glad to see a Coast Guard helo.

Someone opened a door and used a green laser light to blink Morse code. Jake waved when he read the code for *Jukebox*, his radio call sign from his combat deployments. A rope was lowered with two vests attached, along with what appeared to be a handheld radio in a mesh bag.

When the vests came into reach, he removed them and strapped one onto Cody first, then donned the other. With that done, he clipped each vest's carabiner to a metal D-ring on the rope, placing Cody above him. He put the radio in his pocket and held his arms straight out to each side with both thumbs up.

"We're going for a flight, Cody. You ready for this?"

Cody barked once.

"Good dog."

The copter hoisted the duo up into the air just as a shark lunged halfway into the boat with its mouth open, teeth barely missing Jake's feet.

Jake lifted his legs and bent his knees, hanging above the shark. The empty boat flipped over on top of the shark's head and another shark leapt out of the water onto the exposed boat bottom, thrashing and trying to get at Jake.

As Jake rose higher, one of the smaller sharks breached and shot out of the water toward him. Jake was thankful it wasn't a great white shark that could swim thirty-five miles per hour, fly ten feet into the air and remove both of your legs with one bite.

Cursing, he aimed his pistol at the deadly animal, then hesitated and held his fire, instead kicking the airborne shark hard upside the head and deflecting it away.

Rising out of range, Jake yelled, "Better luck next time, *assshoollles!*"

Cody panted loudly, Ha-Ha-Ha.

The helo flew them over the water utilizing a helicopter rope suspension technique often used by combat Marines on Special Patrol Insertion & Extraction (SPIE) missions.

The two war veterans swayed in the breeze, and Jake looked up to see Cody wearing a fearless doggie grin on his face as he sniffed the air, his ears flapping in the breeze. They'd both done SPIE work while serving overseas, but in different platoons at different times, never together.

"Attaboy, Cody," Jake said. He figured this was like a dog putting its head out the car window, but even better.

The copter's hoist began raising the rope and lifting Jake and Cody up to bring them on board.

Jake pulled out the radio and yelled into the wind, "Thanks for the ride, but don't hoist us up to the helo, just let us fly. My war dog is agitated and in no mood to sit quietly in the cramped space. He might bite somebody. Do you copy?"

The reply came from the pilot in a steady, emotionless voice. "Roger that, Jukebox, we copy. Anything for a war dog. And you Marines do like your SPIE flying. Crazy Jarheads."

The hoist stopped, and Jake grinned and enjoyed flying over the water. Few people in the history of the world had ever done this, and he was in awe of the incredible sensation of soaring through the air on a rope suspended below a helicopter with the vast ocean beneath him.

CHAPTER 5

Jake watched the ocean and sky flying past and soon observed a brightly lit Coast Guard cutter in the distance. The copter flew directly toward it. Men and women in uniform stood on deck and peered up as the copter hovered and descended.

The ship and crew were a welcome sight to Jake. *Thank God for the Coasties.*

When Jake was ten feet from the deck, the copter stopped its descent and hovered as the hoist lowered the rope the rest of the way. He braced his legs for impact and touched down without any problem. The helo pilot and crew were good—damn good.

Cody came down right after him, and Jake caught the dog in his arms, setting him carefully on the deck and unclipping his vest from the rope.

He removed the leather belt from his pants and slipped it through Cody's collar as a makeshift leash, then walked away to clear the area, giving a thumbs-up to the helo.

The hoist raised the rope inside, and the pilot slowly brought the aircraft down for a perfect landing.

Jake stood by, waiting to thank everyone on board the helo. He removed Cody's SPIE vest and his own and set them on the deck by his feet along with the radio, planning on returning the items to the helicopter.

A uniformed female Coast Guard Maritime Enforcement Specialist approached and handed him a bottled water. She had short, regulation hair, a toned body and jaded smile. "My orders are to give this water to you for your dog."

"Thank you," Jake said. He removed the cap and slowly poured water into his cupped left hand for Cody to drink.

Cody lapped it up and then wagged his tail and gave the woman a toothy smile.

She smiled back at Cody and whispered to Jake, "They told us not to ask you any questions, but I just wanted to say it was pretty badass seeing you drop in on a rope at night wearing a tux."

Jake reached into his tux jacket pocket, pulled out the empty wineglass, held it up and asked with a straight face, "This is the party boat I heard about. Right?"

She laughed and shook her head but played along. "Nope, you got the wrong boat."

Jake laughed too. Putting the wine glass back in his jacket pocket, he said, "Thanks for helping a couple of salty Marines lost at sea."

"Marines, huh? I guess that explains a lot," she said with a knowing smile.

Jake gave her a playful wink, a nod and a grin in reply. He was used to the constant joking between the various branches of the military. One thing they'd often ask was, "Are Marines really fearless —or are they just *crazy*?" Jake would say it might be a little of both.

He watched as the helicopter powered down and Secret Service Agent Greene stepped out, bending her head and ducking under the rotating blades as she jogged toward him.

Easton remained in the copilot seat, nodding at Jake.

Jake nodded and waved in thanks and respect for Easton, a capable agent and man of few words. He'd requested Easton and Greene to assist on this mission because they all had a history together. He trusted them and thought they were among the best at their jobs.

Greene ran up to him and asked, "Are you two okay? I saw those sharks trying to get at you." She looked at Cody with concern.

"Yes, we're fine, but Cody needs a vacation—a real one this time," Jake answered.

Greene nodded. "Long past due, I'd say. Here's your phone."

Jake accepted the phone and took a quick glance before he put it in his pocket. He saw texts from Agent McKay, but he would report to her momentarily. Sarah had also texted and called. She would have to wait a few more minutes for his reply. This mission was classified Top Secret, and he was duty-bound by federal laws to keep it that way.

Cody woofed happily at Greene and pressed his head against her stomach. She smiled and glanced at Jake.

"Be friends, Cody," Jake said, giving his dog the code words to go off duty and socialize.

Greene went down on one knee and gave Cody a hug. "Hey, you golden furball from hell. How are you doing, huh, big guy?"

Cody accepted the hug and wagged his tail. Greene was one of the few people he ever allowed to hold onto him.

She stood up. Jake gazed into her sea-blue eyes for a moment. She held eye contact and didn't blink.

It seemed to Jake she sensed he was admiring her eye color. He looked away at Cody. "I think this is the second time you've helped save my life. Thank you."

She smoothed the jacket of her dark pantsuit over her pistol and badge. "Anytime. I just go where they tell me to. But I have to admit, when they said Cody might be lost at sea, I was worried sick about him."

Jake held out his hand to shake hers. "Cody appreciates it. You're special to him."

They shook hands, their eyes met again and then she quickly turned away to pat Cody on the back. "Sure. Don't mention it."

An officer approached, his handheld radio crackling, and Jake heard the question, "Status report?"

The officer replied, "Man and dog are on board. Good to go." He then turned to Jake. "The captain wants to have a word with you. Follow me."

Nodding, Jake patted his thigh. "Cody, heel."

Cody came close and stood right next to Jake.

The officer hesitated. "The dog should stay here."

"No, sir. We're partners. He goes where I go," Jake said. "That's nonnegotiable, or else I'll have to skip the captain's meeting. No offense."

The officer stared hard at Jake.

Cody growled.

Greene displayed her Secret Service badge. "With respect, sir, your captain already approved it."

The officer spoke into his radio, listened to the reply, and let out a loud breath. "Fine, let's go."

Jake said to Greene, "We'll be right back—don't leave without us. I know Easton gets impatient with me."

Greene smiled and shook her head. She picked up the two vests and the radio from the deck and walked toward the helo.

Jake followed the officer, with Cody trotting by his side like a shadow.

The officer led Jake into an empty meeting room and told him to wait there, closing the door behind him as he left.

Cody sniffed around the room, searching for any threats, the way he always did.

Jake watched his dog and thought about how Cody hadn't accepted his deprogramming after he'd EAS'd at his end of active service. He still searched rooms, bags and people as if it was his job and his duty. Jake always let him do it. Some dogs need a job, Cody most of all.

Jake heard a click, glanced toward the sound and saw the doorknob turning.

Cody growled protectively, his hackles rising.

CHAPTER 6

The ship's captain opened the door and entered. He was a tall, fit man in his early forties with close-cropped hair and a flat stomach, wearing a starched white uniform shirt and highly shined shoes and projecting an aura of command. "I'm Captain Ballard."

Jake stood ramrod straight and gave him a crisp salute out of respect and old habit, even though he was no longer active-duty. "Jake Wolfe and Cody, sir."

The captain returned the salute, and the look in his eyes said he appreciated Jake's respect.

Cody stared at the man, and his nostrils flared.

"Easy, now," Jake said, holding onto the belt-leash.

The captain appeared unafraid as he looked fondly at the dog. "I had a chocolate lab named Hershey when I was growing up, and she meant the world to me."

"Be friends, Cody," Jake said.

Cody slowly approached the uniformed man who exuded power. He sniffed his hand and then wagged his tail, seeming to decide they might get along okay.

After the doggie sniff "handshake," the captain held out his hand to Jake.

Jake shook hands firmly. He noted the captain's grip was like iron. "Thank you for helping us with our mission tonight, sir," he said.

"Agent McKay can be very persuasive," Ballard said. "And besides, I couldn't leave two Marine combat veterans adrift and hunted in *my* water."

"McKay knows that particular Marine veteran is irreplaceable." Jake gestured at Cody.

"She also told me the government issued you a Letter of Marque and Reprisal. Are you authorized to explain any more about it to me?" Ballard asked.

Jake nodded. "Yes, sir, but only in general terms. The law itself is little known, but it's not top secret."

"She said it allows you to operate in a similar way to the Coast Guard. That sounded farfetched to me. Do I understand it correctly?"

"Let me put on my lawyer hat for a moment and give you a quick summary." Jake mimicked putting on a hat.

Captain Ballard raised his eyebrows. "Wait, you're a lawyer? Flying on a SPIE rope over the ocean with a war dog on a moonless night after doing God-knows-what mission?"

Jake grinned. "Practicing law is my day job. I got myself an internet law degree, studying evenings and weekends, and all the other lawyers hate me for that."

Ballard laughed. "Okay, tell me about your Letter of Marque."

"It officially converts my civilian boat, the *Far Niente*, into a Naval auxiliary. It also makes me a commissioned privateer with jurisdiction to conduct reprisal operations worldwide, and I'm covered by the protection of the laws of war."

"You're serious?"

"Yes, sir, and I'm operating under admiralty and maritime law, giving me broad legal powers on the water similar to what the Coast Guard has. I'm also allowed to *mete out judgment*. It's an old, very powerful and rarely used legal instrument from the swashbuckling pirate days."

The captain stared at him. "That's incredible. Where's your boat? Tell me about her."

"She's a sixty-foot power yacht, berthed in San Francisco Bay at the moment. My home harbor is a midpoint on the West Coast between San Diego to the south and Seattle to the north."

The captain scratched his chin. "If you're going to continue operating against modern-day pirates in my part of the ocean, I want to be aware of it."

Jake wasn't sure what type of top-secret clearances the captain might or might not have regarding these kinds of unusual missions. Rather than argue, all he said was, "The only thing I have planned right now is a long-overdue vacation."

"No more unscheduled helicopter fast rope landings at night on my ship?"

"Not if I can help it, sir."

Captain Ballard held his gaze. "Just for the record, that flight was highly irregular."

"Yes, sir, my work is too, but we both protect America in our own way."

Ballard thought that over for a moment. "All right, young man, enjoy your leave, you're dismissed."

"Yes, sir. Thank you, sir," Jake said, saluting again in thanks to the man who'd bent a few rules to help rescue Cody.

Returning to the deck, Jake held Cody's belt-leash tight as they walked toward the copter. Greene gestured at him to get on board. He and Cody climbed in, and the helo powered up and took off.

As they rose in the air, Jake looked out the window and saw a uniformed woman peering up at the helo, the one who'd given him a bottled water for Cody. He smiled at her and waved. She smiled and waved in reply. Cody woofed and put his right front paw on the window. The woman laughed and nodded, waving at the dog.

Once airborne, Jake asked, "Do you have any food on this bird?"

Greene shook her head. "None."

Jake called out, "Easton, put her down on the roof of the first Super Duper Burger we fly over. Cody likes their organic vanilla ice cream cones."

Cody wagged his tail.

Easton glanced back and shook his head. "They don't have those in San Diego, only in the Bay Area. And besides, you know we're not landing on any damned rooftops."

Jake smiled at how Easton always took everything so literally. He acted shocked and looked at his dog. "That's just wrong. Cody, can you believe this *Bravo Sierra?*"

Cody barked twice and shook his head at the often-heard military alphabet code for *BS*.

Jake called out to Easton again. "What about In-N-Out Burger? Check Google Maps, bro!"

Easton ignored him.

Jake smiled. He could never resist joking around with Easton. He felt a weight lifted off his shoulders now that Cody was safe from the sharks. His heartbeat slowed, his adrenaline levels dropped, exhaustion set in and he craved a drink of Irish whiskey.

Greene took out her phone and called McKay using a program similar to FaceTime or Skype, only encrypted. "We're exfiltrating. Jake and Cody are on board the copter, and their mission was a success."

McKay's exhausted face appeared on the phone display.

Jake noted she was once again putting in long hours of overtime protecting her fellow Americans.

McKay said, "Jake, what is your gut feeling about the op?"

"My feeling is, this was only a temporary fix," Jake said. "As long as a buyer will offer big money for stolen boats, somebody will step in and supply them."

McKay nodded. "We're having the right argument with the wrong person."

"Agreed. The one thing keeping the piracy going is this new cartel buying stolen boats. And the main person keeping the new cartel going is the mysterious leader. If we find that man and remove him from the game along with his top associates, we might stop the piracy and terrorism."

"We can cut the head off a snake, but another cartel might fill the void."

"I'm not so sure. Don't most cartels *buy* boats from their legal owners and pay more than they're worth, to avoid unwanted attention?"

"Yes, but this young new guy is more impatient, greedy and brutal."

"That will be his undoing," Jake said, sounding as if it was already decided and planned.

McKay paused a moment. "Does this mean you're volunteering to hunt down and eliminate the narcoterrorist boss of this new cartel?"

Jake gazed at the phone display and shook his head. "No, my dog needs a rest and I'm finally going to take some time off, like we agreed. Why can't you find someone else to handle the problem instead of me?"

"Because I know your history and how far you'll go to protect innocent lives."

Jake made an effort to suppress the memories of his violent history—years of war and fighting overseas and the death of good friends.

He said, "The Irish writer James Joyce once wrote: 'History is a nightmare from which I'm trying to awake.' I often feel the same."

McKay lifted her chin and held his gaze. "Jake, I understand it's a nightmare, but when you're a patriot with talent, courage and powerful skills, it's your duty to make sacrifices for the good of your country. You are morally obligated and can't just quit when you get tired of it all."

Jake stared at her image for a moment. "Thanks, but I'm not quitting the team, only taking some temporary leave, just like any other active-duty service person who's paid their dues and far more."

McKay appeared to think it over, then said, "All right, you've certainly earned some leave. Rest up and we'll talk again soon."

Jake said, "And I hope you'll please go home now, get some sleep and wake up to a hug from your loved ones." He stared pointedly at her, feeling she was past the point of exhaustion and needed a push from a friend.

McKay held his gaze and nodded, a tired, grateful smile on her face, as if nobody had ever said that to her. The phone went dark, and Jake handed it back to Greene.

Greene glanced at Jake in surprise, as if now understanding more about his complicated relationship with McKay. She asked, "It's none of my business, but what are you going to do on your time off? Party like a sailor on shore leave?"

Jake shook his head as he stared out the helo window at the ocean. "Relax at a beach in Cabo San Lucas, Baja Mexico. With plenty of warm sunshine, tasty tacos, cold beers and margaritas. Did I mention the tacos?"

Cody woofed in apparent approval.

CHAPTER 7

In a beautiful rural area of western Mexico, an ambitious new cartel boss enjoyed life at his luxurious hacienda.

The estate's walled compound featured acres of land on all sides, a twelve-bedroom mansion, and a large swimming pool in the outdoor entertaining area. A fenced corral served as a boxing ring, and a stage for dog fights and cock fights.

Scores of armed guards patrolled the landscaped grounds to ensure his safety from rivals who wanted him dead. A helicopter sat on a landing pad, ready for a quick escape if necessary.

His cartel name was *El Rojo*, "The Red One." He'd earned the name by causing endless bloodshed. Now most people simply referred to him as Rojo—Red.

His appearance was that of a successful businessman, well-dressed in custom-tailored linen suit pants, a sky-blue Armani dress shirt, a Rolex watch and handmade Italian loafers. He was clean-cut, with a short hairstyle and freshly-shaved face. No gang tattoos visible on his neck. He could walk into a bank and appear as if he might be the bank's manager.

He sat at an outdoor table in the shade of a palapa tree, drinking a cup of café con leche and smoking a Padrón Anniversary Series Maduro cigar from Nicaragua. The perfectly handmade stick burned evenly, and the rich velvety smoke tasted of toasty sweet earthiness, dark chocolate, and a hint of caramel. It went well with the coffee and reminded him of his home country of Nicaragua where he'd once owned a successful cigar business.

After he'd worked his way up from nothing, the company had done well and he'd employed hundreds of *torcedors*—cigar rollers—men and women equally, who rolled a variety of cigars by hand.

One day, men from a Colombian drug cartel had insisted he allow them to smuggle cocaine in with his shipments of cigars into the United States. He'd refused at first, until they'd killed his brother, shot many of his employees, and burned down one of his barns filled with tons of valuable fermenting sun-grown tobacco.

Under the threat of death to every member of his family and all of his employees, he'd finally agreed to the smuggling. He was paid a fortune as he learned about the astonishing profits to be made in narcotrafficking.

The US Drug Enforcement Agency in Florida found cocaine hidden in with his cigar shipments and confiscated his entire inventory of cigars throughout the USA. At home, the Nicaraguan National Police arrested him and seized his business, property and bank accounts.

Luckily, he'd hidden away plenty of cash, prepping in case of disaster.

While he served time in prison, one of his mistresses bribed some guards and they allowed him to escape.

Bitter and angry, he made his way north to Guatemala, snuck across Mexico's southern border and joined the endless flood of undocumented migrants from Guatemala, Honduras and El Salvador. Most of them were fleeing crime and violence, and they remained in Mexico.

He traveled to Mexico's west coast and started life over with nothing but a suitcase full of cash, the shirt on his back and the hatred in his heart.

After working for a while as a farm laborer, he decided to go into the crystal meth business and make fast money via chemistry. This second time in business, he vowed to be absolutely ruthless with anyone who threatened him or his family. The dead can't hurt you, and people are easy to kill. It was a truth he'd learned in prison, the gray-walled university of crime.

Birds chirped in nearby trees and woke him from his reverie. Every day, his servants placed small chunks of fruits onto sharpened branch twigs in the trees. It kept the birds busy, so they wouldn't land on his table and try to peck at his meal.

It pleased Rojo to hear their cheerful songs as they happily obeyed his wishes. He looked around at his estate in pride, feeling like the king of his domain and dictator of his people.

He'd quickly become wealthy and powerful, and now he commanded respect and loyalty from his cartel, and instilled fear in everyone else. Many people hated him, while others blessed him for his generosity.

Life was good when you sold an addictive product to a vast market, brought in literally tons of cash money, and didn't pay any taxes. The bribes he paid to officials on both sides of the border were a kind of tax, however. He smiled at his own wit.

Rojo had never planned on being one of the "big bosses" among the cartels. He'd only wanted to carve out his own modest share of what he referred to as the *independent pharmaceutical business*, while remaining below the radar of the DEA.

But it was too late for that now. Musicians were singing *narcocorrido* ballads about his exploits. They'd dubbed his group "Los Carniceros"—the Butchers. The other, more established cartels were not amused by this newcomer who earned millions without their approval.

He'd grown up in poverty but always promised himself he'd find a way to earn a good living and earn respect. He'd started with cigars, but it wasn't his fault if the Colombian cartels had ruined it all.

The American gringos wanted to buy drugs and get high. The United States was the largest consumer of illegal drugs in the entire world. Somebody would supply their needs and get rich quick. Why not him? It was like the failed US alcohol prohibition all over again. History repeating itself. Mexico was the new Chicago. Maybe he would be the next Al Capone, and hopefully avoid any modern-day Eliot Ness and FBI team of Untouchables.

Glancing at the nearby fenced arena, he watched a rooster strutting around with razor-sharp spurs attached to its legs. The fighting cock was being trained to battle another to the death in a bloodsport exhibition.

Rojo and his men would place bets on the outcome. If anyone said the sport was inhumane, he'd tell those hypocrites his fighting cocks lived a far better life and died with more nobility than the mass-produced grocery store chicken they'd had for dinner.

His nephew, Tomás, walked up to him. The young man was in his mid-teens, wore new bluejeans and a Mexico National Team futbol jersey, had an enthusiastic smile and was in need of a haircut.

Tomás said, "I caught another one!" He held a tablet in one hand and gestured at a nearby device that looked similar to a large CCTV camera but was aimed up at the clouds. As they both followed the strange camera's line of sight, they saw a black quadcopter drone falling slowly from the sky.

It landed on the ground, and Tomás picked it up and removed the batteries, carrying it to his uncle. "This is a DJI Tech drone. One of the latest and best models. They cost thousands of dollars and are used by US law enforcement agencies."

Rojo patted Tomás on the back. "Impressive. You can add it to your ever-growing collection. I'm still not sure how you can capture a spy drone and make it land at your feet, but I like it."

Tomás grinned. "I could tell you, but then I'd have to kill you."

Rojo smiled and nodded at the familiar joke. "Indulge me. What black magic do you use?"

Tomás pointed at the camera device, which was once again scanning the skies for threats, then gazed at his phone and read a description. "The device is known as an Airbus Drone Disable System. It uses a new science called smart responsive jamming technology. In plain words, the device automatically detects a drone flying over the property up to a height of around five kilometers, jams its signals, disables it and takes control."

"And it's on duty twenty-four hours a day?"

"Yes, protecting you around the clock."

Rojo raised one eyebrow. "What if someone cut our power?"

"I have it hooked up to its own generator that will kick on instantly in the case of a power outage," Tomás said.

Rojo smiled proudly at his nephew. "You're a young genius. I'm glad you enjoy working with these technological wonders."

Tomás shrugged humbly. "I just love science, inventions and intelligent ideas. For example, I learned the Dutch National Police use large birds of prey such as bald eagles to fly up and grab a small drone in midair with their talons and bring it down to the ground. I'd love to have a bird like that." He held out his tablet and displayed a YouTube video.

Rojo chuckled at the kid's enthusiasm. "If you want one, you shall have one, my brilliant boy."

Tomás clapped his hands in glee.

A dark gray SUV drove up and stopped. The driver stepped out, opened the back hatch and dragged out a man who had his hands zip-tied in front of him. The driver lifted him to his feet and shoved him stumbling toward Rojo.

Several more of Rojo's men approached, carrying machetes, and stood there awaiting orders to kill.

"Go inside, Tomás. You don't need to see this," Rojo said.

CHAPTER 8

Rojo pointed his cigar at the house and gestured for Tomás to go.

"No, please, uncle. I'm old enough to be involved in the business," Tomás said.

"Fifteen is too young. On your eighteenth birthday, we'll talk," Rojo said.

Tomás stood up tall. "Don't I serve you well?"

"Yes, but your father is a successful *gomero*. Why don't you follow in his footsteps and avoid the violence?"

"I hate farming the opium poppies!" Tomás said.

Rojo nodded and took a sip of coffee. "I understand. In the past, I grew tobacco, but farming is a slow way to create a product. When I lost my land, I needed a new product *instantly*. That's why I turned to chemistry."

"Uncle, I'm ready to take on more dangerous responsibilities."

"Young man, I was only teasing about you being a farmer. My dream is for you to attend Universidad Nacional Autónoma de México. It's highly ranked in all of the world. You could study at the Faculty of Sciences and get a bachelor's degree as a computer scientist."

"Thank you, but I'm hyperactive and I can't sit still in school. Please let me into the business. Test me. If I fail, I'll shut my mouth until I'm eighteen."

Rojo scratched his chin and thought it over for a moment. "Fair enough. If you fail, I'll admire you for trying. If you succeed, you'll become a man today."

He called out to the driver. "Enrique, bring him to me."

Enrique was a short man with a scar on his left cheek, black hair, a mustache, and sun-bronzed skin. He dragged the man forward and threatened him with a pistol.

Rojo studied his prisoner for a moment, puffing on his cigar while the man waited to learn his fate. Finally, he set the cigar down in a beautiful ceramic ashtray glazed with hand-painted images of an Aztec legend about the tragic love story of Popocatépetl and Iztaccíhuatl.

"You failed me, *cabrón*. You had one job, to be my backup guard and protect our boat supplier, but you allowed someone to kill him. We need more boats! I warned you what would happen if you failed me, didn't I?"

The man fell to his knees and pressed his palms together with fingers pointing up in supplication. "Please, *jefe*, I was only gone for a few minutes to get some food. The attack came right at dinnertime. When I returned, I took some video of a hotel room service waiter running from the building. He had a pistol. It's on my phone!"

Rojo considered this. He looked at Enrique. "Do you have his phone?"

"Sí, patrón," Enrique said. He reached into his pocket and tossed the phone to Tomás, who smiled, appearing thankful of how Enrique always included him and respected his tech skills.

Rojo asked, "What do you find on there, Tomás?"

Tomás tapped the phone and sought out the video. He played it for his uncle and they both watched. On a dark night, a tall man in a black tuxedo came jogging down some stairs to the beach, ran across the sand and launched a dinghy onto the water. When the man passed by the camera, you could just see his face for one second, and a moment later his jacket flapped up in the breeze and revealed a pistol tucked in the back of his pants.

"I'll take screenshots of his face and pistol, and brighten the images," Tomás said.

Rojo nodded, trusting Tomás to do the strange technical work for him.

Moments later, Tomás said, "There he is, the man who killed our boat supplier, and the pistol he used to do it." He handed the phone to his uncle.

Rojo stared at the two pictures. "Who is this troublemaker?"

"Let me put his face into Google image search," Tomás said.

The prisoner on his knees let out a breath of relief. "You see? I helped find him for you, boss!"

Tomás showed the search results to Rojo. "I didn't get an exact match, but found him in the similar images. It looks like his name is Jake Wolfe and he lives in Sausalito, California, up near San Francisco. In the past he worked as a photojournalist and now he's an attorney. I wonder if he might still be in San Diego, or on his way north."

Rojo cursed. "Why would a damned lawyer kill my boat supplier?"

The nearby anti-drone mechanism turned with a mechanical whine and pointed up at another patch of sky.

Rojo glanced at it and then at his nephew.

Tomás nodded in reply. "He might be working for the US government, and the lawyer job is only a cover."

Rojo looked at the second photo and studied the pistol in the man's waistband. "Is that one of the Glocks carried by DEA agents? No, it's the same kind of pistol our boat supplier and his crew carried. Wolfe obviously took it away from his target and used it against the idiot."

Tomás tapped the phone display and brought up more photos of Wolfe. "Look at this! Jake Wolfe is friends on social media with Sammy Lopez."

Rojo scowled. "Pez Lopez, the man who stole my prized possession?"

"Yes, uncle. Maybe he knows the location of your hard drive."

The prisoner said, "Let me kidnap Wolfe and bring him here so you can question him. I'll go at once, *por favor.*"

Rojo looked at the screenshot of Wolfe's face and saw the eyes of a capable and dangerous no-nonsense man—maybe a combat veteran or former policeman. He pursed his lips, deep in thought. "You're sure you could bring him to me alive?"

"Yes, I swear it!"

Rojo took a sip of coffee and set the cup down. "No. You failed me. I'll have to send Enrique to do your job." He made a chopping motion with his hand.

Enrique and several other men attacked the prisoner from all sides, wielding machetes and hacking him to death as he screamed for mercy.

Rojo spoke to his nephew. "Tomás, this is your test. Prove to me you're old enough to be in the business."

Tomás moved toward the prisoner with a set jaw and a determined walk, his hands clenched in fists. Enrique handed him a machete and gave him a confident nod, waving the other men back to allow Tomás his moment. Tomás raised the machete high and brought it down with all his might into the dying man's neck. He hit a jugular vein, and the man fell over, bleeding to death like an animal in a slaughterhouse.

Enrique and the other men slapped Tomás on the back, congratulating him for his heartless brutality.

Rojo nodded in approval. "Good work, Tomás. I'm impressed."

"Anything for you, patrón," Tomás said, bowing his head in respect.

Rojo smiled. "You are a man now. Welcome to the business."

Tomás stood proudly, at a loss for words. "Gracias."

Enrique said, "Tomás did well."

Rojo met his eyes. "Enrique, I want you to find Jake Wolfe and bring him to me along with Sammy Lopez. We'll torture both of them and learn what Pez did with my damned hard drive."

Enrique nodded. "I'll go at once, patrón."

Tomás said, "I'll use the internet to find Wolfe's current location."

"Excellent, but first, a well-earned drink for my loyal soldiers," Rojo said. He poured shots of Reserva de la Familia Tequila for his killers, his *sicarios*, including one for his young nephew.

Rojo lifted his own glass in a toast. "To our brotherhood, where only the strong survive. Spread the word: I own this territory, I am the boss and *we* are the law."

The men and the boy drank with their boss, their *jefe*. They were among the strong, they were killers, they feared nothing and no one. Who could dare challenge them?

CHAPTER 9

Cabo San Lucas,
Baja California, Mexico

Two days later, Enrique walked into an upscale Cabo hotel, passing through the lobby resplendent with plants and tile, and outside to the beachside cantina. He sat at a table on the sand among the early lunch crowd, sipping a cold beer and pretending to be a clueless tourist, looking at his phone when he should be appreciating the world-class view of the beach and seashore.

He rubbed the scar on his left cheek as he secretly observed his target: Jake Wolfe. That was him, no doubt about it. His orders were to capture Wolfe and his friend Sammy Lopez, and take them to Rojo's hacienda.

Out on the water, Jake stood barefoot on a paddle board, wearing board shorts, sunglasses and a smile as he coasted across the warm turquoise water toward the sugary white sand beach.

He planted the paddle into the salty sea water and pulled it back toward him, alternating strokes on either side of the board: left and right, left and right. The powerful muscles of his bare chest and strong arms bulged under his suntanned skin with every stroke.

Enrique noted with respect how Wolfe's torso was marked by an amazing variety of battle scars. He had received damn near every war wound a man could suffer and survive.

Luckily, Tomás had quickly assembled a sparse intel file on Wolfe, discovered his location and learned that the scars came from wounds he'd survived as an infantry Marine in combat overseas.

Those days were supposed to be behind him now, but Wolfe had killed their boat supplier at the fancy hotel. This man obviously had a lot of secrets and was not to be underestimated.

The dog stood on the board in front of Jake, smiling a retriever dog smile and wagging his tail. His short golden coat looked like it might be the result of a cross between a yellow Lab and a Golden Retriever.

According to gossip, every person at the resort who saw the dog wanted to pet him, but Jake didn't allow it. He'd said there were two reasons. First, Cody was trained as a service dog, wore an official registration tag on his collar, and you shouldn't pet service dogs when they're working. Second, Cody had served overseas as a military working dog (MWD), and if he didn't know you, he didn't trust you.

Cody wore a lightweight yellow nylon vest bearing black lettering in English and Spanish that read: *Service Dog - Perro de Servicio*. Tourists pointed at him and took pictures and video with their phones.

Enrique didn't share their happy enthusiasm. To him, the dog appeared alert and protective, always looking around and sniffing the air, ready for action.

He tore his gaze away from the dog and focused on taking slow, deliberate breaths as he prepared for the abduction.

But where was Sammy Lopez? Where was the girlfriend named Sarah? He planned to kidnap all of the targets together at one time. They'd use the woman as leverage against Wolfe. The man might never break unless he saw her suffering in terrible ways.

The thought of harming an innocent female made Enrique sick to his stomach. It was one thing to kill a violent man, but Jesús would not forgive what Rojo had planned for Sarah.

He closed his eyes for a moment. *I'm going to hell.*

~

Jake paddled toward the beach, his arm muscles straining. Suddenly he felt a tingling at the back of his neck, as if he was being watched and might be facing danger. It was a kind of sixth sense he'd developed in combat. The strange ability had become far more pronounced after a recent near-death experience where he'd nearly drowned.

He peered at the beach, the hotel windows and nearby boats, but didn't see any threats, only tourists enjoying the beautiful resort.

The feeling reminded him of how he wanted a normal life now, and to fit into society. However, after killing enemy combatants in war, going on several covert missions to assassinate high-value targets for the CIA, and now helping Agent McKay and the POETs to protect America's west coast, he feared his life would never be normal again.

He should probably give up any notion of having a wife and kids. His missions would take him away from them, and he could get himself killed in a way no life insurance policy would cover.

He glanced at his dog and saw him sniffing the air and observing the people. Once, while deployed overseas, Cody'd had no choice but to kill an enemy combatant. He'd saved his platoon, but his handler had died in the fighting. The dog had taken it hard. Now he was highly protective of Jake and his pack and was rarely "off duty."

Everywhere Jake looked he saw female tourists in bikinis, their exposed bodies glistening with suntan oil.

One truly spectacular brunette in blue denim shorts, a white tank top and leather sandals walked out of the hotel toward the water and waved at Jake. He smiled at seeing his girlfriend, Sarah. They'd agreed to meet in Cabo for a much-needed vacation. She'd just arrived and was a beautiful sight to see, with long dark hair, a warm smile and cute eyes that sparkled when she laughed. He had strong feelings for her, growing stronger every day. Surfing to the beach, Jake ran the board up onto the sand.

Cody jumped off and trotted over to Sarah, wagging his tail.

Sarah went down on one knee and gave the dog a hug. "Hi, sweetheart. Did you miss me?"

Cody shook his fur and sent drops of water flying in all directions. Sarah smiled at the dog. He'd put water spots all over her shorts and top, but as a veterinarian and dog lover, she just smiled and didn't appear to mind at all.

Jake appreciated how Sarah didn't get upset over every little thing in life, the way his former fiancée had. He pulled the borrowed paddle board up onto the beach, flipped it over and laid the long paddle on the sand next to it, leaving it there for the next hotel guest who might want to use it. He smiled at Sarah and walked up to her as she stood up to greet him.

"Hello, beautiful. Have we met?" Jake asked with a wink.

"Not yet, but I'm here looking for a hot date," Sarah replied with a smile.

Jake smiled in return. "Look no further, I'm here alone and I've got this cool dog."

Sarah laughed. "You had me at cool dog. He's amazing." She put her arms around Jake's neck.

Jake held her tight and they kissed as if they'd been apart for a long time instead of only a few days.

Female tourists relaxing on chaise lounges nearby watched the public display of affection with rapt attention from behind their designer sunglasses.

Jake noticed. He maintained situational awareness and was always observant of his surroundings, but he paid no attention to the tourists; he only had eyes for Sarah. "Do you like our suite?"

"Yes, it's beautiful, and I love our view of the harbor and seashore. But what does a girl have to do to get a cold beer from a cabana boy around here?"

Jake called out to a Mexican boy who looked to be around eighteen. As a war veteran, Jake thought of the civilian as just a kid. Jake was only in his late twenties, but he felt like combat had aged him in dog years. He had an old soul.

"Manuel, can you ask a waitress to bring us dos cervezas, tres aguas, and a bowl for señor perro?" Jake asked.

"Sí, patrón, un momento," Manuel said and ran off fast toward the bar.

Sarah raised her eyebrows at Jake. "You speak Spanglish, El Patrón?"

Jake smiled and shrugged. "Manuel calls me boss because I tip him well. He's a good kid, working to help support his family."

"What have you and Cody been up to?"

"Yesterday we went sport fishing and I caught and released a couple of striped marlins." Jake displayed photos on his phone.

"They're so beautiful. It's nice you released them."

He gazed out at the ocean. "I even said I was sorry for the inconvenience."

She laughed.

~

At a nearby table, Enrique innocently tapped on his phone while secretly taking pictures of Jake and Sarah. He sent a text to Rojo.

Enrique: *The woman joined Wolfe. No sign of Lopez.*

The reply from Rojo came quickly: *Let me know the minute Lopez arrives. And watch out for Wolfe's dog. The rumor is he's trained to bite off your cojones.*

Enrique glanced at the dog again, noticing its teeth, and looked away while crossing his legs. He'd always been afraid of dogs, and he shuddered at the thought of being bitten on the crotch by a military-trained beast.

The cartel would use Cody in dog fight exhibitions, where people would pay money to see a war dog get into the ring with an angry, abused Pit Bull Terrier and fight to the death. They'd place bets on which one would live or die.

Enrique secretly felt sorry for the Bull Mastiff Terrier dogs who were beaten and trained to be violent in the ring, but he could never say so out loud, or he'd appear weak. On a bad day, he often felt like he was an abducted Pit Bull himself, taken from his family and forced into a life of violence he didn't want, with no way to escape until death.

Reaching inside his camera bag, he touched the pistol to boost his confidence and remembered something one of the americano members of the cartel had said to him: *When in doubt, shoot your way out.*

CHAPTER 10

Jake and Sarah ended their embrace just as a pretty Mexican waitress approached them carrying a tray with two bottles of Modelo Especial beer, three bottled waters and an empty bowl, along with a basket of tortilla chips and a dish of salsa. She tilted her head and raised her eyebrows at Jake, indicating an available table in the outdoor cantina.

"Bueno," Jake said, smiling. He led Sarah to the table, signed the tab and added a tip for the waitress.

"Gracias," the waitress said.

"De nada," Jake replied.

Sarah sat down under the shade of a large umbrella and took a sip of her ice-cold beer. "Ahh, I needed this."

Jake filled the bowl with water and set it down for Cody, who lapped up some water and coughed afterward. The waitress continued standing there, smiling at Jake. "Anything else, Señor Lobo?"

Jake smiled when she used the Spanish word for wolf. "Yes, could you please give me a large beach towel for my dog?"

The waitress went to the bar, grabbed a big white towel, and gave it to Jake with a smile before walking away to take another table's order.

Jake removed Cody's vest, used the towel to dry off his dog's fur, and then spread out the towel in the shade for Cody to lie on, snapping his fingers and gesturing with a hand signal.

Cody stretched out prone on the towel and rested his head on his paws.

Sarah smiled at Cody. "How's our boy liking Baja so far?"

Jake noted how she called Cody *our* boy. He liked that. "Cody enjoys the warm water and always wants me to toss a Frisbee into the surf so he can fetch it. Everybody here loves him. They call him *el perro dorado.*"

"The golden dog," Sarah said, reaching down to pat Cody on the head.

Jake nodded. "Yesterday, I sent Cody to fetch a cold beer from the bar, carrying a rolled-up napkin holding some pesos as a tip for the bartender. Cody carried back the beer in a woven basket with a handle, and now everybody is watching him and talking about him."

Sarah said, "Speaking of people watching and talking—if you don't mind me asking, where is your shirt? Aren't you supposed to wear one in a restaurant?"

She glanced at the women pretending not to stare at Jake's muscled chest as they discussed him among themselves. The battle scars all over his torso caused some men to take a second glance too. Jake looked down at his chest, furrowed his brow in pretend confusion.

"Huh, I'm pretty sure I had a shirt on just a few minutes ago."

Sarah smiled and shook her head. "So, we're really going to see mama gray whales and their babies in the morning?"

"Yeah, my buddy Pez has a cousin who runs an approved whale watching service at Magdalena Bay."

"Pez?"

"Pez is the nickname for my infantry Marine friend Sammy Lopez from San Diego," Jake said. "He's going along with us to see the whales."

Sarah dipped a chip in salsa. "I remember you talking about a friend named Sammy."

"With a nickname like Pez, people are always giving him Pez candy dispensers. He has an amazing collection."

"I heard that the Mexican government is protective of the whales and the areas where they give birth," Sarah said.

Jake took a drink of beer and set down the bottle. "True, but the cousin has official permits. He's been doing it for years and years."

Sarah chewed the tortilla chip and took a sip of beer. "The shuttle driver told me this is an especially good time of year to see the baby whales."

Jake looked out at the ocean. "Yes, at the end of February and beginning of March, the babies have nursed and grown, and the mama whales will bring them out and about."

Sarah got an amused look on her face. "So, the gray whale schedule is why you declined an invitation to Daniel Anderson's presidential inauguration?"

Jake lifted a shoulder. "It was the reason I gave to Daniel and Katherine, but mostly I didn't want to take Cody all the way to Washington, or leave him behind."

"Katherine looked so brave on TV, standing there showing a baby bump in her maternity dress, along with a bald head and flat chest," Sarah said.

"She's going to survive the breast cancer and chemo, give birth to a healthy baby, and be a wonderful First Lady," Jake said with emotion in his voice. He'd fought an assassin to the death while protecting Katherine's life. She'd told him they were friends forever, and he agreed.

Sarah gazed at the harbor and the variety of boats. "It used to be, they wouldn't do chemo on pregnant women, but in recent years they've successfully used low-dose treatments for breast cancer in hundreds of cases with no harm to the baby."

"Many women end the pregnancy, but Katherine struggled with infertility for so many years she would not let go. She told Daniel she wanted a child more than her breasts. He supported her, whatever she decided."

She stared at Jake, trying to guess how he'd react to her own pregnancy. "How many people will be on the whale watching boat with us?" She glanced at Cody and then at Jake, her eyes questioning.

"It'll be a small open panga boat with just the boat skipper, you, me, Cody and Pez. They don't usually allow dogs, but I paid extra to bring Cody along. You know how he has a special love of whales."

Cody sat up when he heard the words, wagging his tail and eagerly looking around as if wondering, *Whales? Did somebody mention whales?*

Sarah laughed. "You're so funny, Cody."

Cody gave her a toothy grin.

∾

Sarah took a few sips from her beer and then switched to water. She hadn't planned on starting a family at this stage in life, wasn't ready yet, and felt conflicted about what to do. Her plan had been to wait a few more years, and then decide if and when to bring a child into this crazy world.

Should she talk it over with Jake? End the pregnancy without mentioning it? Go ahead and have the baby, no matter what Jake wanted or didn't want?

For some reason she felt torn, half-fearing and half-hoping Jake might want to raise a child with her. But it was a huge, life-altering responsibility. One they hadn't discussed. A lot could change during the two decades it took to nurture a child into an adult. She knew so many single moms who bravely struggled to survive every day.

How many people stayed *happily* married for *twenty* years? Well, okay, she actually did know quite a few who were happy grandparents now, and it gave her hope.

The only thing she was absolutely sure of was that she hadn't been intimate with anybody else. Jake was the father. However, she'd recently refused his invitation to go together in an exclusive relationship, so would he believe her or ask for a paternity test?

Why had she refused his offer?

Her career was finally taking off and her veterinary clinic had an ever-growing list of happy clients. She'd worked so hard for so long getting to this point, and now an earthquake in her life could bring it all crashing down.

She took a deep breath and let it out, remembering her plan had always been career now and motherhood later.

CHAPTER 11

Jake noticed Sarah lost in thought and wondered what was on her mind. She seemed to be worried about something. If their positions were switched, she'd ask him what he was thinking about. He didn't like being asked that question, so he didn't pose it to her.

The waitress walked past their table carrying a tray with plates of food that smelled delicious.

"How about some lunch?" Jake asked.

"I'd love it," Sarah said.

"They have fresh-caught lobster. Would you like a lobster tail with melted butter, along with some rice, beans and tortillas?"

"Lobster tail? Now you're talking," Sarah said.

Jake waved at Manuel, and the boy took his order. "And dos cervezas, por favor," Jake said.

"No more cervezas for me," Sarah said, holding up a hand to signal stop.

Jake gave her a curious look. "Okay, una cerveza."

Manuel nodded and ran off toward the kitchen.

Sarah took a drink of water. "The beer was making me sleepy because I stayed up late last night catching up on paperwork. That and the jet lag and hot weather have me looking for a hammock to take a siesta."

"We could go to our room for a siesta after lunch. It's a tradition and might even be required by law here," Jake said with an innocent smile.

Sarah gave him a warm smile in reply and her eyes sparkled. "Hmmm, I know how our siesta would end up. You'd be having your way with me in bed and I wouldn't get any rest at all."

~

Enrique observed Sarah and got a bad feeling. She had a confident way about her that told him she was no pushover. He sent a text to his employer.

Enrique: *Send me more men. Sarah appears to be a woman who can take care of herself. And as for the dog, I believe he will fight hard.*

He added a string of curses in Spanish to make his point.

Rojo: *You're afraid of a female, and a perro?*

Enrique: *No, I'm afraid of YOU, patrón. I refuse to fail you. We have plenty of men available, and it's a sign of power to use overwhelming force.*

Rojo: *I appreciate your honesty. Tell me more about this war dog.*

Enrique: *He keeps looking at me. I predict he will quickly kill at least one of our men; maybe take bites out of two or three before he can be tranquilized.*

Rojo: *He'll be worth a fortune in the dog fights.*

Enrique: *Not if he escapes. Please send additional men at once.*

Rojo: *I'll send six extra men, heavily armed. Shoot anyone and everyone you have to, but take my prisoners alive.*

Enrique: *Sí, patrón. Gracias.*

Enrique swore silently to himself. His country's male culture was one of machismo, but he'd seen women who could kill just as well as any man. And the dog appeared smarter than any he'd ever seen. He would not allow himself to be caught off guard by Sarah or Cody.

And if the dog was going to kill a few of Rojo's people, they should be others, not Enrique. This was why the boss had put him in charge of this operation. He always thought ahead and saw the problems to be overcome. He wasn't arrogant; he was thoughtful. Nobody else had his instincts. Some lower-level cartel men would die from Cody's bites, but Enrique would then capture the valuable beast.

He looked around at the hotel guests and staff. Some of these innocent people would be killed as collateral damage and there was nothing he could do about it. They were simply in the wrong place at the wrong time. He said a silent prayer for their souls.

The honest man he used to be would never take part in such a terrible thing. He cursed quietly at himself. How had he ended up here?

Jake enjoyed talking with Sarah about the whale watching boat trip, and soon their waitress reappeared with two plates of lobster tail lunches and one plate of plain beef fajita meat without any onions or bell peppers. The unseasoned beef had been cooked first, and now it was cooled off instead of sizzling on a hot iron plate.

Jake carved off a bite of lobster, dipped it in butter and added it on top of the beef. Setting the plate down on the towel for Cody, he said, "Here you go, buddy. Enjoy."

Cody snapped up the buttery lobster morsel and swallowed it down.

"Did you even chew it, bro?" Jake asked with a laugh.

Cody began chomping on the lukewarm slices of fajita beef, his dog tags clinking against the plate.

Sarah smiled at the dog. "They know Cody's order by now?"

Jake nodded and unrolled a linen napkin to remove the silverware. "Yeah, he's a regular. He barks and tells them he'll have the usual."

Sarah laughed. "I believe it."

Jake savored a bite of lobster with lemon butter, followed by a forkful of seasoned rice. He grabbed a plastic bottle of red sauce and squeezed, adding some to his refried beans.

Sarah suddenly noticed she had an unexpected craving for seafood. She held a warm flour tortilla in her left hand as she used a fork to eat with her right, alternating bites of butter-dipped lobster and tortilla. "Yum, so amazingly good."

Jake smiled. "My girl has a healthy appetite."

Sarah didn't say what crossed her mind, how she was eating for two now. She only gave him a brave smile and said, "This lobster is deliciosa."

Jake pointed at the harbor. "That boat right there brought in these beauties early this morning. I was here taking Cody for a walk, so I helped unload the catch while Cody supervised."

"Can't get any fresher lobster than that," Sarah said.

How was she going to bring up the subject of her pregnancy? It was now or never.

CHAPTER 12

Enrique continued observing his targets, and he received a text from the cartel boss.

Rojo: *The men are almost to your location. What is Wolfe doing now?*

Enrique: *Eating, drinking and enjoying the beach, like every other tourist.*

Rojo: *No sign of Lopez?*

Enrique: *Not yet. If he's coming, he missed lunch. Sometimes the intel is wrong, or people change plans.*

Rojo didn't reply, and he could imagine the boss impatiently seething and cursing. He'd seen it before. When a man had nearly unlimited money and power, he hated to be kept waiting by any person for any reason. Mistakes were unforgivable. Life was cheap. You were easily replaced.

A few minutes later, Rojo sent another text: *I'm on a tight schedule. The hell with it. I'm sending Angel.*

Enrique's stomach dropped. *Ángel de la Muerte*—the Angel of Death—was a woman who not only killed the enemies of her cartel but enjoyed making them suffer as much pain as she could inflict upon them before they died while begging for mercy.

The sociopath even had a rogue doctor who would give her victims injections of lidocaine to keep them from passing out or having a heart attack. She wanted them awake and their hearts beating, so they could suffer longer.

He didn't reply. What was there to say? Soon, Jake Wolfe and his girlfriend would be screaming out answers to questions—and heaven help them if they didn't have the right answers.

Jake finished off his beer just as Manuel delivered another one and brought Jake's camera bag from behind the bar.

Sarah asked, "I'm curious, how can a high-school-aged kid serve beer, and why does the restaurant allow a dog, and what happened to the no-shirt-no-shoes-no-service policy?"

Jake said, "Manuel's mother works at the front desk. She got him a job when he turned eighteen, which is the perfectly legal drinking age here and in almost every country around the entire world. It was once the same in the USA, until we made buying or selling beer a crime during Prohibition. If a grown man or woman bought one cold beer after a hard day's work, they could be arrested. That seems like a fair and reasonable law, right?"

"Does this hotel allow service dogs?"

"Yes, and I gave them a copy of Cody's assistance dog registration tag issued by the San Francisco Department of Animal Care and Control. I also paid the cantina manager a generous tip and promised her my dog would behave himself. The shirt and shoes thing doesn't apply at this beach bar, but I'll put on a T-shirt if you want me to." He gave her a winning smile.

"I guess they're a lot more relaxed here about some of the strict rules we have in the States," Sarah said.

Jake nodded. "It's funny, and kind of sad too. Last night I got invited to a barbecue at a quiet beach. My hosts drove their four-wheel-drive SUVs onto the sand, lit a campfire, cooked some seafood, smoked cigars, drank beers and tossed a Frisbee for Cody. At many beaches up north, all of those things are crimes. You can't drive on the beach, light a campfire, smoke anything, drink alcohol or let your dog run free. We'd have been ticketed or arrested and maybe hauled off to jail as criminals who must be put behind bars."

Sarah rolled her eyes, and Jake knew she was used to hearing his "lawyer talk" about how he thought some laws were as stupid as the congressmen and congresswomen who constantly passed more without bothering to read them.

She asked, "How did Cody handle the flight down here?"

Jake used his linen napkin to dab at his mouth. "He flew like a champ. Bart's corporate jet is amazing. You'll get a chance to see it on our way home."

"Good, I only bought a one-way ticket, like you said to."

"Bart is planning on having you as his guest for the return flight. He'll be on vacation for several more days and can come or go as he pleases."

Sarah looked off in the distance at the beautiful view. "It must be nice to own a jet and fly anywhere you want, anytime you want."

Jake took a sip of beer. "I prefer to know somebody who owns an expensive jet and then suggest they're past due for a spontaneous vacation to sunny beaches."

Sarah gave him a knowing look. "You're a silver-tongued devil, that's for sure."

Cody finished off his fajita beef, drank some water from the bowl and let out a loud doggie burp.

Jake and Sarah both applauded. "Bravo, bravo," they said in unison.

Cody lowered his head as if taking a bow, then stretched out on the towel and sighed contentedly.

Jake reached into his camera bag, withdrew a T-shirt and pulled it over his head. He pulled on a pair of cargo shorts, and then dropped two flip-flops onto the sand and slipped them onto his feet. "Check it out: a shirt and shoes and shorts. Legal in all fifty states—at least for now anyway."

Sarah gave him a smile. "I remember visiting a hotel in Maui with a poolside bar where you could swim up and get a drink."

Jake nodded. "There are lots of them, and they remind me of the song: 'No Shoes, No Shirt, No Problem' by Kenny Chesney."

Sarah stood up. "I'm off to the ladies' room. Too much bottled water today."

"There are restrooms in the hotel lobby, unless you prefer the one in our room," Jake said.

Sarah displayed the room key. "Private versus public? No contest. I'll be right back." She walked into the hotel lobby toward the elevators.

For a moment, Jake watched her go, enjoying the guilty pleasure of admiring the amazing view of his girlfriend's beautiful backside in those formfitting short shorts. Her dark hair shone in the sun, and her toned legs gave testimony to her commitment to running and martial arts classes.

Every other man in the cantina was glancing at her in admiration but pretending not to. A few women stared and frowned.

How had he been so lucky as to meet a woman with such an amazing mind, body and soul?

CHAPTER 13

Sarah walked through the artistically designed lobby and took an elevator to her floor.

Walking down the hallway, she thought of what little she knew about very early pregnancy symptoms. She'd only found out recently, but she had the constant urge to urinate, her breasts felt tender and sore today, and this morning she'd had a touch of nausea.

Arriving at their room, she put her key in the lock and opened the door. As she did, someone stepped out of a nearby stairwell door and sprinted toward her at alarming speed.

A wiry, toned woman with short black hair and an angry look on her face closed in fast. In seconds she would get her outstretched hands onto Sarah's throat.

Sarah's martial arts and urban survival training kicked in and she ran into the room, threw her shoulder against the door and slammed it closed. She almost made it, but the woman leapt forward and put her right boot on the floor in between the door and the frame.

Both women pushed hard against the door, fighting for supremacy.

The attacker reached inside, trying to scratch Sarah's eyes. The back of her hand was tattooed with two black crosses, one of them upside-down.

Sarah bit down on the woman's fingers as hard as she could, and when the attacker cursed and withdrew her hand, Sarah kicked the boot and forced it out of the doorway.

Slamming the door closed, Sarah locked the deadbolt, grabbed her phone and called Jake. When he answered, she spoke quickly and clearly. "I was attacked at the door to our room by a woman with short black hair. I'm inside and she's in the hall. Send hotel security and the police, hurry!"

She heard Jake cursing and yelling orders at people as if he was still in the Marines and the hotel was under enemy attack. Cody barked loudly too.

Sarah's mouth dropped open as she saw a long, thick knife blade appear between the door and doorjamb. It twisted hard to one side and allowed the door lock to release.

The door burst open, and the angry woman pointed a combat knife at Sarah. One of her fingers was bleeding profusely. "Did he give you the package? Tell me where it is and I'll kill you quickly without suffering," she said. Her angry eyes told a different story.

Sarah had no idea what this crazed woman was talking about. She ran to the kitchenette and grabbed a knife from a wooden block.

The woman let the door close behind her as she chased after Sarah. They squared off in fighting stances.

"Police and hotel security are on the way," Sarah said, holding the knife up in front of her.

The woman sneered. "We pay off most of them. Give me the package, or I'll cut you open like a pig at slaughter." She suddenly threw her knife at Sarah's face.

Surprised, Sarah barely dodged the blade in time as it flew past her left eye.

"I don't have a package!" she yelled.

The woman pounced on her, grabbing the wrist of Sarah's knife hand with both of her own hands and twisting hard. "Are you here to buy it? Is it in this room? Give it to me!"

With her wrist in pain, Sarah focused on the martial arts training she practiced in classes every week in San Francisco's Chinatown neighborhood. She purposely allowed her assailant to pull her closer, and then threw a brutal punch with her left hand, the way she'd practiced endless times.

The woman tried for a head butt just as Sarah punched her in the nose. Sarah's hit had even more effect due to the target's head moving closer at the same moment.

When Sarah felt the woman's nose crunch and break under her fist, she yanked her right hand free, but in doing so, she dropped the knife and it clattered on the floor.

Sarah went on the offensive. Raising both fists, she assumed the on-guard position in the fluid style of Jeet Kune Do, the fighting system developed by Bruce Lee. She bent her knees, moved lightly on the balls of her feet and threw a straight-lead punch with her dominant right hand, hitting her opponent on the sternum and knocking a burst of air from her lungs.

The woman grunted, took a deep breath and bellowed in fury as she attacked, fighting like an angry wild animal.

Sarah maintained warrior discipline and used what are known in the art of Jeet Kune Do as intercepting fists, stop hits, stop kicks, and simultaneous parrying and punching. Her fists and feet pounded the assailant in a frenzy of hits like a human jackhammer.

The woman couldn't lay a hand on Sarah, while Sarah used her opponent as a human punching bag, scoring strike after strike on her face and upper body.

This was what she had trained for, what she'd become good at, and now she was using every ounce of skill fighting to protect herself and her pregnancy.

"Come at me and I'll destroy you," Sarah said.

Somebody threw the room's door open, slammed it against the wall with a bang and yelled, "Policia!"

The woman glared at Sarah in hatred through blackened puffy eyes as blood ran from her nose and split lip. "You're a *dead* woman," she hissed.

Sarah held up her fists in defiance, ready to fight another round. "I'm just getting warmed up."

A uniformed policeman came into the room with a pistol in his hand.

The attacker ran out the open sliding door, burst through the thin screen and dove off the balcony into the swimming pool several floors below with a loud splash, accompanied by the screams of tourists.

"Loca!" the policeman said, and yelled orders into his radio.

Sarah held her abdomen in both hands and bent at the waist. "I have to use the bathroom, it's an emergency."

The officer held up his hand with palm out. "Alto."

She disobeyed his order to stop and quickly ran into the bathroom, closed the door and locked it.

As she sat on the toilet, her hands shaking, Sarah heard Jake call out to her.

"Sarah, it's Jake. Where are you?"

Cody barked and scratched on the door with his paw.

The policeman said something in Spanish.

"If you must know, I'm taking a long-delayed and well-deserved pee," Sarah said with a fake calm as tears ran down her cheeks. Not someone to cry very often, she realized the early pregnancy hormones were affecting her body and emotions.

She wondered if this attack had anything to do with Jake's secret life as a government assassin. If it did, there was no chance of him stepping up and being a good father to their baby. No chance in hell. He might put their child in constant danger for years to come.

Maybe it would be best if she went home, paid a visit to the women's clinic and put an end to her unintended pregnancy. She'd almost done it early this morning but had sat in the clinic parking lot crying and missed an appointment with her doctor friend.

However, it broke her heart to think the choice was being pressured by her boyfriend's double life. Of all the men she could have fallen for, why did it have to be Jake, a man with a dangerous past and deadly enemies who continued to hunt him down and might never stop?

She hung her head and sobbed in despair while Cody continued to scratch on the door.

CHAPTER 14

Jake stood with his back to the bathroom door as the policeman checked his passport, driver's license and room key. He saw the officer glance at Cody, who kept pawing at the door. "Out, Cody. Sit," Jake said.

Cody obediently sat, his eyes on the officer, nostrils flaring as he took in every scent of the man's body, weapon, shoes and clothes.

While Jake had his wallet out, he removed a business card featuring the logo of the U.S. Marshals Service.

"Sir, in the past I've assisted law enforcement as a deputized citizen," he said, handing the card to the officer. "I'll be happy to cooperate and help the police in any way I can."

The officer compared Jake's name on the card to that on his driver's license and relaxed a little, pocketing the card with a nod.

Jake had been fired by the U.S. Marshals from his role as a deputized citizen, but he felt no need to explain that detail right now.

He lightly knocked on the door and called out, "Sarah?"

"Yes?"

"If you're okay in there, say the code word."

"Artemis," she said.

"Thank you." Jake let out a loud breath and restrained himself from crashing his shoulder into the door and bursting it open the way he would have if she'd said any other word.

He thought about the origin of their code word. Sarah had a tattoo on her left arm of a goddess carrying a bow and a quiver of arrows, accompanied by two hunting dogs. Many people commented on it, but few understood it. When Jake had first seen it, he'd said it looked like Artemis, the Greek goddess of the hunt and protector of life. A good archetype for a veterinary doctor. Sarah had appeared surprised, but obviously pleased with his accurate guess.

Sarah opened the door and came out, went to Jake and clung to him. He put his arms around her, held her tight and felt her shaking now that the crisis was over and her adrenaline levels were dropping.

Cody pawed at Sarah's thigh and pressed his head in between her stomach and Jake's stomach, with his butt sticking out as he wagged his tail.

After a while, Sarah let go of Jake and wiped her eyes on her sleeve. "A woman came at me with a knife and said if I'd tell her where *it* is, she'd kill me quickly without suffering."

"Where *what* is?" Jake asked.

"I don't know. She told me to give her the *package*, or she'd cut me like a pig."

"A package? It could be anything." Jake looked at her bruised hands. "Did you fight?"

"Yes, and I broke her nose." Sarah raised her fists in the on-guard position Jake knew well, having trained in the art of Jeet Kune Do also. It was a popular form of martial arts in San Francisco's Chinatown.

"I hope you kept your left elbow up," Jake said. "She didn't stand a chance against your superior fighting ability."

Sarah closed her eyes and shuddered. "I think she was criminally insane. Too late for a psychiatrist."

The police officer listened to them and wrote in a small notebook. He noted Sarah's scraped knuckles and looked at her with newfound respect in his eyes. He gestured at the balcony and spoke in accented English. "Did you know that woman?"

"No, I've never seen her before," Sarah said.

The look on the officer's face revealed his doubt. He spoke in Spanish into his radio and returned Jake's passport, driver's license and room key to him.

Sarah asked, "May I go lie down? I'm not feeling well."

The officer nodded in agreement and swept his hand, giving her the go-ahead.

Sarah climbed into bed and lay on her back on top of the covers with her right forearm resting over her eyes.

Cody jumped onto the bed and lay next to her, facing the room and keeping his watchful eyes on the policeman and the open door.

Sarah put her other arm across the loyal dog's back, holding onto him like a life preserver in a stormy sea.

Jake observed Cody and knew his dog was barely under control and would fight anyone who might so much as try to lay a finger on Sarah.

Jake spoke in a forced calm voice to the officer. "I'm sure whoever the woman was, she went to the wrong room by mistake. We don't have any packages, and you're free to search. Please be my guest, sir."

"Yes, we'll search the room," the officer said.

Several other uniformed officers arrived and began a methodical search.

Jake climbed onto the bed and sat with his back against the headboard. He held his dog's collar as Cody growled at the armed strangers.

"Out, Cody. Quiet. Wait for my orders," Jake commanded.

Cody huffed and obeyed.

Jake had invented the command to *wait for my orders*. It meant anything could happen, and Jake would decide how Cody would respond. Jake was amazed Cody had learned and understood the concept. For many years the dogs in his pedigree had been carefully bred for their brains and personalities and Jake was ever grateful to be partners with a best friend he believed might be the smartest dog in the world.

Once the search was completed, a female officer said in broken

English, "Now … search … bed." She motioned with her hands for them to get off.

Jake, Sarah and Cody stood aside as the policewoman tossed the bed, cut slits in the mattress and reached inside but didn't find anything.

After the police officers left the room, Jake closed and locked the door and made a phone call to the front desk. "I'd like to move to another suite on a higher floor. Yes, right now, please. Inmediatamente, por favor. The price is okay. Charge it to my card, and please add one hundred US dollars as a tip for yourself. Thank you."

A maid from housekeeping arrived at the door, shocked at seeing the ransacked room. "Qué pasó?" she asked. "What happened?"

Jake decided to influence the gossip that would surely result. "A woman wanted to rob a guest who was seen wearing expensive jewelry. But she got the wrong room. We never bring any jewelry on vacations. My girlfriend was attacked, and the police tore our room apart by mistake. I'm a lawyer, but I won't sue the hotel owners into bankruptcy over this as long as they make a reasonable effort to keep us happy." He gave her a generous cash tip and a kind smile.

The maid's eyes went wide as she accepted the money and explanation. She then led them up to the top floor and an even more luxurious suite.

Once they were alone, Jake locked the door, opened the minibar and offered an airline-size bottle of tequila to Sarah.

She shook her head. "No, thank you."

"It might help calm your nerves."

"My stomach is upset. Do you have any Alka-Seltzer?"

"Yes." Jake rummaged through his carry-on suitcase, found the item, poured some bottled water into a glass and plopped two tablets into the water.

Sarah drank the fizzy remedy, then went out onto the balcony and sat on a wicker love seat. She stared at the ocean as a tear ran down her cheek.

Jake watched her with concern. She was a tough cookie, and not one who would cry often. He whispered, "Cody, *comfort* her."

Cody jumped onto the love seat, stretched out across her thighs, wagged his tail and shook his head so his ears flopped.

Sarah patted Cody on the back. "You're such a good dog."

～

In another high-rise hotel building nearby, Enrique sat in a room with the lights off as he observed his prey through a small gap in the window shades, using a camera with a long telephoto lens.

This was the hardest part of his job. The sitting and watching for hour upon hour. Perhaps the attractive woman would get undressed before bed. He wondered if she slept in the nude. Maybe he'd take some photos of her to pass the time.

He zoomed in on Sarah's face, saw her tears, and felt bad about himself. What kind of man was he turning into? His dearly departed wife, killed by a rival cartel, must be rolling over in her grave. The thought of his sweet wife gone too soon made his heart ache, and he drank a shot of tequila to ease the pain.

He sent a text to his employer. *The so-called Angel of Death failed to even put a scratch on the woman named Sarah.*

After a pause, the reply came: *The Angel is bruised, bloodied and outraged, but tomorrow is another day for her vengeance. She will start by pulling out their fingernails with a pliers and then move on to the blowtorch.*

Enrique: *I could try to enter the room and take them hostage when they're asleep, but the dog would hear me.*

Rojo: *Don't try it. Better to take them when they're walking, or in a car.*

Enrique: *Do you want me to shoot the dog right now? He's out on the hotel room balcony. My rifle has a scope and a silencer.*

Rojo: *No, that could cause the targets to panic and flee.*

Enrique: *Your orders?*

Rojo: *Keep watch on them all night. We'll follow them tomorrow morning and grab them at the right moment.*

Enrique cursed. Rubbing the scar on his left cheek, he turned on the coffeemaker, brewing a full pot of strong coffee for the long night ahead. Killing people was easy, but kidnapping them alive was a dangerous game either side could lose.

CHAPTER 15

Jake stood on the hotel balcony next to Sarah and Cody and tried to lighten the mood. "Let's cruise the *Far Niente* down to Cabo and live on board. You can open a veterinary clinic for Chihuahuas and I'll take tourists out in the boat to catch fish and get drunk and sunburned."

Sarah shook her head sadly. "Jake, I don't feel safe here any longer."

Jake's smile fell and he nodded. "I understand. We can check out and move to a different hotel."

"That woman might be watching us right now, and she could find our new hotel."

Jake thought about it. "Cabo is one of the safest and best places to visit in all of the world. However, we could leave town, drive up to Magdalena Bay, spend the night there and see the whales in the morning instead of doing it the next day like we'd planned."

Sarah relaxed her shoulders. "It's nice and quiet there, right?"

"Yes. Puerto San Carlos is a humble little fishing town on a quiet peninsula, far away from the big cities."

"How far is it?" Sarah asked.

"Mag Bay is about a five-hour drive from here. We'd arrive in time for dinner, and they catch plenty of lobsters there." Jake wiggled his eyebrows up and down.

That earned a tired smile from Sarah. "You know just what to say to a girl."

Jake smiled in return. "Let's do it. I'll call the hotel up there and let them know we'll be a day early. It's nothing fancy compared to this royal palace, but it's rustic, clean, quiet, and away from the typical crowds. I like the town for its simple, honest way of life. It feels like you've gone back in time to a nice place with good old-fashioned people. I could live there and be a fisherman."

"But you already paid for this penthouse suite," Sarah said.

"I don't care about money, I only care about you," Jake said.

Sarah stood up and put her arms around his neck, laying her head against his chest.

Jake held her for a long time and wondered if there was something more she wanted to say. In his experience, each woman was unique in her likes and dislikes. Sometimes Sarah would jokingly say, "Men are clueless." Jake would joke, "If that's true, would it kill you to give us a clue once in a while? I'll give you twenty dollars for one clue." That would start a silly game, where she'd say something, and he'd pull out a twenty and ask, "Is that a clue? Am I getting a clue here? I'm prepared to buy it, like on that TV game show where you buy a vowel."

After their kiss, they began repacking their suitcases. Sarah was quiet and pensive, as if her mind was far away and something was worrying her. Jake again wondered what she was thinking about. Relationships depended upon communication. If she wouldn't tell him what was going on, what could he do? He was starting to feel left out, as if his opinion and possible contribution didn't matter.

"Sarah, do you want to talk? I'm a good listener."

She shook her head. "I'm just shook up from what happened."

He nodded politely, not believing her.

They went downstairs and checked out. Jake put their bags into the rear cargo area of his rented SUV and opened a back door so Cody could hop onto the backseat and stretch out.

Sarah sat in front next to Jake, who drove them on a roundabout route designed to lose anyone who might be following. He made four right-hand turns and kept his eyes on the rearview mirrors, then drove a few miles and made four left-hand turns. Satisfied they were free of any tail, he headed onto the highway and toward Puerto San Carlos.

On the drive, they talked about whale watching, as Jake tried to keep Sarah's mind off the troubles she'd gone through. Eventually she nodded off and took a nap.

Jake sent a text to Pez: *You said we could go on the whale watching trip tomorrow or the next day, right?*

Pez: *Yeah. Either day is okay. My uncle has lots of boats, and cousins for captains.*

Jake: *Okay, I'd like to go tomorrow morning, if that works for you too.*

Pez: *Sure, no problemo. See you mañana.*

Jake: *Thanks!*

Upon arrival, they enjoyed a dinner of grilled mahi-mahi tacos and cold beers in a tiny restaurant that was more like a homemade shack than a building. Cody ate plain grilled boneless fish with no added toppings. The people were warm and friendly, the food was simple but satisfying, and Jake and Sarah agreed it was a wonderful meal.

After dinner, they went to their humble hotel, climbed into bed and fell asleep.

~

Enrique received a text from Rojo: *Where are they now?*

He replied: *I followed the tracking beacon at a discreet distance. They're at a small hotel in Puerto San Carlos.*

Rojo: *Good. Bring them to the hacienda for questioning.*

Enrique: *Sí, jefe.*

Thinking it over, Enrique decided to wait until early morning and use the element of surprise. If he burst into the room of a US Marine combat veteran and a war dog during the night, he might end up dead. Best to wait until the man was taking a morning shower, naked and defenseless.

He parked near the beach and slept in his SUV like a college kid vacationing on a low budget, drinking some tequila to help him fall asleep. Thank heaven for tequila. He tried not to think about the possibility of the dog biting his crotch when he kidnapped the man and woman at gunpoint.

He had a fishing net ready to throw over the dog. Hopefully, that would render it harmless enough that he could avoid shooting the valuable animal.

CHAPTER 16

Before dawn, Jake and Sarah took a shower together "to conserve water," soaping and massaging each other.

As Jake was about to get out of the shower, he heard Cody barking. Jake wrapped a towel around his waist and went to find his dog facing the door, with his hackles up and teeth bared.

"Do we have trouble, boy?" he asked, loudly, grabbing his pistol and racking a round into the chamber. "After I shoot him in the face, I want you to bite his balls off!"

He heard fast footsteps in the hall and wondered if he'd been followed or if it was just a local petty thief who liked to burglarize hotel rooms.

Jake and Sarah dressed in layers of clothing for the cool air on the water, and Jake put the same lightweight yellow nylon vest on Cody that his dog had worn in Cabo.

Cody stood patiently by the door, wanting to go outside and relieve himself.

They all walked out of the hotel just as the sun was peeking over the horizon and met up with Sammy "Pez" Lopez. Pez was a clean-cut American-born male with a Mexican immigrant mother and a caucasian American father. He'd served in the US Marine Corps infantry, with multiple deployments to combat overseas. He and Jake were brothers in arms, survivors and friends forever.

"Hey, ese," Pez said, smiling at Jake.

Jake smiled in reply and asked, "Cómo estás, vato?"

"Muy bien. I'm good."

They clasped hands and pulled each other close for a man hug and slaps on the back.

Cody barked at Pez and circled around him, sniffing and taking full inventory.

"He's not gonna bite my ass, is he?" Pez asked with a grin. He held out one fist for Cody to sniff, the way he'd done with Marine war dogs overseas.

"Be friends, Cody," Jake said as he clipped a leash onto his dog's collar. "Is there somewhere nearby to get breakfast?"

"Yes, and you'll love it. Follow me," Pez said.

As they walked, Jake made introductions. "Sarah, this is Sammy Lopez, a badass infantry Marine and a close friend. Pez, this is my girlfriend, Sarah. As I mentioned before, she runs the best veterinary clinic in the nation, and she's Cody's doc."

"Pleased to meet you, Sarah," Pez said. "As a veterinarian, would you say Cody is smarter than Jake?"

Sarah laughed. "Yes, he's smarter than all of us. In my work I've met hundreds of dogs, and Cody is exceptional. There is no other dog quite like him."

Cody stopped and peed on various spots along the way, marking his territory.

While Pez and Sarah chatted, Jake maintained his situational awareness, watching out for any signs of danger.

Jake saw Sarah glancing at Pez in curiosity, probably noticing that his friend was a bodybuilder, with muscular arms, a powerful chest and flat stomach. Pez had warm seductive eyes, an easy smile and the confident manner of a Latin lover.

Pez reached into his pocket and pulled out a Pez dispenser toy featuring the head of Snoopy wearing dark sunglasses. Handing it to Sarah, he said, "A gift for the veterinarian."

Sarah smiled and accepted the gift. "Thank you, Pez. I'll treasure it always." She bent the top back and ejected a rectangle of candy. "Mmm, raspberry."

Jake smiled. His friend still had an easy way with the ladies and was being his usual charming self. "Is your favorite Pez toy still R2-D2 from Star Wars?"

"Yes, I've always loved R2," Pez said.

"I still have the Popeye one you gave me," Jake said.

"That one fits you, Jake."

Jake sang the Popeye cartoon theme with ad-libbed lyrics from an old drinking song. "I like to go swimmin' with bow-legged women …"

Lights went on in a few of the humble homes they were passing.

Pez smiled and turned to Sarah. "That's why we called him Jukebox. Always belting out song lyrics at inappropriate moments."

Jake shrugged innocently, and they all laughed.

"Terrell's call sign was Grinds, because he loved coffee so much," Pez said.

"It started out as a joke, Lieutenant Coffee Grinds, but ended up as plain old Grinds and now he's a legend in the Marines," Jake said.

"My girlfriend, Olivia, wanted to be here with us, but she couldn't get time off work," Pez said. "She's looking forward to joining us for dinner."

"Can't wait to meet her," Sarah said.

Pez stopped at a small hand-built house where a family served meals out in their front yard on several rustic wooden picnic tables. They were the only diners at the moment. A smiling middle-aged woman named Carmelita treated them like visiting relatives, serving a home cooked breakfast of huevos rancheros. The dish included eggs simmered in salsa, with sides of chorizo, rice, beans and handmade corn tortillas. She poured them endless cups of rich Mexican coffee and chatted with Pez in Spanish.

Sarah said, "This food is wonderful."

Cody devoured a plate of plain scrambled eggs and looked at Jake for more. Jake smiled and shook his head, gave a hand signal and pointed down. Cody lay on the ground, waiting patiently for orders while sniffing the air and looking left and right.

Pez asked, "Jake, is it true you're a lawyer now?"

"Yes, believe it or not," Jake answered.

"There's a Mexican curse that says: May your life be filled with lawyers."

Jake laughed. "No bueno."

After they finished their meal, a few children came out of the house and shyly gave two old battered acoustic guitars to Pez. "Will you sing for us, tío?"

Pez handed one of the guitars to Jake and held onto the other.

"Tío means uncle," Pez said. "Do you still practice those songs we used to play in the Marines?"

"Yes, I play my guitar all the time to relax," Jake said.

"Let's play 'Mexico,' by James Taylor. The kids like that one."

"Perfect choice," Jake said.

Pez used a pick, but Jake played with his thumb.

They both strummed their guitars and found them well tuned. They played the intro and then sang together in harmony. The kids joined in on the chorus, and Sarah happily sang along with them. Cody stood next to Jake and howled to the music.

Several people from nearby homes gathered around to listen. After the song ended, everyone said hello and good morning to one another. Pez paid Carmelita in pesos, giving her a generous tip and a hug. Jake set down the guitar and quietly left an extra tip under his breakfast plate. Many of the gathered people hugged Pez. Some hugged Jake and Sarah too. Pez handed out small sums of money to the kids, so Jake did the same.

CHAPTER 17

On the walk back to the hotel, Pez said, "Carmelita is a widowed mother, barely making ends meet. I try to buy a meal from her whenever I'm in town. Her husband was a good friend of mine. An honest fisherman, killed by drug-smuggling criminals who stole his boat."

"That's so sad," Sarah said.

"And it's terribly common lately," Pez said, his tone angry, eyes dark. "There is just so much money in the drug trade, billions of dollars, it corrupts everything it touches."

Jake remained quiet, his right hand clenched in a fist as he stared out at the water and thought about the modern-day pirate-terrorist he'd assassinated. He wondered how many honest people on both sides of the border had been murdered or sold into human trafficking by that evil man before he'd put a stop to it. His only regret was that he hadn't killed the beast any sooner. Cody pressed against his handler, as if sensing his mood. Jake took a deep calming breath in an attempt to cool down his anger and patted his dog on the back to reassure him.

Once they'd walked back to the hotel, Pez opened the back hatch of his parked SUV. "I have a few rolled-up sleeping bags in here, but still plenty of room for perro dorado vato."

Cody gave a doggie grin when Pez called him vato.

Sarah asked, "What does vato mean?"

"It means something like dude, man, guy, bro ... you know," Jake said with a smile. He gave a command and Cody hopped into the cargo area, sniffing everything.

"I'll let you close the hatch," Pez said, moving toward the driver's door.

Jake said, "Sarah, can you sit in the backseat and talk to Cody for a moment, so he doesn't get anxious when I close this door?"

Sarah slid into the backseat, reached out and patted Cody on the back. "Hey, sweetie, we get to see whales, huh?"

Cody wagged his tail and gave her his best retriever grin.

Jake was careful of Cody's tail as he closed the hatch. He quickly sat next to Sarah and reached out to give his dog a scratch under the chin.

Pez asked, "All aboard?"

"Good to go," Jake replied.

Pez drove toward the bay and turned on the radio.

Jake was glad to see his old friend Pez again, but their reunion also brought back painful memories of their desert deployments.

The death of his war dog, Duke. His own near death from a bullet wound in the thigh, until he was saved by a blood transfusion from Lieutenant Terrell Hayes. The long days spent recovering in a hospital bed, where he received a Dear John letter from his girl back home.

Lastly, doing a number of secret missions for the CIA Special Activities Division to terminate high-value targets, when he was on record with the Marines as still healing up in the hospital. That was where he should have been. He still walked with a slight limp. The CIA had known his desire for revenge would win out. They'd played on his emotions and used him on what amounted to suicide missions, but he had survived.

The CIA work had only lasted a short time, but it had been intense, and he still had nightmares about a final semi-authorized mission where he'd slaughtered a terrorist group that was beheading women who refused to be sex slaves. The mission was planned and ready, but the agent in charge, Chet Brinkter, hesitated to give the order. Women were dying every day, and Jake went ahead without Brinkter's approval. He'd saved the women and gotten himself fired by Brinkter, and had no regrets.

Jake's heart pounded in his chest as he blocked the past out of his mind. *Block it. Block it. Block it.* Those men were dead, the women were safe, and he had to put it all behind him. *Block. It. Out.*

They continued driving for a while, talking about the natural beauty of Baja. Sarah glanced at him a few times, as if wondering what was on his troubled mind. Jake was bound by federal law not to tell her anything, and he didn't want her to suffer along with him, so he pretended not to notice her attention.

Soon they arrived at a protected area of scenic shoreline with pristine sand and unspoiled blue water. It looked like a visit to a simpler time in the past when there were fewer people and crowds. Jake wondered what it must have been like to live back then, before the population boom that seemed to be causing so many problems all over the world.

"Here we are," Pez said, bringing the SUV to a stop.

Jake saw a man waiting there with several twenty-two-foot pangas, the popular modest-sized open outboard-powered fishing boats. Near him, a folding table was piled with bottled water and packaged snack foods. The man watched their car approach, but he didn't appear happy to see them.

Pez made introductions. After a brief discussion in Spanish with his cousin, Pez said, "Rafael will allow the dog to come along as he promised, but if Cody starts barking and bothering the whales and other boaters, we'll have to turn around and come back here. No refund, agreed?"

Jake nodded at Rafael. "Agreed. Cody will be quiet if I give him his orders. Don't worry, he's highly trained."

"Keep the perro quiet, por favor," Rafael said, apparently unimpressed by Jake's assurances.

Jake held up three fingers. "Cody, how many is this?"

Cody gave three short barks.

"Uno, dos, tres ... you're right," Jake said and patted Cody on the head. Rafael stared at the dog in surprise, and Jake grinned. It was a trick he'd taught Cody. He never asked his dog any other number.

"Cody, fetch a bottled water." Jake pointed at the bottles on the picnic table and snapped his fingers.

Cody trotted over to the table, picked up a plastic bottle with his mouth and brought it to Jake, just the way he and so many other service dogs are trained to do. He looked up at his master as if to say, "That was too easy, what else do you need?"

Jake took the bottle. "Before we get on the boat I'll have him go pee. He's trained to go on command."

Pez nodded. "It's true, I went on patrol with war dogs all the time when Jake and I were deployed."

Jake pointed at a patch of sand. "Cody, pee now. Pee there."

Cody went to the area Jake indicated, emptied his bladder and walked back.

"Good dog," Jake said, getting down on one knee and giving Cody a hug.

Rafael raised his eyebrows in amazement, then turned and led them to one of the boats, where they all climbed on board and donned life jackets. Jake had brought a dog-sized lifejacket for Cody, and now he fitted the orange vest onto his dog. Rafael started up the single engine and cruised slowly out onto the warm, salty turquoise water.

As they were leaving, a small shuttle bus arrived at the beach, carrying a group of tourists and two more boat captains. Behind it followed a few other cars and a dark-windowed SUV.

CHAPTER 18

Enrique parked his SUV, lowered his window and studied the scene using the same camera with the long telephoto lens. If anyone looked in his direction, he presented the image of a typical photographer taking pictures of the bay and whales.

He focused on the boat with Pez and his friends on board, then nodded and tapped his phone to send a text: *Targets acquired. They're on a whale watching panga.*

Rojo replied: *Lopez had his chance to fix this problem. That time has passed. Take him prisoner along with the others, so Angel can question them.*

Enrique set down his phone and again used the camera to gaze at everyone on the panga. He thought to himself, *Oh well, if they all have to die screaming, that's the way it goes. If you want to avoid trouble in life, you should choose your friends wisely.* Family, friends and lovers could make or break you. It was too late for these people, but that wasn't his concern. He had his orders. It was them or him. What else could he do?

A familiar thought crossed his mind, that he should have gone into the restaurant business when his brother, José, asked him to. You didn't get rich quick, but you earned an honest living. And you had good food, cute waitresses and no worries about the cartel's cold-blooded killers.

He cursed at his mistakes and wrong choices in life.

In the panga boat, Jake kept one hand on Cody, just to be safe. Cody wagged his tail.

Sarah asked, "Rafael is the name of a saint, isn't it?"

Rafael smiled proudly. "Sí, señora—arcángel San Rafael."

"There's a beautiful city near where I live named San Rafael. You should visit sometime."

Jake noted how Rafael beamed, clearly enjoying having his name complimented by the pretty lady. But the contented look on his face also said he'd never leave his beloved bay to visit any of the expensive big cities full of stressed-out people running in a rat race, who'd pay big money to spend time in his shoes for a few days on a much-needed vacation. Although he was poor, he was living their dream vacation every day and was grateful for his humble blessings.

It reminded Jake of the old fable about a humble Mexican fisherman who brought in his day's catch to the dock. A business consultant on vacation advised him to buy more boats, hire employees and work more hours. In twenty years, he could retire as a millionaire. The fisherman asked, "And then what?" The businessman said, "And then you could enjoy life, go fishing and spend lots of time with your family." The fisherman shrugged and replied, "But I'm already doing that right now."

Rafael puttered around the bay, slowly and patiently, pointing out telltale spouts in various spots in the distance.

Jake whispered to Cody. "Remember, we're in *stealth* mode. It's *quiet* time, no barking."

Cody nodded, his eyes bright and his tail wagging.

Suddenly, just ahead of them, a mother gray whale surfaced and spouted with a whoosh. Moments later a baby calf came up for air beside her.

Jake guessed the calf was probably eight to twelve feet long, and the mother between thirty-five and forty-five feet.

"Rafael, you are a whale whisperer," Jake said.

Grinning, Rafael turned off the engine and used his hands to splash water in the direction of the whales, getting their attention and saying, "Hola, bonita. Hello, beautiful."

The baby whale calf was inquisitive and playful, swimming right up next to the boat and rolling on its side to get a good look with one large eye.

Everyone took turns petting the calf, and Sarah leaned over to give it a kiss.

Cody whined and pawed at the air toward the baby whale.

Jake said, "Easy, now, Cody. Be a good boy." He carefully held Cody over the edge of the boat so the dog could touch the whale with a front paw.

Rafael spoke reverently about the whales and the water, his voice filled with love for the gentle giants and the beautiful bay, a national treasure of great pride for Mexico.

"On the ocean we are in touch with *alma de la tierra*—the soul of the earth," he said.

Soon, the mother whale popped her head far out of the water and gently put her chin up on the side of the boat.

Cody woofed at her and got what Jake called *happy feet*, lifting each front paw up and down happily, left-right-left-right.

Jake held onto the handle on the back of Cody's life jacket, lifted him close to the mama whale and spoke in a quiet but firm voice. "Easy now. Give mama whale a gentle lick. Good boy. You're a good boy, aren't you? Yes, you are."

Cody licked the mother whale's salty face and gave a retriever dog grin.

Sarah used her phone to take pictures and video of Cody.

Jake noticed that while they interacted with the whales, a police boat cruised into the bay, and one of the two officers used binoculars to observe each panga.

"Why are the police here?" he asked.

Pez said, "Sometimes a police boat will patrol here to make sure people follow the rules. Lately, there's a two-hour time limit for each boat. It protects the whales from being bothered by too much activity."

After their two hours were up, they made their return trip to the beach, motoring past the police boat. It followed them and pulled up alongside their panga with lights flashing. One officer hailed Rafael in Spanish.

Rafael's smile fell and he translated. "Jake, he says the dog is not allowed. You must pay a fine and promise you'll never do that again, or he'll take you and your perro to the police station."

"How much is the fine?" Jake asked quietly, sensing a shakedown.

Rafael named a figure, and Jake handed over the pesos without any negotiation. The officer bumped boats, accepted the fine with a smile and waved at them to proceed.

Jake smiled politely in return and nodded at the officer as they pulled away. "Gracias, patrón."

He saw the man grin and give half of the cash to his police partner.

When they arrived at the beach, Rafael cursed at Pez and said he could have lost his source of income due to a dumb dog.

Jake understood enough Spanish to know what was being discussed. He handed some more cash to Rafael. "I'm sorry, Rafael. Let me pay you extra, and I apologize for the trouble."

Rafael accepted the extra payment and nodded. "Gracias, but next time, no perro. Never again."

Jake, Sarah and Pez thanked Rafael for a wonderful whale watching trip, shook hands and took pictures with him, and then walked to the rental car and drove off.

Enrique sat in his SUV and held the camera to his eye as he watched Jake talking to the police. He cursed and his face reddened in anger, causing the lighter scar on his cheek to be more pronounced.

Setting aside the camera and reaching for his phone, he sent a text: *It's no good. A police boat arrived and demanded a bribe from Wolfe.*

Rojo: *Is it anyone on our payroll?*

Enrique: *No. I don't recognize the two officers.*

Rojo: *Where is Lopez?*

Enrique: *The target is driving away now.*

Rojo: *Follow him and do your job, or you'll be replaced.*

Enrique closed his eyes for a moment in dread. If he didn't succeed, and soon, he was a dead man. Ángel de la Muerte might torture him for hours or days, because she enjoyed it so much.

In self-defense, he sent her a text: *Angel, I need your help to capture that woman who fought you. I can't do it alone, and you're the best. She deserves to feel your wrath.*

The Angel responded to his flattery with a reply text: *Yes, I'll help you. With pleasure.*

He let out the breath he'd been holding. If there was one thing he could always count on, it was Angel's vicious desire to inflict pain on other people. She was a dangerous sociopath, but he needed her skill set right now and didn't care who suffered—man, woman, or dog—if it saved his own life.

CHAPTER 19

Jake held Sarah's hand on the return drive to the hotel. It wasn't something he put a lot of thought into. He just did it instinctively and it felt right.

Sarah glanced at his hand and then smiled at him. "I loved the whales."

"Me too, and Cody was so happy," Jake said.

"When do the gray whales go north to Alaska?" she asked.

"They start migrating at the end of April. Maybe when they pass San Francisco, we could take the *Far Niente* on a whale watching trip."

She smiled and nodded. "I'd love that."

His phone buzzed and he answered. "This is Jake."

"Good morning, it's Bart. One of my clients needs me back in the city right away, so I'm planning on flying home today. Sorry for the short notice, but duty calls. Are you ready to go, or planning to stay a while longer?"

"We'll probably go with you, but I'll talk to Sarah and let you know," Jake said, ending the call.

"Talk about what?" Sarah asked.

"Something came up and Bart has to fly back today. Are you ready to go home, or do you want to spend some more time at the beach? There are still plenty of lobster tails calling to you."

"I'm ready," Sarah said. "I saw the whales and it was a wonderful experience, but clients and their pets are counting on me."

Jake smiled at how dedicated she was to the four-footed residents of her city. "All right, let's head back." He reached out and tapped Pez on the shoulder. "Last minute change of plans, bro. We'll be flying out today."

Pez turned down the music and glanced in the rearview mirror. "Short trip. Got work to do, *hermano*?"

"Yeah, but we'll come back soon to visit you in San Diego. You promised me a grand tour of the best taco trucks, and I'm going to hold you to that."

"Sounds good," Pez said, smiling. "Speaking of food, will you be here for lunch? I know some great places to eat in Cabo."

"Let me ask." Jake sent a text to Bart.

Jake: *We'll be flying home with you. What's our departure time?*

Bart: *Around six o'clock. We'll have a light dinner on the flight.*

Jake: *Okay, thanks. See you then.*

He told Pez, "We'll be here for lunch. The flight isn't until six."

"Great, I'll take you to an amazing seafood place," Pez said.

They stopped by the hotel in Puerto San Carlos, where Jake paid the bill and loaded their two small carry-on bags into the SUV's front passenger seat footwell.

They all chatted on the drive south, making plans for a future return visit. Cody took a nap in the cargo area, among the rolled-up sleeping bags.

When they arrived in Cabo, Pez headed for a restaurant, singing along with Mexican music on the radio and not appearing to pay any attention to Jake and Sarah's conversation.

Jake noticed Sarah giving him a long look and appearing to reach a decision.

She said, "Jake, after seeing those beautiful baby whales, there's something I want to talk about."

"Of course, you can talk to me about anything," Jake said.

"Well, I don't know how to say this, and it's not easy, so I'll just blurt it out. I recently had a surprise and found out you and I are going to become ..."

At that moment, a red Jeep Wrangler crashed into the side of their SUV, hitting the driver's door hard, caving it in and bursting the window. The collision drove their SUV sideways until it slammed into a parked car.

Sarah screamed and bumped her head on the window. The side airbag deployed, but she was halfway bent over from the impact and she partially hit the safety glass.

Cody was protected by the sleeping bags. He woke up from his nap, barked frantically and pawed at Jake's shoulder.

Jake yelled, "Is everyone okay? Cody, hold still."

Cody disobeyed orders and climbed over the seat to be with Jake and Sarah. He sniffed Sarah's face, licked the bump on her forehead, and whined.

Jake took a quick look at Sarah and Cody to make sure they weren't seriously injured. He then leaned in between the front seats and saw Pez's shirt drenched in blood. He unbuttoned the shirt and found an open chest wound that made a sucking sound as it bubbled with each shallow breath. It appeared to Jake a broken rib might have punctured a lung. Pez could die without immediate medical attention.

Vivid memories of combat returned to the surface and flashed through his mind. Shaking his head to clear it, he tapped 911 into his phone, knowing the emergency number was the same in the US, Canada and Mexico. A woman answered in a calm, steady voice.

Jake yelled, "Emergencia—ambulancia por favor!" He repeated the request for an ambulance several times.

As he ended the call, a woman with short-cropped black hair and an angry scowl on her face walked up to Pez's door and tried to pull it open. She had a black eye, along with a nose that was crisscrossed with white medical tape. Next to her stood a man with a long scar on his left cheek. Jake had a feeling he'd seen the man somewhere before. He used his phone to take video of them as the man yelled at the woman, "Are you crazy? Rojo ordered us to capture them, not kill them."

The woman cursed. "Take them prisoner, especially that bitch. Don't worry, I'll make them talk."

Jake had no weapon except for his fists and his dog, but those would have to do. He called 911 again, grabbed the key fob and pressed the red button to set off the car alarm, opened his rear passenger door and stepped out.

"Cody, stay in the car," he said.

Cody disobeyed and leapt out to stand by Jake's side.

Jake closed the door and pressed the key fob to lock it. With the car alarm blaring and lights flashing, he and Cody stood guarding the car as he spoke loudly into his phone. "Policia emergencia!"

The hackles on Cody's neck stood up and he growled in warning. He raised his lips to reveal sharp teeth.

The man with the scar took a step back, his wide eyes on the dog. He held a fishing net in both hands as if prepared to throw it.

Jake held his phone so the duo could see themselves being recorded on his front-facing video camera. With the phone in his left hand, he closed his right into a fist and said, "Police are on the way. This is a war dog, and although I would never hit a woman, this dog will fight both of you to protect me and our friends in the car."

The woman sneered at him and gave a cruel smile, as if looking forward to inflicting pain on him and the dog.

"Not if we kill him first," she said.

The man cursed at her. "Rojo wants the dog alive."

"Cody, *protect* Sarah!" Jake said, giving the command that allowed Cody to go off-leash and fight anyone who threatened his pack.

Cody snarled and opened his mouth that might soon bite into his enemies. His bright eyes flicked over them, watching their hands.

The woman licked her lips and pulled out a large knife. "I'll enjoy this."

Jake took a ballpoint pen from his pocket and placed the end against his palm and the shaft between his two middle fingers. He made a fist, the pointed end of the pen sticking out like a dagger. He'd never harmed a woman but he couldn't stand by and allow her to attack Sarah and Cody.

The man threw his net at Cody, but the dog evaded capture. He then looked at Jake's fist and at the agitated dog and took another step back.

Jake told him, "I'll punch you in the eye with this pen, and then my dog will rip your throat out."

The man drew a pistol and aimed it at Jake. His hand shook as he said, "Call off the dog."

Cody barked twice as he slowly moved closer toward the enemy.

Jake said, "If you shoot me, the dog will kill you. If you shoot the dog, I will kill you. Hold your fire if you want to live."

The man swallowed in fear and began to hyperventilate.

If a Marine war dog's handler was in danger and couldn't give orders, the dog was trained to act on its own and fight independently. The woman might have sensed this, because she tried to circle around the front of the SUV, toward Sarah's side of the car.

Cody moved quickly between the woman and the car, blocking her path.

Jake gave the woman one last chance to avoid having Cody bite the wrist of her knife hand. He yelled, "My attack dog *wants* to bite you, look at him!"

Cody's lips curled back as he snarled at the enemy soldier threatening Sarah. His right rear leg trembled, the one he'd injured in combat. He appeared confused but ready to fight one female to protect another, although he'd never done it before.

A siren filled the air, and blue and red lights strobed on buildings down the street as the police car raced toward them.

The man and woman both turned at the same time and ran to a waiting getaway car. They sped off and the woman glared back through the rear window at Jake. If looks could kill...

Jake said, "Cody, *guard my six.*"

Cody stood guard, protecting Jake's back, sniffing the air and watching for threats.

Jake unlocked the SUV and turned off the alarm. He opened his carry-on bag, grabbed a clean T-shirt and held it against Pez's chest wound to staunch the blood loss. He was careful not to press too hard, so as to avoid causing a collapsed lung.

He glanced at Sarah and saw her passed out with her head against the window. She was breathing steadily and wasn't bleeding externally as far as he could see.

A second siren joined the first, approaching from another direction. Jake continued to apply pressure to Pez's wound. "Hang on, brother. An ambulance is on the way."

CHAPTER 20

A blue-and-silver pickup truck arrived with its police lights flashing. The words painted on the doors read Policía Municipal. The truck stopped and an officer stepped out, dressed in a dark blue uniform and black boots.

Jake said, "Cody, to me. Hold."

Cody went to Jake's side and awaited further orders as his alert eyes and trained nose took in everything that was happening.

Jake nodded at the policeman in respect. "Señor policía."

The officer nodded at Jake in reply, carefully avoiding Cody as he looked inside the SUV at Pez and Sarah, and spoke in Spanish into his radio mic. Moments later, an International Medical Response ambulance drove up. Two EMTs jumped out, dressed in khaki cargo pants and light blue polo shirts. They quickly but carefully placed Pez and Sarah onto stretchers and put them into the ambulance. Cody barked when the EMTs put Sarah on a stretcher, as if giving them orders.

Jake said, "Out, Cody. These are corpsmen."

He used some tissues to clean Pez's blood off his hands, then took out his wallet and showed the EMTs his international travel insurance card. One of the men used his phone to take a picture of the card.

Jake asked, "Can we ride with you to the hospital?"

The EMT glanced at Cody, who appeared agitated. He shook his head. "No, señor. Take a taxicab." He climbed into the ambulance and it roared off toward the hospital.

As Jake called a taxi, he noticed that the abandoned Jeep Wrangler was equipped with a heavy-duty winch mounted on a solid steel front bumper and cage. That rig had crashed through Pez's door like a battering ram. He took a picture of the Jeep and its license plate.

When the police officer finished talking on his radio, he spoke to Jake in accented English. "Señor, I need to ask you some questions, por favor."

Jake watched the departing ambulance in frustration. "Could you ask the questions while you give me a ride to the hospital?"

"No, señor."

Jake cursed in español, and the officer raised his eyebrows, appearing both surprised and impressed with Jake's fluency in the local profanity.

Sarah woke up in the ambulance feeling dizzy and suffering from a pounding headache. Her heart raced and her thoughts were confused. She could feel a bump forming above her right eyebrow. She tried to speak but her mouth was dry and she had trouble forming the words.

She suddenly realized her cotton briefs were moist. Had she wet her pants during the accident? When she tried to raise her head and look down, the EMT held her shoulder firmly and said, "Don't move, señorita."

Sarah's dizziness increased and the world began to spin around in circles as she passed out again and fell into darkness.

At the hospital, Sarah woke up on her back on a rolling gurney as a nurse pushed it quickly along a hallway under bright fluorescent lights. Doctors and nurses shouted to each other, working as a team. The nurse rolled the gurney into a room, removed Sarah's jeans with scissors and tossed them into a plastic bin.

As her pants were removed, Sarah saw a bloodstain on the crotch. She looked down, saw the same red stain on her underwear, and began to cry.

"I'm pregnant," she said. "Can you please give me an ultrasound?"

The nurse gazed at Sarah with pity and understanding, made the sign of the cross and said something in Spanish about an *enfermera de obstetricia y ginecología*. She left the room as an obstetrics and gynecology nurse walked in.

The OB-GYN spoke perfect English as she gently gave Sarah a pelvic examination and an ultrasound. Her sad face revealed the diagnosis before she said, "You've had a miscarriage. I'm very sorry."

Sarah curled up in the fetal position, pulled the covers up to her neck, closed her eyes and cried into the pillow as she wished it was all just a bad dream. Where was Jake when she needed his strong arms around her?

Jake apologized to the officer for cursing and made an effort to politely and carefully answer the man's questions. He reminded himself this wasn't his hometown, where he had a best friend on the force and took the police chief out on his boat for fishing trips. He had to protect Cody from being taken away from him, and get to Sarah as fast as possible.

After checking Jake's ID, the officer said, "That Jeep is stolen. The drivers who ran away might be undocumented foreigners. Yes, we get them here too, over five hundred thousand last year."

Jake showed him the short video he'd taken of the two assailants armed with a pistol and a knife.

The officer watched and listened and said, "Secuestro a plena luz del día—kidnapping in broad daylight. Send that video to my phone." He recited his number.

Jake sent the video and asked, "Am I free to go now, Officer?"

"Yes, you can go," the policeman said.

A brand-new white Suburban drove up, and the taxi driver put his window down. "Señor Lobo?"

Jake nodded. "Yes. Please pop the back hatch for my luggage."

He transferred the two small carry-on bags from the wrecked SUV to the Suburban, then climbed into the backseat with Cody. "Please drive as fast as possible to the hospital."

"A sus ordenes—at your service," the driver said and sped away.

Upon arrival, Jake paid the driver extra to deliver his luggage to Bart's jet at the airport. "My friend will give you a tip when you arrive. There's nothing valuable in the bags, just clothes and such."

The driver noticed traces of blood on Jake's hand. His eyes went wide and he promised all of the bags would arrive with their contents intact. As the Suburban drove away, Jake sent Bart a text and let him know about the situation.

He walked inside the hospital with Cody on a leash, found a nurses station and asked about Sarah and Pez. A nurse frowned sadly. "I'm terribly sorry, but Señor Lopez was pronounced dead on arrival."

Jake felt like he'd been punched in the stomach. His throat tightened and his anger flared. But his anger soon turned to dread as he thought of Sarah's injury and how head wounds were so unpredictable.

"How is the woman, Sarah Chance?" he asked and then held his breath, waiting for the answer.

"She's going to be fine, shaken up and slightly bruised, but no broken bones or internal injuries," the nurse said.

Jake let out a huge sigh of relief. It appeared to him the nurse was leaving something unsaid. What was it? He was going to press for more answers, but just then a doctor ran up and shouted in Spanish. The nurse replied to him and then said to Jake, "Have a seat. Someone will come and find you."

Jake watched the doctor and nurse take off in a hurry and disappear through a doorway.

Time seemed to pass in painfully slow motion as Jake and Cody paced back and forth in frustration while waiting to see Sarah. Jake was about to break the rules, cause trouble and have Cody search for her when finally a nurse led them down a hallway to a room Sarah was sharing with several other people, each in their own bed with a curtain around it.

At the door, Jake heard two nurses whispering in Spanish and mentioning Sarah's name. He knew enough to understand their words *el aborto espontáneo* meant a spontaneous abortion. She'd had a miscarriage.

His heart ached as he walked into the room and found Sarah in bed with tears on her face. He went to her side, put his arms around her and didn't let go.

"Sarah, I heard the nurses talking. I'm so sorry."

"Just hold me," Sarah said. She cried on his shoulder for a while, letting out her pain and sorrow.

After the hug, Cody jumped onto the bed and lay down, holding Sarah's hand in his mouth and gazing at her with sad brown eyes.

CHAPTER 21

A nun came into the room wearing a black-and-white habit. She held Sarah's hand. "My poor child. Let us pray together. Are you Catholic?"

Sarah shook her head. "No, I'm an open-minded agnostic, but thank you for your kindness."

The nun smiled with love and prayed in Spanish and then in English.

"Compassionate God, soothe the hearts of Sarah and Jake, and grant that through the prayers of Mary, who grieved by the cross of her Son, you may enlighten their faith, give hope to their hearts, and peace to their lives. Amen."

A young Mexican female doctor walked in wearing a white coat and round wire-rimmed glasses. The nun kindly patted Sarah on the arm and left the room.

The doctor said, "Hello, my name is Dr. Ocampo. I'm a psychiatrist. Sarah, I'm sorry for your loss. Would you like to talk about what happened? It might help you deal with your feelings. As many as one in five early pregnancies results in a loss. It can happen to anyone, due to chromosome problems that can't be prevented, and nature taking its course."

Sarah wiped her eyes. "I understand."

"Please don't blame yourself," Dr. Ocampo said. "The

chromosome problems would have caused a miscarriage eventually. Your car accident simply made the inevitable happen sooner.

Sarah asked, "Jake, did you have any idea I was pregnant?"

Jake shook his head. "No, only that you had something on your mind you weren't telling me. I knew you were taking the pill, so it didn't occur to me you might be pregnant."

Sarah took deep breaths, her voice wavering. "Birth control pills have a 9% failure rate. The pregnancy came as a total surprise and I wasn't sure what to do."

Jake was careful not to say 'I know how you feel.' He didn't know and couldn't know.

"That must have been a difficult thing to go through alone. You can always talk to me about anything," he said.

Sarah gazed into his eyes. "What would you have said if I'd told you we were expecting a baby?"

Jake held out both hands, palms up. "I guess I would've bought cigars and handed them out to friends."

"You want to be a father?" she asked in surprise.

Jake thought for a moment. No, he didn't want to be a father yet. It wasn't the right time, but if an unplanned pregnancy brought a baby into his life, he'd try to be the best father he could.

He said, "I wasn't planning to right now, but if I got you pregnant, I'd stand by your side, and I could see us moving in together and raising our child as a happy family. Have you ever thought about living on a boat?"

Sarah pulled the bed covers over her face and cried.

Jake looked at the doctor. "Did I say the wrong thing?"

Dr. Ocampo shook her head. "I realize this is no consolation, but remember at this very early stage, the brand-new developing fetus was smaller than a grain of rice and had not yet formed a heart, brain, eyes, arms or legs. It was almost too small to detect on the ultrasound."

Jake gently pulled Sarah's bed covers away from her shoulders, held her in his arms and rubbed her back.

Sarah wept against his shoulder, unconsoled by the doctor's speech. "I want to go home."

"Yes, of course," Jake said. "We can still make the flight on Bart's jet."

Dr. Ocampo glanced at Sarah's chart. "If your flight is leaving, we can release you, but please get another checkup tomorrow at home with your *médico de atención primaria* … I mean, your primary care physician."

"Thank you, I will," Sarah said.

"Sarah, I couldn't help but overhearing that you were on the pill and this was an unplanned pregnancy," Dr. Ocampo said. "May I suggest a higher dose of hormones, and consistently taking your pill at the exact same time every day?"

"Yes, I'll talk to my doctor about that," Sarah said.

"One last thing, no intercourse for a week or two, depending on how quickly your body recovers," Dr. Ocampo said.

Sarah and Jake both nodded in understanding.

She bade them goodbye and left the room.

Cody licked the tears from Sarah's face.

Sarah hugged Cody and looked at Jake with red eyes. "Even though I couldn't make up my mind about what to do, I still feel devastated by my loss."

"It's heartbreaking for me too," Jake said. "I'm so sorry about everything. I feel like this is all my fault."

She held his gaze. "You haven't said a word about Pez."

Jake felt the old familiar pain. Another of his Marine brothers had made it all the way through multiple combat deployments, only to come home safe and then die a pointless death.

He took a deep breath and let it out. "Pez didn't survive the accident," he said, his voice rough.

Sarah held his hand tight. "I'm sorry, Jake."

He nodded in thanks. "The woman driving the truck that hit us had short black hair. Didn't you say the woman who attacked you at the hotel had hair like that?"

Sarah's eyes went wide. "Yes, chopped-off hair, like she'd cut it herself with a knife, and so dark I thought it might be dyed with shoe polish."

"She also appeared to have a broken nose. Did you do that to her?"

"Yes, I punched her hard and felt her nose crunch under my fist."

"I wasn't going to show you the video, but I feel like you need to make a positive ID. Are you up for this?"

Sarah bit her lip and nodded. He held up his phone and played the short video.

Sarah gasped. "Yes, that's her. I remember those two crosses on her right hand."

"She murdered Pez," Jake said.

"Was she after him, or me?" Sarah asked.

"She's after that package you mentioned. I think they wanted to kidnap us. You can hear the man yell at her and say they were supposed to capture, not kill." Jake played the video again, turning up the audio.

Sarah listened carefully and asked, "Why would they want to kidnap us? For ransom?"

Jake stared at her and remembered she was a very strong person, but a good and innocent soul. Not a battle-hardened and jaded war veteran like many of his other friends.

"To make us talk, and tell them where to find the package," he said.

"Make us talk? You mean they'd torture us?" Sarah asked, her face going pale.

He hesitated for a moment, allowing it to sink in, but then gave her the painful truth.

"Yes, I'm afraid so. The cartels do it all the time. But instead, that woman executed my friend, Pez. She appears to be a vicious, bloodthirsty psychopath who belongs locked up in solitary confinement. And her cartel boss needs to die a violent death."

Sarah gazed at Jake, speechless. He guessed she was seeing a familiar look in his eyes that he couldn't hide from her. The enraged desire for justice and retribution. An eye for an eye. Those who were responsible should be punished and stopped from doing it again.

Jake knew she'd seen that look in the past and hoped never to see it again. But what could he do? He had to protect Sarah and

Cody from the threats against them, and he wouldn't let any more of his veteran friends get murdered by this crime cartel. *Not while I'm still breathing.*

He pulled out his black phone and placed an encrypted call to Agent McKay in D.C.

CHAPTER 22

In her office beneath the White House, Agent McKay was hard at work as usual, protecting US citizens who had no idea they were in any danger.

Her black phone buzzed with a secure call from Jake Wolfe, and she stared at the display for a moment before answering. Jake was supposed to be on vacation right now, but the man was a magnet for trouble. He might be in a Mexican jail at the moment, or finding a sunken ship full of Spanish gold, for all she knew.

With a weary sigh, she answered his call. "McKay."

"It's Jake Wolfe. Sorry to bother you, but we were attacked by criminals in Cabo San Lucas. Sarah was injured and a friend of mine died. We need a trusted driver to take us from the hospital to the airport."

"I'm sorry about your friend. Is Sarah going to be okay?" McKay asked, furiously tapping on her computer's keyboard.

"Sarah was hospitalized with a worrisome bump on the head, but she's doing okay now," he said.

"I have assets all over Cabo. You're at the main hospital?"

"Yes," Jake said.

"One of my people is en route to you now, ETA ten minutes. Her name is Lourdes Benitez. Code words are Swiss watch."

She sent Jake a text along with a scan of a Mexican Federal Police ID card featuring the face of an earnest woman.

He said, "One more thing. Sarah asked if someone can bring her a clean pair of pants." Jake recited the size Sarah had requested.

"Something will be done about that, but I can't predict what you'll receive on short notice."

"Thank you, Shannon," Jake said.

McKay paused a moment. "You're welcome … Jake. I'll have assets watching over you all the way back to San Francisco."

She ended the call and gazed at her computer monitor, watching a dot on a map moving toward the hospital.

A few taps on her keyboard brought up the hospital records of Sarah's miscarriage. That gave her pause. Sarah and Jake were going to have a baby? But someone had put an end to that. She felt sorry for Sarah and realized Jake would likely kill whoever did this. There would be no stopping him.

Exhausted but focused, she couldn't help thinking about how Jake was going to give her one of the priceless puppies from Cody and Skye's litter. She imagined her blind daughter bonding with a super-smart guide dog that had Cody's bright eyes and retriever grin. It was a small miracle in her difficult life, and she was deeply grateful. If anyone tried to take that away from her child, she would move mountains to stop them.

Jake stood next to Sarah's bed, and Cody sat by his side, watching the door.

He sent a follow-up text to McKay.

Jake: *Here's a video of the people who killed my friend Sammy Lopez. It was a vehicle-ramming attack. They mentioned someone named Rojo.*

McKay replied: *We just learned Rojo was the cartel gang leader buying stolen boats from the HVT in San Diego.*

Jake: *My priority right now is to get Sarah home safe, but I'm coming back to Mexico and I want in on any mission against Rojo.*

McKay: *We're working on it. I'll keep you apprised of the situation.*

Jake: *One more problem. I choked when it came time to fight a woman. I couldn't bring myself to injure her, even though she deserved it.*

McKay: *We'll give you a Taser shotgun. Packs a punch but doesn't leave any lasting injuries.*

Jake: *Great idea, thank you.*

Seven minutes went by, then there was a knock, and a visitor entered the room. Cody growled, and Jake said, "Out, Cody."

A short, Mexican woman in her early thirties, dressed in a dark pantsuit, stared at Jake in recognition. "I'm Lourdes Benitez, here to pick up and deliver a Swiss watch to the airport." She held up a Mexican Federal Police ID and badge to Jake.

Jake studied the ID and compared it to the picture on his phone. He nodded at her and displayed his California driver's license. "Good to go."

A nurse ran in and handed a simple woven bag to Sarah without a word, then left the room.

Sarah looked inside the bag and climbed out of bed. "I'll be right back."

Sarah went into the bathroom and closed the door.

In the bag was a knee-length dark blue skirt with an elastic waist, a white blouse, a pair of underwear and a few absorbent panty liners. She cried fresh tears as she put on the clothes, grateful for whoever had provided them.

Once Sarah was dressed, she went out of the bathroom and nodded at Jake.

The policewoman opened the room door, beckoned at them and stepped into the hallway, looking both ways for any danger.

Sarah gave Jake a sad look and held his hand as they walked down the hall with Cody trotting along beside them and sniffing at the woman as if he knew she was carrying a concealed weapon but was there to help his pack.

Jake spoke to Cody, giving him commands as they exited the hospital and got into an unmarked SUV with dark windows.

On the drive to the airport, Lourdes handed an automatic pistol to Jake without a word.

Jake accepted the older, well-worn H&K MP5K full-auto submachine gun pistol, equipped with a thirty-round magazine, a laser sight, and no shoulder stock.

He held the compact weapon in both hands and aimed it at the floor, keeping the safety on and his index finger pointed straight alongside the frame just above the trigger.

As they drove, Jake did recon, looking around in all directions and checking the mirrors.

He saw Sarah turn her head and gaze out the window, apparently having been through too much and not wanting to see him holding the frightening weapon and acting as if he was prepared to kill.

With a heavy heart, he wondered if he might be keeping her from a peaceful life with another man.

CHAPTER 23

They arrived at the airport without incident and drove to a private area where Bart's Gulfstream G550 jet waited on the tarmac.

As Lourdes parked near the beautiful jet, she said, "My orders are to see that you get on board and take off."

Jake handed over the MP5K to her. "Gracias."

She accepted the weapon and replied, "De nada."

Jake exited the car along with Sarah and Cody, and they walked away. A slender blonde female member of Bart's flight crew greeted them at the bottom of the stairs. Jake motioned for Sarah to go first. He put a nylon vest on Cody, grabbed the handle on the back and carried his dog like a suitcase as he climbed the steep stairs, being careful of Cody's legs. Cody wagged his tail and gave a toothy grin to the flight attendant. She smiled at him.

As Sarah went into the jet's luxurious cabin, Jake stopped and turned to look back at the federal policewoman, giving her a nod of respect. He saw Lourdes nod in reply, remaining seated in her SUV and watching the jet.

The pilot spoke over the intercom. "Crew, please close the door and prepare for departure."

The flight attendant said, "Please take a seat, Mr. Wolfe." Her name tag read "Dawn."

"Dawn, do you have a cold pack in your first aid kit?" he asked.

"Yes, I'll bring it to you."

"Thanks." Jake walked toward Sarah and waved at Bart, who was relaxing in his own private seating area, talking on his phone.

Jake sat down in the luxurious padded leather seat next to Sarah. "I hope they serve champagne on this cheap flight."

Sarah chuckled at his absurd remark. "Thanks for making me laugh. Otherwise I'll just cry some more."

Jake held her hand to his lips and kissed it. "Crying is good for you. Sometimes life is like that song, 'Between a Laugh and a Tear,' by John Mellencamp."

Cody sat in the spacious area at their feet, putting his head on Sarah's knee and gazing up at her as if sensing her ongoing distress. She gave him a pat. "Good dog. Lay down, Cody."

The dog stretched out on the carpet and made himself comfortable.

Jake raised an eyebrow at how his stubbornly independent dog happily obeyed Sarah's every wish. He took off his shoes and gently rubbed Cody with his right foot. Cody turned onto his back to get a belly rub.

The jet taxied toward the runway and the pilot spoke over the intercom. "Prepare for takeoff."

Soon they were airborne and flying over the picturesque shoreline. Jake thought about how Bart had once said he liked to fly along the coast at a lower altitude and gaze out the window at the seashore. He didn't care about the fastest route; he only wanted to enjoy the ride and the view. Somehow the flight plan of the well-connected attorney was always approved.

Jake looked out the window in awe of the beautiful west coast of the United States. It was an amazing sight to see. Thank God Sarah had survived all the danger and they were now on their way home, safe and sound. What else could go wrong?

He glanced at Cody and saw that his dog was relaxed but keeping an eye on his handler, waiting for orders. Cody also observed Sarah from time to time as she rested with her seat leaned back. The dog appeared as if he was standing by to help her in any way he could.

Jake's heart swelled and he smiled at Cody, ever grateful to have the loyal companion in his life.

Her eyes closed, Sarah said quietly, "I'm so relieved to be on our way home."

Bart walked up and sat near them in one of the large luxurious seats. The distinguished-looking gentleman had touches of gray in his hair and was impeccably dressed in tailored clothes and expensive shoes, even while on vacation.

He appeared worried. "Thank goodness you could make the flight. I understand you were in a car accident and someone died. Are you three okay?" The older man looked at Sarah with parental concern in his eyes.

Jake appreciated Bart's attentiveness. His lawyer mentor had always been fond of Sarah.

Sarah opened her eyes and gave Bart a brave smile. "I was shaken up and got a bump on my head, but your jet is a lifesaver. Thank you so much, Bart."

Bart nodded. "Anything you want, just ask Dawn and she'll take care of you like family. It's only an hour-and-a-half flight, so we'll be having a light dinner of chicken Caesar salad. Plain chicken for Cody."

"That sounds wonderful," Sarah said.

Cody woofed at him.

Bart nodded at the dog and then looked Jake in the eye, appearing curious if he had any details to add but not wanting to cross-examine him due to lawyer etiquette.

Jake held Bart's gaze. "The person who died in the accident was my good friend Sammy Lopez. We served together overseas in the Marines."

"I'm terribly sorry, Jake," Bart said.

"Thank you, my friend."

Bart nodded sadly. "Well, I'll be on the phone billing client hours to rich people so I can pay for this ridiculously expensive jet." He walked off toward a large recliner chair that afforded comfort and privacy.

Sarah glanced around. "This is the most beautiful jet I've ever seen."

"I hope so. This thing costs tens of millions of dollars," Jake said.

"Wait ... *tens* of millions?" Sarah asked.

Jake nodded.

Dawn arrived and offered each of them a champagne flute filled with bubbly.

Sarah accepted a glass, gulped its contents down and handed it back empty.

Dawn smiled and held out another glass to Sarah. "I can bring a bottle if you'd like." She gave Jake an instant cold pack and a hand towel.

"Thank you, Dawn." Jake squeezed the center of the cold pack, made it pop, and shook it until it became ice cold. He wrapped it in the towel and handed it to Sarah. "For your bump."

Sarah pressed it against her head and sighed. "Thanks. It feels good."

Jake held his champagne glass close to his nose, gave it a deep sniff and then drank a noisy slurp as he tasted the bubbly. "Veuve Clicquot Yellow Label?"

Dawn nodded at him. "Yes, good guess."

"We'd both appreciate one more glass of this champagne, and some water, when dinner is served," Jake said.

Dawn smiled and nodded at him. She glanced at her wrist, where she wore a beautiful slender Cartier watch that looked like a gold-and-diamond tennis bracelet, and walked away.

CHAPTER 24

At his ranch in Mexico, Rojo paced back and forth alongside the pool until he received a call from Enrique.

"Wolfe left the hospital, drove to the airport and boarded a private jet," Enrique said.

Rojo cursed and yelled at his phone. "Stop that flight. Don't let Wolfe get away."

"It already took off, jefe."

Rojo's voice went cold. "Do something."

Enrique knew that tone and he chose his words carefully. "I suggest we shoot down the jet with a stinger missile."

"But I want to question Wolfe about the hard drive."

"I don't believe he knows anything about it. If we blow up a multimillion dollar jet and kill everyone on board, it will send a message to whoever actually has the drive."

Rojo kicked a patio table and sent it into the pool. A maid panicked and ran inside the house.

Rojo took a deep breath and nodded to himself. "You may be right that he has no knowledge of the drive, but Angel wants him and his girlfriend taken alive for her pleasure."

"You're smart to keep Angel happy if you can. She's insane," Enrique said.

"Angel had a horrific and painful childhood. Her heart is filled with hatred of all mankind."

"She's a loose cannon."

"Yes, but she's *my* loose cannon. She was on her way to the hospital to capture them, but it's too late now."

"I have a man standing by with a heat-seeking Stinger missile," Enrique said. "Let me conference you into a call."

Enrique put his phone on speaker and a man answered.

"Your orders?" the man asked.

Enrique said, "I have Rojo on the phone with me."

"Sí, I'm in position, awaiting the order," he said, his voice betraying his fear.

Rojo spoke up. "Don't do it."

"Do it? Yes jefe, at once!"

"No, you idiot, I said *don't* do it!"

"It's too late, I fired the missile," the man said.

Rojo cursed, drank a shot of tequila and slammed the glass down on the table.

As the liquor burned down his throat, he drew his pistol and looked around for a target.

He shot at a nearby tree, wishing it was the idiot who'd fired the missile.

Sarah sipped her second glass of champagne, slowly this time, and asked Jake, "How did you guess this? Are you developing a nose like Cody?"

Jake smiled. "I wish. I'd find all my missing socks. Actually, I studied winemaking at UC Davis for a while, so I learned about still wine and sparkling wine. This brut has layers of cherry from the Pinot Noir, some citrus and minerality from the Chardonnay, plus a telltale earthy brambly berry flavor from a black grape nobody has ever heard of named Pinot Meunier."

Sarah took a sip, savoring the flavors he'd described, and nodded. "It's delicious. Why did you stop your wine studies?"

Jake looked past her, out the window. "I left college to join the

Marines and fight terrorism."

They were both quiet for a moment and she steered the conversation back to wine. "My other fave bubbly is Domaine Chandon."

Jake said, "Maybe you like Chandon because we had brunch there after we went for a ride in a hot-air balloon."

"That might have influenced my taste. We'll have to do that again soon."

Cody raised his nose and sniffed, no doubt smelling the chicken being tossed with the Caesar salad.

Jake patted his dog on the back. "Cody only flies first class on private jets. He's the James Bond of dogs."

Sarah scratched Cody behind the ears. "If I'd wanted to stay longer and we'd missed this flight, how were you planning to get our boy back home?"

"Rent a Suburban or Tahoe and drive north. Enjoy a road trip with stops at beaches along the way," Jake said.

"How long does that take?"

"Only a few days, depending on how many beaches you visit."

"Sounds like fun. I might have gone with you two, rather than catch a commercial flight home."

He smiled. "We would've loved that. You're always invited to come with us anywhere we go."

"I'm going to hold you to that," she said, returning his smile.

Jake held her gaze. "Cody misses you desperately if we're apart for very long."

"Oh, *Cody* misses me, huh?" She gave the dog a pat on the head.

"That's a fact," Jake said. Cody nuzzled her hand.

Dawn walked past them, paused a moment and said, "Dinner will be ready for you two in just a minute."

Cody woofed at her.

"Oops, you *three*," Dawn corrected.

Cody gave her his retriever grin and wagged his tail.

A Klaxon alarm suddenly went off with a loud blaring sound.

Sarah gasped.

Jake looked out the window and saw a smoke trail rising from the water off the coastline. He jumped out of his seat and ran to the front of the jet, where the pilot was yelling something to the copilot.

"Incoming missile!" Jake yelled. "Gain altitude. Get above fifteen thousand feet!"

The pilot pulled back on the yoke, increased speed and replied in a controlled voice, "We're at fifteen thousand now, on our way to twenty thousand."

"Roger that," the female copilot replied, busily checking the dashboard instruments with a steady, determined look on her face.

The nose of the plane came up, engine speed increased and Jake had to hang on to avoid falling down the aisle.

CHAPTER 25

A US fighter jet roared past below them, so close it made both pilots sit up straighter and take deep breaths.

Jake peered out the windshield and recognized a US Air Force F-15E Strike Eagle fighter.

The fighter launched a cloud of chaff and heat decoy flares as countermeasures to the incoming missile, causing the weapon to explode harmlessly before it could do any damage.

A shock wave buffeted Bart's jet, but the aircraft remained unharmed and was soon back on course, although at a higher altitude.

"What the hell just happened?" the pilot asked, his jaw set, as he stoically kept his emotions under control.

Jake stepped into the cockpit and went down on one knee, in between the seated pilots. "Off the record, someone on a boat fired a SAM at us—a surface-to-air missile. Officially, though, *nothing* happened. You didn't see that. It's a matter of national security. I hope you understand."

The pilot said, "The only thing Homeland told us was that an Air Force fighter jet would be following our flight to SFO because we had you on board." He started to ask another question but was interrupted by a communication from Homeland, asking for their cooperation and repeating what Jake had said about it being a matter of national security.

Jake said, "Thank you both. You're two of the best pilots I've ever had the honor of flying with." Although he was partial to Marine pilots of Osprey tilt-rotor aircraft flying over hostile war zones, these two were brave and talented pilots who'd done well under threat of death.

They both nodded without a word.

On a hunch, Jake asked, "Air Force veterans?"

"Yes," they said in unison.

"Respect," Jake said.

The male pilot nodded in reply and went back to doing his job. The female copilot stared at Jake curiously for a moment and then turned her head and faced forward.

Jake walked back to his seat.

Cody stood guarding Sarah.

"Good dog," Jake said.

He sat down, leaning across Sarah and watching out the window as, far below them, a boat near the coast exploded in a ball of flame.

"What in the world is going on?" Sarah asked, staring out the window along with Jake.

"Someone on a boat fired a heat-seeking missile at our jet, but an Air Force fighter pilot stopped it by using heat decoy flares. And the boat was destroyed by that same pilot firing an air-to-surface missile."

"Is America under attack?" Sarah asked, her face pale.

"Only this jet as far as I know, but if a boat or ship off the coast fires at a target in the United States, it officially becomes an enemy combatant attacking our nation and may be dealt with accordingly."

"That was a close one," Sarah said.

Jake nodded. "Those fighter pilots are hella good. During the early days of the Iraq war, Air Force F-15Es wiped out half of the Iraqi Republican Guard."

Bart came and sat with them again. Raising one eyebrow, he said in an exaggeratedly calm voice, "Um, Jake, is there something you might want to tell me?"

"Here's what I know. First, Sarah was attacked by a woman with a knife who demanded a package. Second, the same woman was involved in the vehicle-ramming attack that killed Pez, and her partner said they were supposed to kidnap us. Third, your jet was fired upon by what must have been a shoulder-launched heat-seeking missile known as an FIM-92 Stinger."

"Do you think that woman fired a missile at my jet?" Bart asked, incredulous.

"If not her, maybe it was an accomplice. Unless you're handling the divorce of a Russian mafia boss."

"I never handle divorces or take criminals as clients. Who was piloting that military aircraft?"

"All I can say is it was an Air Force fighter jet protecting us on behalf of a clandestine government agency that doesn't want any publicity," Jake said. "I'm a big fan of air support. When I was deployed overseas I used a laser sight to paint targets for the Marine Corps fighter pilots. Very few people know about the Marine aviation squadrons. It's almost a secret—just how the Marines like it."

"Speaking of secrets, I'm aware you do secret work for the federal government, and it's why you asked me to fly you and Cody down the coast on short notice," Bart said. "I was happy to do it, but is that work catching up with you now?"

Jake thought for a moment. "This seems to be related to something my friend Sammy Lopez was involved in."

"Any idea what it entails?"

"I'd like to find out. All we know is someone is demanding a package."

Sarah nodded at Bart. "The woman who attacked me asked about a package, but I have no idea what it might be."

Bart appeared to think it over. "Jake, please thank your friends in high places for saving our lives from the attack."

"I'll be sure to pass that along," Jake said.

Bart pulled out his phone and looked at the screen. "Hmm, I'm getting a call from the 202 area code in Washington, D.C. Isn't that an interesting coincidence?" He thumbed the answer icon and walked away.

Jake wondered if McKay was finally going to give Bart top-secret clearances, as she'd once planned to do so Jake could consult him on the legalities of his acts as a privateer with a Letter of Marque and Reprisal. He hoped so, because this jet was one of the very few Cody would agree to fly on.

~

Rojo accepted the phone from Enrique and watched a delayed livestreamed video. He saw one of his men on a boat fire a stinger missile into the air.

The missile soared into the blue sky, leaving a smoke trail behind it.

Suddenly a cloud of red hot flares popped. The missile exploded and a jet passed over the bloom unharmed.

The idiot using the camera recorded a vapor trail coming straight down at him, and he must have just stood there transfixed like a deer in the headlights as it targeted his boat.

The screen lit up with a blinding flash and then the video went black.

"That cost me another boat. I'm surrounded by idiots," Rojo said, and he threw his phone down against the patio floor tile, breaking it.

Tomás picked it up, removed the SIM card and placed it in an identical phone. He gently set the new phone on the table in front of his uncle. "The good news is, you wanted Wolfe alive, and he's still alive. Also, he's going home, where he might let his guard down and allow your men to capture him."

Rojo nodded and took a moment to light a cigar, his hands shaking with frustration. He then poured another shot of tequila, drank it down in one gulp and bit into a wedge of lime.

"You are a wise young man," he said. "Place a three-way call with Enrique and Angel."

Tomás set up the call and handed the phone to his uncle.

Rojo said, "Wolfe escaped and he cost me a boat. Bring him to me. I want you to ask him where the hard drive is, and I want him to suffer great pain."

"*Sí, patrón,*" Angel said.

"Both of you travel north at once, take Wolfe and his dog and girlfriend hostage and bring them to me. Wolfe may or may not have knowledge of the hard drive, but either way I still want to torture him. Do you agree, Angel?"

Angel said, "Torture requires patience, but we always learn something useful that puts money in our pockets. Once Wolfe sees his girlfriend screaming in agony, he'll tell us anything to make it stop."

Rojo ended the call.

CHAPTER 26

Dawn served dinner salads to Jake and Sarah, along with a plate of plain chicken for Cody.

As they ate their meal, Sarah said,

"Jake, for the record, I've been too busy with my career to even consider having a child anytime in the next few years."

"I understand. Your career is much appreciated by the city's four-footed family members," Jake said.

"I also have this bad boy in my life who exposes me to danger on a regular basis."

Jake set down his fork. "I'm sorry about everything you've been through lately. I feel like it's all my fault."

Sarah took a sip of champagne. "Maybe you could try to compartmentalize your life. Your work in one compartment, your private life in another separate compartment."

"I'll try my best," Jake said. "I could also assign a bodyguard to protect your home and business."

She sighed. "I hope that won't be necessary."

They finished their meals, and Dawn collected the plates. Sarah reclined her seat, pulled a blanket over herself and fell asleep.

Jake was glad she was taking a nap. The rest would do her good. He gazed out the window while the jet flew over Monterey Bay Peninsula, one of the most scenic and beautiful places he'd ever visited. He saw the yacht club, Pebble Beach, and Carmel-by-the Sea. They were all calling to him. He was past due for a return visit.

He wondered if one of the yacht harbor guest berths was available for rent. If so, one day soon he could cruise there in the *Far Niente* and spend a week. They probably had a waiting list, but maybe he could just skip the marina and anchor out offshore, commuting back and forth with his reliable dinghy.

Next, he watched as Santa Cruz came into view, where old growth redwood forests met the sand and sea. Bordered by ocean beaches to the west and Sierra Nevada Mountains in view to the east, there was no place in the world quite like it. He felt an urge to take Cody there for a walk on the beach and a hike in the redwood forests.

Soon the jet landed at SFO and rolled to a private hangar where Vito was waiting in his black limousine to give Jake, Cody and Sarah a ride home.

Jake was glad to see Vito, who belonged to the Amborgetti family and was a trusted friend.

Jake had recently sworn the *omertà* oath of secrecy and was a "made man." At the time, it had been the only way to protect Sarah's life. Jake and Vito were now obligated by honor to protect each other's family and friends.

Exiting the jet, they all walked over to Vito's limo and climbed inside. On the drive, Jake told Vito about the attack on Sarah and how Pez had been murdered by cartel criminals.

Vito cursed and said in Italian, "Give me their names, and I'll make them dead."

Jake glanced at Sarah as she stared out at the city, deep in thought, not understanding the conversation. He replied in Italian. "The government is handling it. They blew up a cartel boat already, and more actions will follow."

Vito nodded, apparently satisfied with the exploding boat, because that was something an Italian on a vendetta might do.

Vendetta was an Italian word, after all.

When they arrived at the restored Victorian home where Sarah rented a studio apartment on the second floor, Jake said, "Sarah, I think Cody and I should spend the night and protect you."

"No, not tonight, Jake," Sarah said. "Thank you, but I want to be alone and think things over."

"All right, but we're going to walk you to your door," Jake said, getting out of the car and saying something in Italian to Vito.

Vito tapped his phone, sending a text.

Opening Sarah's car door for her, Jake held her hand and walked beside her to the building as Cody tagged along behind them.

They climbed the outside stairs and Sarah opened her second-floor apartment door and stood in the doorway, as if knowing Jake would try to follow her inside and charm his way into staying.

"Thank you both, and now I'll say good night," she said.

"Sleep tight," Jake said, giving her a kiss.

Cody put his head under her hand.

She finished her kiss with Jake and patted Cody on the head. "You two take care."

"Talk to you tomorrow," Jake said.

A black sedan pulled up and the driver cut its headlights. The window went down and an Italian man nodded at Jake. He had dark hair, jaded eyes, and wore a pale blue dress shirt along with a black sport coat to hide a pistol and holster.

Jake nodded in reply.

"Who's that?" Sarah asked.

"Beppe is a friend who'll be sitting there all night," Jake said.

Sarah tried to protest, but Jake said, "It's not up for debate, or Cody and I will sleep right here on this deck in front of your door."

"You'd do it, too," she said. "You know, Jake, I'd wished for a more exciting man in my life, but this life-or-death excitement is not what I had in mind." She gave him a tired smile and closed the door.

Jake heard the deadbolt turn and lock with a loud click. It felt like she was pulling away, but he respected her need to be alone. He and Cody walked down the stairs, and Vito drove them toward the harbor and the *Far Niente*.

CHAPTER 27

Sarah looked out her window and watched Jake drive away. *Should I have let him stay? Why do I constantly challenge him?*

The answer came to her mind loud and clear. *Because several times now he's nearly gotten me killed. What other woman do I know who would live this way?*

She observed the Italian bodyguard as he stood next to his car, smoking a cigarette. Beppe's face was devoid of emotion as his eyes flicked up and down the street in both directions. She knew he was armed and would not hesitate to use what Jake called "extrajudicial measures" to protect her.

"I'm not even safe in my own home," she said out loud.

Closing the blinds, she poured herself a glass of wine, no longer interested in the ice cream she'd recently craved. The fact that she could drink now brought back painful memories of the accident and hospital.

Thinking about Jake, she sipped her wine and ruminated on what he'd said about raising a child together on the boat.

Tears ran down her face. Jake was falling in love with her. That much was clear.

But she wasn't the type to trick a man into the eighteen-year commitment and enormous financial cost of parenting a child by purposely allowing a pregnancy and then acting as if it was an accident. If she ever had kids, she wanted it to be with a partner who wanted them just as much as she did.

She hadn't even been looking for a serious relationship, but a chance encounter with Jake when Cody had needed medical help had altered the course of their lives.

Drawing a hot bath and soaking her tired body, she thought it over. This could pull them apart, or bring them closer together.

Taking another drink of wine, she told herself she'd still date Jake because he could make her laugh and give her amazing orgasms, and yes, she was falling in love with him.

Although, if Jake ever asked her to marry him, she'd probably have to say no. He was too deeply involved in dangerous and violent troubles, mostly for the government, but also on an occasional foray into vigilante justice. But he was a smoking hot boyfriend and that's all she wanted right now. No marriage, no babies, no lifetime commitments.

Accepting the situation for what it was, she stepped out of the tub and toweled off. Turning off the lights, she went to bed and fell asleep exhausted but hopeful for the future.

On board the *Far Niente*, Jake sat on his couch, thinking about Sarah and fighting off the urge to drive back to her apartment. He sipped a glass of Redbreast Irish Whiskey and listened to music, wondering if Sarah was asleep.

Should he send her a text? No, that would be intrusive. She wanted some time alone to think. Maybe he was holding her back from true happiness with some other man who lived a normal life.

He didn't feel sleepy at all, but he needed the rest. Sometimes it helped him clear his mind and relax if he played the visually intensive problem-solving game Tetris, or the similar Bejeweled, or Candy Crush Saga. Studies had found the activity refocused the visual processing center of the brain and could overwrite negative images in the mind, lower the symptoms of stress, and help with insomnia.

His friend Paul would play the games on his phone at night when he felt the need to drink alcohol. The theory was that it helped by replacing craving or obsessing or anxiety with a harmless activity that could occupy the mind.

Jake owned every retro game system you could think of and kept all of them on the *Far Niente*. Nintendo 64, Gameboy, Xbox and PlayStation, among others.

He should have played a game, but he sat drinking and brooding instead. Soon, in his mind he saw Pez and his battered, bleeding body at the scene of the accident, and suddenly a rare and surprising bout of PTSD depression came upon him in full force.

His particular symptoms were different from what some of his friends talked about. He gripped his hands into fists and began breathing fast. Images flickered past his vision, and sounds roared in his ears.

A battle at night, rifle muzzle flashes, screams of the wounded. Female hostages crying out for him to rescue them. Jake yelling at the women to lie down. His own rifle firing round after round and dropping enemy terrorists, rapists and murderers. The rescued women crying in thanks as he led them away in the dark of night to rescue aircraft.

Jake stood up, held his arms out by his sides and took slow, deep cleansing breaths to clear away the memories.

Cody came to him and pawed at his thigh. Jake went down on one knee and gave his dog a hug. "Thanks, buddy. I'm okay now. I just had a flashback or something."

Cody whined. If a dog could appear worried, Cody was doing it.

Jake tried to cheer himself up for the sake of Cody. "Who wants to watch a doggie movie?"

Cody woofed and wagged his tail, jumping onto the couch and lying down with his head facing the TV.

Jake sat next to his dog and patted him on the back. Thumbing the remote, he turned on some previews. "We have *Lady and the Tramp*, of course—it's a classic. And that's you playing Tramp's part in the spaghetti dinner scene, no doubt. There's also *Cats & Dogs*. I know how much you like Lou and Butch. Oh, and here's one of your favorite adventure films, *Eight Below,* starring your hero Paul Walker."

Cody barked and his tail wagged faster.

"Eight Below it is," Jake said, turning on the movie he'd seen more times than he could count. "You remember that a dog dies in this movie, and it's very sad, right?"

Cody put his head down on his front paws, as if accepting the heartbreak as part of life.

"All right," Jake said and patted his dog again.

Once Cody was occupied with the movie, Jake made a conscious effort to keep himself distracted and avoid drinking too much whiskey. But he couldn't help thinking about how it was his fault Sarah had suffered a miscarriage. Feeling a tightness in his chest, he took a long drink to empty his glass, then glanced at Cody before quietly pouring another shot from the bottle he'd kept nearby.

He told himself that sometimes a battle-scarred war veteran needed a drink or two, and this was one of those times. Hopefully, he wouldn't go down the road of self-medication to deaden the pain, as so many of his friends had done after returning home from their service and failing to fit in with civilian life.

CHAPTER 28

In the morning, Jake sat at the patio table on the boat's aft deck and sipped a cup of coffee. He sent a text to Sarah: *Good morning. Thinking of you.*

She didn't answer his text, but he guessed she might have gone into work early and was busy treating a dog or cat patient at her pet clinic. She was gifted and skilled and loved her work. He admired her for that.

Gazing at his phone, he noticed all kinds of texts, many from women who would love to hear from him. He didn't reply to their texts, but he didn't delete them either.

A black Suburban drove up and stopped near the dock. Secret Service Agents Easton and Greene climbed out of the vehicle and walked toward him, each carrying a black hard-shell guitar case.

Easton opened the gate with a key, and they continued on until reaching the Far Niente. They came aboard without asking and set down the cases.

Greene said, "Two Taser shotguns, one for your Jeep and one for your boat."

Jake opened one of the cases and examined the shotgun inside. "Tell me more about this thing."

Greene said, "The Taser X12 pump shotgun has a range of one hundred feet and holds five rounds that have hooks that stick to skin or clothes. Each round delivers five hundred volts to stun a target for twenty seconds."

"That will do nicely," Jake said. He picked up one of the rounds and examined it. The thing was similar in size and shape to a D battery.

Greene asked, "So, Jake—you couldn't shoot a female? What about gender equality?"

"I'm all for equal pay and opportunities," Jake said, "but in matters of life or death I live by a personal moral code. I refuse to harm women, children or dogs. And my code is not up for debate or discussion."

"Fair enough," Greene said. "A troubleshooter with an old-fashioned moral compass."

He shook hands with each of them. "Thank you both."

The agents walked back to their Suburban and drove away.

Jake grabbed a leash and took Cody for a walk. As they strolled along the seashore, his phone buzzed with a call from Olivia, girlfriend of the late Sammy "Pez" Lopez.

"I found his journal," Olivia said. "He hid it at my place for some reason. Your name and phone number are in it, and he wrote that you were one of his best friends."

"That's true," Jake said without hesitation. "I'm sorry you and I didn't get a chance to meet when I was there. What else did Pez write in the journal?"

"He was being threatened by a cartel demanding he give them a missing package, or they might kill him and his parents and me too."

Jake felt his pulse quicken. "Where are you right now?"

"I have no idea what the item is. I'm hiding out right now. I want to organize Sammy's funeral, but I'm afraid to show my face in public."

"I thought Pez sold auto parts on the internet."

"Yes, he did, and he made good money. Many smaller auto parts are made in China and assembled in Mexico. He exported the finished products across the border to his US warehouse and sold them on the internet to all fifty states."

"Did he mention any particular package to you, or what was inside it?"

"No, nothing. His journal only says it was a priceless package, nothing more. I've visited his warehouse many times, and it's filled with thousands of boxes of various auto parts. Every day his employees would ship out packages."

Jake thought for a moment. "Is a manager still running the company?"

"No. I told everyone the business was temporarily closed. That's causing financial problems for the employees, but at least they're still alive."

"Good point," Jake said.

"I wish I could help Sammy's parents with the funeral arrangements." She sobbed for a moment.

Jake looked off into the distance. "I met Pez's mother and father a year ago. They're nice people. Tell you what, I'll come to San Diego and help you all with the funeral and everything. Maybe we can get the auto parts business open and running again too."

She sighed in relief. "Thank you, Jake. Sammy wrote in his journal that he could always trust Jake and Terrell, no matter what. And he added in capital letters: SEMPER FI."

Jake felt a tightness in his throat. "Always faithful. Well, now I have to come down there to honor his faith in me. I'll see you in a few days. Lay low and be careful until then, all right?"

"Okay, please call me when you get here," Olivia said.

"Will do, talk to you soon." Jake ended the call.

Cody stared at Jake as if reading his mind.

Jake nodded at his dog. "We're going for a cruise south, down the coast. It'll be a few days at sea. You up for that?"

Cody barked and pawed the deck, as if ready to go anywhere Jake went.

Jake patted Cody on the back, then tapped his phone and called Terrell. "How's your head wound? Healing up okay?"

"Getting better every day," Terrell said. "Mainly because I'm a hard-headed son of a gun. Are you impressed?"

Jake smiled at the typical banter from his friend and made light of the recent operation to remove a shrapnel fragment from his cranium. "Kind of, but actually it's no big deal. You're just another typical Marine jarhead who refuses to die."

"True—and your point?"

"I got a call from Pez's girlfriend, Olivia. She found his journal and it says he was being threatened."

Terrell's voice changed from sarcastic to serious. "I'd like to read that journal, but it's pretty far out of my jurisdiction. You're a lawyer, help me come up with some reason to get a copy."

"I'm going down there, so I'll take pictures and send them to you."

"Flying in Bart's jet again?" Terrell asked.

"No, taking the *Far Niente* on a cruise this time," Jake replied.

"Not the fastest way to get there, but the most enjoyable."

"Yeah, I can cruise to San Diego in just a couple of days. I'm figuring four hundred and fifty miles, running at eighteen knots or so and taking twenty-five hours total. I'll split that into two days, stopping somewhere on the way to sleep. Santa Barbara is two hundred and twenty-eight nautical miles from here, so maybe I'll spend a night in Santa Barbara Harbor and take Cody ashore to exercise his legs."

"I love Santa Barbara. I heard Oprah owns a house in the Montecito area," Terrell said.

"That doesn't surprise me. She can buy houses anywhere, so why not there?" Jake asked.

"She's a smart investor who paid fifty million dollars for the home, and now it's worth twice that."

Jake tapped his phone. "Hmm, a quick look at Zillow shows a bargain house for sale at *only* thirty million."

"What does thirty mill buy you there lately?" Terrell asked.

"Some acreage and a nice big mansion with seven bathrooms."

"Only seven?"

"One for each day of the week. Any more and it might seem excessive," Jake said.

"Wouldn't want to get carried away."

"All things in moderation."

"When's the funeral?" Terrell asked.

Jake gazed toward the south. "I'll work it out with Pez's parents and let you know. Olivia said Pez wrote in the journal that he could always count on Terrell and Jake. Semper Fi."

"Damn. When I fly down for the funeral, maybe you and I can snoop around. We owe that much to Pez," Terrell said.

"I agree," Jake said.

"Later, brother." Terrell ended the call.

Jake stared out at the city. Now he had to tell Sarah he was going out of town. How would she react? Maybe she'd welcome a break from seeing him after all they'd been through together lately. Or maybe she'd break up with him because it was all just too much.

Either way, it would be nice to have a farewell dinner beforehand, to leave her with happy memories.

Following his gut instinct, Jake drove to Sarah's pet clinic, parked nearby and walked in the door with Cody on a leash. "Be friends, Cody."

Sarah's young receptionist, Madison, gazed at Jake with obvious adoration. "Hi, Jake, how are you and Cody today?"

"We're good, Maddie, and you?" Jake said.

Madison had long brown hair, doe eyes and pretty features. Jake could sense her obvious attraction to him but kept her at a distance.

"It's all good," she said and blushed as she often did when Jake spoke to her in his deep voice.

Cody went to her, put his head on her lap and wagged his tail. Madison ruffled Cody's ears.

"Well, hello, handsome," she said.

Sarah walked into the reception area wearing a doctor's white lab coat and leading a Shetland sheepdog on a leash. The dog barked at Cody.

Cody turned and gave a deep growl in reply.

Jake tugged on the leash, and Madison let go of Cody, who returned to Jake's side.

"Easy, fella. Be friends," Jake said.

A woman in a well-tailored designer skirt suit stood up from where she'd been sitting in the waiting area and took hold of the sheltie's leash. "Thank you for the checkup, Dr. Sarah."

"My pleasure, Courtney. It's always nice to see Max, and she's as healthy as can be," Sarah said.

As the woman left the clinic, Sarah turned to Jake and gave him an inquiring look. He gave her a winning smile in return. "We stopped by to say hi and ask if you'd like to have dinner tonight at Amborgetti's."

Sarah blinked. "Wow, what's the occasion?"

"Big Mo invited us. If we don't go, he'll be offended."

"Hmm, we probably don't want to offend a mob boss, do we?"

"That's just a rumor, started by gossip tabloids," Jake said with a straight face.

Sarah laughed at his BS. "I'd love to have dinner there tonight."

Jake glanced at the clock. "Pick you up at your apartment at seven?"

Sarah nodded. "I've never been to Amborgetti's. Is it fancy? Should I wear a dress and heels?"

"Yes, it's absolutely gorgeous, like you. They have an unwritten look-your-celebrity-best dress code, so I'll be wearing a suit and tie. See you at seven." Jake led Cody out the door, and noticed Sarah's reflection in the door glass for a second as she stared at him curiously.

CHAPTER 29

Later that evening, a few minutes before seven o'clock, Enrique drove a minivan with darkened windows and slowly followed a GPS beacon he'd hidden underneath Wolfe's Jeep.

Watching a dot on a map display, he said, "Hopefully, we'll catch Wolfe and his girlfriend together."

Angel de la Muerte ran a hand through her chopped-short black hair and carefully touched her tender nose that was crisscrossed with white tape. "I wanted to ambush Wolfe when he got into his car."

"Rojo said to take all three of them, Wolfe, the dog and the girlfriend. We don't know where she lives."

"That bitch broke my nose. I can't wait to get her in handcuffs and have a little talk," Angel said.

"Sí, Angel, you will get your revenge," Enrique replied. He felt sorry for Sarah, but also relieved Angel's violent temper was focused on someone else besides him.

Enrique sighed quietly. The psycho killer in the van with him was worse than no help at all. He would not only have to capture the targets, he'd have to make sure Angel didn't kill one of them in a fit of rage, the way she'd killed Pez.

~

Jake pulled up in front of Sarah's apartment at seven o'clock on the dot. He sent her a text and stepped out of the Jeep. Sarah came out onto the upstairs balcony, locked her door and carefully walked down the steps in a pair of high-heeled black leather pumps.

Her little black dress was a stretch knit body-con style that fit like a glove and accentuated her curves, the hem ending a few inches above her knees. She'd topped it off with a stylish cropped jacket of butter-soft black leather that matched her shoes and clutch purse. She'd had her hair styled, and her lipstick was a shade Jake had seen her wearing once before. When he'd complimented her on it, she'd said it was named "blushing nude."

Jake stared at her super-hot appearance and thought Sarah looked like a Hollywood movie star. "Wow, you're stunning!" he said.

Sarah smiled, obviously pleased at his reaction. "You like my outfit?"

Jake nodded. "I like it a lot."

She got seated, and he closed her door.

As Jake drove, Sarah said, "Thanks for asking me out to dinner. I'm hoping you can cheer me up. I talked to my therapist about the miscarriage and she said some women go into mourning, while others shake it off and move on. I respect that every person is different. In my case, I want to put the trouble in Cabo behind me and live my life."

Jake thought she sounded like a combat veteran. "My sister Nicole is a psychiatrist. She says every individual has a unique personality and faces life's challenges in their own way."

Sarah thought about that for a moment. "I'm a strong woman, resilient, and grateful for the good things in my life. I want to focus on the positive."

"Speaking of good things, you're going to love Amborgetti's," Jake said.

"What's the specialty of the house?"

"They have all kinds of authentic Italian dishes, but I'm craving their famous combo of New York steak with a side of lasagna," Jake said. "I highly recommend it."

Sarah smiled. "That sounds good. I've been eating a low carb diet and I'm due for some lasagna."

"Add a good Italian red wine and you'll love it." At the next stoplight, Jake tapped his phone and sent a text.

～

"Where is he going?" Angel asked, as Enrique followed the GPS beacon from a distance.

"How do I know? I'm just following a moving dot on a map," Enrique replied.

Staring at the tracking display, Angel said, "He hasn't stopped anywhere except at traffic lights."

"Maybe he's meeting his girlfriend someplace. We heard him ask the dog if he was ready to go see Sarah."

"I'm getting impatient and looking forward to some one-on-one time with them," Angel said.

She pulled out a knife and rubbed the blade's razor-sharp edge against a whetstone, mumbling to herself about what she was going to do, starting with Sarah.

～

Jake drove up to Amborgetti's restaurant and parked right in front of the door. Two tall men in Italian suits stared at the Jeep and nodded in recognition. The looks on their faces said Jake was expected and they knew his license plate. They appeared to be powerfully built, in charge, armed and not to be trifled with.

Jake returned the nod to the men he knew were highly trained bodyguards. He was on a first-name basis with most of the guards but hadn't met these two yet.

A parking valet ran up to the Jeep and stared at Jake in awe and respect. The young Italian man said, "Giacobbe Il Coltello?"

"Yes, I'm Jacob The Knife, but you can call me Jake. Please take good care of my car."

The young man spoke into his phone, then sat in the driver's seat, his eyes taking in the high-tech dash console. Jake pressed his key fob to open Cody's K-9 door on the driver's side of the Jeep. Cody jumped out wearing a service dog vest and the official registration tag on his collar.

Jake pointed at the dashboard, looking the valet in the eye. "I know this looks like some kind of cool spy tech stuff, but do *not* touch anything. You're being recorded on video. Is that understood?"

"Yes, sir," the young man said, nervous at seeing his face on the dashboard computer screen.

Jake handed over enough cash to make sure he gave the valet the most generous tip he'd ever received.

"You're working for me while you're in charge of my vehicle," Jake said.

The man nodded in agreement, his hands on the steering wheel.

Jake walked around the car with Cody following and opened Sarah's door.

Sarah held onto Jake's arm as she stepped onto the sidewalk in her high heels. Cody reacted protectively to Sarah, pawing the pavement, raising his nose and staring at the two powerful men in suits standing nearby, who his highly trained sense of smell told him were armed.

Jake said, "Out, Cody. Be friends." He clipped a leash onto his dog's collar, and the three of them went into the restaurant.

As Cody passed the armed men, he let out a low growl.

The men smiled and nodded at him, acting as if everyone in the Amborgetti organization knew about Cody and considered him a valued member of the family. Just don't get too close or make him mad.

Inside, the hostess glanced at Jake and his dog in recognition. "Mr. Wolfe, so good to see you again. Right this way."

"Grazie, Lucia," Jake said.

Lucia led Jake, Sarah and Cody to one of the best tables in the house.

Sarah asked, "How often do you dine here, Jake?"

Jake said, "Once or twice a month, Anselmo and I have a private lunch to discuss legal questions, protected by attorney-client privilege. I also worked here in high school. My cousins run the place, and it's always been like a second home to me."

Sarah looked around and took it all in, as if learning about a new side of Jake she hadn't known.

Many of the diners smiled at seeing Cody walk past. One of them said, "Is that the dog I saw on TV, riding the bus?" Another said, "He's the dog who found that child in a burning building and saved her life."

Jake noticed some men ogling Sarah's attractive figure on display in the formfitting dress. He didn't blame them. She looked amazing. A few women gave Jake a quick up-and-down glance they thought was stealthy. Jake took it all in stride. People watching was a national pastime, and he was proud to be seen with Sarah.

When they arrived at their table, Jake asked Lucia, "Could you please have a waitress bring us two glasses of champagne?"

"Of course, Mr. Wolfe," Lucia replied.

Jake handed her a tip. He then gave a command, and Cody went under the table to lie down. Jake held Sarah's chair for her, and as she sat down she appeared surprised but pleased at his confident old-world chivalry. He sat across from her, just as a new waiter appeared who Jake had never seen before.

The waiter poured two glasses of champagne, and set down a basket of various Italian breads along with a dish of olive oil infused with herbs and a splash of balsamic vinegar. "Are you ready to order, or do you need a few minutes to look at the menu?"

Jake held his gaze. "My lady and I will both have the New York steak, cooked medium rare, with lasagna on the side. The cooks are friends of mine and are already preparing the meal. I'd appreciate it if you'd stop in the kitchen and check on our order."

The waiter's face paled slightly, but he kept his cool. "Excellent choice, sir. I'll go see how it's coming along." He turned and headed directly for the kitchen at a brisk pace.

Sarah smiled at Jake as if not sure what to think. "No man has ever ordered for me until now—it's kind of fun."

Jake gave her a wink and a smile. He dipped a piece of bread into some of the world's highest-quality olive oil and took a bite, followed by a sip of fine champagne.

Sarah did the same. "I love it when they serve olive oil instead of butter."

Jake looked off into the distance. "I'm torn. My Italian side agrees, but my Irish side wants Kerry Gold."

They noticed a commotion as the hostess led a famous rock star and his entourage of groupies to a nearby table. Sarah stared in disbelief at the popular celebrity. She glanced at Jake, her eyes questioning. He nodded and tilted his head at another table where a well-known Hollywood actor and actress were talking and laughing.

Sarah raised her eyebrows at seeing the movie stars up close. "I'd heard they were shooting a film here in the city."

The waiter returned quickly with two plates of steak and lasagna, along with a bowl of cold meatballs, no red sauce.

A woman walked up and handed the waiter a bottle of wine. He presented it to Jake and asked, "Is this the correct wine for you, Mr. Wolfe?"

Jake noted how the waiter now knew his name. "Yes, that Barolo is the one I asked for."

Sarah glanced at the meatballs. "You ordered for Cody, too?"

Jake nodded. "It was all part of our dinner reservation. On the way, I sent Vito a text, saying we'd arrive on time."

The waiter expertly popped the cork from the bottle, poured two glasses of the red wine and left the bottle on the table.

"Grazie," Jake said.

The waiter nodded and handed Jake a card. "It's a privilege, *Giacobbe Il Coltello*. Here's my mobile phone number. Please call or text if you need anything whatsoever to make this a memorable meal. I am at your service."

Jake shook his hand. "Much appreciated. I'll let Anselmo know you are taking good care of his family."

The waiter walked away, relief on his face.

Sarah tasted the wine and smiled. "This is unbelievably good."

Jake knew the bottle was a rare treasure that cost a fortune but he didn't say so. He savored a bite of lasagna, followed by a sip of wine. "I love it. Let's eat dinner here every night from now on."

Sarah smiled and shook her head. She glanced at Cody's food. "Are you going to feed our boy?"

Jake nodded. "Cody loves those plain meatballs. They don't add any onions or garlic to them."

"Good. Dogs can't have any of that."

"I've purposely been making him wait, because he's getting too damned cocky," Jake said, smiling. He set the plate down under the table and said, "Enjoy your dinner, Cody."

Cody had waited patiently, and now he chomped on the food as his dog tags clinked against the white porcelain dinner plate.

Enrique drove slowly past Amborgetti's restaurant. Angel lowered her darkened window just a few inches, enough to peer at the building and windows. She saw Jake and Sarah sitting at a table, enjoying food and drink.

"There you are, Sarah," she said, gritting her teeth.

CHAPTER 30

Jake was glad to see Sarah enjoying her steak and lasagna, along with the amazing wine. In between bites, he had her laughing at some of his stories from when he worked in the media as a photojournalist.

The dinner was a wonderful treat for both of them, and during a pause in their fun conversation, Sarah asked, "Jake, do you think you'll ever want to try salsa dancing?"

For a moment, Jake felt as if the music had stopped with a screech and he was a deer in the headlights. The question seemed to come out of the blue. He almost said no, which was the simple truth, but he kept an open mind while wondering why she had to ask now, of all times?

"I think we talked about this before and I said … maybe?"

Her face revealed her disappointment. "*Maybe* isn't really an answer, but that's *fine*. The bottom line is, I want to salsa dance, and I'm not going to give it up for you, okay?"

It sounded to Jake like a rehearsed speech—one she'd dwelled on for a while. He tried to read the look on her face and the tone of her voice. No help there; he was lost. However, he knew that if a woman said everything was "fine," it wasn't fine at all—probably the opposite. She'd probably been waiting until he was in a really good mood to ask him this question.

He took a calming breath and decided that after all the things she'd been through because of him, maybe this was the very least he could do for her in return.

However, to avoid setting a precedent where she'd make an unhappy demand and he'd obey like a pussy-whipped guy who'd given up his man card, he negotiated with good-natured cheerfulness.

"Well, let's see. I've asked you to go on a fishing trip and you've said *maybe*, too. That makes us even. Why don't we both do each other a favor? I'll go to salsa lessons with you, and you can go out fishing with me. Fair deal?"

Sarah rolled her eyes. "There are women who like to go fishing? Seems like a guy thing. Not on my to-do list. Good luck with that."

"Yes, of course, lots of women enjoy fishing. Are you kidding me? Here's an example." Jake tapped his phone to show her a YouTube video channel called Fishing with Luiza.

Sarah glanced at the attractive woman and sighed. "Looks like an advertisement for bikinis."

Jake smiled and shrugged. "She's Brazilian, and sometimes she wears a Brazilian bikini. Go figure. And it's just so darn warm in sunny Florida when you go out on a boat."

"Cool story, bro," she said, appearing unimpressed. "And here's my own video of what you're missing out on when you don't go dancing with me." She held out her phone and showed him a video of her dancing with a good-looking man.

Jake tried to make light of it. "He looks familiar … wait … I think he's Luiza's boyfriend!"

Sarah laughed. "That's Bob. He's an architect and a good dancer. This video is from before I met you, in case you're wondering."

"I'm happy for Bob," Jake said, acting as if he couldn't care less, but he took a drink of wine to hide the fact he wanted to find Bob and punch him in the face. Setting down his glass, he said, "Okay, so I'll go to the next lesson I'm able to attend … and when do you want to go fishing?"

Before Sarah could answer, their waiter reappeared. "Could I interest either of you in dessert? Our *tiramisù* is delicious with an after-dinner espresso."

"I couldn't eat another bite," Sarah said, smiling.

Jake said, "Dinner was fantastic, but all I saved room for was a shot of grappa."

The waiter turned to Sarah. "And for you?"

"What is ... grappa?" Sarah asked.

Jake said, "Try it, you might like it."

Sarah shrugged. "Sure, why not?"

After the waiter walked away, Sarah smiled in victory and asked innocently, "What's the weather supposed to be like tomorrow?"

"The forecast is good weather for *fishing*," Jake said. "Nice try to change the subject."

She giggled and her eyes sparkled. "Busted. You have a one-track mind."

He took her hand in his, drew it to his lips and kissed it. "You're what's on my one-track mind."

She took a deep breath after the kiss. "Couldn't we go out on the water and fool around, and just say we'd gone fishing?"

"That's a tempting proposal."

"Would you play the guitar for me?"

Jake nodded. "Of course. Tell you what—I'll go to a dance lesson first and *then* you can go fishing with me on a weekend morning. If we don't catch any fish, we'll go to bed and console each other."

"Okay, it's a deal, and I hope the fish take a day off," she said with a sexy smile.

Vito Amborgetti stopped by their table. The handsome and dangerous-looking young Italian man always had a slightly amused smile on his face. One of the waiters magically appeared with a chair, and Vito sat down.

"How was dinner?" he asked.

From under the table, Cody let out a doggie burp.

Vito smiled. "That's one yes vote."

Sarah said, "Dinner was wonderful. How have you been, Vito?"

"I'm good. How's the veterinarian work going?"

"My business is growing every month, thanks for asking.

Recently some Italian nonnas came in with their fur babies and said you recommended me."

Vito shrugged. "I knew you'd take good care of my friends and family."

A cocktail waitress arrived to drop off three small glasses of grappa, the fiery liquor distilled from the pressed grape pomace left over after making wine.

Jake held a glass near his nose, but not too close, and sniffed the high-alcohol bouquet of grapes, plums, vanilla, flowers and spices. "This is amazing."

"Only the very best," Vito said.

Sarah gave her glass a skeptical look.

Vito said teasingly, "No obligation to taste it, but speaking of grandmas, my nonna swears it adds years to her life. If you do try some, take small sips. It's powerful stuff."

Sarah smiled at Vito's absurd charm. Ignoring his warning, she picked up the shot and boldly drank it down in one gulp as if thinking, *That'll show them.* Her face then turned red, she coughed hard and her eyes watered.

Jake watched this, smiled and shook his head. He turned to Vito. "She's a handful."

Vito laughed. "I noticed."

Once Sarah caught her breath, with a tear rolling down one cheek, she asked, "What's in that stuff, rocket fuel?"

Vito nodded in mock seriousness. He cupped a hand near his mouth as if revealing a secret and whispered, "We distill extra and send it to NASA."

Jake said, "Wow, you're brave, Sarah. Don't worry if your tongue is numb. That's normal the first time you drink it down in one gulp. Most people work their way up to that."

Vito picked up his glass, held it out to Jake and toasted, "All'amicizia."

Jake repeated the toast in English. "To friendship."

They both drank the strong liquor, coughing afterward.

Vito looked Jake in the eye. "What have you been up to? Anything you can talk about?"

"I'm going to be taking salsa dancing lessons with Sarah." Jake turned to her and said, "I meant to ask, do they serve margaritas, or what?"

She smiled and shook her head, still recovering from the potent shot of alcohol.

Vito raised an eyebrow at Jake. "Salsa, huh? How did she talk you into that?"

"Sarah could talk me into just about damn near anything, but don't tell her I said that."

Vito nodded, all serious, and whispered in reply, "Your secret is safe with me."

Sarah laughed. "You two are absurd."

Jake said, "And in return, I *demand* that she go out on a fishing trip at five in the morning, catch a big smelly fish, drink beer, smoke a mild cigar and hopefully not get seasick and puke over the rail." He gave her a winning smile.

"Good grief, you drive a hard bargain," Sarah said, returning his smile. "Do I have to wear a Brazilian bikini like Luiza? Maybe I'll start my own YouTube channel called *Fishing with Sarah*."

Jake rubbed his chin. "Huh, I hadn't thought of that, but I like your bikini idea."

"I can go along with the bikini, but no cigar for me. I draw the line there."

"No worries, I was kidding about the cigar, but I'm happy as hell about the bikini. This is working out great."

Vito smiled and stood up. "My work here is done. The grappa has magic powers, I'm telling you. By the way, this dinner is on the house, for all that overtime you worked here in high school, Giacobbe Il Coltello."

"Grazie, amico," Jake said, meeting Vito's eyes.

"Prego," Vito answered and walked away to visit the rock star's table, where a waiter was preparing a flaming dessert.

"Whoa, should I grab a fire extinguisher?" Vito asked, winking at the rock star and getting a laugh from the groupies.

CHAPTER 31

On their way out of the restaurant, Jake deliberately led Sarah past the rock star's table. The man was famous for being an unabashed flirt.

The singer gazed at Sarah as she passed by and called out, "Hi, beautiful. What's your name? You're invited to join us."

Sarah laughed, flattered by the attention, and took Jake's hand in hers.

Jake held on possessively, and smiled at seeing her so happy.

They made their way to the front entrance, where he saw the same two armed men outside, standing ready to protect the customers.

As Jake opened the front door, a van with darkened windows drove up and a woman stared out the passenger window. She wore a black stocking cap and had a wild look in her eyes.

The van screeched to a stop, the automatic sliding door opened on the side and the woman stepped out wearing a blast vest. She aimed a pistol at Jake and Sarah and yelled, "Get in the van!"

Both bodyguards drew their pistols.

Cody barked at her, and she reflexively swung her hand down to aim her weapon at the agitated dog.

Jake quickly closed the restaurant door and used it to protect Sarah and Cody.

Although the door looked like any other restaurant entryway, he knew it was three-and-a-half-inch-thick bulletproof Plexiglass, similar to what protected many bank tellers and jewelry store windows.

Cody bared his teeth, lips curled, snarling.

Jake held on to his pistol and waited as both of the bodyguards fired at the woman and the van.

The woman took two hits to her vest and staggered backward as if she'd been hit with a baseball bat. She fell into the open door of the van, cursed at the driver and screamed in rage, "You drove up too soon!"

The driver hit the gas and roared off as the automatic door closed and the woman scooted her legs out of the way. A black SUV gave chase.

One guard entered the restaurant and said, "It's clear now, Mr. Wolfe."

Jake nodded at him. "Grazie."

The bodyguard spoke loudly to the restaurant clientele. "Nothing to worry about, folks. Just some gangbanger punks who drove down the wrong street and fired a few shots, trying to be gangsta. These windows are bulletproof, and the police are here to ensure public safety."

The dinner guests looked out the windows and saw a police SUV arrive with blue and red lights flashing. A uniformed female officer stepped out, appearing calm and in control of the situation.

Italian men in suits blocked traffic and redirected cars down side streets. Nobody was allowed to drive past the restaurant.

Most of the guests relaxed and went back to their conversations, but a few asked for their checks, wanting to leave ASAP.

Jake and Sarah went outside onto the sidewalk and saw the same valet driver pull up in the Jeep. The young man respectfully held the passenger door open for Sarah.

Thanking him, she worriedly glanced left and right and climbed into her seat while he turned his head politely and made sure not to gawk at her pretty legs on display.

Jake pressed the key fob to open the K-9 door. Once Cody was in and safely seated, he tapped the button and closed the door on automatic hinges. He tipped the valet again. "What's your name?"

"Nicky."

"Nicky, do me a favor. Please go under the car and look for a tracking device."

The young man didn't hesitate. He dropped to the ground, rolled under the vehicle and began a careful search.

Jake stood there and waited, holding up one finger to Sarah to indicate a momentary delay.

Nicky came out from under the car and stood up, brandishing a real time GPS tracker that fit in the palm of his hand.

"Here it is, just like you thought," he said.

Jake nodded. "Give that to Vito. Tell him I want a guy to put it in his car, get on the highway and drive all night toward LA. In the morning he can toss it in the trash and drive back. I'll pay him well for his time."

Nicky smiled and nodded, tapped his phone and called Vito.

Jake climbed into the Jeep and drove away. As he passed the police SUV he nodded in respect at Officer Tammi Martinelli. She secretly belonged to the Family and had no doubt responded to a call from Anselmo.

Tammi nodded at Jake in reply and then her dark eyes flicked to Sarah, appearing curious about who Jake was dating.

Sarah met her gaze with a challenging look.

On the drive, Sarah asked, "I couldn't see who was doing the shooting at the restaurant. What was that about?"

Jake said, "Probably some nutcase, angry because he or she can't get a dinner reservation until a year later."

She shook her head. "I can't help but wonder if the trouble in Cabo followed us home."

"I think you're right, so be extra careful and carry your pistol," Jake said. "Beppe will be protecting you for a while until we know it's safe."

Sarah turned and looked at him. "That reminds me of something I meant to ask. Why is Vito so polite and protective of me?"

"Maybe he has a special love of veterinarians?"

"Is it because he considers me a potential future in-law?"

Jake paused a moment as he pondered the loaded question, then nodded at her. "Vito and I are very close, like brothers. As long as you and I are together, he'd do anything to protect my girl."

She smiled. "So, I'm your girl?"

"Vito seems to think so," Jake said, returning her smile.

Cody stuck his head between the front seats and nodded.

Sarah patted Cody on the head.

Hoping to avoid the dreaded *where is this relationship going?* talk, Jake turned on the stereo and played an old song: "Wonderful Tonight," by Eric Clapton. "This song makes me think of you," he said.

Sarah listened to the song, smiling in spite of her worries. She looked out at the city lights, lost in thought.

When they arrived at Sarah's building, she said, "Come upstairs, Jake."

"My pleasure," he said.

Once inside the apartment, Sarah lit some candles, dimmed the lights and sat on the couch.

Jake opened the door into the inner hallway of the Victorian house converted to studios. "Cody, *wait* here and *guard* the door."

Cody stretched out on the carpet runner and rested his head on his front paws, acting as if this was familiar to him and he felt right at home.

Jake closed and locked the door, turned around and walked to the couch.

Before he could sit down, Sarah lifted a cushion off of the couch, dropped it on the hardwood floor, went down on her knees and reached for his belt buckle. "The doctor said no intercourse, so let me give you a goodbye kiss you won't forget."

"Have mercy," Jake said.

CHAPTER 32

The next morning, after a night of restful sleep in each other's arms, Jake cooked breakfast for Sarah and sent Cody to fetch a loaf of freshly baked sourdough bread.

He called ahead to the bakery and then held out a saved bread wrapper so Cody could smell it. "Go see *Vicky*. Fetch the *bread*."

Jake opened the door, and Cody went down the outside stairs and trotted along the sidewalk toward the corner. A woman wearing a white apron and with a dusting of flour on her arms stepped out of the small neighborhood bakery. She held a long paper-wrapped baguette and gave the dog a big smile.

"Hello, Cody! How's my favorite dog this morning?"

Cody woofed at her and wagged his tail.

"Good boy, here's a treat for you, sweetie." Vicky took the wrapper off a cold, hard pat of butter and held it in her palm. Cody lapped it up and gave her a toothy grin.

She smiled. "Okay, now, take the bread home. Off you go."

Cody held the long loaf in his mouth, biting gently right in the middle, with both ends protruding from either side. Holding it with a soft bite, the way some retrievers carry a duck back to a hunter, he trotted back toward Sarah's apartment.

Vicky saw Jake waving at her from the balcony. She smiled and waved in return and went back inside her bakery.

People walking on the street smiled, pointed and took video of Cody as he trotted past carrying the bread.

Cody climbed the stairs, and the right end of the baguette bumped across the handrail balusters, bump-bump-bump.

"Thank you, Cody," Jake said, taking the loaf and patting him on the back.

Jake looked at a dark sedan parked across the street. The driver's window went down, revealing the same Italian man as before, sitting and guarding Sarah's apartment. Jake waved at Beppe in thanks and closed the door.

While singing loudly along with songs on the stereo, Jake cooked bacon, scrambled eggs and made toast. He set two plates on the table and one on the floor, minus the bread. Cody devoured the scrambled eggs with small bacon bits and cheddar cheese.

Sarah poured two mimosas, and as they ate breakfast, Jake told her about his plans.

"I really should go to San Diego for a short visit and help Pez's mother and father bury their son," he said.

Sarah took a sip of mimosa. "Did they call you? How are they taking it?"

"They're taking it hard. Pez wrote in his journal that he could always count on me and Terrell. Semper Fi. I feel obligated by duty to my friend and fellow Marine."

She nodded at him. "I'm not surprised at all. I've seen firsthand how you value loyalty."

"You're invited to come along with us if you have time."

It seemed to Jake that Sarah was in a good mood from the nice dinner the night before, and him agreeing to be her dance partner.

"It's okay, I get it," she said. "You're a good man for helping Pez's mother and father when they need you there."

He reached out and held her hand. "Thanks for understanding. It means a lot to me."

"No worries. This week I have an impossibly busy schedule, so I would've neglected you anyway. But I'm glad that last night I gave you something to think about while you're away from home." She smiled at him.

"I'll be seeing you in my dreams," he said, returning her smile.

After breakfast, Jake and Sarah hugged and kissed each other goodbye.

She said, "One more thing, Jake. A wise person once said, if you want to get even with somebody, get even with a person who was good to you."

Jake considered her words. "Don't worry, I'm only going to San Diego so I can help Pez's family, not to seek revenge," he said, lying to protect her.

She smiled, obviously relieved. "Take your time going, but hurry back."

Jake smiled and nodded. He went downstairs with Cody by his side and drove away while Sarah stood on the deck and watched them go. He waved at her as he drove off, noticing the conflicted look on her face. He could tell she wanted him to stay but understood he had to go when the family of a fellow Marine needed him.

He was glad she'd agreed to it, because he would've gone even if she hadn't. It was good to know Mo Amborgetti's people would be protecting her while he was gone.

Soon he arrived at Pier 39 Yacht Harbor, already missing Sarah as he prepared to leave town. That woman had a hold on his heart like no other before. Cody loved her too. Was it going to work out? He honestly didn't know.

An endless parade of tourists walked around the pier. The crowd was thick, even this early in the day. The big city had a lot to offer, but he missed the peace and quiet of Juanita Yacht Harbor in the small town of Sausalito. Once he returned from this trip, he'd probably take the *Far Niente* back over to Juanita and good old boat slip number A-37. Sometimes you took the best parts of your life for granted because they were so right and good.

Parking the Jeep, he walked down the dock to the *Far Niente* with Cody and boarded. Untying the lines, he motored over to the fuel dock and topped off the tanks, double-checking to make sure the fresh water tanks were full too.

"Are you ready to go cruising on the ocean, Badass Boat Dog?"

Cody trotted back and forth on the deck happily.

Jake laughed. "Let's do it."

A man with dark hair stood among the tourists at Pier 39 and gazed out at the water through binoculars. He tapped his phone and called Rojo. "El Patrón, I've been watching señor Wolfe's boat, as you ordered. He just now boarded the *Far Niente* and took it out on the bay, heading toward the open ocean."

Rojo said, "See which way he goes once he's on open water."

"Yes, sir. I'll have somebody stand watch on the Golden Gate Bridge, and let you know if Wolfe heads north or south."

"Wait a minute. Enrique and Angel are following Wolfe's Jeep on the highway to Los Angeles. Are you sure you saw him on the boat?" Rojo said.

"Enrique and Angel must be following the tracking device, not Wolfe's Jeep. It was obviously a trick, since Wolfe drove up in the Jeep and boarded his boat."

He held the phone away from his ear as Rojo cursed loudly.

CHAPTER 33

Jake motored across the bay, passing beneath the Golden Gate Bridge and onto the Pacific Ocean, and then turned to port and headed south. He pushed the twin throttles forward, felt her respond and come up on plane, and began cruising down the California coast.

Two dolphins leapt from the water near the starboard bow. Cody barked at them happily.

Jake saw the dolphins as a good sign. He opened the custom-made ventilation hatch windows on the enclosed skybridge and stood tall at the wheel with a salty breeze in his hair, feeling like this was where he belonged, at the helm of a boat on the water. The golden sun was shining bright in a beautiful blue sky. The ocean air smelled fresh, and the growl of the twin engines sounded unstoppable.

A quote by the Irishman John F. Kennedy came to mind: "All of us have, in our veins, the exact same percentage of salt in our blood that exists in the ocean, and therefore, we have salt in our blood, our sweat, and our tears. We are tied to the ocean. And when we go back to the sea, whether it is to sail or to watch it, we are going back from whence we came."

Jake also thought about something McKay had said recently: "A privateer is a pirate operating on behalf of a government."

The Letter of Marque made him a privateer—a pirate who had a government license to fight other pirates. And he'd recently killed a modern-day pirate on orders from Washington, D.C. His boat, the *Far Niente* was designated a Naval auxiliary vessel. He worked for a secret branch of the CIA—or a CIA branch of the Secret Service—he wasn't sure which. He had millions of dollars hidden in offshore bank accounts in the Bahamas, taken from a foreign assassin he'd killed with a knife to the heart.

Yes, for all intents and purposes, he was a pirate, secretly working for Uncle Sam.

He turned the sound system on high volume and played the Jimmy Buffett song, "A Pirate Looks at Forty." The story Jimmy told spoke to his soul.

The song cascaded out of the loudspeakers and he sang along, belting out the heartfelt lyrics while Cody howled in harmony.

When the song ended, Jake glanced over his shoulder to gaze far behind him at Point Reyes peninsula and Drake's Bay. The bay was named after English privateer Sir Francis Drake, who'd sailed his ship, the *Golden Hind,* all the way around the world, landing along the Pacific coast of North America in 1579 at what is now known as San Francisco, California.

In those days, Spanish ships known as Manila Galleons traveled across the Pacific Ocean between Acapulco in Mexico and Manila in the Philippines. On Drake's privateering journeys, he'd captured many Spanish conquistador ships and seized their cargos of treasure. The plundered booty included Inca gold and silver, Philippine jewelry, Cambodian ivory, jade from China, spices from Indonesia and Malaysia, and precious gems such as opals, amethysts and pearls from Siam, Burma, and Ceylon.

And a number of treasure ships sank in the Pacific. A total of 130 Manila Galleon's rested on the sea bottom, hiding rich cargoes worth fortunes. Jake hoped to dive one of the wrecks someday and find some Spanish Doubloon gold coins.

He glanced at the *Far Niente's* dash panel and watched another boat come up on the radar. That wasn't unusual, but this one seemed to be pacing his course. Grabbing a pair of binos, he trained them on the horizon and studied the boat in the distance. It was a power yacht similar in size to the *Far Niente* and appeared to be powered by large twin engines. Fast and sleek. Hard to outrun. He tapped the GPS and activated the Save Location feature, wanting a record of the encounter. He was well armed and ready to fight off an attack at sea if necessary, but he'd hoped to have an enjoyable journey.

Jake cruised past the charming seaside town of Capitola and wished he had time to stop at Zelda's on the Beach, sit outside on their deck and have some good food and drink. Maybe he could pay a visit on his return trip.

He and Cody enjoyed cruising along the coast the rest of the day, and Jake felt the urge to keep on traveling for many months in the future to get away from it all.

If only life was that simple.

CHAPTER 34

Twelve hours later, the *Far Niente* approached Santa Barbara.

The sun began to set, painting the sea and sky beautiful shades of purple and gold. The ocean also became quieter. There were fewer boats on the water as many people went ashore for the evening.

Darkness fell and Jake spotted a boat running without lights, which was dangerous and illegal. The boat was hard to see but appearing to mirror his progress. He tapped the GPS and activated the Save Location again. "Bring it on. Let's see what you've got."

He ran without lights for a while and scanned the horizon with night vision binoculars, but he didn't see the mystery boat. It might have been involved in some kind of illegal activity and long gone by now.

Heading for the harbor, he cruised along at a slower pace, enjoying the quiet and thinking about how peaceful it could be in a boat on the water, far from cars and traffic. It was one of the last remaining places of intellectual refuge. A quiet place to drop anchor was like a sanctuary. And now, more than ever in history, any kind of safe harbor for thoughtful people was a scarce commodity.

When he reached the beautiful seaside city of Santa Barbara, Jake motored slowly into the harbor and bought over five hundred gallons of fuel, topping up the tank and spending a small fortune.

He pulled into the reserved guest berth, tied up, went ashore and took an Uber to the hillside home of a married couple he knew. He'd called them before leaving San Francisco, and they were expecting him. They had a pleasant evening grilling burgers, drinking cold beers and enjoying talking in person instead of on social media.

Early in the morning, Jake started out on another day of cruising. He made an effort to adhere to routine, and all was well.

His gunny sergeant had always said, "If you take care of your routine, your routine will take care of you."

He and Cody cruised past Malibu, Los Angeles, Beverly Hills and Huntington Beach. He thought about how Jimmy Buffett owned a home in Beverly Hills, in addition to his homes in Florida. It made sense if you earned his kind of millions and loved the oceans. Why not enjoy more than one seashore of America the beautiful?

That reminded Jake he was past due for a trip to Key West, Florida. He had Marine veteran friends there, and the local fishing, scuba diving and friendly southern hospitality were beyond compare.

Cruising past the Marine Corps base at Camp Pendleton, Jake saluted in respect toward the base where he'd graduated from boot camp and the School of Infantry.

He was in the mood for a cigar, and lit one with a Connecticut wrapper. The mini-fridge supplied a cup of cold coffee with a splash of Bailey's and brandy.

As he cruised along with the sun shining brightly on the sparkling water, Jake noticed another boat that might be shadowing him on his course. A power yacht, around thirty-five feet long with a white hull. That could describe a lot of boats, and any one of them could be heading down the coast.

Looking through binos, he could tell it wasn't the same boat he'd seen up near the San Francisco Bay, but he again tapped the GPS and activated Save Location. Either he was being paranoid, or someone highly resourceful was stalking him.

His ego told him to race straight toward the boat and hail it on the loudspeaker. Maybe they'd have a shoot-out.

Moving to a tall cabinet, he removed a sniper rifle and placed it within arm's reach.

CHAPTER 35

Taking a deep calming breath, Jake continued south and stayed on mission.

During the day, the weather kept getting warmer and he noticed the temperature rise on the display.

Toward evening, he arrived near Naval Base Coronado and motored into Kona Kai Marina, where he'd reserved a temporary guest boat slip on Dock E, closest to the open ocean. Someone had gone out of town on a cruise and rented their slip in the same way people rented homes on Airbnb.

Checking the fuel gauge, he saw that he'd burned forty-five gallons per hour (GPH), using up over eleven hundred gallons. It was expensive to cruise at eighteen knots, but he'd been in a hurry. The AMEX Black Card given to him by McKay was paying the bills.

He called Pez's parents to let them know he was in town. They invited him over for dinner, and he was pleased to accept. After the call, Jake looked out at the city of San Diego and south toward Mexico.

"Listen up, you assholes who murdered Pez," he said quietly, "I'm going to find you, and I'm going to kill you."

Cody watched him closely. Jake noticed it and gave an explanation to his highly intelligent dog. "Yes, we're here for the funeral, but we're also going to find the *bastardos* who killed Pez and crush their balls like this." He slammed his right fist into his left palm.

Cody growled and showed his teeth, ready to rumble.

"And, yeah, I lied to Sarah, because she doesn't need to know and doesn't have top-secret clearances. General Patton once said you should do your duty as you see it, and damn the consequences. That's exactly what we're going to do here, brother dog."

Cody huffed and pawed at the deck as if he understood the feelings behind Jake's words, if not every detail.

Jake patted his dog on the back. "Attaboy. I can always count on you."

An employee of Enterprise Rent-a-Car pulled up in a minivan and gave them a ride to the office. That was the reason they earned all of Jake's business—they'd come and get him or drop him off. Why didn't every car rental company provide that service? It seemed like a no-brainer.

Upon arrival, Jake tipped the driver, then went inside and rented a silver Chevy Tahoe SUV. He drove to the Lopezes' house, parked on the street and knocked on their door. When the parents answered, Jake introduced himself and then Cody.

The parents, Brent and Michelle, said they remembered meeting Jake last year and were so pleased to meet Cody. They in turn presented Pez's girlfriend, Olivia.

Olivia was a short, young Latina with a pretty face and the sad eyes of someone who'd recently lost her beloved. "They asked me to live here a while, for my own safety," she said, appearing afraid and confused.

Jake nodded. "Good idea."

Michelle said, "My husband and I both have paid time off from our jobs, for making arrangements, settling affairs, bereavement and attending the funeral. We insisted on providing Olivia with a place to stay out of sight."

"That's kind of you," Jake said. He turned to Olivia. "You're now also under the protection of two Marine combat veterans—myself and my dog, Cody."

Olivia glanced at Cody. "He's a beautiful dog. May I pet him?"

Jake nodded. "Be friends, Cody."

Cody went to Olivia, put his head under her hand and nodded, wagging his tail.

"Now you can pet him," Jake said.

Olivia patted Cody on the head and finally smiled. "What a good dog you are, Cody."

Cody woofed and gave her a toothy grin.

She said, "I feel safe with Cody here."

"Yes, you're safe. Cody is highly protective," Jake said.

Olivia's shoulders relaxed. She sat down on the couch and let out a long sigh, and a single tear rolled down her cheek.

"Cody, *comfort* her," Jake said. "Allow her to hug you."

Cody was beginning to let a few more rare people hug him and hold onto him. He jumped onto the couch and sat next to Olivia, wagging his tail.

She hugged the golden dog and held onto him like a life preserver. Cody licked the tears from her face. Michelle watched this and gave Jake a sad smile.

He asked her, "How are *you* holding up, ma'am?"

Michelle started to say something but stopped and took a deep breath. "I'm doing the best I can."

Jake stepped closer and held his arms wide, and she leaned in and wept on his strong shoulder, hanging onto him as if he reminded her of Sammy, her lost son.

Later that night, Jake and Cody slept side by side on the large couch. It reminded Jake of when he was deployed overseas at a forward operating base (FOB) and had a folding cot for a bed. He and his war dog, Duke, barely fit on the cot together, but sometimes his dog wouldn't leave his side or sleep in his crate.

Duke hadn't survived combat, and Jake had taken it hard. In truth, he'd never gotten over the loss of his friend. His heart still burned with anger toward terrorists and anyone who might deliberately harm a dog.

His sister, Nicole, was a psychiatrist and she said Cody was helping Jake avoid becoming an angry vigilante. Nicole had no idea about the full extent of Jake's secret life, only seeing a glimpse of some things he'd done to protect people in the USA since coming home from war.

If she only knew...

He did some deep breathing exercises and visualized a walk along the seashore with Cody and Sarah, until finally drifting off to sleep.

In the morning, Cody woke him with a cold nose and a huff to his ear.

Jake stood up and clipped a leash onto his dog's collar.

While heading for the door to take a walk, he gratefully accepted an insulated travel mug of coffee from Mrs. Lopez.

"Thank you, ma'am. I have to go outside, walk my dog and make a phone call," he said.

"When you come back, I'll make breakfast for you," Michelle said.

Jake took a sip from the mug. "Wow, this is probably the best coffee I've ever tasted."

She smiled and shook her head. "Flatterer."

Jake returned the smile and led Cody outside. Once he'd closed the front door, Jake glanced around the street and checked for any threats. He wondered if one of the neighbors was being paid to watch the house.

CHAPTER 36

Jake kept his right hand on the pistol inside his coat, but everything in the residential neighborhood appeared normal.

Cody sniffed the morning air, his eyes alert.

"Cody, pee now," Jake said.

His dog lifted a leg and peed on a bush.

Jake unlocked the SUV, and they both climbed in. Tapping on his phone, he called Terrell as he drove around the neighborhood, getting the lay of the land. In his mind, the Lopezes' house was a base of operations that might need to be defended from attack.

Terrell answered the call with the sarcasm they often shared. "Hey, ugly."

Jake smiled and imitated the voice of Tom Hanks in the movie Forrest Gump, but toned down to a grouchy Marine level. "Lootenant Haayyys."

Terrell snorted. "You're a Forrest Gump, for sure."

"That makes you Bubba, the shrimp boat captain."

"Nah, I love Bubba, but I'm more Lieutenant Dan, since he was a badass lieutenant like me."

"Yeah, that's a fact. What are you up to on your medical leave time off, you LEO mofo?" Jake asked.

"Well I *was* eating a bacon-and-egg sandwich until you so rudely interrupted me."

"Oh man, now I gotta find some sandwich places around here, too."

"Yours can't match this one. It's a work of art, made by an angel," Terrell said.

"Your Wonder Woman wife Alicia is too good for you," Jake said matter-of-factly.

"Yeah, but I got lucky, because I'm part lucky Irish from drinking all that Guinness."

"Glad I was a positive influence on your drinking of Guinness. Are you having a pint with your breakfast, like they used to do in the old country?" Jake asked.

"No, I'm having a cup of black coffee with two sugars. I like my coffee the way I like my women."

They both said, "Black and sweet."

Jake smiled. "You always say that."

"That's coz it's true, and the truth bears repeating," Terrell said.

"Fair enough, but how come no angel woman is making bacon-and-egg sandwiches for me this morning?" Jake asked.

"Maybe you're not sandwich worthy."

"Oh ... that *hurts,* bro."

"That's what you get for interrupting my breakfast."

"Maybe I'll console myself with a breakfast burrito filled with bacon, eggs, pinto beans and avocado," Jake said. "The Mexican food in San Diego is amazing."

"Avocado? What is it with you people who eat that green thing?" Terrell asked.

Jake pretended to be offended. *"You people?* Anti-avocado bias is rampant. The struggle is real."

Terrell's tone of voice changed, growing lower and more melancholy. "I remember how Pez would always order avocado or guacamole anytime he saw it on a menu."

"And you'd tell him nature made avocado bright green as a warning not to eat it. I can still hear him laughing about that."

Terrell blew out a breath. "How are the plans for his funeral coming along?"

"That's why I called, to let you know the day and time of the memorial service. Also, Cody and I have *troubles* here that require your expert assistance—if you can read between the lines."

"Troubles?" Terrell asked.

"Yeah, serious troubles," Jake said, referring to his code for the history of Irish Troubles in Belfast, when nobody knew who might get killed on any given day.

"Give me a sitrep."

"I'm going to try to find out why Pez was murdered. Some folks are not going to like that."

"No kidding. Murderers are funny that way."

"I thought maybe you could fly down here a few days early. You're the smartest detective I know, and currently goofing off pretending to have a head injury."

"Huh, I guess I'll be on the next flight. Otherwise I might be attending your funeral, and nobody has time for two in one month."

"Thank you, brother," Jake said with a smile, grateful for Terrell's unquestioningly loyal friendship.

Two men in a black Ford Explorer followed Jake's rental car from a discreet distance. They listened to Jake's side of the conversation, thanks to a bugging device they'd planted in the SUV during the night. One of the rental car employees had been happy to give them a spare key fob, once they'd shown him their stolen police badges and offered a big cash reward for helping them catch a terrible criminal, instead of being arrested for helping him.

They'd placed the bug under the dashboard, alongside many other electronic car parts, in hopes the dog would not smell anything out of the ordinary.

One of the men said, "It would be best to let Jake pick up the police detective from the airport and then capture both of them together."

The other agreed. "Two are better than one, and the out of town cop might even find the hard drive for us. We'd get the reward money from Rojo, and move up in the cartel organization."

They both smiled.

～

Later that day, Jake met Terrell as he walked out of the San Diego International Airport and stood on the sidewalk.

In spite of the warm weather, Terrell wore his trademark dark suit, white shirt, plain tie and perfectly shined black dress shoes. He looked around with a frown on his face.

Jake pulled to the curb in the rented SUV, and Terrell climbed into the front passenger seat.

By way of greeting, Jake said, "I've been driving around in circles. Fun times."

"I love the airport," Terrell said, deadpan.

Cody put his paws on the center console lid and happily licked Terrell on the face.

"Ewww, jarhead war dog slobber," Terrell said. "What could be worse?"

Cody panted Ha-Ha-Ha.

"And what's that all about, anyway?" Terrell asked Jake.

"Cody is glad you didn't die, I guess," Jake said, smiling at his friend.

Terrell nodded and scratched the dog behind his ears. "Who's the best boy?"

Cody wagged his tail.

As Jake drove off, he saw a black Ford Explorer pull out at the same time and follow behind them, but it didn't appear to be a threat, only a coincidence.

"Wearing that nice suit with a bandage on your head makes you look badass," Jake said.

"I already looked badass, so I guess this just adds to my badass image," Terrell said. He tapped on the controls of the car's air conditioner, setting the temperature as cold as it could get.

"Did you have fun going through airport security?" Jake asked.

Terrell rolled his eyes. "Oh, a ton of fun. I have TSA Precheck and CLEAR, and I showed them my badge and my 'Notice of LEO

Flying Armed' document. I should have passed right through, but an overly ambitious young rookie dude was just sure I was hiding something in my cranium under my bandage."

"But we all know your cranium is empty," Jake said.

Terrell laughed. "Speak for yourself, genius."

Jake glanced at his friend. "Having a hole in your head must be a pain. Does the wind blow through there and whistle and moan?"

"Yeah, it howls through my empty head and out my ass. It's a pain for sure, but I'll take that temporary pain any day in trade for my shrapnel headache pain."

"Seriously, I'll bet it feels amazing to have those headaches gone."

"It actually feels weird, but in a good way," Terrell said.

"Glad I could help you with that," Jake said, nodding.

Terrell snorted. "What? You almost got me killed."

"My methods *are* a little unorthodox."

"That's enough help for now."

"You're sure?"

"Mm-hmm."

Jake shrugged. "Okay, fine. Some people are just so ungrateful when I make an extra effort."

Terrell took off his suit jacket, folded it in half and laid it across his lap. "Costco called and asked why I didn't buy a beer-keg-sized bottle of ibuprofen this month."

"I heard they had to lay off folks at the ibu factory because of you," Jake said.

Terrell adjusted the A/C outlets so they blew cold air on his chest and face. He looked out the window and asked, "How hot is it here today? I'm roasting."

"My guess is, it's hot as hell, but let's check." Jake tapped the dashboard display for a few seconds as he drove. The screen lit up with an image of a cute woman in a formfitting dress, standing in front of a weather map. "I was right. Mexican weather girl says it's *muy caliente.*"

Terrell raised his eyebrows. "Very hot? That's *muy* helpful and so specific, thanks."

Jake looked in the mirror. "A black Ford Explorer has been behind us for a while. What do you think?"

Terrell looked in the sideview mirror. "When did you first see it?"

"At the airport, and then again a few miles back. I'm going to drive around four corners."

Jake took a right, and then another, until he returned to where he started. They both checked the mirrors but the Explorer was no longer behind them.

CHAPTER 37

Jake drove past a street corner where a man stood wearing a long coat in the heat, apparently dealing hard drugs to some girls who had yet to see their eighteenth birthday.

Terrell gave him his battle stare, and the man turned and quickly walked down an alley, as if he knew serious trouble when he spotted it.

"Do we have time for me to bust a perp?" Terrell asked.

"No, sorry," Jake said.

"Next time pull over so I can kick some ass real quick. Only take a sec to break an arm."

"Fine with me, saves you all that paperwork. I'll keep the motor running," Jake said, but he just kept driving.

Terrell put his window down, lit a cigarette and held it outside between puffs so as not to bother Cody with the secondhand smoke. He turned up the air conditioning fan to blow full blast, trying to compensate for the open window. "Now that my headaches are gone, I'm gonna try to quit smoking these damned cigarettes," Terrell said.

Jake thought Terrell didn't sound as if he believed himself, but he nodded in agreement. "Heck, yeah. Jimbo found a way that worked for him. He switched to small cigars and quit inhaling."

They drove to the funeral home and met with two

representatives. Jake made it clear he'd be paying for everything and that he'd be closely auditing the bill, and the look on Terrell's face told them not to mess with the friends of a Marine. The management folks were nice, honest people and they kindly worked with Jake to do whatever he wanted at a fair cost. With that done, Jake gratefully shook their hands and then drove toward the home of Mr. and Mrs. Lopez.

As they passed a Mexican restaurant, Jake said, "Let's grab some tacos real quick."

"Sounds good to me," Terrell said.

Jake parked in front of an older cinderblock building converted into a restaurant, and they all walked inside. The place was empty at the moment and the hostess greeted them cheerfully but appeared surprised to see the dog.

Three SUVs drove up fast and screeched to a halt in front of the restaurant. Four men jumped out of each car, wearing black hoods and carrying AK-47 rifles.

Terrell drew his pistol. "Jukebox, we've got company."

Jake cursed. "Twelve against three, I don't like those odds."

The hostess stared out the window in fear. "*Qué pasa?*" she asked.

Jake pointed at the street and yelled, "*Narcotraficantes!*"

She cried out, and a man wearing a cook's white apron around his waist ran to her, grabbed her arm and pulled her toward the back of the restaurant.

"Follow us. Let's go. *Vámonos!*" he said.

Jake, Cody and Terrell ran after the man and woman and followed them up a flight of stairs to the roof.

A waist-high railing of cinder blocks went all around the roof dining area, which held several patio tables for guests to enjoy outdoor seating. No customers were there at the moment.

Twelve AK-47s all began firing at once, sounding like a string of loud firecrackers going off.

Jake listened to the loud tat-tat-tat of the automatic weapons fire, along with what he guessed was a vehicle being shot to pieces. He observed Cody, hoping his dog didn't suffer from a bout of PTSD.

"*Cuernos de chivo,*" the man whispered, with a fearful look on his face.

Jake nodded at him and said to Terrell, "It means, horns of the goat—the narco nickname for AKs."

After what sounded like hundreds of rounds being fired, the racket stopped and several car doors slammed. Tires squealed and engines roared as the three SUVs drove away. Terrell talked on the phone using his police voice as he headed for the stairs.

Jake and Cody followed Terrell to the main room of the restaurant and looked out the shattered front window. Out on the street, Jake's rented Chevy Tahoe had been riddled with bullet holes and was on fire, burning like a torch.

Sirens filled the air as Terrell went outside. Jake and Cody followed. The killers were gone, but they'd left behind what looked like hundreds and hundreds of 7.62-mm shell casings littering the pavement.

Jake said, "If each of the twelve men fired one forty-round magazine, there must be four hundred and eighty casings on the ground."

Terrell kicked at some casings that appeared different from the rest. "Plus some tracer rounds to the gas tank."

"Do they think we're dead, or was that a warning?" Jake asked.

Terrell shook his head. "I don't know."

San Diego Police cars arrived and a plainclothes female homicide inspector with short light brown hair walked over to Terrell and asked questions.

Jake went back inside the restaurant to keep Cody away from the blazing car and armed police. He sat at a table and called his rental car company. "Hello, Enterprise? Um, yeah, I need you to pick me up."

While he waited for the driver, Jake used his phone to search online for a local window glass company. He asked them to replace the restaurant window and charge it to his Amex Black Card. McKay wouldn't mind paying for the window; that was one of the reasons for the card. Keep people happy and quiet, instead of calling lawyers and the media.

Jake talked to the man who'd led them upstairs. "Thank you for helping us. You saved my dog's life. In gratitude, I'm paying for a new window, and all I ask is that you don't talk to the media."

The man shook hands and said, "Muchas gracias, and I promise, no media. That kind of news story would be bad for business."

The Enterprise driver picked them up, staring wide-eyed at the Tahoe. On the drive to the car rental office, he said, "Well, sir, I'm glad you bought our full insurance coverage for the rental."

Jake laughed. "Best money I ever spent."

Terrell said, "The worst part of this is we didn't get any damned tacos."

Cody barked in agreement.

At the office, Jake rented another "lucky" Chevy Tahoe. They drove to Pez's parents' house and knocked. Brent Lopez invited them inside for coffee. Jake was pleased to let them know all the funeral arrangements were taken care of and paid for. The mother seemed relieved and thankful, but the father appeared skeptical.

"Who paid for everything?" Brent asked.

Jake thought of the black card. "It's a new veterans program."

Terrell kept his face blank and nodded in agreement.

Cody wagged his tail.

"*Comfort* those in need, Cody," Jake said.

Cody went to where the parents sat on the couch, side by side. He put his right paw on the father's knee, wagged his tail, moved his head to flap his ears, and let his tongue hang out. Both of the parents smiled and patted the golden dog on his back, saying what a good boy he was.

The father began to warm up to them. "Terrell, you're a Marine too, like Sammy?"

"Yes, sir," Terrell answered.

"I served in the Navy. Do you guys know what we'd say the word Marine stands for?"

Terrell smiled. "We do, but you're going to tell us anyway."

Brent smiled for the first time since they'd arrived. "It stands for Marines Always Ride In Navy Equipment."

"That's true, and so do Navy SEALs, Top Gun fighter pilots, and admirals," Terrell said. "It's great equipment, the best. Thanks for the ride."

Brent chuckled. "You're welcome. That's what my boy always said, too." He then hung his head, obviously still heartbroken over his son as he tried to be brave for his wife.

Outside of the house, a black Ford Explorer drove slowly past with two men inside.

"They came here just like we thought," the passenger said. "Should we grab them now, along with the mother and father?"

"No, the *jefe* said to wait for his order."

"Seems like a wasted opportunity to me."

"Call the boss right now and tell him you think he's wrong," the driver said as he cruised on past the house.

The passenger said, "That other cartel shot up their SUV and then blamed it on us."

"Most people know if we'd done it, those fools would be dead now. We're going to take them alive, force them to help us find the hard drive, and then leave their heads in the city square."

The passenger spat out the window in frustration while holding the AK-47 assault rifle between his knees, pointed at the floorboard.

CHAPTER 38

Jake and Terrell drove to the funeral and found many of their veteran friends in attendance.

One Marine was now a local sheriff's deputy, who arrived in a marked car wearing his uniform.

Jake gave his friend a man hug and pounded him on the back. "Deputy Kowalski. You're a stud."

Kowalski returned the one-armed hug and slapped Jake on the back. He then did the same with Terrell.

They all glanced over at the gravesite and Kowalski said, "It's a damned shame about Pez."

It was a bittersweet reunion as everyone milled around, talking quietly, shaking hands and giving hugs. Jake felt glad to see old friends, but heartbroken about the reason they were all together again. There had been too many funerals lately for young veterans with their whole lives ahead of them.

When people asked Jake about Pez's car accident, he told a white lie, saying Pez had died instantly at the scene and hadn't felt any pain. People nodded, appearing relieved and thankful to hear that. Jake could tell it helped to ease their sorrow.

But it didn't help ease Jake's sorrow.

Everyone gathered together near the casket draped with an

American flag. Two uniformed Marines stood at attention, ready to perform the flag ceremony.

Jake stood up in front of the mourners. "Could everybody please take a seat?"

Once everyone took their seats and the crowd quieted, Jake said, "Mr. and Mrs. Lopez asked me to give the eulogy for Sammy, who we all affectionately called Pez."

He took a deep breath. "We'll always remember how he collected Pez dispensers, loved guacamole, and had such a wonderful laugh that you just had to laugh along with him. He served with honor in the Marine Corps infantry, was awarded a Purple Heart, and afterward built a successful auto parts business here in sunny San Diego. Recently, he met and fell in love with Olivia."

Olivia bowed her head, tears on her face.

Jake continued. "Although many of us served with Pez and loved him like a brother, we didn't really know all that much about his private life. He liked to talk about sports and cars and food, but not much about himself.

"I once told him a story about how a childhood friend of mine named Charlie had died too young, and Pez said it motivated him to enjoy each day of life as if it might be his last. I'd like to repeat the story now, briefly, in tribute to Pez."

Jake paused, took a deep breath and let it out.

"When I was nine, my best friend died. I was lucky to have a friend like Charlie. He always had a smile on his face and was quick with a laugh or a joke. He never walked past a dog without petting it, a tree without climbing it, or a puddle without jumping in it.

"All good things come to an end, and one day our lives changed. For some reason, Charlie couldn't run as fast as he used to run. He got tired easily, and he kept getting weaker as time went by. It seemed like he was always going to the doctor.

"We both wore those sneakers that TV ads claimed would help you 'run faster and jump higher.' Our theory was that his shoes were wearing out and he needed new ones. When we told this idea to his mother, she got tears in her eyes. We thought she was upset about the cost. We didn't know what she knew. It wasn't her little boy's shoes that were wearing out; it was something inside his body.

"Charlie continued to get weaker as the days passed. I tried to help him when we played sports. I pushed his bike to get it rolling when he felt too tired to pedal, and I protected him from older bullies who tried to take advantage of his weakened condition. He stopped climbing trees, and he spent more and more time lying on the couch and watching TV. Soon he stopped going to school.

"One day I went to his house and his mother told me Charlie was bedridden and couldn't have visitors. Those were the doctor's orders. He was very sick and needed to rest. I asked if there was anything I could do for Charlie. She said no, thanked me with tears in her eyes, and quickly went inside the house. Through the window I saw her sit down at the dining table, put her face in her hands and say, 'Please God, I'm begging you!' As I walked home, I realized my best friend might never get well.

"Soon after that, my mom got a brief phone call that upset her. I heard her tell my dad, 'Little Charlie is gone.' My dad held her while she wept.

"I ran all the way to my friend's house and banged on the door. His mother answered and she seemed to have aged ten years. I asked her, 'Where did Charlie *go*? Is he at the doctor again? When will he be coming home?' She was a brave woman who had tried to be strong for so long, but a mother can only take so much. When I asked my childish questions, it was more than she could bear. She began sobbing, and her whole body shook with grief. She put her trembling hand against the door frame to steady herself, but then slumped against it for support and slid down onto her knees. With a ragged voice, she managed to say Charlie had died and gone to heaven, and he wasn't coming back.

"I liked to think I was a tough and brave little soldier, as I'd seen in the movies, but tears began to pour from my eyes too. Something merciless had killed my best friend, something I couldn't pronounce, something frightening that no doctor could stop. Something called leukemia.

"I didn't know what it was. All I knew was that my best friend was gone, forever, and there was nothing I could do to save him. It was the most helpless feeling I'd ever known. And I did the only thing I could: I tried to hug his mother like a man as she poured out her heart, grieving the loss of that beloved happy soul who'd meant the world to everyone who had known him during his brief time here.

"That night I lay awake in bed, unable to sleep. In my imagination, I thought leukemia must be some kind of evil creature, maybe like the wild and crazed animals with rabies who could bite you and make you sick. Whatever it was, I wanted to hunt it down and fight it with my Boy Scout sheath knife. That way it couldn't take away anyone else's child or best friend.

"For a week afterward, I slept with that knife under my pillow, vowing if the 'thing' came for anyone in my house, it would have to get past me first. I hoped it would come at me. I wanted to fight it. I wanted to kill it. I wanted *justice*.

"My parents found the knife under my pillow and I heard my dad tell my mom they'd have to keep me busy and my mind on positive things.

"After a time of mourning, Charlie's family packed up and moved away. I was told they wanted to start life over somewhere new, without the painful memories. Before they drove off, his mother hugged me goodbye and said something remarkable. This brave woman who had just lost her only son thought not of herself, but only of how this tragedy might affect me and my life. She asked me to promise something to her.

"She said, 'Promise me, Jake, that you won't stay sad for too long. Promise me you'll try your best every day to be happy and enjoy life. You have to be twice as happy, so you can make up for what Charlie will miss out on. When you laugh, I want you to laugh twice as much. When you love, I want you to love doubly strong. And when you live your life, I want you to live it with twice the joy and hope and happiness that other people do. Avoid being like those who go through life half-asleep. It will help make *me* happier if I know *you* are happy. Can you do that for me, Jake? Will you promise me? Cross your heart?

"I looked up at her kind face, and in my most solemn nine-year-old voice, I vowed, 'Yes, I double pinkie swear.'

"She laughed softly, held out her pinkie fingers to hook with mine, and then patted me on the head, ruffling my hair. Then she got in the car, waved goodbye and drove away, and a part of my lost childhood and innocence drove away with her.

"I've tried my best to keep my word and live with joy and happiness, love and laughter, as if I were doing it for two people instead of one. This actually got me into a lot of trouble, first in school and later in the workplace, where stern authority figures would get angry and say I was being 'too happy' or 'too funny,' and they were going to wipe the smile right off of my face.

"To my long-lost friend Charlie, I can only say, thank you for being such a good buddy to me and a great son to your mom and dad. Our lives were made so much richer by your brief visit here. In my imagination I see you in heaven, jumping in puddles, petting dogs and climbing trees.

"To my good friend Sammy Lopez, I'm glad the story about Charlie had such a profound effect on you and helped motivate you to enjoy each day to the fullest during your brief life.

"To all of you here today, it would honor the memory of our mutual friend Pez if you'd make the same promise to yourself that I made to Charlie's mother and Pez made to me. Promise you'll try every day to appreciate and enjoy life. When you laugh, laugh twice as much. When you love, love doubly strong. And when you live each day, live it with twice the joy and hope and happiness that other people do.

"Our friend Pez did that, and he would want us to do the same.

"Amen."

Everyone in the crowd murmured, "Amen."

Jake held out his hand to Cody and gave him a Pez dispenser toy featuring R2-D2. Cody held the toy in his mouth and walked over to the freshly dug grave. He laid the Pez dispenser on top of the flag-draped casket, hung his head and stood there with his tail down and head bowed.

All of the people in the crowd wept openly now; nobody could hold back the tears.

Inside a black Ford Explorer parked nearby, two cartel members watched the funeral through binoculars.

"I see a sheriff's car and at least one uniformed deputy."

The other nodded. "Sheriffs will eff you up, and several of those veterans are probably carrying."

"We'll wait until after the funeral, follow Wolfe's car and take him and the detective and the dog."

CHAPTER 39

The two uniformed Marines conducted the flag-folding ceremony and gave the flag to Brent and Michelle Lopez. When the funeral employees went to lower Pez's casket into the ground, Olivia asked them to keep the R2-D2 Pez dispenser on top. They complied with her request. Cody huffed at them as if saying to be careful and show respect to his fallen Marine friend.

As the funeral ended, people said their goodbyes, then walked to their cars and drove away. Jake, Cody and Terrell drove toward Pez's house. On the way, Terrell asked to stop at a store, where he bought zip-top plastic bags and nitrile gloves.

They arrived at Pez's empty home and found his extra key under one of the dozens of terra-cotta planter pots, where Olivia had said it would be. Jake and Terrell gloved up and went inside.

Terrell held his pistol in front of him and called out in a commanding voice, "Police are entering the house!"

The home had been ransacked. Couch cushions slit open with the stuffing pulled out, the refrigerator and kitchen cabinets emptied of their contents, carpet pulled up from the floor in several places.

"It looks like we're late to the party," Terrell said. "And what is that smell?"

Jake spoke to his dog. "*Search*, Cody. Search for *people*."

Cody huffed, sniffed high and low, and went down the hall and to a guest bathroom, stopping in front of the closed door. Jake and Terrell followed, holding pistols ready to fire.

Jake opened the door and saw and smelled that someone had emptied their bowels in the toilet and neglected to flush afterward. "DNA evidence from a dumbass?" Jake asked.

"Literally," Terrell said. "The San Diego PD can deal with that. Let's keep moving." He turned on the bathroom's overhead fan and closed the door.

Cody searched and cleared the rest of the house, ending up in the master bedroom. He led Jake to a nightstand next to a bed that had been tossed, with the mattress ripped apart.

The nightstand was a beautiful wooden Lauderdale End Table Humidor, about the size of a mini fridge, sitting flush on the floor. The single door hung open to reveal an empty space where a top drawer had been removed, and three empty shelves below it that could hold hundreds of cigars.

Terrell said, "That looks like the same humi you have on the *Far Niente*."

Jake nodded. "Yeah. Pez asked me about humidors and I sent him a pic of Stuart's end table. He loved it and bought one online."

He went down on one knee and ran his glove along the inner walls of Spanish cedar, knocking on them to see if there might be any hollowed-out concealed spaces.

"I guess whoever searched the house stole the cigars," Jake said. "Pez had quite a collection and would text me a photo once in a while of an especially good one he was smoking. I'd fire up one of mine and text a photo in reply."

Terrell nodded. "Speaking of collections, he had all kinds of Pez dispensers. I haven't seen them anywhere."

Cody dug at the carpet in front of the humidor with both front paws, letting out a low growl.

"You want me to *dig*?" Jake asked.

Cody barked and nodded.

"Cody smells a gun or something underneath." Jake grabbed the top edges of the humidor with both hands and tipped the heavy piece of furniture over to look at the bottom. It was solid, but moving the humidor had revealed a floor vent for air conditioning.

Cody pawed at the vent that was about the size of a shoe box lid.

Jake took ahold of the lightweight metal register and lifted. It came up, exposing a locked door of a floor safe underneath, installed into the HVAC air duct.

"Good work, Cody," Jake said, patting his dog on the back.

Cody sniffed at the floor safe, and the hackles on his neck stood up.

The safe was built of gray-painted metal, with a black plastic combination dial lock.

Terrell said, "That's a pretty cheap-looking dial. It reminds me of the Master combo lock I had in high school."

Jake nodded. "My friend Levi said the weakest part of most safes is the combination lock."

"What now? Hit the dial with a sledgehammer?" Terrell asked. "I've seen a few opened that way." The look on his face told Jake he'd done it himself.

Jake took out his phone and searched YouTube for a video by a super smart hacker about how to break open a Master combo lock. He and Terrell watched the video, followed directions and improvised some steps. A few minutes later, the safe clicked and unlocked.

"That genius dude gives advice to the FBI," Jake said. He pulled the door open to reveal some bundles of cash, a passport, a loaded pistol, a set of keys and a small black velvet ring box.

Cody growled when the pistol was revealed. Jake stroked his back.

Terrell said, "If I hadn't seen you watching that video, I'd think lock picking was a skill you learned from the CIA black ops folks."

"No, I never went to The Farm. I received a crash course in field spycraft and covert killing from an agent who trained me overseas while I was healing up in the hospital from that near-fatal bullet wound to my thigh," Jake said, patting his leg.

Terrell nodded. "That time I donated my blood to your sorry ass."

Jake smiled. "My sorry ass thanks you, blood brother."

"All of your fellow Marines believed you were still in the hospital, but you were on missions and killing high value targets."

Jake nodded. "It was top secret. Sorry if I had to make folks worry about me."

"We would've worried more if we'd known you were limping on that leg while shooting terrorists up close and personal," Terrell said.

"What can I say? The CIA offered me a chance to get revenge on the lowlifes who killed my war dog."

Terrell glanced at the cash bundles. "Should we turn that money over to the SDPD or give it to Pez's mother and father?"

Jake followed his gaze and guesstimated there must be at least a few hundred thousand dollars there. "I vote we give it to the grieving parents."

"Agreed."

"One of these keys might get us into the warehouse. What about the passport, jewelry and pistol?" Jake asked.

"Take all of it. We might need it later and I don't want to come back." Terrell handed a zip-top plastic bag to Jake.

Jake emptied out the safe and put everything in the bag except the ring box. Opening it, he saw a woman's gold-and-diamond engagement ring. He was no expert, but this thing appeared unique, beautiful and expensive. He held it out so Terrell could see it. "Looks like Pez was going to pop the question to Olivia."

Terrell frowned. "It's a damned shame. Let's get out of here, grab a coffee and see what's on the drive." He began walking toward the front door.

Jake closed and locked the safe, put the vented cover back in place and rearranged the end table on top of it. Dropping the plastic bags into his camera backpack, he gave a command to Cody and they both followed Terrell outside.

In the car, Jake set the backpack behind his seat and started the engine. A black-and-white police car pulled up next to them, and the driver's window went down.

CHAPTER 40

A uniformed officer sat behind the wheel, the name Fincke displayed above his shirt pocket. He asked, "Terrell Hayes, right?"

Terrell gave him a nod. "Officer Fincke. This is a pleasant surprise. What brings you here?"

"Just doing my job," Fincke said. "Find anything useful in the house?"

Terrell said, "No. Somebody ransacked the place. Feel free to take a look. If Sammy Lopez died in a simple hit-and-run, why would somebody search his home?"

Officer Fincke lifted a shoulder. "It was probably just teenagers having a party, getting drunk and trashing an empty house. Happens all the time, and the realtors hate it."

"Hmm, that could be it," Terrell said. "See you around, Fincke." He patted Jake on the shoulder.

Jake waved innocently and drove away. "You made a friend on the force?"

"I stopped by the local police station and talked to a few people who all think I'm wasting my time on this. And I met that baby-faced rookie who seems to be obsessed with me."

"What do we tell that cop if he happens to go in Pez's house and finds the safe?"

"We tell him it was empty."

"Empty?"

"Empty as a banker's heart."

Jake stopped for a red light. "Well, we didn't find any so-called package. What do you think it is?"

"I don't know, but the criminals near both sides of this border thrive on drugs, guns and money."

"Sounds like a Warren Zevon song."

Terrell turned and looked at Jake, raising his eyebrows. "Zevon?"

"Don't tell me you've never heard the 'Lawyers, Guns and Money' song."

"Never had the pleasure. Is it a lawyer thing? Your theme song?"

Jake tapped the dashboard display. The sound system played Warren Zevon singing the famous song.

"Catchy tune," Terrell said. "Sounds like the dude who sang 'Werewolves of London.'"

"Yeah, that's him. His life was cut short by cancer."

"That's sad. Screw cancer."

"Agreed. When an interviewer asked Zevon what he learned from facing certain death, he said you should enjoy every sandwich."

"That's good advice, and it reminds me we should get a sandwich soon," Terrell said as he flipped through Sammy's passport.

Jake glanced at the passport as he drove. "Did Pez travel much?"

Terrell flipped a few more pages. "He went on vacations down south to Panama, Bermuda, and the Cayman Islands."

Jake's shoulders slumped. "Offshore banking destinations."

"Yep," Terrell said sadly. "What was our bro up to?"

"Maybe he was in trouble, but why not ask us for help?" Jake said.

Terrell's phone vibrated and he answered, "Hayes." Listening a moment, he said, "You have time now? Okay, I'm on my way." He ended the call. "My contact at San Diego Homicide says she wants to talk about Pez."

"What's the address? I'll drive you there," Jake said.

"No. Drop me at that row of taxis up ahead," Terrell said. "I'll take a cab, and while I'm in the meeting, you and Cody can get started searching Pez's warehouse."

"Okay, that works," Jake said. "Gotta keep our plans flexible."

"Semper Gumby," Terrell said, repeating an old Marine Corps joke about flexibility.

"Does your contact believe our theory that Pez was murdered?"

"No, not so much. Pez died in another country, and the Los Cabos police report said it was just a car accident."

Jake pulled over and parked in front of a hotel. "If she doesn't believe you, why don't you meet with her later?"

"I want the SDPD to take a hard look at this case before I leave town. They're good cops, but once I'm gone they'll drop it and move on to more urgent matters." Terrell climbed out of the SUV. "After the meeting, I'll take an Uber and meet up with you."

"Okay, see you soon," Jake said.

Terrell closed the car door and walked toward a waiting taxi.

Cody placed a paw on the window control, lowered the glass and barked at Terrell.

Terrell nodded without turning around.

Jake drove away and followed his dashboard GPS guidance to the warehouse. It was located in an industrial area immediately north of the border, between the Otay Mesa port of entry and the California Highway Patrol's border facility. The warehouse district was home to a wide variety of businesses. He noted plenty of nondescript buildings on both sides of the border.

Jake parked in front of the warehouse and office building. He put on gloves and tried several of Pez's keys until he found one that opened the front door. Inside the reception area, Jake turned on some lights.

"Cody, *search*."

Cody sniffed high and low, walking along the hallway and going into one of the offices. He sniffed at a desk drawer and pawed at it.

Jake pulled on the drawer, but it was locked. He used a key on the ring to open it. Inside he found a pistol. Jake praised Cody and pushed the drawer closed. "Good dog. Keep searching."

Cody sniffed his way around the room, stopped in front of a closet and sat down.

Jake opened the closet door and found a tall stack of white cardboard file boxes. Next to them, a long raincoat hung on a hook. Cody got to his feet and sniffed at the raincoat.

Jake lifted up the coat and found an AR-15 rifle leaning against the wall. It appeared that Pez had been armed against surprises, like any veteran might be.

"Good boy, continue," Jake said and closed the closet door.

Cody led Jake out of the office, down the hall and into the warehouse. He sniffed at shelves of auto parts and pallets stacked with boxes, ending up in a break room.

Suddenly stopping in his tracks, Cody moved his head from side to side, his nostrils flaring. He let out a low growl, then slowly approached a refrigerator and stopped.

"Bad news?" Jake asked.

Cody growled again, his hackles bristling.

Jake opened the fridge door. The items inside were typical: a few cans of soda, a carton of individual coffee creamers, and plenty of bottled water.

Cody stuck his nose in between the fridge and the wall, taking deep sniffs, his tail sticking straight out.

"Easy, boy. I'm going to pull this thing out and look behind it." Jake unclipped Cody and let him off-leash, then grabbed the refrigerator on both sides and pulled it toward himself.

The fridge appeared to be stuck, so Jake went down on one knee and looked underneath. It had locking wheels. He used the toe of his right foot to work the locks on the front two wheels at each corner and tried again to move the appliance. This time, the fridge glided forward easily on well-oiled wheels.

Behind the appliance he saw a metal panel access door with a sign saying DANGER — HIGH VOLTAGE. Jake unplugged the fridge and pulled it further out into the break room.

Cody went to the panel door, sniffed it and let out a growl.

Jake drew his pistol and whispered, "Quiet, now."

Cody stood still like a statue, waiting for orders.

Jake tried the recessed handle, but the panel door was locked. He pressed an ear to the metal and listened for a moment. Hearing nothing, he pointed at a spot on the floor off to the side, in a safe place. Giving a hand signal, he directed Cody to that spot, and his dog moved there and sat down, keeping his bright eyes on his handler.

Jake tried several keys on the ring until he found one that worked. He pulled the door open and stepped away in case someone inside fired a weapon. No shots came, and he glanced into the opening to find a hidden storage area.

He didn't see anybody waiting in ambush, so he turned and aimed his pistol inside, ready to kill a criminal in self-defense.

What he saw next was mind-boggling. It wasn't just a storage area—there was a large manhole-shaped opening in the floor and a wrought-iron spiral staircase leading down underground.

"Wait here one minute, and *guard* this door," he said to Cody.

Cody growled in protest and separation anxiety, but obeyed orders.

Jake went through the panel door and stepped onto the circular staircase. Climbing down the stairs into the subterranean earth, he flipped a switch to turn on bare lightbulbs strung on wires overhead.

He held his pistol up and ready as he quietly studied the area and found the entrance of a tunnel leading south toward the border. It went off into the distance so far it vanished.

The tunnel appeared serviceable enough to travel through on a regular basis. It featured support beams, ventilation PVC pipes pumping fresh air, a wood plank floor and a pulley system for winching goods in and out. The plywood ceiling was high enough to walk standing up, maybe seven feet tall. Various sections of the walls were plywood too. Other sections were heavy clay held back by chicken wire fencing.

Standing at the bottom of the stairwell hole, where he could get two bars of phone reception, he took a picture and texted it to Terrell:

Cody found a tunnel under Pez's warehouse leading south toward the border.

Jake remembered reading something about how the authorities had found hundreds of drug-smuggling tunnels under the border. Mostly near San Diego, California, and Nogales, Arizona. One of the biggest and most sophisticated tunnels was even equipped with electric railcars and elevators. It was hard to believe, but true. And it made sense when you considered the billions of dollars to be made in smuggling. Even a small operation might bring in several million dollars a month. Any tunnel of any kind was priceless.

He had no doubt the people who built these sophisticated underground smuggling routes were professional criminals who would kill you without a second thought to protect their incredible profits.

Jake knew he should call the cops and let them send a tactical robot "SWAT BOT" through the tunnel to investigate, but he shook his head as anger burned in his chest. Too many criminals got away with their crimes due to slow-moving bureaucracies, gullible juries and early parole from over-crowded prisons. Ask any cop and they'd tell you the stories that haunted them.

No, these criminals had killed his Marine brother Pez. He would find them and deal with them personally, to be absolutely sure they received the measure of justice they deserved.

Climbing the stairs back up to the break room, Jake holstered his pistol and patted his dog on the back. "Cody, we're going down into an underground bunker. Are you up for that?"

Cody huffed and pawed at the floor as if there was no way in hell he'd let Jake go down there without him.

Jake grabbed the handle on the back of Cody's vest, picked him up like a suitcase and carefully went through the panel door. He climbed down the stairway while holding Cody up so his legs were safe from harm.

At the bottom, Jake set Cody on his feet, clipped a leash onto his collar and gazed down the claustrophobia-inducing tunnel that was so long he couldn't see the end.

Drawing his pistol, he said, "Search, Cody. Hunt for the enemy."

CHAPTER 41

Cody observed Jake's tense body language, smelled the cortisol stress hormone emanating from his adrenal cortex, and sensed his anger.

He listened to Jake's commands and obeyed his orders, sniffing the dank air and then the wood planks on the floor beneath his feet. He slowly walked forward, pulling on the leash, heading down the tunnel with his head moving back and forth and his nostrils flaring.

Cody smelled traces of sweaty men, weapons and drug chemicals, along with rats, moles, gophers, earthworms, ants, termites, the pungently fragrant plant Jake called cannabis, and ... human blood, recently spilled.

His hackles stood up, and he moved forward slowly, hunting the enemy while also protecting his handler from potential threats.

Cody would kill for Jake, and give his life for him. Jake was his alpha, pack mate and best friend. Cody was devoted to serving by his side and doing the dangerous Marine Corps duty Jake said was *patriotic*.

This dug-out tunnel smelled far different from the hot desert where he'd done most of his patrols. Damp, dark and earthy, instead of baked sand, simmering with heat in the blazing sun.

As he walked along the wooden floor that smelled of pine boards and plywood, he felt a tremble in his right rear leg. It was something he'd noted ever since he'd been injured after biting an enemy attacker on the throat to protect his Marine platoon. He hadn't wanted to bite the man, but when his pack had come under a surprise attack, what else could he do?

And then a bomb had exploded, and he'd awakened in a hospital with his leg bandaged and taped up. His handler hadn't survived. That gave him a heavy feeling in his chest whenever he remembered it.

Now he was below the earth. In a tunnel. Like a rat. This must be what it was like to be a dachshund and go into a badger's lair. How did he know that? A memory came to him of a movie his breeder had shown him, one of so many movies about dogs and their jobs and capabilities. He now understood their goal had been to increase his knowledge and intelligence.

Sniffing multiple scent trails, he proceeded further and growled when he came closer to a large amount of cannabis, along with at least two loaded weapons.

Jake followed closely behind Cody, with his pistol up and ready to fire. He felt naked without his Marine rifle and realized he should have grabbed that AR, but a pistol would have to do.

As the two war veterans walked quietly along the tunnel, Jake thought of his older friends who'd served in Vietnam, where they'd found tunnels and hidden rooms dug into the earth under the jungle. They told him stories that made his hair stand on end. The argument he always had with them was whether it was worse in the wet, humid jungle, or in the dry, blazing hot desert with no alcohol or women. They eventually agreed that the lack of beer and female company was the worst of fates under any circumstances.

After walking what seemed like several football fields, Jake and Cody approached a matching pair of open spaces dug out on each side of the tunnel, like a way station. Both spaces held large shrink-wrapped bundles of marijuana stacked high on warehouse racks.

Jake guessed there must be thousands of pounds there—literally tons of weed.

He'd heard the tunnels were extra helpful for moving cannabis because it took up a lot of space and was hard to smuggle in large quantities. Maybe the legalization and regulation in so many US states and Canada would end the need for criminals to supply the herb. Only time would tell.

Cody stopped abruptly and Jake did too.

Cody sniffed the air and moved to the right, raising his nose toward the open area before they entered it. He did the same on the left side, and then went rigid, let out a low growl and sat down, blocking Jake's path.

Jake's heart pounded in his chest. His war dog was indicating dangerous chemical smells. Was a hidden IED ready to blow the support beams and bury them alive?

Suddenly, Jake thought he saw a ghost. A pale shimmering image of his deceased war dog appeared in front of him.

"Duke?" Jake said, a cold tingling at the nape of his neck and gooseflesh dimpling his arms. The ghostly image of a Belgian Malinois war dog pawed at the ground, looked Jake in the eye and then vanished.

Cody gave a low growl, pressed against Jake and prevented him from moving forward. Jake felt a knot in his gut as he used a flashlight app on his phone to take a better look in this dim section of tunnel.

There. A tripwire of clear fishing line ran across the tunnel at about six inches above the wood floor planks. Right where Duke had pawed. A few steps closer and Jake would've tripped it.

"Cody, sit. Stay."

Jake stepped forward, leaned his head in and peeked into the open area on his right. He studied the wall and found a sawed-off shotgun mounted onto two wooden support beams, aimed toward where his chest and head would be as he passed by. He drew a deep, calming breath, turned to the left and glanced across the tunnel to see another shotgun mounted there, aimed at where his stomach and crotch would take the hit.

Jake swallowed hard and retreated back several feet away from the open area, taking Cody with him. "Cody, you and Duke saved our lives," he said with a forced calm. "And it's not the first time. Thank you, my friend."

Cody huffed, obviously knowing they were in danger but not understanding the reference to Duke. His bright eyes watched Jake and his nostrils flared as he sniffed the air for further threats.

Jake snapped his fingers and pointed to the wooden floor. "Stand back. Stay."

Cody stood still, but he whined, wanting to be closer to Jake and struggling to obey.

Jake took off his backpack and removed a Leatherman multitool. He lay down on the wood floor, stretched his right arm out to its full length and carefully used the built-in wire cutter to snip the fishing line on the right and then on the left. He pulled the cut strand away and tossed it aside. Staying low, he commando-crawled on the wood floor planks, moving past the weapons.

Turning to look back, he noticed his dog's separation anxiety. Cody kept his eyes on Jake and shifted his weight from either front paw as if struggling to remain in place. Jake held up his hand.

"Good dog. Hold your position. *Hold*."

He studied the weapon mounted on his left. An older Remington 870 Express twelve-gauge pump-action shotgun, with part of the barrel sawed off. Getting to his knees and reaching out, he carefully pressed his finger on the safety, then turned and did the same to the matching shotgun on his right.

Jake let out a relieved breath and patted his thigh. "Clear. Come here, Cody."

His dog trotted over and pressed against him.

Jake gave him a reassuring hug and a scratch behind the ears.

"Good dog. Now *search* this area." Jake waved his hand at the open space.

Cody began a thorough search, sniffing his way around the two cave-like rooms on either side of the tunnel. He stopped at each shotgun and then moved on. The only things he found among the large stacked bundles of weed were two boxes of twelve-gauge double-aught buckshot shells, and a plastic gallon-size water bottle full of urine.

Jake holstered his pistol and used the multitool to snip the multiple zip ties holding one of the shotguns to a support beam. He pulled it free, emptied and reloaded it with shells, and then opened a box and added a number of extra rounds to his jacket pockets.

"Continue the search, Cody," Jake said, pointing at the tunnel ahead.

They carefully walked forward, with Jake carrying the shotgun up and ready.

Cody found the other end, where they saw a long, solidly built wooden ramp leading upward to a steel door with a deadbolt lock.

CHAPTER 42

Jake whispered, "Cody, stealth." He quietly walked up the ramp to a landing that looked like the inside of a coat closet. Pressing his ear to the crack between door and frame, he heard *narcocorrido* music playing, and at least two men singing along with the ballad.

As far as Jake could understand, the Spanish lyrics told about how Rojo would cut your head off if you crossed him, like a butcher cutting the head off a cow. Heads would roll in the town square and everybody would know who was the boss.

Jake took a closer look at the door. It featured dozens of nuts and bolts in two vertical rows and several horizontal rows. The pattern reminded him of train tracks.

What's bolted to the other side?

He carefully tried the doorknob, but the door was locked. Studying the deadbolt, he saw the brand name Kwikset imprinted on the lock face above the keyhole. He took out the key ring and found a key with the same name.

The key fit, and he quietly unlocked the door, turned off the tunnel lights and pulled the door open a few inches. Peering into the area beyond the door, he saw a large area that appeared to be a home's living room, dining room and kitchen which had been converted into a warehouse. Moving his head, he saw another open area to his left. They must have also knocked out a wall to a bedroom.

Painter's tarps covered the windows. Rows and rows of folding tables and freestanding shelving units were stacked high with shoebox-sized plastic bags, taped securely, full of what looked like crushed glass. Each one marked with a number that Jake guessed to be the weight of what was probably crystal methamphetamine. There were also stacks of cash and rounds of various ammunition. A set of six metal lockers stood against a far wall.

Two men sat at an empty table off to the right in the dining room, playing cards and drinking tequila. One man appeared to be Mexican, the other Caucasian. They faced each other, neither one had eyes on the door, and a number of shelving units partially blocked their view.

Something colorful caught Jake's eye, a collection of Pez dispensers stacked on the table in front of each man. His stomach churned. They were using his murdered friend's Pez dispensers for betting on their card game.

One of them lifted a toy and popped a candy into his mouth.

Jake again thought about how he should let the police handle this, but when he saw the Pez dispensers, something inside of him snapped. He whispered an order for Cody to stay and gave him a hand signal. Cody obeyed but bit his teeth onto Jake's pant cuff, pulling on it as he struggled to follow orders.

Jake gently eased the door further open. Shaking his pant leg free from Cody, he silently stepped into the room. Closing the door behind him, he noticed this side of the door had a metal shelving unit bolted onto it and stacked with cardboard boxes, in an attempt to keep the tunnel entrance disguised and hidden. There were several more shelves along the wall on either side, and this one blended in.

He stayed out of sight and spied on the men, preparing to capture the predators and drag them back across the border to be arrested by Terrell and put in a cage.

The Mexican man joked, "It was worth killing Pez just to get all this candy."

MARK NOLAN

"Yeah, and soon we'll have fun with his girlfriend, too," the other man said.

They both laughed and drank shots of tequila.

Jake's vision turned red as he felt a flash of his dormant violent temper rise to the surface and take control of his heart and soul. He moved further into the room and aimed the shotgun as he yelled, "Police! Hands above your heads!"

The surprised men dropped their cards, drew weapons and fired wildly in his direction. They held their pistols like tough guys who didn't practice at the pistol range. Hands up too high, pistols turned sideways to look badass and "gangsta," with terrible aim and no adjustment for recoil.

Jake had four years of experience as an infantry Marine and endless hours of practice at the firing range. He was well trained at using deadly force, had killed uncounted enemies, and knew that with a sawed-off shotgun at this range he couldn't miss.

In what seemed like slow motion, he fired twice in self-defense. With practiced control, he blasted one cloud of buckshot at each man's head, cutting down the criminals without remorse.

This gang had murdered Pez, his good friend, fellow Marine and brother in arms. This was war and they were enemy combatants who deserved to die. That was his belief, his vow and his duty.

He killed the killers with a professional's detachment, the same way a sheriff in the old west would have done when he was the only thing standing between evil predators and honest townsfolk. This was the OK Corral, and he was Doc Holiday blasting the shotgun.

He was actually glad they'd tried to kill him. That made his job easier. Both targets went down, dead or dying. There was no coming back from a headshot of double-ought delivered up close and personal.

Jake reloaded two more shells into the shotgun out of habit and self-discipline. He walked to the table, grabbed a plastic trash bag and scooped all of the Pez dispensers into it. Adding them to another bag on the floor, he said a few choice words and wished the criminals a fast trip straight to hell.

One of the barely surviving killers wheezed a final curse at Jake with his dying breath. Jake aimed his shotgun close to the man's chest. "You screw with one Marine—you screw with *every* Marine." He pulled the trigger and blasted the man's evil heart, putting him out of his misery.

He then fired at the chest of the other man, who appeared to be dead, but now there was absolutely no doubt.

The narco song continued to play on repeat as Jake took a quick survey of his surroundings. He saw stockpiles of handguns and AK-47s. Worse, there were armor-piercing rounds known as *matapolicías* —cop killers. Even some grenade launchers.

"Oh, hell no."

He glanced over at one wall and saw a stainless-steel operating table like you'd find at a hospital. He noted a body bag on the table, zipped shut. By the shape of the bag, the body inside seemed to be missing its head.

A refrigerator sat next to the table. Expecting the worst, Jake opened the fridge for just a second and when the light flicked on he saw a man's severed head on a plate, dead eyes staring back at him. He slammed the door shut, gagging and choking down the bile rising in his throat.

Seething with righteous anger at the killers, he felt tempted to set the piles of cannabis and money on fire, toss in a few grenades, and blow up the cop-killer rounds so they couldn't be used. However, that might harm innocent bystanders in neighboring houses. He took deep breaths, exercised self-control and walked away, leaving the evidence for Mexican police to find and use to shut down this crime cartel.

It was time to get out of there, before the booming shotgun noise brought people to investigate. But first, he wanted Cody to conduct a quick search. He had a bad feeling the severed head wasn't the worst of what might be found here.

CHAPTER 43

Jake turned back toward the tall metal shelving unit hiding the door, found the doorknob and pulled on it, revealing the closet and ramp. Cody stood there in the semi-darkness, anxious and whining. Jake beckoned his dog to enter the house, and Cody quickly alerted to the aromas of gunpowder and blood. His hackles stood up and his lips pulled back to bare his teeth as his right rear leg trembled.

Jake scratched Cody on the nape of his neck. "Easy, boy. I've secured this area. *Search* it now." He closed the secret door, held up the shotgun and let Cody continue walking off leash.

Cody moved further into the house, raised his nose high and then held it down low. He moved his head back and forth from side to side and went straight to the set of six metal lockers against a far wall, where he pawed at one of the doors. Jake opened the locker door and found Olivia stuffed in there upright. She was bound with rope, gagged, blindfolded and wearing headphone-style shooting range earmuffs to block out sound.

Olivia didn't move and it appeared she might be high on drugs, unconscious, or dead.

Jake felt his heart flip. He took off her blindfold, gag and earmuffs. Beneath the earmuffs, she also wore earplugs. He removed them and worked at untying the ropes from her wrists and feet.

Once she was free, he gently put his arms around her waist, pulled her against his shoulder, picked her up and lifted her out.

He was relieved to find her still breathing, her skin warm and her pulse slow but steady.

She blinked her eyes, took a breath and moaned, "Please let me go. *Por favor!*"

Jake spoke close to her ear. "Olivia, it's Jake Wolfe and Cody. We're going to get you out of here." She squinted at him as her eyes adjusted to the lights, and he wondered how bad off she was. "How many fingers am I holding up?"

She peered at his hand. "Two fingers."

"That's right. Good."

He grabbed an unopened bottled water from one of the nearby tables, twisted off the cap and held it to her lips.

She drank thirstily and seemed to partially come back to life. "Jake, is it really you?"

Jake held his face close to hers so she could see him clearly. "Yes, and something only you and I would know is, Pez wrote in his journal that he could always count on Jake and Terrell. Semper Fi."

"Oh, thank God." She clung to him and cried.

He hugged her. "Cody is here too, see? He found you."

Cody woofed at her.

She nodded against Jake's shoulder and sobbed. "I love Cody."

Jake continued holding her as she adjusted to the fact she might survive this nightmare.

After a moment he said, "Okay, stand still and wait right here with Cody guarding you while I handle a situation real quick."

"Yes, Jake. Whatever you say."

"Listen, those men who held you captive are dead. Please face that wall so you don't see their bodies. I'm going to call 911 and fire my weapon to make a loud noise and bring them here fast. I need you to be silent. Don't scream."

He handed her the earmuffs, and she nodded in agreement, then turned away and donned them.

Jake snapped his fingers. "Cody, stay. Protect."

Cody moved to her side and stood at attention, his bright eyes glancing around the room, nose up and sniffing the air.

Jake searched the dead men and found a disposable phone. Tapping on the display, he called 911. When the operator answered, Jake set the phone on a table, fired two loud shotgun blasts at a far wall, ended the call and tossed the phone next to one of the bodies.

Grabbing the trash bag full of Pez dispensers, he moved toward Olivia and removed her earmuffs. "Hold on to my belt at the back of my waist as we go through that door. Stay close and keep both hands on me."

"Yes, Jake." Olivia's eyes went wide at the sight of the ramp leading down into a tunnel. "Where are we going?"

"Do you trust me?" Jake asked.

"Yes, I trust you, Jake," she replied.

"Good, then follow my orders without question," Jake said.

She nodded.

He went through the doorway, pulling Olivia along, with Cody trotting ahead of them.

Jake closed the door behind him and locked the deadbolt with his key. "Cody, lead the way."

The dog walked in front of his handler, head up, sniffing the air, ready to defend and protect.

Olivia followed Jake into the tunnel that was dimly lit by bare overhead bulbs, and she let out a frightened moan.

Jake guessed Olivia had been brought here blindfolded and probably wearing earplugs—maybe unconscious. He spoke slowly and chose his words carefully to avoid giving her a panic attack.

"This is an *escape passage* that will take us to safety in San Diego," he said. "Cody will go first to make sure there are no surprises."

"Oh, thank God." She nodded, confused, and holding tight to Jake's belt.

It occurred to Jake she might be high. "Did they give you any drugs?" he asked as they walked along and followed Cody down the ramp.

She nodded. "Yes, I was driving my car and a cop pulled me over. Someone got in the backseat and placed a cloth over my mouth. It knocked me out for a while, and I woke up in that room with those two men. They stuck a needle in my arm and I felt like I was drunk." She shuddered at the memory.

Jake led Olivia further through the tunnel, making their way under the border with Cody in front. He held the shotgun up and ready to fire over his dog's head.

"Stay close to me, Cody," he said.

On the long walk, they passed the open area and the other shotgun mounted alongside the tunnel. Olivia saw it and gasped in shock but held tight to Jake's belt. He could feel her hands trembling as she clung to him.

Jake said, "We're okay, Olivia. Almost to the exit, fresh air and sunshine."

Olivia began crying again. "I heard them say they were going to sell me to a pimp in Tenancingo, Tlaxcala, and that it was the sex trafficking capital of the world. The pimp would then send me to the United States to work as a sex slave in a big city." Her body shook as she sobbed quietly for a while and then stumbled and fell to her knees.

Jake stopped for a moment, helped her up and hugged her. "Those men are dead now. They can never bother you again."

She nodded, her face wet against his neck. "Thank you for rescuing me. I'd almost lost hope."

"Cody did it. I just follow him around," Jake said, giving a shrug and trying to perk up her spirits enough to complete the escape.

Olivia glanced at Cody and saw the dog watching her and waiting patiently to guide them further. She took a deep breath, wiped her eyes and continued on the trek.

CHAPTER 44

When the trio arrived at the stairway leading upward, Terrell stood up above them in the lunchroom, gazing through the panel doorway with an angry scowl on his face, holding his pistol and aiming it downward. Jake might have accidentally shot his friend but he instantly recognized the face and commanding voice of his Marine lieutenant yelling at him.

"Jukebox, lower your weapon!" Terrell said.

"Roger that, Grinds!" Jake said, lowering the shotgun.

Cody barked at Terrell.

"Good work, Sergeant Cody," Terrell said.

"Rescued hostage coming out." Jake sent Olivia up the stairway first, patting her on the back, then picked up Cody and carried him by the handle on the dog's vest. They exited through the panel door at the top and ended up in the lunchroom of Pez's auto parts business.

Terrell closed the door to block out the underground area. He let out a loud breath.

Jake saw his friend's shoulders slump in relief from the powerful claustrophobia he suffered.

Terrell said, "The radio is buzzing with chatter about Mexican police finding a house full of crystal meth along with two recently shot dead men. It's very close to the border here. Somebody at that location called 911." He raised his eyebrows at Jake.

Jake nodded. "When I rescued Olivia, two sicarios tried to stop me. In war, when you see the enemy, you shoot them. Am I right?"

Terrell nodded in agreement. "And on a hostage rescue mission, cops are quick to use deadly force to protect innocent civilians."

"That's how it went down," Jake said. "Do they know who owns the house?"

"The cartel can buy any house. They pay ten times what it's worth, pay in cash and threaten to kill your family if you don't sell. Who would say no?"

Terrell opened the lunchroom door to reveal SDPD Police Sergeant Fincke facedown on the floor of the hallway with his hands cuffed behind his back. His legs were up, ankles cuffed to his wrists.

Olivia gasped. "That's the cop who pulled me over."

Jake asked Terrell, "What is Fincke doing here?"

"He was waiting in ambush to kill you with Pez's AR," Terrell said, waving a hand at the rifle lying on a table.

Jake moved to the hallway and stood over the prisoner, glaring down at him. He placed the warm end of the shotgun barrel against Fincke's neck.

Fincke froze still.

Jake said, "You're working for the cartel that killed our friend Pez?"

Quaking in fear, Fincke took a deep breath and attempted to speak in a tone that made him sound like the voice of reason. "Yes, of course I work for them. I had no choice. It's not too late for you to make a deal like I did. You'll be well paid. Otherwise, your families will be tortured and they'll die horrific deaths while you watch. I'm … *sorry*."

"You're going to prison for a long time," Jake said.

"Maybe not. My fellow cops will believe me instead of you."

Jake thought about kicking the man, or having Cody bite him. Instead he reached into his top left shirt pocket and tapped his phone to turn off the video recording. He then opened his small backpack and removed a fist-sized bag of crystal and a stack of cash.

Still wearing gloves, he went down on one knee and planted the drugs and money in Fincke's pockets. "Your fellow cops will find this evidence on you. Enjoy prison life."

Terrell frowned at Jake. "No. We're not going to plant evidence on a suspect. He's dirty and we're clean. I draw the line right here."

Jake took a deep breath and let it out. He nodded resignedly. "I was only putting the fear into him. But yeah, you're right as usual. That's why I look up to you, brother. Sorry I got carried away. This video might be useful, though." He tapped his phone and played a video of Fincke admitting he worked for the crime cartel.

"Send that to my phone," Terrell said. He took a small cigar out of his pocket, sniffed the wrapper and then looked around and put it back.

As Jake removed the planted evidence, Fincke said, "I saw you come out of Lopez's house carrying a backpack. You found the cartel's missing package, didn't you?"

Jake shook his head. "No, I'm still looking for it. Tell me everything you know about it and maybe the judge will go easy on you."

"Who the hell are you, anyway?" Fincke asked.

Jake replied, "Charles Bukowski."

"Are you DEA?"

Jake shook his head. "I work for the post office."

Fincke cursed. "Your name's Wolfe and you're looking for the package. Why? Who's paying you?" He struggled against his bonds muttering what he'd like to do to Jake. Cody growled close to the man's ear. Fincke closed his eyes in fear.

Jake said a code word. Cody growled louder and put his teeth on the man's throat but didn't bite him, only breathed hot, angry breaths on his skin. Fincke moaned in fear. His whole body shook with tremors as if he was having a seizure.

Terrell observed Fincke, and in an overly casual voice asked Jake, "Ever had a panic attack like that?"

"No, but Cody and I often give them to people," Jake said.

Terrell nodded, a grim smile on his face. "Got a sitrep for your lieutenant?"

"Yes, sir," Jake said, out of old habit from their deployments.

"Follow me," Terrell said and went back into the breakroom.

Jake slapped his thigh twice, and Cody appeared by his side. They followed Terrell and closed the door behind them.

Once they were out of Fincke's earshot, Jake said, "There's no doubt this cartel killed Pez. One of them admitted it. They're preparing for war, with armor-piercing rounds, grenade launchers, you name it."

Terrell nodded. "American drug addicts funding cop-killer terrorist weapons. Lately in the US, people are more likely to die from an opioid overdose than in a car accident."

"I think this stuff is crystal meth." Jake held out the small zip-top bag.

Terrell stared at it. "Yeah. Looks like glass."

"Chemistry that kills you," Jake said.

"And causes a crime wave of epic proportions. My Mexican police colleagues on the other side of the tunnel found a body with its head cut off," Terrell said.

Jake glanced toward the panel door. "They kept the head in a refrigerator. Hope I can forget I saw that."

Terrell said, "Sometimes the cartels keep a severed head cold and fresh until they deliver it to whoever they want to intimidate." He checked his phone and continued. "The DEA and border patrol will be crawling all over this place any minute now. Get going, and take Olivia with you. When I called my local police contact here, I left you out of it."

"Thanks, brother," Jake said. "The Mexican police are locked out of the tunnel on the other end, until they find a key or break down the door."

"For all they know, someone from their side of the border killed those men," Terrell said.

"That works for me. And when they see the stacks of cash and cop-killer rounds, they might not care who did them the favor anyway."

Jake led Olivia and Cody outside and saw a parked police car. He tried the driver's door and found it unlocked. In spite of his talk with Terrell, he shoved the zip-top bag of meth and the stack of cash under the driver's seat, locked the doors and said, "That's payback for Sammy Lopez."

He moved on to his rented SUV, tossed the bag of Pez dispensers in the back, helped Olivia and Cody get situated and drove off.

"Olivia, lean your seat back. Lay low and hide," Jake said.

Olivia didn't ask why, just did exactly what Jake told her to do, trusting and obeying the man who'd rescued her.

Jake removed his blue nitrile gloves moments before Police, DEA and CBP cars raced past them with lights flashing. He stared straight ahead, face devoid of emotion.

CHAPTER 45

After Jake drove a few more blocks and the law enforcement vehicles had gone past, he said, "Olivia, you can sit up now. Tell me more about when they pulled you over and snatched you."

Olivia sat up, raising the back of her seat to its upright position. "I risked taking a drive to get fast food, and somebody saw me. I was so stupid." She wiped her wet eyes with her sleeve.

Jake reached into the center console and handed her a few paper napkins left over from one of his lunches. "Don't feel bad. They probably had snitches all over the place watching for you, to earn a reward. But you were safe at the Lopezes' house? The parents are okay?"

She blew her nose. "Yes. I want to go there now, please. A while ago they came home from church and their house had been ransacked, just like Sammy's place, so the cartel knows they don't have the package. Mr. Lopez bought a hunting rifle and isn't afraid to use it in self-defense."

They drove in silence toward the house. After a while Jake asked, "Those men who kidnapped you, did they ever say what was in the package?"

"They said it was a hard drive containing a database listing the home address of every law enforcement officer in the United States."

Jake felt his stomach drop. Could that be possible? If so, the package absolutely must not be allowed to fall into the hands of criminals and terrorists. He cursed under his breath.

Arriving at the parents' house, Jake walked Olivia to the door, carrying the black garbage bag and wearing his small backpack on one shoulder.

Cody sniffed the air, on alert. He stared hard at a neighbor who checked his mailbox.

Pez's parents answered the door and Michelle cried and hugged Olivia.

Brent said, "We were worried sick about you young lady."

They all went inside, and Jake gave the trash bag to Brent. "I thought you'd want to have these, sir."

When Brent opened the bag and saw his son's Pez collection, he choked up and blinked back a few tears. "This means a lot to us. Thank you, Jake."

Jake said, "Olivia, I have something for you, too. It's wonderful, but it will make you cry."

"Did it belong to Pez?" she asked.

"Yes, and he planned on giving it to you."

"Please let me see it." She bit her lip.

Jake reached into his backpack, took out a black velvet ring box and opened it to reveal a diamond wedding ring.

Olivia gasped. She took the box and slipped the ring onto her finger. "Oh my God." She sat on the couch and sobbed.

Michelle hugged the girl that would have been her daughter-in-law, and she began to cry too.

"There's one other thing," Jake said to Brent, opening his backpack, removing several clear plastic bags full of cash and setting them on the dining table.

"What in the world? That's a lot of money," Brent said.

"Sammy kept some of his life savings in a floor safe," Jake said. "It belongs to you now."

Michelle said, "Thank you, Jake. You could've kept that money and we never would've known, but you're an honest man. Sammy spoke highly of you."

"He spoke highly of you too. He was like a brother to me, and now we're family. I guess you're stuck with me and Cody," Jake said.

Michelle smiled sadly. "Mi casa es su casa. My house is your house."

As if he understood her words, Cody walked to a dog bowl on the kitchen floor and noisily drank water.

"Make yourself right at home, Cody," Jake said.

Cody gave them a toothy grin, water dripping from his mouth. At a screen door leading to the backyard, a small dog yapped at Cody and jumped up and down. Cody gave one fierce bark to show the dog who was boss and walked away with head held high, as if he thought of himself as a dangerous Marine war veteran who had no time to argue with a harmless little civilian pet.

"I'm sorry, but we have to be going now," Jake said.

"Are you sure you can't stay for dinner?" Michelle asked.

"I'd love to, but there are things to take care of." Jake shook hands with Brent.

"Son, you be careful when you're *taking care of things*," Brent said with a worried frown.

"I will, sir," Jake said. "I have a war dog to protect me. Right, Cody?"

Cody barked once.

Both parents stared at the dog in wonder as he appeared to nod his head.

Michelle and Olivia stood up. Jake hugged Michelle, then Olivia. "No trips for fast food, Olivia, until I let you know it's safe, okay? And no deliveries to the house, either."

Olivia nodded against his chest, hanging onto him as if he were a life preserver. "I lost my job, so I'm not going anywhere. I just wish you and Cody could stay with us."

"I wish we could too, but we have to go." Jake pried himself loose from the hug, patted his thigh for Cody to follow and walked out of the house.

As Cody hopped into the car, Jake surveyed the street in both directions, looking for anything out of place. All appeared safe and normal, but you just never knew.

Driving away from the Lopezes' house, Jake sent a text to Terrell.

Jake: *Olivia heard them say the package is a database listing the home address of every LEO in America.*

Terrell: *Damn. Give that intel to McKay.*

Jake: *Will do.*

Jake then called Agent McKay in D.C.

"You found a tunnel," McKay answered his call.

"Yes, and we followed it into Mexico," Jake said.

"I'm getting reports from both sides of the border. Dead bodies, weapon stockpiles, cop-killer rounds, grenade launchers, stacks of cash and enough crystal meth to indicate a large-scale laboratory in operation."

Jake asked, "Is a tunnel under our borders considered a threat to national security?"

"Yes, it is. I've alerted Homeland and the CIA. A task force in Nogales, Arizona is finding a new tunnel every month, except for last month when they found three."

"Why is Nogales tunnel central?" Jake asked.

"There is a vast underground drainage system that connects the two border cities. It's a smuggler's dream come true."

"Olivia said she overheard Rojo's men talking about the package. They said it's a hard drive containing the home address of every LEO in the USA."

McKay cursed. "I'll alert Homeland to that new intel."

"If it's a matter for the POETs, I'm right here on location and ready for action."

"No. The local authorities are handling it now. And they're seeking a mystery man with a shotgun. I need you to leave town."

"All right, but if they fail to catch Rojo, I'll come back, with or without your support."

"Give them time to do their jobs," McKay said.

Jake hesitated a moment and took a deep breath before answering.

"I'll try to be patient," he said, not sounding convincing, even to himself.

"Jake, I'm not asking you to try, I'm ordering you not to go rogue assassin on me. Stand down and go home."

"Yes, ma'am," Jake said and ended the call before she could add any further rules of engagement.

CHAPTER 46

Rojo paced back and forth next to the beautiful swimming pool at his hacienda, as he barked angry orders into his phone. "Get it done, you idiots!"

He ended the call, cursed and picked up his pistol from a nearby table. First, he took aim at the fighting cock strutting in its fenced area nearby. No, it was too valuable, and a thing of fierce beauty in its own way. He swung the barrel toward a blue-nose Pit Bull Terrier puppy playing fetch with Tomás.

Tomás saw this and his face went pale. "No, uncle!" He picked up the dog protectively and held her to his chest.

"You dare oppose me?" Rojo asked.

"I can't stand to see a dog harmed," Tomás said.

Rojo shook his head in disgust. "That's weak."

Tomás met his eyes. "No, it's brave. You always said a man has to stand up for himself and his family. This dog is family to me and I'm standing up for her. Standing up to *you!*" Tomás added a string of blistering curses he'd heard Rojo say.

Rojo raised his eyebrows and considered this. "Hmmm, that's an impressive argument."

He fired the pistol at a potted tree, bursting the clay pot and making the tree fall over. Next he aimed at the deep end of the pool, firing a few rounds into the water.

Tomás spoke in a forced calm voice, still hanging onto the dog. "Is it that same man, Señor Lobo, making you angry again?"

Rojo set down the pistol, made a fist and pounded it on his table. "Yes, it's Jake Wolfe. When we capture him and bring him here, I want you to be among those who chop him to death with machetes."

"I'll be proud to follow your orders, Patrón," Tomás said, setting down the dog and patting her on the back. "Let me pour you a shot of tequila, and brainstorm ways to capture Wolfe and reclaim the hard drive."

Rojo accepted the glass and drank the tequila down in one gulp. "I'm listening."

Tomás said, "You said a policeman in San Diego named Fincke saw Wolfe and the detective leaving Pez's house."

"What about it? That idiot Fincke let them get away."

"Tell Fincke to bring a K9 cop and dog to search the house. The K9 can follow the scent of Wolfe's dog, and maybe learn where it stopped and found something."

Rojo gaped at the young man. "You're smarter than all of my cartel put together."

He made a phone call to Fincke, but the man who answered had a different voice.

"Hello?"

Rojo ended the call and handed the phone to Tomás. "Remove that SIMM card and destroy it," he said.

Tomás removed the phone's memory card, held it with a pair of needle nose pliers, and torched it with a butane lighter until it melted.

Another burner phone among the many on the table buzzed, and Rojo received a text message that read: *Jake Wolfe is living on a boat at Kona Kai Marina.*

"We found Wolfe," Rojo said.

Jake drove to San Diego's Kona Kai Marina and parked his rented SUV.

As he and Cody walked toward the rented guest slip where the *Far Niente* was berthed, he caught a glimpse of a man sitting at the table on his boat's aft deck and smoking a cigar as if he owned the place, or would soon.

Jake ducked low out of sight, whispering a command and giving a hand signal to Cody, and they split up on separate missions.

Cody snuck on board, stealthily circling around the bow and down the starboard side of the boat, out of sight of the visitor and coming up behind him.

Jake quietly walked on board and down the port side, stopping in front of his uninvited guest and aiming his silenced pistol at him.

"What's your excuse for illegally trespassing?" Jake asked, calmly, but boiling in anger inside and ready to fire his weapon.

The man blew out some cigar smoke, waved his cigar as if Jake was an insignificant mosquito, and smiled an evil smile. "Do I look like someone who cares about laws, *cabrón*?"

"No, you look like an asshole who's about to be executed," Jake said, raising his pistol and aiming at the man's forehead.

The man shrugged and brought his other hand out from beneath the table, which held a pistol similar to the one Jake was using.

"I see you still have the pistol you stole from my boss," the man said.

Jake noted the man's pistol was the same as his, and was aimed at Jake's stomach.

Cody approached the man quietly from behind, and Jake gave a soft, whistled command.

The man stared at Jake in confusion, but Cody appeared out of nowhere and bit down on his wrist, holding his gun hand down against the tabletop.

Jake leapt forward and shot the man up close, so as not to risk hitting Cody. He fired one round into the man's chest and then disarmed him.

As Jake removed the pistol from the dying man's hand, the

sicario made one last effort to kill him, squeezing off a shot and grazing Jake's left biceps.

Cursing, Jake took the man's weapon and pistol-whipped him with it. Cody darted under the table to threaten the man's crotch, snarling and baring his teeth.

Jake said, "We're clear, Cody. *Bite him!*"

Cody snarled and bit down on the man's crotch as hard as he could. And even though the man was bleeding out and near dead, he screamed one last time in ultimate agony on his way to hell.

"Cody, heel," Jake said.

Cody came to Jake's side, and Jake went down on one knee to hug his dog. "Good boy. You're such a brave and noble savage, aren't you, Cody?"

Cody whined and licked at the blood on Jake's arm.

"It's just a scratch, don't worry," Jake said, but he knew he had to stanch the blood loss. Reaching into a drawer, he grabbed a QuikClot packet, applied the mesh bandage to his wound and used medical tape to hold it in place. Better safe than sorry.

Moving quickly, he untied the lines from the dock, climbed the steps to the bridge and motored away from the harbor, out into the open ocean.

CHAPTER 47

Once on the open ocean, he bumped the throttles and pointed the bow toward empty water.

Soon he had the motor yacht many miles offshore. Stopping the engines, he let her drift, went downstairs to the lower decks and found his diving gear. Grabbing two weight belts, he climbed back up to the aft deck. He then put the heavy belts onto the man he'd killed.

Tossing the body overboard and watching it sink, Jake wondered if this man had been forced to join the cartel. Did sicarios threaten to torture his wife and kids to death? He felt as if he should say a few words. He recited the Lord's Prayer from memory, quoting the gospel of Matthew—mouthing the words he'd heard endless times in Catholic school when he just wanted to be out walking the seashore or sailing on a boat.

Climbing upstairs to the bridge, Jake cruised away until he put several miles between his boat and the burial at sea. He then eased back on the throttles, returned to the aft deck, grabbed a hose and began cleaning the deck. Spraying water, he washed the blood off and sent it down both curved steps onto the twin swim platforms and into the ocean.

Glancing at the horizon as he worked, Jake saw a Coast Guard cutter heading in his direction. He then sprayed and cleaned the deck with renewed determination.

The Coast Guard hailed Jake on VHF marine radio channel 16 and asked him to switch to channel 22A, which is reserved for communication between US Coast Guard vessels and private vessels.

The cutter advised, *"Far Niente,* prepare to be boarded for inspection."

Jake grabbed the aft deck mic and replied with fake cheer, "My pleasure. Coasties are always welcome here. I'll get the coffeemaker going."

Pulling out his encrypted black phone, he placed a call to Washington.

"McKay."

"It's Wolfe. I'm in international waters off San Diego. The Coast Guard is preparing to board the *Far Niente,* and there's blood on the aft deck."

She paused for a moment. "I thought I ordered you to leave town."

"I was trying to."

"How bad is the deck?"

"I cleaned it pretty well, but it won't stand up to a thorough inspection."

"How well hidden are your POET-issued weapons?"

"They won't find those unless they bring a dog on board, in which case I'm hosed. Their dogs are good. They can smell drugs, weapons, currency, etc."

"Right, and you have weapons, suspiciously large sums of cash, passports in other names and from other countries."

"Am I authorized to show the captain my letter of Marque and Reprisal?"

McKay said, "Yes, you are, and I'll assist you. Hang on a minute while I call the cutter."

Jake heard McKay talking to someone on another phone. Her tone was brisk, authoritative and demanding.

His radio crackled with a call from the Coast Guard cutter. *"Far Niente,* please stand by."

"Aye, sir," Jake said respectfully.

Minutes later the radio crackled again. *"Far Niente,* please disregard. Captain Ballard says to have a nice day, Jake, and say hi to Cody for him."

Jake smiled. "Thank you, my friends. Give my best to the captain. If any of you are ever up the coast near San Francisco, stop by Juanita Yacht Harbor in Sausalito for beers and a barbecue."

"Roger that, but ... do jarheads know *how* to barbecue?"

Jake chuckled at the friendly jibe. "Yeah, we use a flamethrower."

He heard laughter, and then silence.

Once the cutter had cruised away, Jake went to the galley, reached up into a cupboard with his good arm and pulled out a bottle of Redbreast Irish Whiskey. He took a long pull directly from the bottle and exhaled loudly. "That's what I'm talking about. God bless Irish barley growers and distillers."

The three-hundred-year-old tradition of copper pot still distillation, followed by aging in the finest sherry barrels, produced a whiskey like no other. Redbreast was the most popular pot-stilled Irish whiskey in the world, and Jake guessed his own constant purchases had made a contribution to that status. He faced east and waved toward Ireland, where his money went.

Cody pawed at Jake, sniffed the bloody bandage on his arm and growled.

"I know, it's worse than I thought. I need to see a doctor soon, and I will, I promise," Jake said. "Right now, this Irish painkiller will have to do."

Jake drank another pull, then went upstairs to the bridge, pushed the throttles forward and cruised back toward the boat harbor. Yes, he needed to visit a hospital, but how would he explain the wound? And would there be police at the harbor now, due to the suppressed gunfire, or had the muted sound escaped notice?

CHAPTER 48

Jake returned to the harbor and didn't see any police. He and Cody walked to the rental car, and as Jake drove off, he called McKay again.

"One more thing—I've been shot. Know any doctors in San Diego who don't ask questions?"

McKay exhaled loudly. "You're just now telling me this minor detail?"

"Apparently."

"Drive to Hotel del Coronado and wait in the parking lot. I'll send a SARC from the Naval Amphibious Base to find you."

Jake drove to the famous hotel and waited for the Special Amphibious Reconnaissance Corpsman. A plain dark blue van with federal plates pulled up, and the driver studied Jake's face and motioned for him to get in. Jake and Cody hopped inside. The interior looked similar to an ambulance.

The driver said, "I'm Logan. They sent me to patch you up."

"Thanks, Doc," Jake said.

Cody sniffed the driver and growled.

Logan held still and raised his eyebrows. "What's he doing?"

"He's a Marine war dog, and he knows you're armed. Wait a minute while he checks you out."

Logan held still. "I love war dogs, but yours is kind of scary-smart."

"Be friends, Cody," Jake said.

Cody inspected Logan, seemed to approve of him, and then began to sniff all around the inside of the van.

Logan let out a sigh of relief and drove them to a quiet spot down at the empty far end of a row in the large parking lot.

"Okay, let's see your injury." Logan studied the wound and frowned. "You were lucky. Another inch over and you'd be in the hospital right now."

"This dog is my good luck charm," Jake said.

"Want a pain pill?"

"Ibuprofen will do."

"Where did you serve?"

Jake paused and looked the man in the eye. "All over the place," he said vaguely due to operational security (OPSEC).

"Good to go." Logan nodded in understanding and treated Jake's wound using a local anesthetic.

Jake bit down on a rolled-up white washcloth and groaned a few times as Logan sewed him up. Cody sniffed at Jake's injury and whined.

Logan said, "The local ladies say you Marines are all the same. Tough as nails. Got something to prove. Big swinging dicks and an even bigger attitude. But you're gentlemen who always pay for dinner and treat them right, the way they like."

"And you NAVY SARCs are the most badass docs ever," Jake said.

Cody woofed and nodded.

Logan stared at the dog in wonder.

Jake smiled. "Navy Corpsmen saved his life when he got injured overseas. He knows a medic when he sees one."

Logan finished taping up Jake's wound and he joked, "No charge for this repair. You were never here."

Jake considered him for a moment. "I'm guessing you have some top-secret clearances."

"Yes. McKay recruited me for situations that require discretion," Logan said.

Jake reached out and shook hands. "Thanks again, Logan."

"No problem. Maybe I'll see you and Cody again someday, Jake."

"And hopefully I won't be wounded," Jake said.

He climbed out and walked toward the SUV with Cody at his heels. As he walked he called Terrell.

"Any more news?"

Terrell said, "I did a door-knock-and-talk, up and down the street. One guy across the way told me he'd been working past midnight recently when about thirty Chinese men and women came out of Pez's building, climbed into a box truck and drove off."

"Undocumented immigrants, smuggled through the tunnel?"

"Yeah. Who rides in a box truck?"

"That's a good way to die of heat stroke in this weather."

"Speaking of which, it's too hot here for my ass, so I'm going to head home," Terrell said.

"You miss your wife."

"Well, duh. Alicia is the best wife in the universe."

"McKay ordered me to leave town. Why not cruise back home with me and Cody and catch a few fish along the way?" Jake asked.

"I'd like to, but Beth is covering for me and doing all of my work in addition to hers. And Chief Pierce is asking me if I'm going to get a job at the San Diego PD."

Jake opened the car's back passenger door for Cody, and his dog hopped in. He closed the door and slid into the driver's seat. "Nope. You're on injury leave. I'm gonna call Alicia and Beth and Pierce and tell them you need this fishing trip to relax and heal up your head wound, or else you'll blow a fuse."

"That's a good line of BS, keep talking," Terrell said.

"We'll explain it to them after we're on the ocean. You spent the night, woke up and we were underway. I shanghaied you. It'll be something that's already happening. They'll have to deal with it."

"You lawyers always have a lie for every contingency. They'll blame you for this, you know."

"What else is new? I always get blamed for damn near

everything. Same as when I was a kid. Every mom was like, *It can't be my perfect child's fault, so we'll blame it on that Wolfe boy who dares to talk back to adults and question our commands.*"

Terrell laughed. "All right, Jukebox, I'm in, but you'd better have lots of good food and brewskis."

"Of course. I'll hit a mini-mart on the way, to stock up on peanuts and light beer. Nothing but the best for you, Loo-tenant Grinds."

Terrell jokingly uttered some poetic profanity and ended the call.

Once they were all on board the *Far Niente*, Terrell sat in the captain's chair, known as the first seat. Jake sat in the chair next to him, known as the second seat, and gave newly commissioned "Captain Terrell" a hands-on crash course on how to cruise the boat. He pointed at a harbor sign that read: Idle Speed - No Wake Zone.

"You've seen me do this before. We're going to slowly make our way out to the ocean. Bump the throttles forward a little, but easy does it, don't get carried away."

Terrell bumped the throttles a bit too hard and the *Far Niente*'s twin engines roared to life as she leapt forward and surged across the water. People on nearby boats turned and stared. One man yelled at them on his PA system.

Jake waved, nodded in apology and eased back on the throttles. "That's okay, Grinds. You have the need for speed."

Cody woofed at Terrell and wagged his tail.

Terrell smiled. "Cody likes to go fast."

Jake slowed the yacht down to a little over the posted speed limit. They left the harbor and he said, "Okay, we're on open ocean now. Ease the throttle forward some more."

Terrell handled the throttle just the way he'd seen Jake doing it so many times, and the boat surged ahead smoothly and came up on plane.

"You're a natural," Jake said and nodded in satisfaction. He reached into a mini fridge and handed Terrell a cold bottle of Modelo

Especial. He then opened a drawer and took out a Halloween costume pirate's black eye patch on an elastic string. Putting the costume accessory on Terrell, he used his phone to take a picture of his friend standing tall at the wheel, shirt off, holding a beer in one hand, with a bandage on his head and a pirate eye patch over one eye.

Terrell had a big confident smile on his face for the first time since he'd sustained the nearly fatal head injury. His badass self was back. Look out, world.

Jake sent the photo to Terrell's wife, Alicia, with a text. *Your man is a stud, on his way home to you, the love of his life. He can't wait to see you but needs this boat trip to heal his mind, body and soul on the journey.*

Alicia replied: *Agreed. Thank you, Jake. You're invited over for dinner this weekend. And you'd better bring some good wine!*

Jake: *Yes, only the best wine for you, BFF.*

That made Jake think of Sarah, and he sent the photo of Terrell to her, along with a text: *Pirates have taken over the Far Niente!*

Sarah didn't reply.

Jake observed Terrell enjoying himself, piloting the boat across the blue water, with a salty breeze in his hair and the sun on his back. He thought the cruise was doing a world of good for his best friend.

"We need to do this more often," he said.

Terrell took a deep breath of clean ocean air. "Damned right."

Jake tapped the controls and played a music video on the bridge TV at high volume: The Lonely Island - I'm On A Boat, the explicit version featuring T-Pain. The official video on YouTube.

Jake and Terrell sang along, belting out the profane lyrics, and Cody howled. The men had a good laugh afterward. Jake knew Alicia didn't approve of the song, but he and Terrell thoroughly enjoyed yelling the ridiculous curse words. Sometimes combat veterans needed to swear and let off steam and have a few laughs. You couldn't do it in "polite society," but out on the ocean you were alone and free.

After an enjoyable day of cruising, they stopped for the night and anchored out, offshore.

Jake said, "I'm taking it easier on the engines on the way home. We'll make the trip in three days instead of two. I pushed her hard on the way down, but this is a pleasure cruise heading home."

Terrell bit on the foot of a lit cigar in the corner of his mouth and answered, "It's all good. This is so much better than flying in a crowded tin can."

Jake nodded, aware of how Terrell's claustrophobia made him hate airline travel.

He fired up the outdoor grill and barbecued a beef tri-tip medium rare. Carving off thin slices, he piled it high on toasted French rolls.

Cody ate his beef plain, devouring it quickly and licking his snout afterward.

Terrell savored a bite of sandwich, followed by a sip of cold beer. "This tri-tip is hella good. It reminds me of when we visited our buddy Rick in Santa Maria."

"Thanks. This one turned out all right, but in Santa Maria they cook it over red oak coals and nothing can compare to the genuine thing," Jake said.

Cody burped loudly, apparently saying he'd eat *any* tri-tip, *any*time, *any* place.

Jake and Terrell laughed, and Cody gave them a big grin.

After a few more beers, they all turned in for the night. Terrell slept on the couch in the salon, preferring it to the guest staterooms downstairs below decks, due to his claustrophobia.

Jake and Cody slept well, but were awakened before dawn by a ding from the security system.

Lifting his head, Cody growled and hopped off the bed, his eyes watching Jake.

Jake checked his phone and saw the view from a surveillance camera. A rubber dinghy bumped against the hull, tied off with the painter on its bow ring to the *Far Niente's* starboard rail. A dark figure climbed on board uninvited.

CHAPTER 49

"Oh, hell no," Jake said. He stood up, pulled on his pants, and sent a text to Terrell's phone.

Cody trotted to the stateroom door, turned his head and looked back over his shoulder at Jake.

Jake said, "*Stealth*. Shhhh."

With pistol in hand, Jake exited the room and walked toward the aft deck sliding door, leaving the interior lights off.

Cody followed along silently.

Terrell went to the nearby galley and reached for a pistol hidden behind the bar.

Jake pointed at himself and then at the stairs toward the bridge. Next, he pointed at Terrell and then at the sliding door.

Terrell nodded and gave a thumbs-up.

Jake climbed the stairs with Cody at his heels. On the bridge he quietly opened a cabinet and removed a rifle.

He sent Terrell another text: *In position.*

Jake peered down at the unwelcome visitor and saw a man holding a pistol up in front of him as he slowly and quietly crept toward the aft sliding door.

Terrell suddenly turned on the lights, inside and outside. He stepped in front of the Plexiglass door and aimed his pistol at the intruder.

The man reacted instantly and fired several shots at Terrell. His rounds bounced off the thick bulletproof Plexiglass and one ricochet hit him in the face, dropping him onto his back, dead.

Cody growled and his right rear leg trembled.

"Easy, boy," Jake said, patting his dog on the back. "Grinds took care of business."

Jake and Cody went down the stairs and met Terrell coming out the door.

Cody sniffed the bleeding enemy and his smoking pistol. He growled low in his throat.

"Marines, clear the boat and perimeter," Terrell ordered in a practiced, calm and commanding voice that did not expect any disagreement.

"Roger that," Jake said. He patted his thigh for Cody to follow and moved toward the port side, while holding his rifle up and ready.

Terrell patrolled the starboard side.

They met up at the bow.

"Clear," Terrell said.

"Clear," Jake said in reply.

Everyone returned to where the empty dinghy remained tied to the gunwale, and Cody sniffed at the boat and growled.

Jake asked, "Well, Detective Grinds, should we dump the body for the sharks and let the raft drift away empty?"

Terrell appeared conflicted as he wrestled with the decision. "Turn off all boat cameras."

"Roger." Jake tapped his phone and shut down the boat's security cams.

Terrell walked back to the dead body. "We have video evidence he committed piracy, assault with a deadly weapon, attempted murder, and … stupid suicide."

Jake nodded. "Served him right, too. Am I a bad person if his stupid self-inflicted headshot made me happy?"

"Nope, that made all of us happy," Terrell said. He looked at the dark, empty water all around them. "I'm leaning toward your sharks idea, but let me check his ID first. Do you have gloves?"

Jake walked to the aft deck, opened a drawer and grabbed a dispenser box of blue nitrile gloves. He returned and held out the box to Terrell.

Terrell plucked two and gloved up. He patted down the dead man and didn't find anything on him. "He's incognito, but we can guess who sent him."

"Yeah, and now let's send him to hell," Jake said. He gloved up and grabbed the man's wrists. Terrell nodded and grabbed the ankles. They swung the body back and forth, with Terrell saying, "One, two, three!"

The dead man sailed over the gunwale and hit the water with a splash. Jake untied the painter of the dinghy and gave the small boat a shove, sending it drifting away.

They all walked to the aft sliding door, and Terrell said, "Swab the deck."

Jake raised his eyebrows. "I'm pretty sure you have to wear the pirate patch when you say that, Loo-tenant."

He pulled out a hose with a spray head, told Cody to hop onto a bench seat, and began to spray off the aft deck.

"I'll go get the patch," Terrell said jokingly. "And where is our pirate flag, with the skull and crossbones? You're slacking off."

As Jake sprayed the deck and Terrell observed, Jake joked in reply, "Are you going to get us some damned cigars and beers or just stand there and supervise like a brass-hole who has shiny stars on your collars?"

"Keep swabbing, squid," Terrell said with a grin as he went inside to the galley.

Jake called after him, "I'm a jarhead, not a squid, and it's *Mister* Jarhead to you, pal."

Terrell returned with two cigars but no beers. "I turned on the coffeemaker."

Jake finished up spraying the last of the blood off the deck. "This is getting to be a routine, and I don't like it," he said.

Sharks arrived in response to the blood in the water, and began tearing the floating body limb from limb, thrashing in the water as they fought for bites of food.

The sight reminded Jake of how he and Cody had almost ended up as shark food.

Cody apparently felt the same. He barked at the deadly animals, and his hackles stood up.

"Heel, Cody." Jake picked up the rifle, turned to Terrell and said, "Let's get underway."

They all headed upstairs to the bridge, and Jake raised anchor and motored away from the area.

Jake bumped the throttles and brought the *Far Niente* up on plane. He and Terrell sat in the two black-leather-and-chrome captain's chairs, smoked cigars and drank coffee, waiting to see the beautiful sunrise.

Terrell waved his cigar and gestured at the rifle that Jake had set on a countertop. "Good idea to keep that handy. We might need it again."

Jake nodded. "You never know."

They continued cruising up the coast, and on the way they watched the sun come up in the east, painting the sky with brushstrokes of orange, purple, red and gold. They cruised for two more days without any trouble, catching some fish and grilling them for lunches and dinners. In the late afternoon of day three, they were rewarded with the sight of the Golden Gate Bridge in the distance. A humpback whale breached off the port bow and Cody barked at it happily.

Upon arrival at the Pier 39 Marina, Alicia stood waiting at Jake's boat slip. A cute black woman with full lips, a warm smile and sparkling eyes, who wore her dark hair in the latest style. Dressed casually in bluejeans and a white blouse, she waved excitedly at the boat, all smiles and eager to greet Terrell and welcome him home.

Terrell said, "I've never seen a more beautiful sight." He turned on the stereo and played "Come Monday" by Jimmy Buffett, a song about traveling to San Francisco, missing his beloved woman and longing to see her again.

Alicia listened to the song and smiled.

Once the boat eased into the slip and bumped the dock, Jake

hurried down the stairs, grabbed the lines, leapt onto the dock and tied up.

Alicia asked, "Permission to come aboard?"

"Yes, please do," Terrell said, holding his arms wide open to her. They embraced and kissed as if reunited after a long separation.

Alicia kept her arms around his neck. "I like this song."

"I played it just for you," Terrell said.

"You're sweet. Is that Jimmy Buffett?"

"Yep. His music is great for boat bums and good-hearted pirates," Terrell said. He reached into his pocket for the pirate eye patch, put it on, and said, "Ahrrr m'lady."

She grinned. "Wow, you look *hot* as a pirate! Maybe you should wear that to bed tonight, hmm?"

"Why wait until tonight? We could hurry home right now."

She giggled. "You talked me into it."

"Ayyee, lass."

Alicia kissed him again and hugged him tight. "I missed you so much."

"I missed you more," Terrell said.

Jake observed his friends and felt happy for them. It made him wonder what it was like to have that kind of happy relationship. He was reminded of when he'd recently deplaned a flight and walked into the airport. He'd noticed a fellow male traveler being greeted by his joyful wife and kids, who'd made a big fuss, obviously delighted to have him home again.

Would Jake ever experience that in his life? No, probably not. It didn't seem to be in the cards he'd been dealt. The man he'd seen returning to his family wasn't coming home from a mission where he'd assassinated a high-value target for Uncle Sam.

After the hug, Cody woofed at Alicia.

Jake said, "Say hi to your friend, Cody."

Alicia patted Cody on the back and gave him a fond smile. "Hey, fuzzy butt doggie. How'd you get so fuzzy, huh?"

Cody wagged his tail and pressed his head against her stomach. The dog often made it clear Alicia was one of the people he loved most. Cody was trained to ride the city bus to Terrell and Alicia's house if he got separated from Jake and had done so more than once. All the bus drivers knew Cody and looked after him like he was their lucky mascot. There was a dog up in Seattle who rode the bus to a dog park. Now San Francisco had its own bus-riding dog, and every person who rode the bus loved him.

Jake smiled. "Hi Alicia, good to see you." He finished tying up.

"Hi, Jake. Thanks for bringing my man back home to me."

"It was my pleasure. You two should go out with us on a whale watching trip one weekend soon."

"That sounds like fun, let's do it," she said.

They bid their goodbyes, Terrell and Alicia moved toward her car, and Jake locked the aft sliding door of the *Far Niente*.

Walking up the dock with Cody by his side, Jake asked, "Ready to go visit Sarah?"

Cody ran to the Jeep, wagging his tail.

Jake sent a text to Sarah: *Cody and I are back. Want to have dinner?*

Sarah didn't reply.

Jake felt his pulse quicken. He sent a text to the Italian man he had guarding her.

Jake: *Beppe, report.*

Beppe: *I'm at Sarah's clinic. She's inside, working. No threats.*

Jake: *Do you have eyes on her at the moment?*

Beppe: *Yes. She's in the reception area, busy with a client.*

Jake: *Good work. Thanks.*

His phone buzzed and he received a short video from Beppe. He saw the pet clinic window and glass door. Inside, Sarah stood holding a small dog and talking to a woman.

Jake nodded. Too busy working to answer the phone. More importantly, he'd put her in danger and they'd had cartels stalking both of them. She might be pulling away. He couldn't blame her if she did.

Would he ever teach a son or daughter how to pilot a boat, care for a dog, go camping and make a fire? He felt an ache in his chest as he realized it might never happen for him. If he had a wife and kids, his clandestine missions could put them at risk.

Maybe their relationship just wasn't meant to be more than two lovers, dating whenever time permitted.

Am I Sarah's friend with benefits?

"Who knows?" he asked out loud.

Cody studied him quizzically.

They climbed into the Jeep and drove off toward Sarah's clinic.

CHAPTER 50

Sarah stood in her pet clinic's reception area talking with Madison, both of them working overtime. Her phone buzzed in her pocket with calls and texts, nearly nonstop, but she ignored it for the moment.

The desk phone rang and Madison reached for it, but Sarah held up her hand. "It's after hours, Maddie. You can let it go to voicemail."

"Okay, Dr. Sarah," Madison said.

Sarah smiled at how Madison always called her that. The informal title embossed on her name tag gave clients the feeling she was part of their extended family. Madison used the title with clients all day, every day, and now said it out of habit even when they were alone.

The clinic front door opened and a woman who appeared tired, hungry, and in need of a shower and some clean clothes walked in carrying an unhappy-looking Beagle dog.

"I'm sorry, we're closed," Madison said. "But the twenty-four-hour pet hospital is always open. Would you like me to give you their address?"

The woman teared up and said, "We went for a walk and she stepped on a piece of broken bottle glass in the street. She's been limping ever since and I'm afraid the cut might get infected. Can't you please put some dog salve on her paw, wrap it up and give her some Tramadol for the pain?"

As a veterinarian, Sarah knew that sometimes drug addicts would deliberately harm a dog or cat in hopes of getting their hands on pain pills. One of the warning signs was when a brand-new client came in and asked for a drug by name, one that had opiate-like effects.

She smiled kindly. "Let me take a quick look at her paw."

One glance at the perfectly straight cut on the dog's paw told her it hadn't been cut by bottle glass, which would have created a ragged edge. This wound had been inflicted upon the poor little thing with a razor blade by this criminal woman or an accomplice.

Sarah felt anger in her heart and barely kept herself from yelling at the woman and punching her in the face. She gritted her teeth for a moment, making an effort to remain calm and professional, and then lied. "Yes, we have that medicine in stock. I'll go take a quick X-ray of her paw, bandage her wound and write you a prescription. Please wait here and help yourself to a cup of coffee or a soft drink. I'll only be a few minutes."

The woman handed over the dog and sat down in the reception area, nervously chewing on a fingernail as she glanced out the window. Sarah followed her gaze and noted a man waiting in a dark green parked car. He had a gang tattoo on his face and glanced about as if worried.

She carried the dog into an exam room, closed the door, set her on a table and scratched her behind the ears with one hand while reaching into her pocket for her phone with the other hand.

She sent a text message to her police friend, Sergeant Beth Cushman of the SFPD.

Sarah: *Suspected drug addict deliberately harmed a dog to get pain pills. Currently sitting in my reception area. Accomplice outside in a parked car. What should I do?*

Beth: *Stall for time. I'm on my way.*

Sarah: *Will do. Thanks.*

Sarah sent a similar text to her assistant, Madison, and then used a device to check the dog for a microchip. Yes, the pet was registered to someone living in the Cow Hollow neighborhood. She placed a call.

When a woman answered, Sarah spoke quietly. "Hello, is this Paige?"

"Yes, speaking," Paige said.

"This is Dr. Sarah. I'm a veterinarian here in the city. Is your dog missing?"

"Yes! Did you find Lulu? We've been frantic with worry."

"Please describe her to me."

"She's a full-grown beagle wearing a red collar with a bone-shaped dog tag. My phone number is on the tag."

"She isn't wearing the dog tag right now, but I found your information on her chip. Please confirm your address and driver's license number."

Paige recited the address and number. "Is Lulu okay? May I come and get my baby, *please?*"

"Yes, come to my office and show me your driver's license and I'll release Lulu into your custody."

"Oh my God, thank you so much. Today a dark green car pulled over at our house and a man just reached over the fence, snatched Lulu from the front yard and sped away before we could even blink."

"You might want to let her play in the backyard from now on. This kind of thing is becoming more common every day." Sarah recited her clinic's address and ended the call, then glanced out the window and saw Beth drive up in her unmarked police SUV.

She sent Beth a text: *It's the dark green car with a man in the driver's seat.*

Beth stopped in the street behind the suspect's car, blocking it from backing out of the angled parking spot. There were cars parked on either side, and a light pole in front.

Gotcha.

She turned on her car's blue and red lights and stepped out, wearing her pistol and badge on her belt and carrying a pair of handcuffs in her hand.

She reached into the suspect's open driver door window and quickly pulled the key out of the ignition. The man grabbed her wrist, just as she'd planned. She used her other hand to cuff his wrist to the steering wheel, and wrenched herself free.

In a panic, he frantically reached for her holstered pistol with his left hand, but she took a step back and Tasered him. He shook like a leaf in a storm.

"Have a nice nap, asshat."

Turning toward the clinic, she walked to the front door with a determined stride.

CHAPTER 51

Sarah stepped away from the exam room window, opened the door and looked down the hall toward her reception area.

The nervous female suspect leapt to her feet and glanced out the window.

Beth walked in and presented an intimidating sight to see. Wearing a dark pantsuit, with fiery red short hair, piercing blue eyes, a badge on her belt and a pistol in her hand.

The woman whirled around and ran down the hall.

Sarah stepped into the hallway and closed the door behind her, blocking the woman's path with both fists raised in a Jeet Kune Do stance, ready to fight.

"Stop! You can't come in here," she said. "The only way out is the front door."

Panicked, the woman opened a folding knife and charged straight at Sarah. "You're lying. Get out of my way!"

Sarah felt herself losing her temper. "Is that the knife you used to hurt an innocent dog? I'm going to drop you like a bag of dirt."

Beth appeared in the hallway behind the suspect and yelled, "Police! Lie facedown on the floor! Do it!"

Sarah threw a punch with her left fist, deflecting the woman's knife hand, and then followed up with her right, hitting the woman in the face with a knockout punch. The woman's head snapped back, her feet flew out from under her and she crashed to the floor, hitting the back of her head and lying there groaning in pain.

"Turn over facedown and put your hands behind your head. Do it *now!*" Beth yelled.

The woman didn't move. Sarah held her breath, afraid she'd killed the suspect. She hadn't meant to hit her that hard. What had gotten into her?

Beth kicked the knife away from the woman's hand, grabbed her and flipped her over. "Don't move! You're under arrest for animal abuse and conspiring to obtain a controlled substance by fraud." She pulled the woman's wrists behind the small of her back and slapped on zip-tie handcuffs.

The Beagle barked at them from inside the exam room.

"Thank you, Beth," Sarah said, taking a deep calming breath and letting it out.

"Happy to help, but you looked like you were doing just fine by yourself. Is the dog going to be okay?"

"Yes, her paw will heal up in due time."

"I need to put the suspects in my car. I'll be right back." Beth yanked on the prisoner's biceps, lifting her up.

The woman came to her senses and began crying. "He made me do it."

"Yeah, right," Beth said. She lifted the criminal to her feet, held on to her arm and the back of her belt, and perp-walked her out to the police SUV.

Sarah went into the exam room and quickly treated the dog, putting salve on the cut and wrapping its paw in a bandage.

She carried Lulu up to the reception area and gently set her down in a dog playpen corral. The dog sniffed around and began to chew on a yellow duck squeaky toy.

Madison said, "That's sinking low to hurt a dog so they could get high."

Sarah cursed and looked out the window as Beth shoved the criminal into her SUV's backseat, behind the partition cage.

"I can't believe I punched that woman so hard," Sarah said.

Madison smiled. "You were a badass. She has a black eye."

Sarah thought to herself that she'd done it before and could do it again, but felt surprised at how she'd taken the law into her own hands. She hadn't just defended herself, she'd delivered a punishing blow meant to deliver a message.

Beth came back into the clinic. "Sarah, can you send me the video?" She pointed at a camera up in the corner.

"Yes, I'll send it right now. Thanks again for getting here so fast."

Beth nodded. "You can always contact me. If I can't get here quick I'll send a uniformed cop."

"I appreciate that, Beth. I know as a homicide detective, this isn't your typical work."

Beth nodded. "A cop is a cop. You're my friend and I'm always ready to help you."

Sarah smiled at her friend. "Were you home, off duty?"

"Yes, but Kyle is over at a friend's house right now." Beth gestured at the Beagle. "Is that their dog, or did they steal it?"

"They stole her. They're dognappers. Luckily, she was chipped."

"Dogs are only considered to be low-value property in the state of California, but I'll add petty theft to the crimes I'm going to charge them with."

"The real owner will be here soon."

"Well, that'll be a happy reunion."

As if on cue, the clinic door burst open and a middle-aged woman came inside. She took one look at the dog and cried out, "Lulu!"

The Beagle barked happily, stood on her hind legs and put her front paws on the top of the gate to the pen, wagging her tail.

"What did they do to your foot, sweetie?"

Sarah walked over and shook the woman's hand. "I'm Dr. Sarah, and this is Detective Cushman. You must be Paige."

Paige cried as Sarah took a photo of her driver's license and allowed her to pick up her dog and hold her.

Beth said, "It would help us prosecute the criminals if you'd take a moment to file a formal complaint."

"Yes, please. I want them to go to jail," Paige said.

As Beth took her statement, asking questions and tapping on her

236

phone, Sarah felt her racing heart begin to slow down. She realized this was a less dangerous example of the kind of thing Jake had always been fighting against. He protected innocents from being harmed by criminals. If these two people would kidnap dogs from loving families and harm them to feed their out of control addiction, what worse things might they do next? Kidnap a child? Rob a bank? Commit murder? They belonged in prison.

Sarah thought of how Beth was so dedicated to making a positive difference in her community. Beth's husband had left her because she worked too many hours. Sarah could understand his selfish needs, but she wouldn't leave Jake. The good-hearted bad boy meant too much to her. And Cody too—especially Cody.

It was all becoming clear to her now. Sarah felt like she finally understood Jake. She got it. He would get angry at the injustice and feel like he had to do something.

She checked her phone and saw that he'd been trying to get in touch. As she thought about Jake and Cody, they drove up in the Jeep, parked, and walked toward her door.

CHAPTER 52

Jake saw his Italian friend, Beppe, sitting in the dark sedan and watching Sarah's clinic.

Beppe waved Jake over and said, "There's a cop inside. I can see Sarah and she's okay. So far, no danger from the cartel. It's just some young idiots getting arrested."

"Thanks, I'll go find out what's happening," Jake said.

Beth walked out of Sarah's clinic and Jake stopped to talk with her.

"Be friends, Cody," he said.

Cody went to Beth and pressed against her. Beth patted Cody on the head, and told Jake what had happened.

Sarah came outside and hugged Jake.

"Are you okay?" Jake asked.

"Yes, other than sore knuckles from punching a criminal in the face." Sarah held up her hand to show him.

Cody pressed against Sarah, and she went down on one knee and hugged him. Cody sniffed her knuckles and gave them a medicinal lick.

Jake said, "We just got home from San Diego after cruising up the coast with Terrell. We were going to surprise you."

Sarah stood up. "Did Terrell enjoy the boat trip? Alicia is so worried about him."

Jake nodded. "It was the perfect therapy for his injuries—both physical and emotional."

As everyone talked in front of the clinic, a teenaged Latina woman walked past on the sidewalk across the street, pushing a baby stroller. She glanced over at them and stopped, a frightened look on her face.

Cody alerted to the stroller, his nose up and twitching, his tail down. He barked several times in warning.

Jake felt the hair on the back of his neck stand up. The woman appeared to be acting under duress. *Did the baby stroller contain a bomb?*

He drew his pistol and yelled, "Get behind my armored Jeep! Do it now!"

Beth stared at him in surprise and drew her pistol.

Jake, Cody and Sarah moved toward the Jeep.

Beth stood her ground. "Police! This is a crime scene. Move along."

Across the street, a man with a scar on the left side of his face appeared out of a recessed doorway and walked to the woman. When he passed the stroller, he reached in and removed a submachine gun pistol, raising it and opening fire.

Abandoning the stroller, the young woman sprinted down the street to an alley and disappeared.

Jake said, "Cody, on me." He grabbed Sarah's arm and pulled her behind the Jeep.

Cody followed Jake and stood close to Sarah, bright eyes glancing back and forth for anyone he might have to bite.

Several bullets hit the Jeep, along with the cars parked on either side. A nearby store window shattered.

Beth ducked behind the front of the Jeep and returned fire over the hood, wounding the perpetrator. The man dropped his weapon and fell to the pavement, bleeding. Beth ran to him, kicked the weapon away and placed handcuffs on his wrists and ankles.

Jake opened the Jeep and grabbed the Taser shotgun. "Cody, get in the car. You too, Sarah. Get in and close the door."

Sarah shook her head. "No. I'm going into my office. I'll lock the door and protect Madison."

"Dammit, Sarah."

As Sarah opened the clinic door, a car drove up and screeched to a stop. A woman with chopped-off black hair jumped out and ran at Sarah with a knife in her hand.

The woman yelled, "Remember me, bitch?"

Sarah tried to get inside the clinic and lock the door, but Angel ran too fast. Sarah reached into her purse and drew a pocket-sized Seecamp .32-caliber that was only four inches long and loaded with jacketed hollow-point rounds. Aiming the pistol at Angel, Sarah had only a few seconds to pull the trigger or else get stabbed.

A teenaged boy stepped out of the car and aimed a pistol at Jake and Cody but then hesitated, gazing at the dog with a conflicted look on his face.

Jake felt déjà vu and for a split second had a flashback to when he'd shot a boy in combat in the Middle East. The young man had driven up in a junker car and shot the canteen right out of Terrell's hand as he was taking a drink. Jake had shot and killed the terrorist, and then the young man's bomb vest had blown up. Luckily the car packed full of IEDs hadn't detonated. Jake had only been nineteen at the time, and while he'd saved a lot of lives, he still had nightmares about the teenager he'd killed.

Cody snarled and ran at Angel, trying to bite down on her knife hand and defend Sarah. Angel dodged his teeth and raised her knife, preparing to bring it down on the dog. Jake fired the Taser shotgun at Angel, even though the boy was aiming a pistol at him.

The spinning round punched Angel on the chest and hooked onto her clothing, shocking her with hundreds of volts. She tripped and fell to the sidewalk, writhing in pain and convulsing, arms and legs flailing.

Sarah kept her pistol aimed at Angel. "Shoot her again, Jake. Or else I might have to."

Jake shot the boy instead.

The young man dropped to the pavement, letting go of the pistol and rolling around as his body jerked in spasms. Jake then turned and shot Angel again to prevent Sarah from pulling the trigger. He reached into his Jeep and handed some thick plastic zip ties to her.

"When she stops twitching, cuff her hands and feet."

Sarah nodded and got to work. "My pleasure."

Jake ran to the boy and placed zip ties on him before the shock wore off.

Beth walked up. "Damn, that attack happened fast."

"I almost shot and killed her," Sarah said, her face pale.

Jake put the boy over his shoulder, carried him to Beth and set him down on the sidewalk next to Angel.

Beth said, "Jake, the man I wounded wants to talk to you. He asked for you by name." She gave him a questioning look.

"First I want this psycho locked in your car's backseat cage," Jake said, pointing at Angel. He slung the shotgun across his back using the attached leather strap.

Angel lay on her back, still groggy. Beth searched her and found a burner phone. She grabbed her by the armpits, and Jake grabbed her ankles. They carried her to the police SUV and loaded her into the backseat.

Angel began to come out of her fog, and she cursed at Jake in Spanish, her words slurred.

Jake said, "Do you want another five hundred volts? I have lots of rounds."

That shut her up for a moment. Beth slammed the door, locking the woman inside. The man who'd fired a rifle at them lay on the street, wearing handcuffs.

Jake approached him. "You look familiar. What did you want to say to me?"

"My name is Enrique, and I'll tell you everything about Rojo's cartel, in exchange for one small favor."

Jake stared at him without mercy. "What favor?"

"Let the boy go. Tomás is a good kid who was corrupted by his uncle. Let him go and I'll be your star witness, even if it kills me."

"Let me bring him to you," Jake said. He walked over to the Jeep, picked up Tomás and carried him to Beth's SUV.

Beth held up her hand. "Wait a minute, Jake."

"Let's hear them out, Beth," Jake said.

He sat the boy on the pavement next to Enrique, "Your name is Tomás?"

"Sí, señor," Tomás said.

"Why didn't you fire your pistol?"

"I can't harm a dog. My heart won't let me," Tomás said.

Jake glanced at Enrique and the man nodded in affirmation.

"But you could have shot me," Jake said.

Tomás shook his head. "If I shot you, the dog would attack me, and then I'd have to shoot it too."

Jake felt conflicted about what to do with the kid.

CHAPTER 53

Jake said, "Tomás, if I let you go, you'd have to promise me you'll stay far away from the narcos."

Enrique spoke up. "He can get a job at my brother's restaurant." He turned to Tomás and said, "You met José when we had dinner there. Tell him what happened and that I sent you."

Tomás stared at Enrique for a moment in surprise and then nodded his agreement.

Jake pressed Enrique for more. "Give me your best intel about Rojo first, as a show of good faith. Where is the hard drive with the database? You give me that, or you get nothing but pain." He held out his phone, taking video.

Enrique got a tortured look on his face. "I don't know, but I'll tell you something else that will make Rojo go insane with rage. He bought an oil company pipeline drill that can bore a tunnel and lay pipe. It could quickly drill dozens or even hundreds of pipelines under the border."

Jake felt his jaw drop. "Where is this pipeline drill located right now? Tell me."

Enrique took a deep breath and let it out. "It's hidden in an empty factory building near the border." He recited the address.

Jake sent the video to Agent McKay in D.C.

"Thank you, Enrique. We have a deal," he said. He used his knife to cut the zip ties off Tomás.

Enrique said, "Tomás, take the money from my wallet, get on Amtrak to San Diego and then walk across the border. Go straight to José's restaurant."

Jake gloved up and patted Enrique down, finding his wallet and a cheap phone. He gave the money to Tomás.

"Tomás, I'm letting you go because you refused to shoot my dog. The world needs men like you to do the right thing."

Tomás stood up straighter. "I've learned my lesson. I promise I'll work at the restaurant and do my best to be a good man."

Enrique nodded sadly, as if proud of the boy, but knowing he'd never see him again. "God bless you, Tomás. Adiós."

"Adiós, Enrique," Tomás said, fighting back tears.

Jake pointed at the corner. "Jog to that street, turn right and hail a cab to take you to the Amtrak station. Go on!"

Tomás jogged to the corner. He took a long look back, and Cody woofed at him as if urging him on. He went around the corner and disappeared from sight.

Beth scowled at Jake. "Don't ever interfere with one of my arrests again."

Jake held out his hand and gave her the wallet and phone. "We traded Tomás for the pipeline drill. He wasn't eighteen anyway, so you couldn't charge him as an adult. He'd have made bail from juvenile hall in an hour."

"Oh, really? And who would've bailed him out?"

"I would have," Jake said.

Beth let out an exasperated breath. "Try to make yourself useful and help me get Enrique into the back seat."

They loaded Enrique into the car, and Angel sneered at Beth. "I wasn't expecting you to be here, but I have a surprise for you. You think you've won? No, we've kidnapped your son. You lose."

Beth's pale cheeks flushed. She cursed at Angel and slammed the door closed. Pulling out her phone, she tapped an icon to call Kyle and received no answer. Next, she called her roommate and sitter, Zoey.

Zoey said, "I was just about to call you. Kyle went to Tyler's house to play video games, but he's late coming home and isn't answering his phone."

Police cars arrived and uniformed officers ran toward Beth.

Jake opened the door to Beth's SUV and aimed his pistol at Angel. "How did you even know about Beth and Kyle?"

"Tomás found a news story online about Kyle flying a swarm of drones. You and Beth were featured in the story." She laughed.

Jake said, "Tell me where you took Kyle, or I'll shoot you in the head."

Angel scoffed. "You're too *noble* to kill a woman. And the child is hidden where you'll never find him. Lucky for you we didn't find Sarah's last name and address until just now or I'd have cut off her ears."

Jake clenched his jaw and pressed the barrel of his pistol against her forehead. His breathing became ragged and he swallowed hard.

Angel leaned forward against his pistol, her eyes glinting. "Go ahead and shoot me. I want to be the first dead woman haunting your conscience. Rojo will take good care of my family, and musicians will sing *narcocorrido* ballads about my death." She cursed at him in Spanish.

Jake blew out a breath, holstered his pistol and forced himself to remain calm. He studied her for clues, noticing her dirt-encrusted boots. "What's this on your shoes?" He yanked off one of her boots and examined the fresh dirt and flower petals.

The woman fell silent, staring at him with hatred.

Jake slammed the door shut and held out the boot toward Beth. "I know a forensic botanist, and I'm going to ask her to examine this."

Tech Officer Roxanne Poole walked up to them. A uniformed cop with brunette hair and determined brown eyes, she wore tortoise shell style glasses and was known for being curious about anything to do with science.

Overhearing Jake, she used one finger to push her glasses farther up her nose. "Seriously? A forensic botanist? I'm going with you."

"All right, let's go. Beth, if we find out anything, you'll be the first to know," Jake said.

Beth clenched and unclenched her fists. "Thank you. I'll call Tyler's mother and send cops to their house." She put her hand on the butt of her pistol. Her left eye twitched with a nervous tic as she hyperventilated.

A male cop named Wilson stood listening, stone-faced. "We'll get everybody in the department working on finding Kyle, stat."

Beth grabbed the radio and called in the kidnapping of a police officer's child. In moments, every cop in the city would be laser-focused on solving this one crime.

Jake and Cody ran to the Jeep, followed by Roxanne. Jake stopped to hug Sarah.

"Come with us," he said.

Sarah shook her head. "No, I have to get Madison home safe. She's scared to death right now."

"All right, I have to go help find Kyle," Jake said. He glanced over at his Italian friend.

The man was being questioned by a police officer and showing his ID. He caught Jake's eye and tilted his head toward the other cops.

Jake turned to one of the uniformed officers he knew. "Wilson, can you assist Sarah? She was targeted by one of the perps."

Wilson nodded. "Young lady, you are now under the protection of the SFPD."

Sarah smiled at the older man with flecks of gray in his hair and laugh lines near his eyes and mouth. "I feel safer already," she said.

Jake shook hands with Wilson, climbed into the Jeep along with Cody and Roxanne, and drove away. As he drove, he grabbed his phone and scrolled through the contacts to find Professor Hannah Haskett. He called the forensic botanist he'd once met at a fundraising dinner, and put the call on speaker. "Hannah, it's Jake Wolfe, formerly a news photographer. Do you remember meeting me at that fundraising event for the Make-A-Wish Foundation? We talked about your forensic botany work."

"Yes, Jake. If this is about botany, I have a minute to talk. If it's a ploy to ask me out to coffee, I'm happily married, so I'll just say no and save us both time."

Jake smiled at how some women were propositioned quite often and thought every friendly man wanted to get them into bed. They were probably right ninety percent of the time.

"It's only about botany, and you might help find a kidnapped child. I have a female police officer with me. Can we please have a few minutes of your valuable time?"

She paused a moment. "A kidnapped child? Please come to my office at once!"

"On our way now. Be there soon."

Jake switched on the Jeep's police lights and siren and turned to Roxanne. "You're a cop, so I can use these now, right?"

Roxanne stared at him. "Why ask? You're already doing it."

Jake nodded. McKay's little-known federal agency had given him the vehicle equipped with all kinds of technology. He wasn't sure how much he could say about it to Rox, so he didn't say anything.

CHAPTER 54

Arriving at Hannah's lab in record time, Jake went inside and handed over the suspect's boot.

Hannah went right to work. She scraped off a specimen of flowers and dirt and gazed at it under a high-tech microscope that looked to Jake as if it was the latest and greatest.

She lectured him the way a professor would teach a class of students. "These flower petals come from a Peggy Martin Rose, a thornless climbing rose that's great for attracting bees."

"Where can I find them?" Jake asked.

"It's also known as the Hurricane Katrina Rose, an antique flower of unknown origin that was growing in New Orleans resident Peggy Martin's garden when Hurricane Katrina hit. The plant withstood hundred-and-fifty-mile-per-hour winds, being submerged in twenty feet of saltwater for more than two weeks, and the scorching heat that followed, and it still survived. It's a plant that inspired folks in the south to stay strong and carry on."

"*Where* do they grow? Remember, a child's life is at stake," Jake said.

She nodded. "The regular kind with dark pink flowers are popular and grow in lots of places."

"But these are orange petals."

"Correct. This is a very rare hybrid invented by Dr. Emily

Lindstadt, a local horticulturist. She's a modern-day Luther Burbank. Nobody else has any of these rose plants, only her."

Roxanne said, "Please give us the *address*, ma'am. It's urgent."

Hannah said, "Yes, of course. You'll only find these orange roses on Dr. Lindstadt's wooded property, adjacent to her home. I have her address on my phone." She reached into her jacket pocket, pulled out her phone, tapped the screen and then held the device out toward Roxanne, who was closer to her.

Roxanne took a picture and then quickly tapped the address into her own phone and texted it to Jake, along with the photo.

Jake said, "Thank you, Hannah. I'm sorry we pushed so hard for information, but this could save a child's life. Your assistance has been invaluable."

"I'm glad I could help. Are you working for the police now, Jake?"

Jake headed for the door. "I often volunteer to have Cody work as a search and rescue dog," he said over his shoulder.

Cody woofed in agreement as he followed Jake.

Hannah gazed at the dog. "A botanist and a search dog is a highly sound combination."

Jake reached the door. "Thanks again."

"Good luck," Hannah said.

Rox asked, "Hannah, could I buy you lunch one day soon and hear your stories about forensic botany?"

"Yes, I'd enjoy that," Hannah said.

Jake ran out of the lab with Cody and Roxanne following close behind him.

He drove at high speed to the address and pulled up in front of Dr. Lindstadt's large home and grounds, leaving his police lights flashing behind the Jeep's front grille. Everyone jumped out of the car and Jake grabbed the Taser pump shotgun from the cargo area, along with extra rounds.

He took off running toward the tall greenhouse and wooded acres in back that were visible from the street.

Roxanne chased after him. "I'll cover your six."

Jake said, "Cody, *search*. Find the *hostage*."

Cody ran free, off leash. He raised his nose high, tasting the air, then sniffed near the ground as he trotted purposefully toward the home, a dog on a mission. He veered around the side of the house and across a lawn, heading for the greenhouse in back.

Jake and Roxanne made eye contact, nodded at each other and followed closely behind Cody, working as an impromptu team. Jake's respect for Roxanne's skills grew every time they met.

Cody went to the greenhouse door and pawed at it. Jake opened the door and held his shotgun up and ready to fire. Cody went inside and moved faster now, his nostrils flaring. Jake was right behind him, ready to shoot anyone who threatened his dog.

They rushed though the vast greenhouse and Cody went out the other side. The dog took off following a scent trail into the wooded acres of property behind the home.

Kyle Cushman woke up lying on his back in a dark, enclosed place. Next to him, a glow-stick gave off an eerie green light. He felt disoriented and suddenly realized he was trapped inside a giant fish tank without any water. The kind of large aquarium he'd once seen in a restaurant. He guessed it was around six feet long, two feet wide and four feet tall. Outside of the thick clear acrylic walls, everything appeared to be pitch black. In a panic, he found a small flashlight near the glow-stick and turned it on.

What he saw made his mouth open in shock, but no words came out. Gooseflesh raced up his arms and he shivered in fear.

I'm buried alive?

The entire oblong aquarium was surrounded by freshly dug earth. Above his head was a narrow air tube leading upward into the dirt. A slight breath of fresh air came in from the tube. Near the glow stick, on the floor of the small prison cell, he noted a single bottle of water, a printed note, and a digital timer. The note read: *How long will you last after your water runs out?* The digital timer counted down the time. He'd been buried for over an hour already.

The second line of the note read: *Nobody can hear you scream.*

He screamed anyway, at the top of his lungs. He couldn't help himself.

Afterward, when his heart stopped racing as if it might burst, he made an effort to control his breathing and avoid using up all the oxygen while he tried to brainstorm a way to survive.

Think think think!

Maybe he could break a wall and dig his way upward like a mole. He lay on his back and kicked at a side panel but found it to be hard as a rock. That was probably better than having the pile of earth crush and smother him.

Jake ran after his dog through the woods with his shotgun up. They came to a small clearing with a coffin-sized patch of earth that looked like a freshly dug and refilled grave.

A man with dark hair and a gold front tooth sat on a log holding a cheap phone, as if waiting for orders. He startled and jumped to his feet in surprise. When he turned to run, Jake shot him in the back with the Taser shotgun, knocking him facedown and senseless. Jake used two zip ties to bind the man's hands behind his back and then bind his ankles.

Cody stood next to the fresh patch of dirt and sniffed at a tube sticking out of the ground. He whined, pawing the fresh soil.

Jake put his ear to the tube and heard what sounded like sobbing. He felt his pulse increase as he called 911, and sent texts to Beth and Terrell.

His guess was, the cartel gang soldier he'd subdued had been standing by to dig up the prisoner and exchange him for the hard drive, or to block the air tube and let him choke to death.

Roxanne ran up. "What have we got?"

Jake pointed at the stunned suspect. "Cuff him. I only had zip ties."

Roxanne handcuffed the stunned man's hands with metal police cuffs and used her phone to take video for evidence.

Jake saw a shovel on the ground with fresh earth on its blade. He grabbed it and began furiously digging up the grave.

Police sirens filled the air, getting closer and louder.

Pausing for a moment, Jake yelled at the tube. "Kyle? If you can hear me, put your mouth near the tube and take deep breaths. Hang on, we're going to get you out of there."

Cody barked at the tube several times and pawed at the dirt.

CHAPTER 55

Kyle could barely hear some sounds through the tube, as if an echo coming from far away. Did he hear a dog barking?

He yelled at the tube opening. "Help! I'm buried alive! Please get me out of here!"

Had somebody said to take air from the tube?

He put his mouth onto the opening and inhaled hard. Sweet air filled his lungs and fed his brain and body. He repeated the process several times.

"Please, God, get me out of here and I swear I'll never again sneak out my window and go watch baseball games."

He sobbed quietly, sorry for all he had put his mother through. Would he ever see her again? Feel her strong arms around him? Curl up on the couch to eat pizza and watch television together, and fall asleep by her side?

A shovel scraped against the Plexiglass lid of the tank, and sunlight shone in. A golden dog looked over the edge of the hole and barked, as if giving orders.

A tall, muscular man stood over the tank with one foot on either side. He continued to shovel off the earth with his powerful arms, like an unstoppable machine, until the entire lid was uncovered.

Kyle saw Jake Wolfe put both hands under the lip of the cover and lift it like the lid of a coffin.

Fresh air rushed into the crypt, and Kyle cried in relief. "Jake and Cody! Thank God!"

Jake held the cover open with his left hand and reached out to Kyle with his right. "Grab onto my wrist, little bro."

Kyle grabbed on tight. Jake did the same and pulled Kyle up and out of the tank, hoisting the boy into the air and onto solid ground as if he weighed nothing.

Kyle stood and looked around at his surroundings. They were in the woods? He glanced down and realized the tank had only been buried a few feet deep. Yet, it'd seemed like the center of the earth.

A cop Kyle knew named Roxanne said, "Kyle, your mother is on her way here right now."

Cody pressed his head against Kyle's stomach, nodding and wagging his tail.

Jake said, "Cody, be friends. Comfort."

Overcome with relief, Kyle dropped to his knees, hugged the dog and cried, his tears spilling onto Cody's golden fur.

Jake put his hand on the boy's shoulder. "You were brave, Kyle. Try to inspire other young people to have courage in the face of adversity. It's a tough world out there, and your peer group could benefit from your leadership. Do you understand me, young man?"

Kyle stood up straight and nodded at Jake, wiping his wet eyes on his sleeve. "Yes, I'll do my best."

Jake shook his hand, hoping to give the boy a positive mission and goal to focus on, instead of the negativity and victimhood of his terrible ordeal. It was something his sister the psychiatrist had suggested he do with fellow combat veterans who had frightening memories and lingering injuries.

Beth Cushman roared up in her police SUV, driving across the grass past the greenhouse and four-wheeling it into the woods. Skidding to a stop, she jumped out of her car and ran to her son, lifted him off his feet and held on tight. Kyle wept on his mother's shoulder.

Jake went down on one knee and scratched Cody behind his ears. "You did good, Cody. Look at that."

After a long and emotional hug, Beth turned to Cody and spoke over Kyle's shoulder. "You're a good dog."

Cody wagged his tail.

"And what am I, chopped liver?" Jake asked, with a grin.

Cody panted loudly, Ha-Ha-Ha.

Jake smiled at his dog. "Oh, fine, I see how it is, Cody. Laugh it up, fur face."

Cody gave him a retriever dog's smile.

Beth hugged Kyle again, as if she was afraid to let go.

Roxanne moved cautiously toward Cody, looking at Jake with questioning eyes.

Jake nodded at her. "Cody, be friends with Rox."

Roxanne bravely went down on one knee to pet the dog. "I'm so proud of you, Cody."

Jake raised his eyebrows. This was a first. Roxanne was usually very cautious around Cody. She was so smart, she understood he was a fellow genius and not a normal canine in any way, shape or form.

Roxanne held out her hand, and Cody placed his paw there so she could give it a shake. He then pressed against her shoulder, and she gave him a tentative scratch behind his ears. Cody happily wagged his tail.

Jake reached into a jacket pocket, opened a zip-top bag and held out a dog biscuit to Roxanne. "Hold this in your open palm, just like I'm doing."

Roxanne took the biscuit and held it out to Cody. The dog gently nuzzled her hand, lapped up the biscuit and chomped it down.

Roxanne stood up. "I never thought I'd be friends with an animal who has PTSD."

Jake nodded. "And besides being friends with me, you've got Cody too."

She smiled and shook her head. "You're a wild wolf animal, huh?"

"Wild and free, unlike so many folks," Jake said.

"Do you think Cody might help me get some DNA from that dirtbag?" Roxanne asked.

"How can he help?"

"I don't have a swab kit with me, but if the suspect pees his pants, it's a voluntary donation of a urine sample."

Jake smiled. "Easy peasy." He whispered commands to Cody and gave him hand signals. The two of them ran toward the handcuffed suspect, who had recovered from the Taser round.

Jake pulled his KA-BAR knife with the black blade and gold lettering that read "Operation Enduring Freedom." Holding the blade out in front of the man's face, he yelled, "Tell us who you're working for!"

Cody snarled at the man's crotch, and snapped his jaws as if he was going to surgically remove body parts.

The man screamed, "Get the dog away from me!" A wet stain appeared on the crotch of his pants.

Jake glanced at Roxanne, who nodded in thanks. He watched Beth and Kyle holding onto each other. His heart felt conflicted—happy the mother and son were reunited, but angry that anyone would kidnap an innocent child. He knew the cartels often kidnapped people, and that it was a profitable business for them. Steal a human being and sell him or her back to their family for huge money.

This time, however, they wanted the database. No way. He was determined to make sure they never got their hands on it again, no matter what kind of hell he might have to go through to get it. He was now on a quest.

The handcuffed man said, "I work for Rojo. He'll kill you soon." He spat on the ground.

Jake held out the large knife blade with the point near the man's right nostril. "Small world. I've killed several of Rojo's men. Care to make the list? Go ahead, spit again. Spit at my dog. I want you to."

Cody moved closer, letting out a low snarl, his lips curled to display sharp teeth.

The man glanced at the dog, then closed his eyes and held still.

Roxanne cleared her throat, her demeanor businesslike,

interrupting Jake. "Listen carefully," she told the suspect. "I can offer you protective immunity, but you have to start talking right now and not stop until you tell us *everything*. Otherwise you'll go into the jail's general population, and tonight somebody from a rival cartel will stick a shiv in your neck."

Opening his eyes, the man cursed at Roxanne and shook his head. "It would be better to die in a fight than be tortured slowly by *Ángel de la Muerte*," he said.

Roxanne stared him down. "That's fine with me. I'd be happy to see you dead. Hopefully there'll be a prison video of your murder, so I can post it on the internet for everyone to laugh at."

Jake raised his eyebrows. This was a fierce side of Rox he hadn't seen. The kidnapping of a fellow cop's child had brought out her killer instinct.

Roxanne kept arguing and wore the criminal down. He relented and began talking about how Rojo had forced him to do it. He'd had no choice.

Roxanne shook her head. "That's what every criminal says. Give me details to prove what you're saying is true." She wore a small body camera and recorded him on video.

Jake heard a car engine and turned to see Wilson drive up and get out of his black-and-white car. Jake waved the uniformed officer toward himself.

Wilson said, "We gave your veterinarian friends police escorts and they're both safe at home now."

"Thanks, Wilson. I'm glad you're here. Roxanne could use backup and an official witness while she interviews this suspect."

"I'm always happy to help *Box of Rox*," Wilson said, with a grin.

Jake smiled at hearing the SFPD's unofficial term of endearment for Rox, one of the smartest cops in the city, who was admired by all.

Wilson put his hand on the pistol at his belt and moved toward the suspect with an exaggerated swagger, glaring at him as if he might shoot him for practice if he didn't show respect to Roxanne, his favorite cop.

Jake led Cody to the Jeep and thought about how he absolutely had to put Rojo out of business. The man was spreading a crime wave across the entire west coast of the United States. He was so bold he'd kidnapped a homicide detective's child. Once he had the database, he'd know the home address of every law enforcement officer in the USA.

There was no way that could be allowed to happen. But how could he get close to the secretive criminal?

He sent a text to McKay on his encrypted phone: *If you've authorized a mission against Rojo as an HVT, assign me to him, right now. I'll take him down. Anytime, anyplace, any way. Otherwise I'll go after him alone, on my own, off the books.*

McKay didn't reply immediately.

Jake cursed, put his phone away and began thinking of plans to search and destroy every branch of Rojo's cartel.

CHAPTER 56

As the sun set, Jake drove to Pier 39 and boarded the *Far Niente*. He locked the sliding door, turned off the lights and fell into bed.

Cody jumped onto Jake's bed, turned around three times, lay down and let out a sigh.

Jake closed his eyes. A light wind blew through the harbor, seabirds called, small waves lapped against the hull and he felt the boat rock gently beneath him.

They slept like two exhausted and lost souls who appreciated feeling the movement of Mother Ocean rocking them to sleep.

At sunrise, they got up and went for a walk. Jake bought a plain black coffee from a food cart, along with two breakfast sausage patties for his dog. Cody chomped the sausage and licked his snout.

The tourists were out in force, so Jake drove to Aquatic Park, the urban beach across from Ghirardelli Square. The two war veterans walked on the sand at the water's edge, following the shoreline of the cove. Jake deep in thought, Cody sniffing at various pieces of driftwood the tide had brought in.

Jake studied Greek philosophy in his spare time, and had read the ideas of Diogenes. Two thousand years ago, the cynic had written, "*Solvitur ambulando*—It is solved by walking."

Jake agreed with the claim. In his experience, many problems could be solved by spending time in mindful thought while walking —preferably walking a dog near water or in a forest.

They came upon a torn piece of netting the size of a garage door, and Jake stopped to gather it up into a ball. He belonged to a local NOAA community cleanup group. This netting could trap and kill air-breathing organisms such as sea turtles, which are protected under the Endangered Species Act.

As he deposited the balled-up netting next to a trash bin, his phone buzzed with a call from McKay.

"Good morning," Jake said.

McKay replied, "Morning. Enrique talked to the police and confirmed what Olivia told you. The package is a hard drive containing the names, home addresses, credit reports and medical records of every law enforcement official in the United States."

Jake cursed. "How is that even possible?"

"Somebody may have hacked multiple databases," McKay said. "We're looking into it."

"Why do they want credit reports and medical records?"

"If someone is deep in debt or has crippling medical bills, they're in a desperate situation and easier to bribe."

"Did he say where to find this hard drive?"

"No—only that Rojo will kill to get it back."

"I'm going to find it before he does," Jake said.

"I called to ask if you'd begin searching for it full-time, seven days a week."

"Yes. I'll dedicate every waking hour from now on to finding the damned thing," Jake said.

"Thank you, Jake. I'll share intel as it becomes available. Carry on." McKay ended the call.

As Jake continued walking, he asked himself, "Who would know how to track down the source of an evil hacker's dream database?"

An idea came to him, and he sent a text to Roxanne Poole.

Jake: *Hey, Rox. Can I get your expert opinion on something?*

Roxanne texted in reply: *Unsubscribe.*

Jake smiled. Rox was gifted and she always gave him a ton of grief, but not in a flirty way, just as a colleague. He valued her friendship and appreciated her sense of humor.

Jake: *Cody wants to know if you'd help him solve a mystery.*

Roxanne: *Anything for Cody, but he has to buy me a coffee. I've only had five so far this morning.*

Jake: *Only five? Cody would be happy to buy number six. What time is convenient?*

Roxanne: *Right now works. I need caffeine, stat. Where do you want to meet?*

Jake: *Ladies' choice. We'll come to you.*

Roxanne: *I'm in the Richmond district at the moment, so I'll take a ten-seven at Home Café on Clement Street.*

Jake: *Cody says, 'Okay-woof.'*

He and Cody ran to the Jeep, hopping in and driving to the coffee shop as fast as possible without causing an accident. A passing cop waved, recognizing the Jeep and allowing Jake to break the speed limit.

Jake returned the wave to his client. He did pro bono lawyer work for most of the SFPD officers nowadays. They weren't going to pull over their cost-free lawyer and write him a ticket. Besides that, every cop now knew Jake and Cody had found and rescued Detective Beth Cushman's kidnapped son, Kyle. Rox had texted the video to a few people who quickly shared it, and now every cop had it on their phone.

Jake arrived at the neighborhood known as Little Russia. It had been settled by Russian immigrants in the 1920s, and their cultural influence was still noticeable to him when he passed by the Russian Orthodox Church featuring five onion domes covered in twenty-four-carat gold leaf.

These days the neighborhood included a diverse mix of all kinds of people. Every variety of restaurant you could think of was there too, offering food from numerous countries around the world.

Parking near Home Café, he dressed Cody in a service dog vest, put him on a leash and went inside. "Be friends, Cody. Off duty."

Cody relaxed and wagged his tail, sniffing the air and smelling the aromas of various foods he would be happy to try.

A cheerful barista called out to them. "Welcome home! How are you doing today?"

Jake smiled, surprised at the lively greeting. "I'm good, thanks." He saw Roxanne standing at the register and joined her. "Our orders are together," he said to the cashier, paying for Roxanne's drink and ordering a cup of plain black drip coffee for himself.

They sat at a table decorated with a four-by-six-inch mini chalkboard that read, "Enjoy each other's company. No laptops here please. Thanks."

Jake nodded in approval. He glanced at Roxanne's coffee cup with its foamed milk, rainbow swirls and candy sprinkles on top. "What kind of coffee is that?" he asked.

She smiled. "It's a birthday cake rainbow vanilla latte. You should try one."

"I'll pass," he said with a laugh and took a sip of his black coffee, glancing out the window to check the street for any potential threats.

Cody watched him with bright eyes.

As Jake looked for danger, he thought of how Roxanne's life might become like his if he got her involved with Agent McKay.

An Asian woman walked past, wearing plenty of makeup and a bright blue wig with straight bangs. She smiled happily as she passed their table on her way out and said, "Cute dog."

Jake thought she was doing a pretty good Katy Perry imitation at this early hour. Maybe she'd been up all night drinking and dancing at clubs. "Thanks," he said, realizing that if he wasn't dating Sarah, he might have replied, "My dog thinks you're cute too."

Cody gave her a toothy grin.

A couple sat next to them and placed their order on the table. Cappuccinos with whimsical designs on top, one the face of a cute cat and the other a smiling dog—and plates of avocado toast sprinkled with bacon crumbles.

Cody sniffed at the bacon, and Jake said, "No, Cody. Lie down." Cody gave one last longing look at the food, ducked under the table and lay at Jake's feet.

Roxanne said, "This place is known for their fun coffee drinks and unusual toast toppings."

"That's probably why I've never been here," Jake said with a jaded smile. "What's your favorite, uh, toast?" He glanced up at the wall menu in doubt, as if it was written in hieroglyphics.

"I like their pesto toast with slices of chicken meatballs, and I add a fried egg on top," she said.

He shrugged. "Sure, why not? I'll eat damn near anything. Add another slice of bread and you have a sandwich—my favorite meal. And Cody is always interested in a side order of meatballs."

Cody wagged his tail and it thumped on the floor, thump-thump-thump. Roxanne leaned over to her right and smiled at the dog. It occurred to Jake this meeting was starting to feel like a coffee date. He didn't want to complicate his friendship with Rox, so he got down to business. "Okay, so I was really hoping your amazing mind could solve a puzzle for me."

"Crossword puzzle?" she asked with a grin, taking a sip of coffee.

He lowered his voice. "It's a question about computer hacking by … criminal groups." He looked around. "Actually, why don't we go outside and sit at one of those tables on the sidewalk?"

Roxanne nodded, appearing curious. "Sure, let's go."

CHAPTER 57

They took their coffees and sat at one of the tiny outdoor tables. Cody sat on the sidewalk next to Jake's chair. There weren't any other people around to hear them talk.

Once seated, Jake set his phone on the table and tapped the screen. It emitted a hissing sound along with projecting a green grid light pattern that quickly disappeared.

Roxanne stared at the phone for a moment in surprise. "How did you get your hands on that new privacy technology? Only top-level federal agencies have access at this time."

Jake ignored the question and asked in a low voice, "How would a terrorist hacker go about finding the name, home address, credit report and medical records of every law enforcement officer in America?"

She peered at him, took her glasses off, polished them with a napkin and put them back on. "Every single LEO in the USA? That's a frightening thought. It might be possible if a talented hacker gained access to a city's police computer system, which includes data trails to other agencies, such as Homeland and the FBI."

"What would be an example of a vulnerable computer? How locked down are yours at the SFPD?"

She stared at him, her face revealing the paranoia felt by all network security officers who knew foreign hackers were attacking their employer's website 24 hours a day. "Most successful hacks come from the inside. If you have a suspicion, you need to give me a name, right now."

Jake leaned forward and whispered, "What if an authorized person was bribed, blackmailed or impersonated?"

She frowned. "That's my worst nightmare."

"Your network is connected to the internet, right?"

"Our firewall is the best you can get, but every kind can be breached by hackers if you aren't ever-vigilant."

"Okay, what about a police car's dashboard laptop? If someone broke into a parked cop car, could they use a thumb drive to upload a virus directly onto that one computer?"

She stared at him in alarm. "Yes. A new, custom-written program that doesn't set off any virus flags could go undetected for a while."

"Would the one infected computer be able to get into the main system?"

She looked off into the distance. "Possibly, but I'm telling you it would *not* work. It'd be blocked, quarantined and removed."

"Now you're lying to me," Jake said. "The only secure computer is turned off, and in a locked room. Any other system is hackable."

Roxanne bowed her head and let out a loud breath. "I'm supposed to say it can't happen, but anything is possible, Jake."

Jake nodded and gazed at his coffee cup, thinking. "Imagine if it was some new kind of super virus from hell, designed to be unstoppable."

"What are you suggesting?" she asked, taking a sip of her latte and licking the colorful foam off her upper lip.

"You might want to run a thorough scan on the SFPD computer system," Jake replied.

"I already run a routine scan every night."

"Run another one twenty-four hours a day that goes as deep as it can. Have it look closely at the dashboard laptops, if that's possible."

"No, you don't get it. I'll look for logins to the agency databases hosting the information that was stolen, and work back from there to find the culprit."

"I'm slowly grasping what you're talking about, but that's why you get the big bucks," Jake said. "I'll pass your thoughts along to people who are tracking this situation."

She looked him in the eye. "You know something you're not telling me. What is it?" Spill the details."

"This concerns a federal case that's classified top secret, but I can ask Agent McKay in D.C to bring you on board."

Roxanne nodded. "Do it, Jake. I want in on this. You're talking about *my* police computers. I'm a tech officer. You have to include me."

"That's my opinion as well. When we finish our coffee, we can sit in my car in privacy and talk to D.C. on an encrypted conference call."

"Let's go now. I'll pour this in a to-go cup." She stood up and headed inside.

Jake carefully pushed his seat back and stood up, avoiding Cody's front legs. He patted his thigh. "Time to go, boy."

Cody got to his feet and shook his fur from head to toe.

A woman arrived carrying a Pekingese dog in her large purse. The dog barked at Jake, and Cody growled in response, showing his teeth. Jake tugged on his dog's leash as the woman went inside the coffee shop. Roxanne came out the door and they all walked to the Jeep and took their seats.

Jake locked the doors and turned to Roxanne. "One word of caution, first. If you get involved with federal agencies it can change your life for the worse."

"What exactly do you mean?" she asked.

"At times, police work has made you paranoid, jaded and stressed beyond words, hasn't it?"

"That's a fair assessment, yes." She lifted a shoulder. "It goes with the job."

"Adding this work to your job will double every negative aspect."

She nodded. "I can handle it."

"Okay, but don't say I didn't warn you." He sent a text to McKay and waited for her to respond. His phone buzzed and he accepted an encrypted video call, tapping a control on the dashboard to make the video appear on the in-dash display screen.

"Agent McKay, I have you on speaker," he said.

McKay appeared on screen wearing her trademark suit and tie, a serious expression on her face.

"You have a question?" McKay asked.

"Yes, I'm here with Roxanne Poole, the SFPD tech officer. I think she could be of great help to us and should be given top-secret clearances for this one case."

McKay gazed at Roxanne. "Sergeant Poole. I know all about you and I'm impressed with your work."

"Thank you," Roxanne said, sounding surprised.

"Before you commit to this, I want to explain what you'd be getting into," McKay said.

"Okay."

McKay continued. "You'd agree to a full background check, a credit check including tax returns, a drug test and a polygraph. Once vetted, you'd sign an agreement and swear an oath to protect confidential information that can affect national security."

"I agree to the vetting process," Roxanne said.

McKay nodded. "This intel Jake is referring to bears the classification of Above Top Secret. The highest level of classified information under Executive Order 13526."

"I understand it would be a serious responsibility."

McKay paused for effect. "Let me tell you just how serious it is. If you violate above top-secret clearances, you could be charged with high treason and face life in prison or the death penalty. What do you say now?"

Roxanne got a determined look on her face. "Put me in, coach."

That brought out a rare smile from McKay. "You're in. Go to the Secret Service Field Office, meet with Special Agents Easton and Greene, get vetted and sign the paperwork."

Roxanne sat up straighter. "Thank you. I'll go right now."

"I'll call Police Chief Pierce and let him know you're assisting us," McKay said and ended the call.

Roxanne smiled at Jake. "This is exciting!"

Jake returned her smile and reached out to shake hands. "Welcome to the team."

Cody woofed and pawed at her shoulder.

Roxanne climbed out of the Jeep, ran to her vehicle and drove off fast.

CHAPTER 58

Roxanne passed the vetting process in record time, thanks to McKay's order to expedite every step. After a briefing with Agent Easton, she returned to her office in the public safety building and tried three different strategies.

First, she ran some deep scans on the SFPD computer system.

While the scans were running, she reverse-engineered the virus and wrote an app to search for it. She had several officers from other precincts use the app to check every police car's dashboard laptop computer, one-by-one.

She then went online to some of the breached databases and attempted to track logins back to their source. Hours later, she found one suspicious login from Detective Ray Kirby's laptop.

"Gotcha."

To be safe, she let her team continue checking all of the other laptops and making sure Kirby's was the only one infected.

Getting into her van, she called Kirby and explained matters as she drove to meet up with him.

They both parked in a lot, and Kirby said, "This is ridiculous. I always lock my car."

"Cars can be unlocked with a substitute key fob," Roxanne said.

Running a scan with her app, she checked his dashboard laptop and quickly discovered a breach in security.

"Someone broke into your SUV and installed a virus on your computer," she said.

Kirby stared at the computer, open-mouthed. "I can't believe it."

"I have to take your laptop and give you another one," she said, removing the laptop from its base and replacing it with one from her van.

"That's it, Rox? Were done?" Kirby asked.

"That's it. See you later." she said.

Kirby drove off muttering to himself about hackers.

Roxanne sat in her van and copied the computer's hard drive onto a brand-new blank one. She then ran a program that would clean every trace of the virus from the laptop and overwrite the existing contents with random alphanumeric characters to a DoD level of erasure, using the Guttman algorithm with thirty-five passes. In spite of the over-write, that particular computer hard drive could never be trusted again. It would be destroyed.

With that done, she tapped on the encrypted black phone she'd been given by Secret Service Agent Easton.

Gazing at the display, she noticed the time. Hours and hours had gone by. Her eyes felt watery from staring at various computer screens for so long. She blotted her wet eyes with a tissue.

"I need more coffee," she said and waited for an answer to her call.

McKay answered the phone and her face appeared on the display using the encrypted app similar to FaceTime. "Sergeant Poole, report."

"I have you on speaker, but I'm in my van with the doors and windows closed for privacy."

"Please tell me you found something useful."

"Yes, I discovered a virus. It appears to be Russian in origin, and was uploaded to a dashboard laptop in Sergeant Ray Kirby's police SUV."

"Kill it, erase it, shut it down," McKay said.

Roxanne nodded at McKay's image. "Already done, but before removing it I did some hacking of my own and found out the day it was installed. The time frame matches up with the arrest of a criminal named Elena Savina."

"The Russian hacker who tried to become the crime queen of California," McKay said.

"My guess is Elena planted the virus program, which crawled the networks and harvested the records. What I don't understand is how Rojo ended up with a copy of the data."

McKay pursed her lips. "Maybe Elena put the word out via the prison grapevine that she had valuable information to sell."

Roxanne took off her glasses and pinched the bridge of her nose. "And Rojo bought it from her? I wonder if he bought a copy or the original she'd hidden somewhere."

"Let's hope he bought the one and only, but I have bad news—he plans to sell the database to North Korea," McKay said.

Roxanne squinted at the display in surprise. "How can we put a stop to that?"

"Someone on my team will attempt to troubleshoot the problem."

"Troubleshoot how?"

McKay paused a moment as if making a decision. "A troubleshooter will hunt down the trouble-causing terrorist and *kill* him or her. No more trouble. All legal under the laws of international warfare."

Roxanne put her glasses on and returned McKay's stare. "You mean like a Navy SEAL sniper?"

"Yes, a sniper, a drone, a black ops team, or whatever it takes— but that's top-secret intel and you can never breathe a word about it to anyone."

"Why did you tell me?" Roxanne asked.

"Because in the days ahead, someone on our team might need your help at a moment's notice. And when you respond, I want you aware it could be a matter of life or death."

Roxanne's jaw dropped. *Life or death. The government was planning to assassinate Rojo. What had she gotten herself into?*

She said, "I understand, and I'll try to help if you need me, but being involved with killing is not what I signed up for."

On the display, McKay stared at her. "I believe Agents Easton and Greene told you to be careful what you wished for, but if you're uncomfortable with the mission parameters you can resign right now and walk away."

Roxanne wrestled with the decision, took a deep breath and shook her head. "No, wait. I have more work to do. I'm going to use data mining software to find out if there are any other copies of Elena's stolen database stored in the cloud or on any computer connected to the internet."

McKay frowned. "One day soon a big city police department is going to regret moving data and bodycam video to the cloud. There will be a massive hack at some point. No system is 100% secure."

"I've voiced that same concern to my chief of police," Roxanne said.

"Keep up the good work." McKay ended the call abruptly.

Roxanne stared out the window and asked herself, "What is Jake Wolfe's role in all of this? Did I have coffee with a government assassin?"

She drove back to police HQ, went inside and sat at her desk, unleashing a swarm of search bots onto the internet. They were similar to the famous Googlebot that crawled and indexed billions of webpages all over the world. The ultra-powerful bots she used were based on a clone of Googlebot, and a bootleg copy of Google's artificial intelligence (AI) software named AlphaZero. The AI was programmed to learn and evolve. She found it more than a little unnerving. Roxanne had improved upon it and written a searchbot of her own, leveraging the Google technology.

The unauthorized copies of Googlebot and AlphaZero had been given to her secretly when she was dating a genius who worked for the parent corporation, Alphabet, Inc. Living in San Francisco near Silicon Valley had its perks for an attractive, brainy young woman among the many nerdy engineer males. Some of them had no girlfriends due to their introverted shyness, moving to a new city and working too much overtime.

In addition, several of her female friends who were tech

professionals provided her with mentorship, networking, advice and code snippets.

She'd leveraged all of this help to tweak, develop and clone many more unique bots in her spare time to entertain herself. Her bots crawled websites, cloud storage, databases and even individual computers that had WiFi routers using factory default usernames and passwords that many people never changed.

The intelligence gathering violated some privacy laws, but if she ever got caught, she'd say it was a confidential police matter and part of an investigation. That would make people back off. She'd found secrets that could result in news headlines, or be used for blackmail, but she kept her findings to herself.

Taking a deep breath and letting it out, she added her own name and address to the search parameters, tapped on her keyboard, started the programs running, and watched as a humorous satire gif of the Ms. Pac-Man game played on the monitor.

She said under her breath, "Go get 'em, Ms. Pac-Man. Seek and find any other copies of the LEO database listing me and every other cop in America."

At that moment Chief Pierce walked past. He stopped and stared in surprise at the Ms. Pac-Man image. "Is *this* the top-secret BS the feds have you doing on *my* time?" he asked in his trademark gruff voice.

Roxanne stood up straight, hands by her sides. "Chief, sir. I can't give you specifics, but I promise you I'm kicking ass and taking names."

Pierce stared at her for a moment. "You've never let me down, Rox, so I'm going to take you at your word. Carry on." He walked away, muttering to himself about the feds, city budget cuts and damned computers.

CHAPTER 59

Jake and Cody returned to Pier 39. The tourist crowds were thick and the sidewalks were crowded and chaotic. Jake was happy for the tourists who were enjoying their day, but he craved peace and quiet.

After working his way through the crowd and walking down a ramp to the boat harbor, he lost patience and decided to leave the big city and return to Sausalito.

Once on board the *Far Niente*, he called Vito. "Hey, can I borrow your valet guy to drive my Jeep over to Sausalito?"

"Are you moving back to Juanita Yacht Harbor?"

"Yeah."

"Nicky is working the lunch crowd, but I'll have someone else fill in and send him right over."

"Thanks, I appreciate it," Jake said.

Fifteen minutes later, Nicky arrived. Jake gave him the keys to the Jeep and told him the address. "And don't touch anything on the dashboard."

"I remember," Nicky said as he saw his face appearing on the in-dash display screen. He drove away.

Jake returned to the *Far Niente*, untied the lines and cast off. He enjoyed cruising the motor yacht across San Francisco Bay, and soon arrived at the beautiful small town of Sausalito. He slowly idled into

Juanita Yacht Harbor, berthed the *Far Niente* at his boat slip, and tied up.

"Home sweet home," he said, with a feeling of gratitude

Cody looked around at the familiar surroundings, sniffed the air and wagged his tail.

Jake walked Cody to a landscaped area where the dog peed on several different plants, marking his territory once again.

Two women on bicycles rode past, waved at Jake and said hello. He returned the greeting. It felt good to be home at the peaceful marina and among friends, like putting on an old familiar shoe.

Nicky walked up to Jake and handed him the Jeep keys.

Jake gave him a generous tip. "Thank you, Nicky."

"Wow, thank *you*," Nicky said. "Call me anytime you need a driver."

"Will do," Jake said.

A car drove up and Nicky waved at it. "That's my Uber. See you around, Jake." Cody woofed a goodbye. "And you too, Cody."

Jake and Cody went for a walk and to grab some lunch. As they passed by some colorful houseboats, Jake thought of the late, great soul singer Otis Redding, who'd lived on a boat in Sausalito when he wrote the hit song, "(Sittin' On) The Dock of the Bay."

Cody happily patrolled his old familiar stomping grounds. People walking past said hello to Jake and Cody and asked where they'd been. Folks on boats or working at nearby restaurants waved at them. Cody was a popular resident of the harbor and everybody knew him and loved him.

Later that day, at dinnertime, Jake stood on the aft deck of the *Far Niente* and grilled two bone-in ribeye steaks on the outdoor gas grill while drinking a cold Modelo Especial beer and looking out at the blue sky and white clouds over the sparkling water. Cody sat nearby and watched his master's every move while sniffing the aroma of sizzling beef.

Jake turned off the grill, set the steaks on a platter and carried it high above Cody's head as he walked into the galley through the open sliding glass door. Cody followed, his nose high and nostrils flaring as he smelled the food. Jake put Cody's steak on its own plate, used a knife and fork to cut it into bite-sized slices, and then set it in the freezer to quickly cool it down.

Stirring a pan of garlic mashed potatoes warming on a back burner of the stove, Jake dished up a scoop onto his plate alongside his steak. He set his plate on the bar counter and wagged a finger at Cody. "That's my food. Don't touch it, yours is right here."

Cody waited patiently and followed orders while sniffing the air and salivating. His bright eyes went back and forth from Jake to the dinner plate on the bar as he struggled to control his appetite.

Jake smiled. He constantly tested Cody and worked every day to improve the independent dog's obedience to his commands—his and his alone.

"Here you go, buddy," Jake said. He set Cody's plate on the floor and smiled as his dog attacked the slices of steak.

Jake sat on a barstool and poured himself a glass of a dark red wine blend inspired by the "mixed black grapes" wines first made by the Italian immigrants who'd originally settled in Napa Valley. They'd blended special batches of rich, dark fruit to create something humble, unique, and delicious.

While Cody chomped on his food, Jake savored a bite of steak, followed by a forkful of mashed potatoes and then a drink of red wine. Putting his nose into the wineglass, he inhaled enticing aromas of blackberry and chocolate, followed by a slurp of the purple juice that coated his tongue with delicious flavors of black cherry, boysenberry, cocoa, coffee, vanilla and a slight touch of oak and earth. Ahhh, it went well with the medium-rare grilled beef, and the mashed potatoes that had just the right amount of butter, garlic, sea salt and fresh ground pepper.

He let out a satisfied sigh. This was an amazing dinner. The only thing missing was Sarah.

"This is the rough life, eh, Cody?"

Cody raised his head, let out a dog burp, and went back to devouring his meal.

Jake smiled. "Good boy." He felt deep gratitude for his dog, the good food and wine, and this amazing boat he was borrowing from his friend Dylan, a software millionaire currently living in Dublin, Ireland.

He lifted his glass in a toast to Dylan. His friend had bought an impressive collection of highly rated wines before he'd developed health problems and his doctor had insisted he stop drinking. Dylan had told Jake to enjoy any or all of the collectible bottles he might want to, and Jake was doing just that, every chance he got. He decided he'd have to ask Father O'Leary to pray for his liver.

For some reason, he felt like this was the night before the storm. As if something big was about to happen. The feeling was magnified when his encrypted black phone buzzed with a call from Secret Service Agent Shannon McKay in Washington, D.C.

CHAPTER 60

Staring at the phone, Jake let out a long breath. "No rest for the wicked, huh, Cody?"

Cody licked his snout, having finished off the beef in record time. He went to a watercooler, pressed his paw down on the lever, sent water down a plastic tube to fill his bowl and took a noisy drink.

Jake set down his fork and answered the call, using the encrypted program similar to FaceTime. "Wolfe."

McKay's face appeared on his phone. "We have a situation. It's go-time for a mission off the coast of San Francisco. I'm sending you a file."

"I'm still on a break," Jake said, just to give her a hard time.

"You wanted in on a mission against Rojo. This is it. Cowboy up."

Jake paused a moment to let that sink in. "How are the events in Baja and San Diego connected to San Francisco?"

"It's classified top secret and on a need-to-know basis. I'll explain it if you're on board; otherwise I'll find someone else to avenge the death of your Marine friend, Pez, and the attack on your pregnant girlfriend, Sarah."

Jake stood up as he felt his anger flare, but he kept it in check out of respect for her. "Don't go too far. Yes, of course I'll do the mission."

"You'll thank me for this, Jake. I'm doing you a favor here," she said.

He made an effort to keep his voice calm. "Please send me the file."

His phone buzzed. He opened the docs and saw various facts and photos about two high-value targets.

One of the soon-to-be-dead men was a short North Korean male named Yeong, who had celebrity good looks due to obvious plastic surgery. He was currently visiting the California coast in a megayacht. The young, wealthy and privileged communist man loved to party and spend a fortune on booze, cocaine and high-priced hookers.

Jake thought of the millions of undernourished people in the North Korean dictatorship suffering from stunted growth. A theme from George Orwell's *Animal Farm* came to mind, about how all animals are equal, but some animals are more equal than others.

The second target was the new and ambitious cartel leader named El Rojo, "The Red One." Current location: San Francisco. Now Jake understood why this was like a gift handed to him on a silver platter by McKay.

"Rojo is here, now?" he asked.

McKay nodded. "He's visiting San Francisco Bay and has been designated a high-value target."

"Mission brief?" Jake asked, his tone of voice suddenly businesslike.

"Are you on board?"

"One hundred percent."

"The megayacht is twenty-five miles offshore of San Francisco right now with Yeong, the North Korean spy, on board."

Jake watched a drone video playing on his phone. "One mile into international waters. What's he doing there?"

"His yacht is carrying millions in counterfeit US currency, printed by his government on nearly-perfect printing presses."

"And the Secret Service investigates counterfeiting."

"Exactly. There's also a freighter heading for Mexico to deliver literally tons of precursor chemicals that are used for cooking methamphetamine."

"Korea manufactures the chemicals?"

"No, he bought them from China, and his freighter is registered under a Panamanian flag."

"I had no idea China supplied the meth cooks."

"Almost all meth-making chemicals come from China and are transported to Mexico, where they're cooked by cartels into crystal and smuggled across or under the border to eager buyers in the USA."

"What about in other countries?"

"Myanmar supplies most of Asia."

Jake looked out at the ocean. "Myanmar, the tiny Buddhist country near Thailand?"

"Yes, impoverished people there cook tons of meth into *billions* of little pills that meth addicts all over Asia smoke in pipes. It's Myanmar's number one export. China is right nearby to supply them with precursor chemicals."

Jake shook his head. "I have a question. If the shipment of chemicals from China is going directly to Mexico, why are they doing the trade of counterfeit money up here?"

"The freighter with the chemicals is on its own schedule and also carries tons of legitimate goods. Rojo bribes the port authority to quickly load his one shipping container onto a truck and turn a blind eye."

"Okay, but why is the North Korean's yacht delivering his counterfeit cash here?"

"Yeong is afraid of Naval Base Coronado, and Mexican cartels," she said. "He believes he can get away with the cash trade off the coast of northern California, far away from the southern border. Rojo will meet him and buy the fake cash for half the face value, thereby doubling his investment."

"Any word on the location of the hard drive with the law enforcement officer database?"

"I saved the worst news for last. We've received word Rojo found the hard drive and is going to sell it to the Korean."

Jake cursed. "No. That cannot be allowed to happen. No matter what we have to do."

McKay said, "President Anderson wants you, personally, to terminate Yeong and Rojo, retrieve the hard drive of LEO data, and report to him afterward."

Jake paused a moment. "Did Daniel give an executive order?"

McKay raised one eyebrow, as if a bit surprised at how Jake discussed the new president on a first-name basis. "Yes. We have confirmation Rojo's cartel is planning to kill a number of law enforcement officers in the US and Mexico. He's been designated a Tier I drug kingpin and terrorist, pursuant to the Foreign Narcotics Kingpin Designation Act. Your orders are to kill Rojo and Yeong as high-value targets."

Jake slammed his fist down on the bar. "Where is Rojo right now, at this very moment?"

McKay gave him a tired smile. "That's why the president wants you, Jake. The anger and fury, the protective streak, the deep-seated need for justice. He knows you'll do whatever must be done to protect innocent lives."

CHAPTER 61

Jake cursed. "The damned psychiatrists must have a field day with my psych file."

"It's interesting reading, I won't deny it," McKay said.

Jake let out a loud breath. "Why would the cartel kill LEOs and start a war with every person in US law enforcement? That's insane."

"Yeong wants to temporarily destabilize an American city. It's a test to probe our vulnerabilities. And Rojo wants to assassinate selectively targeted law enforcement officers on the West Coast who can't be bribed, while striking terror into the rest so they accept his money and do his bidding."

"It sounds like Al Capone in Chicago during Prohibition. Not going to happen, not on my watch."

"Agreed, we're hoping you can put a stop to it."

"Where do I handle this situation? On the yacht?"

"Correct. Yeong doesn't plan on coming ashore. Rojo will visit the yacht for a secret meeting. When they're both on board, you'll terminate them, retrieve the hard drive, and remove three major threats against American citizens."

"How many bodyguards are there to deal with?"

"Four soldiers of the North Korean Special Operation Force,

disguised as crew. The rest of the yacht's personnel are civilians working on a chartered boat. Yeong thinks he's incognito."

"Six targets, total?" Jake asked.

"Right. Once the targets are eliminated, you'll withdraw and allow the Coast Guard to board the yacht and find the counterfeit cash."

"It's too bad the San Francisco Police Marine division can't take part in the boarding along with the Coasties. I know Captain Leeds would want to participate."

"I'll give Leeds the chance as a favor to you. The yacht is still within twenty-four miles of the Farallon Islands, which are officially part of San Francisco."

"I didn't think of those little islands."

"Neither did the yacht captain. And in your case, you don't have to worry about borders because the Letter of Marque and Reprisal gives you the authority to operate worldwide."

"I'm still kind of in awe of that letter and its power," Jake said.

"Use it or lose it, Jake. I gave it to you and I can take it away. Make no mistake, I'm in charge of the very few privateers and that includes you."

"How many privateers are there?"

"That's on a need-to-know basis and you don't need to know."

"Agreed. Does the cartel have boats and crews nearby for the transfer of cash? Who'll capture them?"

"Navy SEALs will deal with that problem, on the ocean."

"Yeah, they certainly will. I've seen them in action."

"Is there anything you haven't seen?"

"A ship full of counterfeit money. Maybe I'll take command and cruise to Tahiti or Fiji, buy my own beach and marry a pretty brown-skinned island girl," Jake said.

"Good luck with that."

"I think it's one of my better ideas."

"No, not really," McKay said.

"I need intel about the yacht."

McKay sent him texts with photos and ship schematics. "Make

no mistake, if you're caught assassinating Yeong, North Korea will consider it an act of war."

"And if criminals are being armed by a hostile foreign government and targeting US law enforcement personnel, I consider them enemy combatants and insurgents who are attacking America."

"Exactly. You can put a stop to it tonight."

"I'm going to leave Cody at home for this mission. He can stay with Sarah for the night."

McKay paused a moment. "Is Cody okay?"

"He's fine. I'm just being careful. Boarding a hostile ship at sea in the dark is risky business, and there's nowhere for Cody to run and escape to."

"Before you go on this mission, they want you to attend a meeting at a fusion center."

"Why? You know I hate meetings. Will they allow me to bring Cody along?"

"No. I'm sorry, but his file notes him as an unstable military weapon."

Jake cursed. "Does my file say the same?"

"I can't tell you what it says."

"I'm not surprised."

"One last thing, Jake. On this mission involving a North Korean official, if you're compromised, you'll be disavowed."

Jake took a deep breath and let it out, knowing disavowal might cause him to be kidnapped by North Koreans, imprisoned, tortured and executed.

"Understood. Send me all the files, but tell them I'm going to skip the meeting." Jake ended the call.

His phone lit up as he received the files. He studied them and learned more about the yacht and HVTs.

He said quietly, "I'm going to kill you evil bastards and make the world a better place for everyone to live."

Cody growled deeply, low in his throat.

Jake put his unfinished dinner into the refrigerator, replaced the cork in the wine bottle and disembarked the boat. He and Cody walked to the Jeep, climbed in and drove across the Golden Gate Bridge. When they reached the city, Jake said, "Cody, I have to leave you with Sarah for a while tonight. I'm sorry, but I'll be back soon."

Cody growled at him as if asking how Jake could do such a thing. If a dog could frown, Cody was frowning.

Jake's phone buzzed and he took a FaceTime call via the dashboard computer display.

Roxanne Poole said, "Jake, I have orders from McKay to attend a meeting. Will you be there?"

"No. They won't allow Cody inside the secure building, so I said no thanks."

Roxanne paused. "I'm nervous, Jake. It would help a lot if you were there with me."

Cody woofed at Jake.

Jake looked at his dog in the rearview mirror. "You're fine with waiting in the car, Cody?"

Cody barked once.

Jake nodded at the image of Roxanne. "Okay, you and Cody talked me into it. Send me the coordinates."

"Thank you, Jake." Roxanne ended the call.

The display lit up with a GPS route to an address in a business complex of office buildings and warehouses.

CHAPTER 62

Jake drove to the fusion center and parked in the private lot. It appeared to be a somewhat ordinary building, but was probably designed that way on purpose. He imagined there might even be a vast complex underground.

He said, "Cody, *stay* in the Jeep and *guard* it until I return. That's an *order*, Marine."

Cody stretched out on the back seat.

Jake went inside and met an armed Marine in uniform who escorted him to a windowless meeting room with a long table where several people sat. He was surprised to see his friend Howard "Levi" Strauss, who owned a private security company named Executive Security Services. The man was supposed to be a retired "former" CIA agent, and yet here he sat.

Levi was dressed in a suit and tie and had close-cropped hair with a dash of salt and pepper on the sides. He nodded at Jake.

Secret Service Agents Easton and Greene were also in attendance, along with one man Jake didn't recognize and who watched him enter the room, his eyes never wavering. He looked like someone with a military background who'd seen combat. Jake knew a fellow warrior when he saw one.

Jake met his gaze for a moment, unintimidated, and then turned away, ignoring him. On the monitor he saw the face of Shannon McKay.

"Agent McKay. I have a question," he said.

"Shoot."

"Who's the tough guy staring at my back?"

"Shall I introduce you two gentlemen who have so much in common?"

The man behind Jake said, "Yes, please do. It's high time I met Mr. Wolfe, in spite of his smart mouth."

Jake turned. They stared at each other and neither one blinked.

McKay said, "Jake Wolfe, meet Chris Shafer, a CIA paramilitary operations officer who serves on missions overseas."

Jake raised his eyebrows in surprise and held out his hand. "Pleased to meet you."

The man stood. "I'm honored to meet you as well, Jake. We share a similar history."

They shook hands with a crushing viselike grip. A half smile appeared on Jake's face. Shafer raised one eyebrow.

"We could stand here all day," Jake said.

Shafer smiled. "But let's not. We have business to discuss." He withdrew his hand first.

Jake turned to Levi. "Friend of yours?"

Levi nodded. "A trusted friend."

Jake sat down at the table. "Can we get the meeting underway? My dog is waiting in the car, unless you're brave enough to allow Cody into your building."

Shafer ignored Jake's request about Cody and said, "I called for this quick meeting to explain what we do, and to ask if you'd like to become more deeply involved in protecting our nation."

Jake stared at him as if the man was stupid. "I've already shed blood for this country and nearly died doing it. How much more deeply involved could I get? Are you asking me to donate a kidney?"

Shafer took a breath and calmly said, "I'm talking about your secret work with the POETs: the President's Operational Emergency Team."

"I agreed to work with McKay approximately once a month, or twelve times in a twelve-month period."

"Correct, and you've been a valuable asset. Thank you for your service."

Jake nodded. "But you want more. Of course you do."

Shafer paused for a moment. "You're very perceptive. The situation has changed. We have a new president and First Lady, and you're their friend. They trust you because you risked your life to protect Katherine."

"I was only doing my duty," Jake said. "Any veteran would've done the same."

"The Andersons told McKay they want you to visit them in the White House," Shafer said, appearing slightly surprised.

Jake stared at him. "Is it a problem I'm friends with the new president and First Lady?"

"No, it's helpful. Anderson wants you in on some crisis meetings, along with McKay and myself."

"I'm honored, but no, I can't live in D.C. That will never happen. No offense."

"None taken. You could visit for a few days at a time. Fly there first class and stay in a fine hotel."

Jake tilted his head and cracked his neck, tired of this line of thought. "No, I'm sorry but that's not going to work. Thank you for the offer, though. I'm honored you asked."

Shafer glanced at McKay's image on the TV and then back at Jake. "I was told you didn't want to leave your boat and harbor. And your adopted war dog doesn't like long rides on airplanes. Is that correct?"

"Did Shannon McKay tell you that?" Jake asked.

"Well, yes."

"Then you should believe her and not question me as to whether what she said was true or not."

On the TV screen, McKay lifted a coffee cup to her mouth, apparently pretending to drink while hiding her grin.

Shafer took a patient breath and let it out. "Of course, I'm only confirming it with you so we're all on the same page."

Jake stared at him a moment. "My dog, Cody, is my right-hand man, and he's fought by my side through thick and thin. When Sergeant Cody was a Marine, he had to kill an enemy combatant in a war zone to protect his platoon. He saved their lives but he's had a touch of PTSD ever since. I can't put that war hero in a kennel and stow him in a plane's cargo area for hours on end like he's a piece of luggage. Hell no, I refuse to do that. Don't ever ask me again, and put that in my effing file on the first page."

When Jake's eyes flashed in anger, Shafer held his hands out, palms up. "You could fly there in a private jet, and Cody would ride next to you in luxury. The owners of a famous internet company in San Francisco will loan us a jet and crew, anytime we need it."

"A private jet worked fine when we flew down to Cabo, but D.C. is too far away," Jake said.

McKay spoke up. "Jake, that reminds me, I talked with Bart Bartholomew about you traveling on his jet occasionally, up and down the West Coast. He agreed to it as long as we're buying the fuel."

"Good to know, thanks," Jake said, not making any commitment.

Shafer asked, "Most dog owners who go traveling leave their pet behind with a friend, and I'm assuming you could do that for a few days, right?"

"No, sorry, you assumed wrong." Jake said. "First you say Cody is an unstable weapon and isn't safe to come in here, and then you call him a pet who can be left with a friend for days on end." He shook his head and looked at the door, wanting to exit the meeting.

The man blew out a breath. "I guess we'll have to meet in teleconferences, long distance via encrypted satellite link. You can come to this secure location and sit in on our meetings via a technology similar to FaceTime, but highly secure." He gestured at the monitor where McKay appeared.

"I'm familiar with the tech, and I'd be willing to do that, but only if I can bring my dog in here with me. Otherwise, if you're afraid of him, I'll sit in my Jeep and participate via my dashboard computer instead of here with you folks who can't abide war dogs who served their nation with honor. Frankly, I'm embarrassed for you, but let's move on to what the meetings will be about," Jake said.

Shafer scowled. "President Daniel Anderson wants your input."

"What for?"

"Now that he's president, we told him more about what you do for our group. He suggested you should have some say in the planning stages."

Jake glanced at McKay, who gave him an almost imperceptible nod.

"Planning the termination of high value targets?" Jake asked.

"Correct. You'd help us decide on who, what, when, where, how and why," Shafer said.

He shook his head. "I'm not an expert at planning covert ops."

"No, but you've carried out those plans. None of the rest of us, except for me, has your combat experience. Your opinion is valuable, Jake. It's an honor to be invited into the top circle. Your country needs you. President Anderson won't settle for anybody else."

Shafer tapped his phone and glanced at McKay, who said, "Stand by."

A large TV on the wall lit up, displaying a blank, blue screen. That changed to show the official symbol of the White House.

Moments later, newly elected President Daniel Anderson appeared. A tall man who exuded power, good judgment and calm confidence, Anderson sat at the famous desk in the Oval Office and gazed at Jake as if relieved to see him there.

The president said, "Jake Wolfe. Good to see you. How are you, young man?"

Jake stood up and squared his shoulders. In spirit, he was still among the Marines, some of whom helped to protect the president and flew his helicopters. Once a Marine, always a Marine. "I'm doing well, Mr. President. How is Katherine?"

Anderson smiled. "Always concerned about Kat and the baby, aren't you, son?"

"Yes, sir," Jake said.

"Good man. Kat is handling her chemo like a trooper, but it's not easy being pregnant and undergoing those treatments simultaneously."

"No, sir. I can't imagine what she's going through." Jake thought about Kat battling breast cancer *and* carrying a child at the same time, and he felt heartbroken for her, but also inspired by her courage. He knew the couple had tried for years to conceive and had finally overcome their infertility challenges at long last.

"Kat said you two talked at the hospital in San Francisco before she flew here for the inauguration, and she told you how the doctors had performed her double mastectomy."

Jake had no words. He only nodded at his friend. In the corner of his eye, he noticed Shafer closely watching this interplay as his face indicated he was beginning to understand the depth of friendship Jake shared with the Andersons. They talked to each other like family, as if Jake was their adopted son.

Daniel turned and beckoned to his wife, Katherine, the First Lady. She appeared at his side, bald and flat-chested, with her swollen tummy pressing against the well-tailored maternity clothing. In spite of it all, her face was glowing with the vitality of a soon-to-be mom.

CHAPTER 63

"Kat, you're looking well," Jake said.

Katherine smiled at him. "Hello, Jake. You're finally calling me Kat instead of Mrs. Anderson. Is Cody there with you?"

"No, ma'am, he's waiting in my Jeep. They wouldn't allow him in here because he's considered to be an unstable military weapon."

Katherine, the former prosecuting attorney, set her jaw. "Nonsense. Recently, that *unstable* weapon helped save my life from an assassin."

"Yes, ma'am. He sure did."

"When are you two coming to the White House?" she asked.

Jake looked down for a moment. "We won't be visiting anytime soon. I'm sorry, but Cody can't make that long flight. I won't let him do it. The next time you visit California, we'd love to have you over for dinner, along with all of the Secret Service Agents protecting you, of course."

Katherine smiled at him. "It warms my heart to see how you protect your dog like he's family."

"He *is* family."

"Of course he is."

Daniel said, "Let's hear the short version of this briefing about El Rojo."

Shafer nodded. "One: cartels in Mexico control most of the drug trade in the United States. Their reach extends all the way to Washington, D.C. Two: some time ago a rogue group entered the market for cheap black tar heroin and caused escalating violence between the many criminal entities. Three: recently, Rojo arrived from Nicaragua and wanted to avoid the heroin turf wars, so he went into the manufacture and distribution of crystal meth on a massive scale."

Jake said, "Have you seen before-and-after photos of meth addicts? It's truly frightening what that poison does to people."

On one of the TV screens, McKay replied, "Yes, it's devastating. Rojo cooks large quantities with high purity, sells it cheap, and leaves a wake of destruction in his path."

President Anderson said, "Tell me about the database."

Shafer said, "We've learned the database holds a copy of the name, address, credit report and medical history of every law enforcement officer in the United States."

Anderson frowned. "That could be used as a murder hit list."

Shafer said, "Exactly. I believe Rojo used threats and bribes to make someone in the government give him a password to a police computer."

McKay said, "I have recent intel on that. You should be getting a visitor from the San Francisco Police Department right about now. She has top-secret clearance."

They heard a knock at the door. A Marine opened it and escorted SFPD officer Roxanne Poole into the room. She wore her police uniform, and the look on her face indicated she was not used to the top-secret protocol but was hanging tough through it all.

Jake stood up and improvised on behalf of his friend. He'd dragged Roxanne into this situation and felt protective of her now. "Sergeant Poole. I was hoping you'd be joining us." He pulled out the chair next to him and held her gaze.

Looking at him with a hint of gratitude in her eyes, she walked over and sat down beside him as everyone in the room stared at her.

"What can you tell the president about the tech aspect of this problem?" Jake asked, opening the door for whatever she might want to say.

She gaped at the president's image on the TV screen for a moment, then sat up straight and said, "A Russian criminal named Elena Savina broke into one of our police SUVs. She loaded a virus onto its dashboard laptop and gained access to data trails leading … everywhere."

McKay said, "Elena sold a copy of the hard drive to Rojo, and then hid the original before she was arrested and put in prison. Sammy 'Pez' Lopez took the copy away from Rojo, but claimed it had gone missing and he would try to find it."

Jake nodded. "Which explains the meeting off the coast of San Francisco. Rojo came here to buy the original hard drive and retrieve it from where Elena had it stashed."

"Why didn't he buy it before now?" Anderson asked.

McKay answered, "He didn't know about it. Elena lied and said he'd bought the only copy."

"Has anyone found the copy stolen by Lopez?" Anderson asked.

"Rojo's people found the drive, but it was blank," McKay said. "Pez had erased the data, reformatted the drive and cleared the empty disk space with a software program that wrote nulls over it with 100 repeat passes."

Jake asked, "How did Rojo find out about Elena's original hard drive she kept hidden?"

McKay leaned forward. "Incarcerated women from Rojo's cartel got to Elena in prison. They beat her up and offered her a choice, money, or death."

"And she took the money, like they all do," Shafer said. "Okay, we know Rojo has the hard drive, but what is the current status of the virus Elena planted in a police computer?"

"I reverse-engineered the virus and wrote a program to find it," Roxanne said. "Then I destroyed the one laptop's infected hard drive."

"Did you make a copy of the virus before you destroyed it?" Shafer asked.

She reached into a pocket and set a hard drive on the table in front of her, handling it gently as if it held poison. "This is highly dangerous, appears to be of Russian origin, and I advise—"

"Please give it to me," Shafer interrupted her, holding out his hand.

Roxanne looked at McKay's image on the monitor, waiting for her go-ahead, but Jake picked up the drive, took control of it and held it in the palm of his hand, letting Roxanne off the hook. He was always a lightning rod for trouble, so why not now?

"My guess is, the CIA will want this so they can use it against our enemies," he said.

Shafer said, "Exactly, and as a CIA field agent, I'm officially requesting to take possession of it."

"I don't work for the CIA any longer," Jake said.

Shafer stared at him. "Don't kid yourself."

CHAPTER 64

Jake turned to McKay. "Your orders?"

McKay nodded. "Give it to him, Jake. I've never told you this, but our group works closely with the CIA. They can't operate on domestic soil unless they liaise with a local investigative agency."

Jake nodded. "The Secret Service is perfect for that, and you're already in the White House. It's genius."

"I'm glad you think so. And thank you, Sergeant Poole, for your good work."

Roxanne nodded. "Just doing my job."

Jake gave the drive a brisk shove along the table and it skidded across the smooth surface until Shafer put his palm down on top of it and stopped its progress. He stared at Jake and held his gaze.

"You're welcome," Jake said. "Send that virus to Iran's military computers."

Shafer finally smiled. "Mind reader."

Jake returned the smile, thinking they might get along. He had a buddy in the Mossad, Israel's version of the CIA, who knew secrets about Iran that would blow your mind. They were attempting to build neutron bombs, the nuclear weapons that killed every living thing but left the cities and oil wells standing. Neutron bombs could be used to take over a small country such as Israel by liquidating the citizens—literally—and then sending in millions of new people to repopulate the area.

McKay said, "Jake, there's something you need to know about Sammy Lopez."

He stared at her a moment, not sure if he wanted to hear it, but said, "Go ahead."

"Pez had been threatened with the brutal torture of his parents if he didn't cooperate with smuggling cannabis through the underground tunnel. He went along with it for a while because cannabis is becoming legal in many US states anyway. However, in the end, he found out about the crystal meth, the human trafficking and the LEO database hard drive. Pez stole the hard drive and claimed it had gone missing. He was murdered for protecting America's law enforcement community."

Jake took a deep breath and let it out. Pez had been a good man in an impossibly bad situation, and he'd found redemption in the end. He felt proud of his friend. "Thank you for telling me that."

Anderson asked, "How can we be sure the database Rojo is selling to Yeong is the only copy?"

McKay said, "Roxanne, I'll let you explain this."

Roxanne lifted her chin. "I conducted a deep web crawl with bots, searching for any copy on any cloud or individual computer connected to the internet, and came up with nothing. My guess is, it's encrypted with a code so it can only be duplicated by Elena. If anyone else tries, the copy becomes a jumble of unintelligible gibberish. I've seen that before in a few rare cases."

Jake said, "Pez died for that hard drive. There's no way in hell I'm going to let Rojo sell it to North Korea." He stood up and began pacing back and forth, clenching his fists.

McKay observed him. "Jake, I want you to see the tunnel drilling machine we captured thanks to you making a deal with Enrique."

Another TV screen lit up with drone footage of Mexican Marines driving pickup trucks mounted with machine guns in the back beds. They raced toward a two-story building with tall garage doors. Surrounding the building, they blew the lock on one of the doors and rushed inside.

The view changed to that of a body camera worn by a Marine who ran into the building along with others, all of them firing rifles and killing armed men. The chaotic gun battle was over quickly. The camera then focused on a large machine and moved slowly around it.

The machine was about the size of a bus, painted red, with a glass enclosed driver cabin in front and Army tank treads below.

McKay said, "That's a Ditch Witch JT-8020—a horizontal directional drill (HDD). These are used by major energy corporations to drill conduits and lay pipe for oil pipelines, natural gas pipelines, and utility cable pipelines. This is the biggest one you can buy. When it was brand-new, it sold for half a million dollars. Rojo bought this rig used from a bankrupt company for only a hundred thousand. One big drug haul through a tunnel could bring in millions."

Jake stopped pacing and stared at the TV. "Had Rojo used the drill yet?"

"Yes, he'd drilled and laid pipe to make a conduit that's one-thousand feet long and comes up under a house in the United States. It only took a matter of weeks to drill that tunnel."

Jake asked, "What size pipelines does this machine create?"

"They can range from ten inches to five feet in diameter, large enough for a human to walk through with head bowed. The smaller ones work with ropes and pulleys, dragging drugs into America and money back to Mexico."

"If the cartels buy dozens of those horizontal drills, the ground beneath the border will be like Swiss cheese. How can we put a stop to it?" Jake asked.

"That's the question. The newer machines have cameras to display your progress and a self-feeding pipe-laying system. Everything is automatic. All the operator has to do is learn how to aim and deploy the drill. We've found half a dozen pipelines in other areas, but only by luck, when the operators didn't drill at a proper depth and ran into city infrastructure such as water lines and electric cables."

Jake blew out a heavy breath and walked toward the door. "I

suggest we tag every machine with a hidden transponder, like we do with animals such as bears and orcas. Keep tabs on every single one."

McKay said, "Jake, we found this horizontal directional drill because of you. Thank you, and keep up the good work." She called an end to the meeting and her TV screen went blank as Jake walked out of the room.

∼

Roxanne hurried to follow Jake outside and caught up with him near the Jeep. Jake pressed a key fob and let Cody out of the car so the dog could relieve himself on a patch of grass.

Roxanne gazed at Jake. Their eyes met and she said, "Thanks for being a friend in there." She tilted her head at the building.

"I'll always stick up for you, Box of Rox," he said, smiling and lightening the mood.

"Okay ... Troubleshooter," she said and then closely watched his facial reaction, taking a wild guess he might be one of the government assassins Agent McKay said would troubleshoot the terrorist problem.

Jake appeared surprised, raising his eyebrows. "What in the world are you talking about?" he asked innocently.

Roxanne shrugged, as if almost feeling disappointed. "Nothing. See you around." She walked to her police van and drove away.

CHAPTER 65

Jake sent a text to Sarah: *Any chance you could dog-sit Cody for a few hours tonight? Terrell and Alicia are busy.*

Sarah: *Tonight is our salsa dancing lesson. Did you forget?*

Jake: *Yes, I'm sorry. The government needs me to solve a problem.*

Sarah: *I see. Fine. Bring Cody to my office.*

Jake: *Thank you. I'm on my way.*

As he and Cody drove to Sarah's clinic, Jake thought if a woman said things were fine, you were doomed. The missions were damaging his relationship, but he had to do this one.

At the clinic, Jake parked and led Cody on a leash as they went inside.

Sarah's attractive young assistant, Madison, smiled shyly and bit her lip. "Hi, Jake."

"Hi, Madison, it's nice to see you again," Jake said, his voice neutral.

She blushed and turned away to Cody. "Hey, Cody. How's my favorite golden boy?"

Cody woofed at her and wagged his tail.

"Be friends, Cody," Jake said.

Cody went around behind the counter and put his head on Madison's lap.

She smiled and scratched him behind the ears. "You're the best dog ever."

Sarah came out of her office. "Jake, I'll agree to watch Cody if you tell me what you're doing."

He shook his head. "Ask me no questions and I'll tell you no lies."

"That's your answer?" Sarah asked, her eyes searching his face.

"You begged me to keep Cody safe, and you specifically said *not* to tell you about my missions. That's exactly what I'm doing, and I'm also bound by federal secrecy laws."

Sarah looked at Cody and then at Jake. "Okay, but of all the nights you could've abandoned me … I guess I'll have to dance with Bob instead."

"Mr. Bob Instead?"

"You remember Bob. He's that architect I was dancing with in the video … who, unlike you, shows up for the lessons and enjoys spending time with me."

Jake wondered if Sarah was so angry at him she might do something they'd both regret. He stepped closer to her. "I'll be back soon, but before I go on the mission, please give me a kiss for good luck."

Sarah stared at him as conflicted emotions pulled at her heart. What was she going to do about her rocky relationship with this dangerous bad boy?

"Jake, after I gave a knockout punch to that woman who cut a dog's paw to get drugs, and then I almost shot and killed Angel, I feel like I understand you better now. I get it, but that doesn't make it any easier for me. Do you understand?"

As her heart struggled with her brain, Jake reached out and gently picked her up with one arm around her shoulders and the other under her knees, as if he was going to carry her across the threshold after they'd said their vows. By reflex, she put her arms around his neck and hung on. He leaned in.

"Thank you, Sarah. And now I *need* your kiss for good luck."

"In that case, make it a good one, Jake." She closed her eyes and tilted her head. When he pressed his lips against hers and gave a heartfelt passionate kiss, she felt like he was going away on a journey and it might be their last kiss, forever. That scared her a little.

Jake set her down carefully and turned to Cody. "Sarah is in charge while I'm gone. Obey and protect."

Cody went to Sarah and leaned against her thigh.

Sarah looked at Jake, worried. "Please be safe."

Jake nodded. "I will. See you soon." He walked toward the door, and Cody followed him automatically, like his shadow. Jake stopped and turned. "No. I'm sorry, buddy. You have to stay here and protect Sarah. Remember? I'll be back soon, I promise. Sit and stay."

Cody turned his head back and forth between Sarah and Jake, appearing conflicted. He barked, then bit down on the ankle hem of Jake's pant leg and pulled at it.

Jake went down on one knee and hugged his dog. "I'll be back tomorrow morning at the latest. I swear."

Sarah frowned. "You'll be gone overnight?"

"You were worried about Cody. This way you won't have to," Jake replied in a firm voice that didn't leave any room for debate.

"I'm worried about you too, you fool," Sarah said, her voice thick with emotion.

"Thank you, but this fool will survive."

They stared at each other, their eyes saying more than words ever could.

"Don't do this to me, to us," Sarah said.

"This isn't about you or me. It's bigger than the both of us. You have no idea. I'm sorry, but I have to go."

"Jake, if you walk out that door, our relationship might be over."

Jake appeared resigned as he looked her in the eye and said, "I understand how you feel, Sarah. Maybe someday you'll understand my feelings too." He went out the door and closed it behind him without another word.

Cody howled as Jake drove off without him. Sarah took deep breaths, cursed at Jake and pounded her fist on the counter.

Madison stared at Sarah with wide eyes. "Are you okay?"

Sarah didn't answer. She just stared at the door Jake had gone through. How could one man make her so happy and so angry?

Cody whined.

Madison said, "Cody, do you want a biscuit?"

Cody moved toward the cookie jar on the counter. Madison removed a glass lid from the jar and held out a big bone-shaped biscuit to Cody. He took it and chomped it down and then licked the crumbs off the tile floor.

Madison said, "Sarah, the way Jake looks at you. He's so possessive. It makes my heart beat faster. Maybe you could meet him halfway."

Sarah felt her heart racing too. "He makes me weak in the knees, damn him. But this might be the last straw. I'm thinking it's hopeless and we're just incompatible."

"Is this why you still have other guys in dating rotation?"

"Yes, but they're only platonic dinner dates. I'm not sleeping around, only maintaining my male friendships because Jake and I might break up. He almost got you and me killed that time. Remember?"

"How could I forget? I was never so scared in my life."

Sarah didn't mention her pregnancy or miscarriage. "Jake asked me to go exclusive, but I said no, I'm not ready. I still want to keep my options open."

Madison looked her in the eye. "They say wolves mate for life."

Sarah shook her head. "Wolfe is just his name. It doesn't mean anything."

"It might to Jake."

"Right now he's running off to do something dangerous and maybe illegal, but for the greater good. I just can't live that way."

Madison got a worried look on her face. "What's he doing?"

"He can't say. He has top-secret clearances with the government, from his service in the Marines."

"Wow, that's scary, but it's also kind of hot."

"Would we ever be able to have a normal life together? No, probably not."

Madison shook her head. "Normal is boring. I'm sorry, you two seem meant for each other. I have a crush on him, but he only has eyes for you."

Sarah gazed out the window at the city lights with a sad look on her face. She shook her head and grabbed her purse and coat. "Come on, it's time to go home."

Cody stayed right by Sarah's side, protecting her the way Jake told him to.

CHAPTER 66

Jake drove through the city grumbling to himself. "I feel lost without my dog. And I'm losing touch with my girl, but I won't let her cut off my balls and keep them in her purse. I hope one day she can accept me for who I am."

He arrived at the private estate of Lauren Stephens in Pacific Heights. They'd met when Jake had protected Lauren and her young children from the Russian Mafia. After Jake earned an online law degree, she paid him a quarter million-dollar retainer to be her friendly advisor. He was bound by attorney-client confidentiality to keep her private business private. She often said he was the one man she could trust no matter what.

Today she was allowing the Secret Service to use her private property as a staging area for a covert operation.

Two wrought-iron gates in front of the mansion swung open on silent hinges. Jake drove into the lavishly landscaped grounds and saw a plain black helicopter sitting on the acre of lawn in front. Parked next to it was a black Suburban SUV, where Agent Easton stood waiting.

Jake parked his Jeep, climbed out and walked toward Easton. "That doesn't look like a Secret Service helicopter," he said.

Easton nodded. "An anonymous CIA shell corporation owns it. Virtually untraceable." He dropped a garment bag onto the grass.

Jake leaned down, flipped the folded bag open and pulled the zipper. It contained a white dress shirt, dark gray slacks, shiny black shoes and a navy-blue sport coat.

"I'm in management now?" Jake asked.

"Just put the clothes on," Easton said.

"Roger that."

Jake took off his jacket, two pistols, KABAR Knife, shirt, pants and boots. Standing there wearing nothing but black boxer shorts, he saw a reflection in the darkened windows of the SUV. Lauren was standing at an upstairs window, staring down at him.

He pretended not to notice her as he donned the new clothing, strapped on both his shoulder-holstered and ankle-holstered weapons, and the knife in a small-of-the-back SOB sheath. Once he was dressed, he turned and noticed Lauren, waved at her and received an embarrassed wave back.

Jake's friend, Paul, walked up. "Good luck out there, Jake."

Paul had long black hair and the facial features of a Native American. He was of the Zuni people and he'd served in the Army Rangers, losing a leg in combat overseas.

Here in the city, he'd once seen Cody trotting down the street, searching. He followed the dog and helped him rescue Jake from a house where he'd been held hostage and interrogated.

"Thanks, Paul," Jake said and put on the sport coat. He turned and looked Paul in the eye, feeling that the man had something to say.

Paul held his gaze. "I have no idea what you're doing, but you know I'd go along and help you, right?"

Jake nodded. "I asked, and they said no. Maybe one day soon, though, brother."

"Thanks for asking," Paul said, shaking Jake's hand with a firm grip.

Easton opened a door to the back seat of his SUV, and Jake saw a pair of long stocking-clad female legs on display. The legs swung out and stepped down on expensive-looking white high heels.

Agent Greene stood there wearing a designer silk dress that stopped at mid-thigh. Her hair was intricately styled in an updo, like a bride on her wedding day, and her makeup looked as if it had been applied by a professional makeup artist for a Hollywood movie or a fashion photoshoot. Jake had done his share of fashion model photoshoots in a previous career, and he thought she looked drop-dead gorgeous. For a moment he was speechless.

Greene smiled. "Cat got your tongue, Jake?"

He returned the smile. "Uhm, you clean up good."

"Surprised?"

"That you're a beautiful woman? No, I was already aware of that."

She blinked her eyes and turned her back on him, hiding her facial reaction. Reaching into the SUV, she retrieved her purse.

Jake turned away so as not to stand there gazing at her attractive legs and rear as she bent at the waist in her clingy dress, although most men naturally would have done so because she was a beautiful sight to behold. He felt an ache in his chest, craving variety, something new and different. Thinking of Sarah, he did his best to ignore the age-old animal instinct to be unfaithful, blocking it out of his mind.

Greene closed the car door and moved toward the helicopter. Jake walked beside her, leaving his street clothes and boots on the grass. At the copter door, Jake held out his arm because she was in sky-high heels instead of her usual tactical boots. She grasped his arm and climbed inside. He followed and they sat next to each other.

The pilot started up the engines. Easton climbed into the copilot seat, closed his door and turned to Jake. "Sergeant Cody?"

Jake shook his head. "He's not coming along on this one."

Easton nodded and put on his seat belt and headphones. He spoke to the pilot and they took off.

Once they were flying over the bay, Greene brought Jake up to speed on the mission. "Yeong hires a new and different call girl twice a week. Tonight I'm playing the part."

"Do his guards search the female visitors?" Jake asked.

"Yes, thoroughly, but we thought of a way around that." She turned and lifted the back of her hair to reveal a small stun device hidden at the nape of her neck. "My fancy hairdo is keeping that thing in place. A pat-down of my shoulders won't find it."

"What about Yeong's guest, Rojo?"

"They ordered two girls, but I'll tell them the other one had an emergency, and I'm into threesomes."

"That could be a bad scene if things go wrong."

"Yeah, I could be totally screwed. Literally."

Jake shook his head. "No. I don't like the plan. There has to be another way."

"It's too late, Jake." They stared at each other.

"Once you gain entry to Yeong's room, you'll stun both of them senseless?"

"Correct. You'll take out the two on-duty bodyguards, one on the bridge and one in the hallway by his stateroom." She held out a tablet showing a diagram of the route to the stateroom.

Jake nodded. "And then I'll join your party and terminate the two main targets."

Greene looked out the window at the water below, fear on her face. Jake noticed how stressed she appeared to be.

"Stun Rojo first, and then Yeong. You can wait in the passageway when I take them out."

"Thanks. I'd prefer not to see that."

"Right. Once you see it, you can never forget it."

She nodded and searched his face, as if she knew Jake had seen more deaths than he could count.

Jake said, "That plan leaves two guards unaccounted for, somewhere on the yacht."

"We'll be gone before they know what happened."

They talked about the plan until they both had it clear and gazed into each other's eyes, understanding they were partners and their lives depended on each other. If they failed, they would soon be dead, or wish they were.

Greene took a deep breath and let it out. "McKay said you requested me and Easton to assist you on missions."

"I asked for her best people, who I know and trust. Sorry if it's not something you wanted. You're not obligated to work with me. We can abort this mission and head back."

"No, it's okay. I feel like you respect my skills, and I appreciate that."

Jake looked her in the eye. "I have the utmost respect for you. Some time ago, you stopped Officer Denton from shooting me in the back. Recently, you helped rescue Cody and me from a raft adrift in shark-filled waters. I'm in your debt. Don't forget that."

She nodded, taking some more deep breaths.

Jake saw that she was afraid. It was the normal response to this situation, and that was okay. Fear could sharpen your mind and keep you alive.

The pilot said, "Prepare for landing."

Greene opened her purse and showed Jake a burner phone and a small pistol. "The guard will find these and think he's disarmed me."

"Good idea," Jake said.

As the copter descended, Jake felt his stomach drop. He moved into a tight concealed space equipped with a sniper rifle and a hidden port he could open and fire through.

They landed on the deck with a thud, and a well-dressed guard approached the helicopter. He had on the same clothing as Jake, a crisp white shirt, a navy-blue blazer and dark gray slacks. He held a metal detector wand in one hand and a pistol in the other. The threatening look on his face said that if the wand went off, the pistol would go off next and nobody would be spared.

CHAPTER 67

Jake drew his pistol and looked through a spy port on the copter, ready to shoot the guard if he found Greene's stun device.

Greene opened the helicopter door and paused there for a moment to let the wind from the copter blades blow her skirt up in Marilyn Monroe style.

The guard's eyes widened at the sight of her honeymoon bride white satin panties and matching garter belt. He held out his hand to her.

She grabbed his hand and stepped onto the boat deck, deliberately bumping up against him. "Hi, I'm Chloe," she said in a breathless voice.

"Pleased to meet you, miss," he said. "We're going to walk to that door over there, and I'll escort you to meet your new friend."

"Thank you, kind sir," she said with a seductive smile.

"Pardon me, but first I have to search you and your purse." The guard started with her purse, finding the pistol and phone, and pocketing them. "I'll return those when you leave."

She nodded. "No worries, I always carry them with me."

He ran the wand over her, and the plastic stun device at the nape of her neck didn't set off the alarm. He then patted her down, remaining professional for the most part but enjoying himself a little too much nonetheless.

She let out an impatient breath. "Are you quite done feeling up the merchandise your boss is paying for?"

His smile faded. "This way, please." He gestured toward the door and they walked across the open deck in that direction.

~

In the copter, Jake holstered his pistol, grabbed the sniper rifle, gazed through a night vision scope and found the other guard up on the bridge. The guard aimed a rifle and scope at the copter, ready for any sign of trouble.

The moment Greene and her escort went inside the yacht and closed the door, Jake fired his silenced rifle at the guard on the bridge. The man staggered and fell off the yacht into the ocean, taking his rifle with him.

Jake used the scope to check for any other threats. Nobody appeared on deck. His briefing said the highly paid yacht crew stayed out of sight and turned a blind eye when this kind of thing was going on. He set down the rifle, exited the copter and walked quickly to the door Greene had gone through.

Easton climbed out of the copilot seat and stepped out of the copter. He opened the engine cowling and did a safety check while tapping his phone and starting a timer.

Jake went inside the boat and quietly made his way down a passageway toward the stateroom he'd seen on a diagram. Reaching inside his jacket to the shoulder holster and drawing his pistol with the silencer attached, he approached the room with his gun up. Peeking around a corner, he saw the man who'd escorted Green now standing guard outside a door. He fired a silenced headshot and killed the bodyguard, dropping him to the deck.

Moving quickly to the door, he reached for the doorknob and found it locked. He used a KRONOS lock pick device to quietly pick the lock and opened the door a few inches.

Peering inside, he saw Yeong lying on the carpet, momentarily stunned.

Rojo brandished a knife and threatened Greene, who held the

small Taser device in her fist, her face pale, jaw clenched, eyes determined.

Jake walked in and shot Rojo in the chest. The man fell back onto the floor, squirming in pain but still alive.

"Go into the hallway," Jake said to Greene. "Retrieve your pistol from the guard and wait there."

She turned and went out without a word, closing the door behind her.

Jake approached Rojo and the man suddenly swept his legs and tripped him. As Jake lost his footing, Rojo jumped to his feet and charged at him, grabbing the wrist of his gun hand. They grappled and fell to the deck, wrestling for control of the pistol.

Rojo tried for a head butt and missed. "I'm wearing a vest. You should have gone for a headshot," he said with a sneer.

Yeong woke up, groaning and mumbling in Korean. He grabbed Jake by the hair and helped Rojo come out on top.

Rojo tried again for a head butt. Jake elbowed him in the nose, drawing blood. Rojo sat on Jake's stomach, clamped both hands onto his right wrist and twisted hard, fighting for the pistol. He pressed the gun hand closer and closer to Jake's face.

Jake used his left hand to draw the KABAR knife from the small of his back and shove it through the side opening of Rojo's vest and into his body.

Rojo exhaled sharply, moved both hands to clutch at the knife handle protruding from his side, and groaned through clenched teeth, "Get it ... out."

Jake bucked Rojo off of him, rolled over and shot Yeong in the gut. Yeong fell backwards with a cry of pain, holding his stomach with both hands.

Jake stood up and turned to where Rojo lay on the floor, dying. He mercilessly aimed the pistol at the man's forehead and pulled the trigger twice, killing him.

Pulling his knife out of Rojo, Jake wiped the blade clean on the dead man's shirt. He moved to Yeong, who said, "I'll pay you any amount of money to let me go!"

Jake's voice went cold as he recited a Bible verse. "The avenger of blood shall put the murderers to death." He looked Yeong in the eyes and executed his second target with two rounds in the heart and two more in the head.

He holstered his pistol and knife, and quickly searched both men, finding a hard drive similar in size to a mobile phone. He put it in his pocket and moved toward the door.

He heard shots fired, the door opened and Greene ran inside, closing and locking it behind her. She gripped the small pistol in her hand.

"A guard is coming and he's huge!"

Jake heard heavy stomping footsteps, thud-thud-thud, as if a rhinoceros was running toward them. Something hit the polished oak door hard, like a battering ram. Once, twice, three times, and the door burst open.

A giant of a man rushed through the doorway.

The massive, muscular, herculean guard was dressed in the same style of slacks and sport coat as Jake. His nose had been broken in the past and not treated by a competent doctor. He raised big calloused fists the size of beef roasts and ran straight at Jake, using a surprising burst of speed to fearlessly pounce on Jake and grab his biceps.

Jake staggered backwards, fired his pistol and hit his opponent's left shoulder.

The guard roared in pain as his left arm hung useless. He kneed Jake so hard in the stomach it lifted him off his feet and sent him staggering backwards as the man also tore the pistol from his hand.

Greene raised her small pistol and shot the guard in the back several times. He turned and slapped her hand so hard it caused her to spin sideways, stagger and fall down, dropping the weapon.

Jake leapt to his feet and used Jeet Kune Do as he punched and kicked the guard with every ounce of his strength. The giant took all of the hits, sneered at Jake and then charged him again.

With nowhere to run, Jake dove at the attacker's shins, tripped him and sent him flying. The man landed on his face with a smack of his forehead to the polished wood deck.

Jake tried to quickly draw the small pistol from his ankle holster, but his opponent recovered and was on him in an instant, moving fast like an angry grizzly bear. He crashed into Jake, knocked him down and then grabbed him by the back of the neck with his massive right hand. Leaping to his feet, he swung Jake through the air like a rag doll, slamming his face against a wall.

Jake turned his left shoulder just in time for it to take most of the hit instead of his nose and chin. He felt dizzy from the impact but managed to twist to the side and kick his knee into the man's crotch as hard as he could.

Bellowing in pain and fury, the big man put his meaty right hand on Jake's throat and began to squeeze.

Jake tried to punch his opponent's face, but the man's arm was too long and Jake couldn't reach him. He kicked at the man's knees, but saw stars as his oxygen was cut off and he began to asphyxiate.

Fighting for his life, Jake drew his knife and stabbed the man's wrist, in-between the radius and ulna bones, and then twisted the knife as hard as he could. The man screamed in pain, but his eyes burned with victory as Jake weakened and his body sagged.

At that moment, Jake saw his own pistol appear next to the guard's face, and Greene fired a headshot into the man's temple. The hollow point round expanded inside the guard's head, bursting his brain. He let go of Jake and crumpled to the deck, twitching in his death throes.

Greene stood there in shock, holding Jake's pistol and her own, one in each hand, while looking down at the man she'd killed.

Jake tried to speak, but no words came out, only a raspy croak. He held out his hand to Greene and she gave him his pistol. They opened the door, ran down the passageway and out onto the deck, where they saw Easton walking fast in their direction.

When Easton saw them, he spun on his heel and returned to the copter, climbing inside and giving orders to the pilot.

The pilot increased power, and Jake and Greene ducked as they ran beneath the spinning blades, jumped inside and closed the door.

"Go, go, go," Greene yelled. Her face pale as she leaned over and dry-retched several times.

The copter rose into the night sky, running without lights, and disappeared into the darkness, flying low over the ocean.

Jake put the pistol in his shoulder holster and tried to focus on breathing in and out. Easton turned and looked at Jake with a question in his eyes. Jake nodded, held up the hard drive for him to see and gave a thumbs-up.

Easton spoke into the headset mic. "We're exfiltrating. Targets down. Package retrieved. Mission accomplished."

Jake then began turning blue in the face as he struggled to catch a breath. He went to the first aid kit on the wall, checking the contents. Not finding what he wanted, he began opening every storage compartment he could find.

Greene came over next to Jake. "What do you need?"

"Oxygen," he rasped, and fell to his knees, wheezing.

CHAPTER 68

Greene turned toward Easton and yelled, "Do we have oxygen?"

Easton spoke into his mic to the pilot. "Are you carrying portable oxygen?"

"Affirmative." The pilot nodded and pointed at a cabinet.

Easton quickly took off his headset and seat belt, opened the cabinet and found a portable aviation oxygen system. A green cylinder about the size of a 1.5-liter wine bottle, along with a clear mask connected by tubing.

Greene said to Jake, "Lie on your back, I'm trained in CPR."

Jake felt groggy, but he followed her orders.

She gave him mouth-to-mouth resuscitation. In between breaths, she said, "Focus on your breathing. Don't you die on us, dammit. Cody is counting on you."

Easton appeared by her side and gave her the bottle. She placed the mask over Jake's face and turned on the oxygen.

Jake took deep breaths, and after a while returned to breathing regularly. He removed the mask, sat up and tried to speak.

Greene turned off the oxygen and put a finger to his lips. "Shhh, save it for later."

Easton returned to the copilot's seat and spoke on the radio to McKay.

Jake staggered to his feet, sat down in his seat and opened his small black nylon backpack. He removed a half-pint stainless-steel hip flask and took a drink, feeling the brandy burn its way down his throat.

"Ahhhhh, that's good," he said, and coughed, holding the flask out to Greene.

She accepted it gladly with a shaking hand, and took a swig. Jake noticed her body trembling, and saw that her right hand was speckled with blood from the man she'd shot up close and personal. A tear rolled down her cheek, and she turned to Jake, head bent as if in prayer.

Jake knew what she was feeling, the first time taking a human life by violence. He gave her a hug and she buried her face against his shoulder.

While she wept, he patted her back and in a hoarse voice murmured assurances that she was a brave warrior who'd had no choice but to protect her partner, and that this too shall pass.

When the helicopter landed at Lauren's estate, Easton jumped out and opened the sliding passenger door. Greene stepped down and hugged Easton for the very first time ever. Easton appeared surprised. The stoic agent studied the tear-stained mascara streaks on her face as if unsure what to say.

Jake rasped out, "We were attacked, and she shot a man in the head at point blank range who was choking me to death."

Easton looked closer at Jake's bruised neck, then at Greene's blood-splattered hand. "Understood."

Greene said, "Jake, I've never killed anyone before. Can we talk about this? How do you deal with it afterwards?"

"Let's go to the boat and have a drink, and I'll give you *the talk*," Jake said. He coughed several times and cleared his throat.

Greene reached into the SUV, retrieved her carry-on-sized suitcase and set it down.

Easton held out an empty hand toward Jake. "The hard drive."

Jake handed the drive to him.

Easton accepted it and said, "Good work, you two." He climbed into his black Suburban and drove away.

Paul walked up and handed Jake a dark green plastic lawn-and-leaf bag that held his clothes and boots.

"Sitrep?" Paul asked.

Jake coughed. "Mission accomplished."

Paul glanced at the bruises on Jake's neck. "I swear I'm going with you next time. With official permission or without."

They shook hands.

Lauren opened the front door of the mansion and stepped onto the porch, gazing at Jake with a worried expression on her face.

She was an attractive woman close to thirty years of age, average height and weight, with wavy dark hair and smart eyes. She owned an apparel company that had grown into an internet sensation and made her a multi-millionaire. Several months ago she'd become a widow, and hadn't dated anyone since.

He gave her a thumbs-up, and she waved at him to come closer.

Jake joined her on the porch and he noticed her staring in concern at his bruised neck.

Lauren said, "Jake, I have no idea what you were doing tonight, only that it was top secret and helped to protect American citizens. That was good enough for me because I trust you, but now I'm worried about your injuries."

"It's nothing serious, I'll be fine," he said.

"Did you achieve your … objective?" she asked.

"Yes. I can't give you any details, but thank you for helping the Secret Service."

She took a step closer and gave him a hug. "You're my hero, you know."

He laughed heartily and his chest shook as he returned the hug. "Hero? No, I'm not a hero, but thanks for the kind words."

She let go of him but stayed close, smiling. "You once risked your life to rescue my children. They both think you and Cody are heroes. It's the right word for how I—how we—feel about you."

Jake was not expecting this declaration of her feelings. He blinked and said, "How are Chrissy and Ben doing these days?"

"They're doing great, and they've been asking when you're coming over for dinner again."

Jake thought about Sarah. "My evenings are busy, but maybe we can set up a Sunday brunch."

She smiled. "Sounds good, and for now, please go see a doctor."

"I will. Thanks again, Lauren."

Jake and Greene picked up their bags and drove toward the harbor and the *Far Niente*. On their way, the Jeep seemed to have a mind of its own as it took a slight detour and swung past Sarah's apartment. Jake looked up at her second-floor window and saw two people, shadows behind the curtains. It appeared they were dancing. Sarah's window was partly open, and as Jake passed by, he heard salsa music. Cody barked and peeked out the window with his head between the curtains.

Jake quickly turned a corner, went out of sight and kept driving.

Greene reached over and put a hand on his shoulder. "Was that Sarah's place, and Cody looking out the window after recognizing the sound of your Jeep?"

Jake said, "Yeah. Let's go have those drinks."

Once they were on board the *Far Niente*, Greene went into the guest head, bringing her suitcase along and saying she wanted to shower and change clothes.

Nodding in understanding, Jake walked into his stateroom head and took a shower. The hot water helped to relax his sore neck, and the steam cleared his throat. It occurred to him they were both naked in separate showers, but he blocked any thoughts of a nude Agent Greene out of his mind.

After their showers, they met in the galley and smiled at each other. They were survivors.

Greene's elaborate hairdo, sexy dress and high heels were gone, replaced by damp straight auburn hair, blue jeans, a casual blouse and bare feet.

"I'm having a shot of Irish whiskey to end the day," Jake said matter-of-factly. "What can I pour for you? You name it, I have it."

"Whiskey will do nicely," she said.

Jake poured Redbreast into two highball glasses, without ice. "Here's to surviving a mission."

"Amen," Greene said.

They clinked their glasses, sipped the whiskey and made small talk while waiting for takeout food to be delivered.

His phone buzzed with a call from McKay on the encrypted FaceTime program. He held his phone out in front of him, where he and Greene could both see it.

McKay said, "Congratulations on the successful mission tonight."

"It almost went sideways, but we had some good luck," Jake said.

"From what the Coast Guard found, I'd say you created your own luck."

"What's the status of the assault on Rojo's hacienda?" Jake asked.

"One hundred elite Mexican Marines are attacking the compound from all sides right now. Rojo's gang will be arrested and his bank accounts seized," McKay said.

She showed a split-screen video of the attack. One side gave the view from a vehicle, the other from a drone in the sky above.

"Those Marines are good," Jake said.

"The cartels fear them; they refuse to be bribed or intimidated."

"The untouchables, like Elliot Ness and the FBI back in the day," Jake said.

The cartels call them, *los rapidos*—the fast ones. The Mexican Marines drive high-powered pickup trucks with machine guns mounted in the back. They race toward the fight at full speed."

"They sound like my kind of Marines," Jake said.

McKay said, "I have more good news. The Philippine National Police Anti-Kidnapping Group found the families who were taken off boats near San Diego and sold into human trafficking. The pirate sold all of them to one buyer for slave labor on his shrimp farms. The victims have all been rescued and are safe on board a US Navy ship."

She displayed a photo of dozens of people eating meals at tables in a Navy mess deck.

"Thank God," Jake said.

McKay nodded in satisfaction. "That ties up most of the loose ends."

Jake stared at her for a moment. "Could we help Olivia get Pez's auto parts business up and running again?"

"That's a fine idea. I'll have some of my people in San Diego work on that," she said.

Jake smiled, glad to know Pez's legacy would live on.

McKay glanced at Greene and then back at Jake as if wondering why they were together on his boat at this time of night.

Jake noted the look of doubt on McKay's face, but he didn't offer any comment. He agreed with the Disraeli maxim of *never complain and never explain*. That could often make matters worse.

"Good night," McKay said and ended the call, holding Jake's gaze as the screen went dark.

Jake sensed her disapproval, and set the phone down just as his security system beeped in warning.

CHAPTER 69

Jake checked his phone and used his surveillance cams to see the delivery driver walking up to the *Far Niente*.

He went out to the aft deck, tipped the driver and walked back inside, setting the food on the coffee table along with two plates.

"I called the deli and had them bring us the makings for sandwiches. Help yourself."

Greene piled sliced turkey, cheese and lettuce onto sourdough bread and took a bite.

Jake opened a Staglin Cabernet, an aged bottle of fine red wine from an exceptional year, worth hundreds of dollars. He silently thanked his friend Dylan for the boat and wine collection.

"Simple food and amazing wine. It's good for what ails you," Jake said.

"This wine is delicious. What's that hint of an earthy flavor?" Greene asked.

Jake tasted the wine. "According to legend, it's known as the Rutherford dust, a quality only found in grapes grown in Napa Valley's Rutherford Bench. Georges de Latour of Beaulieu Vineyard discovered it long ago."

"It's incredible," she said.

"Beaulieu means beautiful place. It's what de Latour named the pristine grape-growing land he found here."

"And now Napa is a tourist mecca," she said.

Jake shrugged, and he realized he didn't know her first name. "Agent Greene, what's your full name?"

"You just said it," she replied.

"Is Greene your real surname? Not a code name?"

"Yes, it's real."

"I want to know your *first* name."

She hesitated a moment. "Yvonne."

"Yvonne?"

"Yeah, it's kind of old-fashioned," she said, looking down and nodding in resignation.

It appeared to Jake she was used to being teased about it, maybe bullied growing up. He said, "Yvonne is a beautiful name, very classy and special, with a musical sound. I like it."

She stared at him in disbelief. "Thank you ... Jake."

"After all we've been through together, I think we can be on a first-name basis," Jake said, smiling.

"Sounds reasonable," she deadpanned, but the sparkle in her eyes revealed she was pleased.

After dinner, they sat on the couch and Jake played a song on the stereo: "Let Her Cry," by Hootie and the Blowfish. He strummed his guitar and sang along karaoke style with Darius Rucker.

When the song ended, Greene said, "Quit that. You're making me cry." Tears ran down her face.

"That's why I played it. I want you to cry and let it all out," Jake said.

"Okay, I will." Greene wept and her body was wracked with sobs.

Setting his guitar on the coffee table, Jake felt the urge to hold her, but he thought of Sarah. He sat back and said, "It's time to have the talk."

Greene wrung her hands. "I took a life. I killed a human being, and I'm still in shock. How do you ever get over it?"

"You don't get over it. You learn to live with it," Jake said.

"Live with it?" she asked.

Jake said, "Repeat this thought process to yourself until it's as ingrained in you as the history of this night: A murderer tried to kill you, but you were a better warrior and you killed him in self-defense. He was one hundred percent committed to ending your life. You had two choices: kill or be killed. You made the right choice—the only choice. You're the victim of an attempted homicide by someone who has killed countless other people. If you hadn't fought for survival, you'd be dead now, and so would I. You saved my life and I can never repay you, but I'll always be in your debt. Thank you."

She thought about it for a minute. "That helps me, thank you, but I don't want to go home and be alone. Can I couch surf here and drink some more wine until I conk out?"

Jake smiled kindly. "Of course, my couch is your couch." He stood up and went to the galley to open another bottle of wine.

After sitting on the couch and enjoying more wine and conversation, they were both drunk and she fell over on her side. She pulled at Jake's arm, but he said, "No can do."

She smiled. "You're no fun. Still burning a candle for Sarah, huh?"

"It seems so."

"Fair enough, I admire loyalty in a man. Are you exclusive?"

"No. I asked and she turned me down, but I don't give up easily."

"It sounds complicated," Greene said, with raised eyebrows.

Jake changed the subject.

They talked some more, and after a while she sat up and cried on his shoulder, and he let her do it. Her feeling of shock seemed to come and go.

Jake held her until she passed out, drunk on wine and emotionally exhausted. He laid her down and covered her with a blanket.

For several hours, he sat there on the end of the couch and stayed awake, holding her hand. Whenever she stirred in her sleep, he quietly spoke reassuring words until she relaxed and went back to dreaming.

At one point she mumbled in her sleep, "Damn you, Jake. You could have comforted me in your bed."

Jake whispered, "Someday, maybe, but not tonight."

He felt it was a mistake having her spend the night, but he didn't know how to avoid it.

Later on, sometime past two in the morning, Jake nodded off, slumped over on his side. He accidentally curled up to Greene and dreamed he was with Sarah.

~

In the morning, Jake woke up with a painful hangover. He heard a security speaker beeping, his phone vibrating somewhere nearby, and Cody barking out on the aft deck.

The sliding door opened. Had he forgotten to lock the door? Oh well, if Cody was here, he didn't have to worry about security.

Sarah and Cody walked in and Sarah stopped in surprise at seeing Jake lying on the couch, under a blanket with another woman. "Well, isn't this cozy? I guess the truth is you asked me to keep Cody overnight so you could go to bed with ... whoever she is."

"No, Sarah, it's not what you think." Jake got out from under the blanket and stood up. Cody came to his side, and Jake ruffled his ears.

Sarah's eyes roamed over Jake. "You slept in your clothes?"

Greene woke up and tossed the blanket aside. Standing up with a groan, she said, "We both did. Jake offered me a shoulder to cry on. I got drunk and passed out."

"Agent Greene? Why, what's wrong?" Sarah asked.

"I served my country last night and..." Greene looked at her hands as if seeing them clean now, but not in her memories.

Sarah glanced at the bruises on Jake's neck, and her face went pale. "And someone died," she said.

Greene didn't reply. She went into the head and closed the door.

Jake said, "One of the men who died was the cartel boss who sent that woman to attack us, kill Pez and cause your miscarriage."

A shadow passed across Sarah's eyes. "In that case, I'm glad he's in hell now where he belongs."

Jake nodded. "I looked him in the eye as he took his last breath."

Cody pressed against Jake.

Jake went down on one knee and hugged his dog. "I missed you, buddy."

Cody licked Jake's bruised neck and whined.

"I'll be okay. Somebody tried to choke me to death, but it didn't work out so well for him, thanks to Greene."

Sarah moved closer to Jake. "You should go to the hospital and get that examined."

He stood up. "Don't you have some horse liniment that's good for man or beast?"

"I have some Arnica." Sarah opened her purse and took out a tube of cream. She removed his shirt and began applying the cream to his many bruises with a doctor's gentle touch.

Jake said, "I'd be dead if not for Yvonne."

Sarah glanced up at him. "Yvonne?"

He nodded. "Agent Greene. She saved my life and then felt the terrible burden that goes along with killing someone up close. She's never served in any branch of the military. Never been in combat. It was her first time having blood on her hands … literally. So, we had a drink and I gave her the talk about how to deal with her emotions. Just like I used to do in the Marines when a newly deployed boot killed an enemy combatant."

Sarah shook her head. "Thank God she was there when you needed her."

Jake appreciated Sarah's healing hands on his skin, and he felt she might be caressing his neck and chest longer than necessary. Maybe also hoping to heal his emotionally wounded heart and soul? For a moment, he thought of the Marvin Gaye song, "Sexual Healing." He could definitely use some of that kind of healing from Sarah.

The coffeemaker bubbled and hissed as it brewed a fresh pot, controlled by the timer Jake had set the night before. He went to the galley, poured a cup and added a shot of Baileys, drinking the coffee like a drug.

"Would you like some coffee, Sarah?"

"Yes, please."

Jake poured her a cup, adding Baileys, and set it on the coffee table as he sat on the couch with his shirt off. "Please join me."

Sarah sat down next to him.

He took a sip of coffee. "Last night when I accidentally fell asleep next to that woman, I dreamt of you."

She gazed into his eyes. "I had a dream about you last night as well." Her face flushed slightly.

CHAPTER 70

"How was your date with Bob the architect?" Jake asked, keeping his voice polite and neutral.

Sarah studied her fingernails. "It wasn't a date. It was a dance lesson you agreed to attend as my partner. You stood me up, so I danced with a replacement."

"Oh well, I guess I'm easily replaced. What did you two do after the non-date?"

She hesitated. "If you must know, we went back to my place for a drink and to practice some more. He's a really good dancer, but..."

"But what?" He looked her in the eye.

She paused again. "It wasn't the same as when I'm with you. We didn't have that powerful energy between us. At my place, he tried a clumsy ill-timed move to kiss me. I put my hand on his chest and said to stop. And I was going to explain things to him, but the instant I pushed against him and said the word *stop*, Cody appeared out of nowhere and bit him on the crotch."

Jake burst out laughing. "Attaboy, Cody."

Cody panted, Ha-Ha-Ha.

Sarah couldn't help but laugh along. "It's not funny," she said, covering her mouth to hide her smile.

"Yes, it is." Jake laughed again and patted his dog on the back.

Cody wagged his tail and gave Jake a big grin.

Sarah said, "Cody and I missed you last night, but I'm glad your mission was a success."

"It was important to national security. I'm sorry I do this work for Uncle Sam, but I can't seem to break free of the responsibility to my country."

Sarah got a resigned look on her face. "Someone has to do it, and you're the best. I'll just have to get used to it."

"Thanks for understanding," Jake said.

"Sometimes I can't help but wonder if you might be better off with a woman who lives the same kind of life." She gestured at the door Greene had gone through.

Jake reached out and took her hand in his. "No, Sarah. I want you. I choose you. I need you."

Sarah smiled. "And after one year you can end your service in this dangerous work?"

Jake held her hand to his lips and kissed it. "Yes. I'm trying to put it all behind me, but I committed to a year."

"Why did you have to be the one who went on that mission last night?"

"There was a massive threat against American law enforcement officers. I'm trained for the job that needed to be done and I was in the right place at the right time. What else could I do? How could I say no?"

She studied his face. "Are you sure you didn't do it for revenge against the man who killed Pez and caused my miscarriage?"

Jake held her gaze. "I won't deny that was a big part of it. Yes, I wanted justice, and to put that cartel boss out of business, permanently."

Sarah let out a sigh. "I'll have to ask Alicia for advice on being married to a man who risks his life every day of the week. I don't know how she does it with Terrell."

Jake raised his eyebrows. The corner on one side of his mouth twitched in a half smile. "Married? Who said anything about being married?"

Flustered, Sarah blinked several times. "What I meant was …"

He stood up, pushed the coffee table aside and pulled on her hand.

She let him pull her to her feet, and then fell into his arms.

Opening the door to the head, Greene stepped out and saw Jake and Sarah embracing. Jake's shirt was off. Sarah was quietly saying something about how her body was now fully recovered from the miscarriage.

She tiptoed past them to the aft door, pulling along her small wheeled suitcase.

Cody followed, escorting her up the dock to the parking lot, trotting beside her protectively and sniffing the air for any threats. Easton pulled up in his black Suburban and stopped.

Greene went down on one knee and gave the dog a hug. "I love you Cody, even though you're a golden furball from hell."

Cody pressed his head against her stomach and nodded, wagging his tail.

She patted him on the back and climbed into the Suburban. Easton drove off and Greene looked back, seeing Cody standing there watching her go away—so loyal and protective. She wondered if Jake and Sarah would work things out. She wished them the best, but if it wasn't meant to be, she'd be back to see Jake and Cody.

Easton drove in silence for a while, as he usually did. Greene opened her purse, took out some aspirin and swallowed several pills with a drink of bottled water.

"I have the worst hangover in history," she said. "Not sure if I'm going to live through it."

Easton glanced at her and said only one word. "Breakfast?"

She gave him a tired smile. "Bacon and eggs, hash browns, biscuits and gravy … and coffee, lots of coffee."

Easton nodded and drove to their favorite greasy spoon diner.

Cody watched Greene drive away in the SUV. Once it was out of sight, he gazed around at the familiar sights, and took in all of the favorite aromas of the seashore.

He loved Sausalito, the ocean, beaches, parks, and this quiet harbor. It was good to be back home.

He trotted back down the dock to the boat slip, boarded the *Far Niente* and went inside. Hearing a loud music video playing on the TV, he saw Jake dancing with Sarah. They'd pushed the salon furniture aside and were moving back and forth on the deck in some strange mating ritual Cody didn't understand.

What was the point of this thing called dancing? What did it mean? He sat and watched them for a while, tilting his head to the right and then the left. The scent of happy pheromones from Sarah told him her mood had changed from worried to joyous.

After the song ended, his two favorite people went into the stateroom and closed the door. Cody heard sounds from the bed telling him Jake and Sarah were still in love. That was good.

He pressed his paw down on the lever of the watercooler, filled his bowl and took a noisy drink.

Going back outside, Cody patrolled the sixty-foot boat and walked the perimeter all the way around the deck in a circular route, past the bow and back to the stern.

Sitting on the aft deck, he observed the harbor, docks and nearby park, while thinking about recent events.

He liked the woman named Greene. She was special and might be a good mate for his alpha. But Sarah was first and foremost. She'd captured his heart. He hoped Jake would see that too and retire from the fighting so they could all be together.

Hadn't he and his alpha done enough? When would they ever get to live in peace?

Maybe some human people and dog people never got to retire from war. Maybe they kept on fighting until their dying breaths. If that was the case, he'd fight at Jake's side forever. But he wished with all his heart they could move on and live a peaceful life, along with Sarah, the special woman who looked into his eyes and understood his feelings.

Maybe Jake could just do that lawyer work where people asked him odd questions and he looked in thick books and on the computer-thing for answers, saying big words Cody didn't understand. Jake often joked about only being paid one dollar, whatever that meant, but the work seemed to make him happy, and nobody tried to kill him.

Cody gazed out at the sky and water, smelled the salty breeze and felt the boat rock gently beneath him.

Small fish splashed nearby. Seabirds called to their mates. The morning sun shone down on the sparkling blue bay, and Cody took deep breaths of the clean sea air, enjoying the peace and quiet of the yacht harbor. He liked living here more than when they visited busy Pier 39 in the big city.

Cody rested his chin on his front paws and kept one eye open and watching the dock. This was his home, and Jake and Sarah were his pack. He'd protect them so they could protect others. That was his job and he'd do it faithfully, no matter what.

Thank you for reading *San Diego Dead*. Have you read all of the Jake and Cody books?

Please visit my author page on Amazon to see the entire series and find out what's happening next. While you're there, tap the "+ Follow" button under my photo, and Amazon will let you know when my next book comes out.

Go to: amazon.com/author/marknolan

DEAR READER

Dear Reader,

I do a lot of research while writing novels for you, and I try to include interesting tech, gadgets, and weapons for your reading entertainment.

Quite a few readers send emails asking me which things in my books are real. To answer that for everyone, I've put together a quick list pertaining to this book.

Note: The following list contains spoilers, so if anybody skipped to the back, I advise them to please read the book before reading this list.

First, what is *not* real:

There is no cartel named *Los Carniceros* (the Butchers), and no boss named *El Rojo* (the Red One). I invented an imaginary cartel and boss that don't exist, except in my imagination.

As in every book, names, characters, places, events, incidents, and dialogue are all products of the author's imagination or are used fictitiously. Any resemblance to actual persons living or dead, businesses, organizations, events, or locales is entirely coincidental.

Second, what *is* real:

The following things really do exist but are used fictitiously in this novel. You probably know many of these, but a few might surprise you. Noted in order of appearance:

There really is such a thing as a Letter of Marque and Reprisal. Congress is empowered to grant the letter to a specific person or persons. It would legally convert their private vessel into a Naval auxiliary. They would become a commissioned privateer with jurisdiction to conduct reprisal operations worldwide, and they'd be covered by the protection of the laws of war. In addition, they would be operating under admiralty and maritime law, which would give them broad legal powers on the water similar to what the Coast Guard has. A congressman formally proposed using this old law to fight terrorism, but so far it has not been officially adopted (as far as we know, hmmm).

The Tetris game has a noted "cognitive vaccine" technique and may help with insomnia, calm anxiety, reduce cravings, and ease PTSD. The research came from game designer genius Jane McGonigal, PhD, who wrote a bestselling book titled *Reality Is Broken: Why Games Make Us Better and How They Can Change The World.* Her TED Talks have been viewed more than 10 million times.

The Taser X12 pump shotgun has a range of 100 feet and holds five rounds complete with hooks that stick to skin or clothes. Each round delivers 500 volts to stun a perp for 20 seconds.

Officials have found over 200 tunnels that go under the border between the United States and Mexico. Some have elevators, railcars, etc. Many are quite long. One, dubbed the James Bond, tunnel was hidden beneath a pool table that would rise on hydraulic lifts when someone turned a water faucet.

In an infamous murder in Mexico, an individual was gunned down by one dozen cartel gang members wielding AK-47s who fired approximately 500 rounds into his car.

According to the US-China Economic and Security Review Commission, Mexican cartels produce 90 percent of the crystal methamphetamine used in the USA. China supplies most (around 80 percent) of the precursor chemicals used to cook that meth. Despite international counternarcotic efforts, meth precursor chemical manufacturers in China continue to thrive because the country's vast chemical industries are weakly regulated and poorly monitored. The bottom line: China is the single major supplier of chemicals. If that could be stopped, it would cut off 80 percent of the entire meth chain of supply. Sadly, that will probably never happen.

When I was nine, my best friend died of leukemia. It was a painful, heartbreaking time for everyone. He and his family and friends, including me, were devastated. In this book I've done my best to honor his memory, and that of his brave mother. I'm not naming names, out of respect for the family's privacy. I know you understand, thank you.

EMAIL SIGNUP

If you'd like to be the first to know about specials and upcoming books, please sign up for my reader newsletter on my website: www. marknolan.com

ACKNOWLEDGMENTS

First and foremost, I want to thank *you* for reading my books. My readers mean the world to me. Your kind reviews and friendly emails help motivate me to keep writing. I hope to write a dozen or more books about Jake and Cody for you.

A big thanks to my team of volunteer typo hunter beta readers who proofread the manuscript, found problems and offered suggestions.

Thank you to the dedicated professionals who worked hard to put the final polishing touches on this novel for your reading enjoyment. Beta reading by Maia Sepp. Comprehensive editing by Eliza Dee of Clio Editing. Final proofreading by Leo Bricker.

Thanks to the talented artists at Damonza for designing a beautiful book cover that included Cody.

Thank you to Jane H. Bock, PhD, for her kind help with the character named Hannah Haskett. Jane is a plant ecologist and an expert in the use of plant evidence in criminal investigations. She is a co-author of the book "Forensic Plant Science" and was featured in a Sierra Magazine article titled: "Of murder and microscopes: How botanist Jane Bock became a crime fighter." Haskett is Jane's maiden name, and we thought it would be fun to give that name to the character.

Thanks to Robert Lurz for writing the book *Mindreading Animals:*

The Debate Over What Animals Know About Other Minds. Have you ever felt like your dog could read your mind or guess what you were going to do? You may also have heard about service dogs who can tell when people are about to have a seizure, or are in need of insulin.

Lurz presents a cognitive-science-based argument that nonhuman animals, including dogs, are social, intelligent beings who can be tested for their perceptual state, empathy and ability to sense what other animals (including you and me) might be thinking or feeling.

The debated question is whether this sensing goes beyond animal-human empathy or is simply the animal acting as a clever behavior-reader and interpreting clues as signs, such as when a dog smells your body chemistry, observes your body language, and hears your tone of voice. Maybe it's some of both—behavior-reading and unexplained animal instincts. This was not an inexpensive book or an easy read, but I'm a total nerd for data about dog intelligence, and what Cody might be thinking.

Thank you to Andrew Hogan and Douglas Century for writing the book *Hunting El Chapo*. It reveals the crimes and the capture of the world's most-wanted drug lord. The story of this criminal genius and billionaire is simply mind-boggling. The truth is stranger than fiction.

Thanks to Jason Kersten for researching and writing an astonishing story for GQ about the drug cartels using horizontal directional drills (HDDs) to drill and lay pipe at deep depths and over long distances with the push of a button.

Thanks to everyone at Hotel Del Coronado in San Diego. We enjoyed a nice room with a beautiful view, fun on the beach and seashore, and it was a rare treat to see Navy SEALs swim past during a training exercise at night.

Thanks to the many Mexican friends we met in Cabo San Lucas. The friendly people, warm turquoise ocean, sandy beaches, lobster dinners and cold Modelo beers made for an enjoyable vacation in a beautiful area of Baja California, Mexico.

ABOUT THE AUTHOR

Mark Nolan is author of the Jake Wolfe thriller novel series.

If you'd like to be the first to know about upcoming books, please join the reader newsletter at:

www.marknolan.com

To be notified by Amazon when a new book is available in the Kindle store, visit Mark's author page and click on the gold "Follow" button under his photo:

Mark Nolan's page on Amazon.com

JAKE WOLFE SERIES

Novels about Jake Wolfe.

Have you read them all?

Dead Lawyers Don't Lie

Vigilante Assassin

Killer Lawyer

San Diego Dead

Deadly Weapon

Key West Dead

Subscribe to my reader newsletter at marknolan.com and I'll send you an email when I publish another book or give away a Kindle.